Dark

TEMPTATION

Dark Hearts - Book One

SARAH AMELLE

Dark TEMPTATION

Limitless Publishing, LLC
Kailua, HI 96734
www.limitlesspublishing.com

Formatting: Book Pages By Design
Cover Design: Deranged Doctor Design

ISBN-13: 978-1-954194-11-3

Dedication

This story is dedicated to those who believed in me, when I couldn't even believe in myself.

Prologue

"Stay with me." I whisper the words in his ear as my arms cradle his battered body. I knew it was already too late, the damage was already palpable. His pulse was fading and his warm hands beginning to grow cold. I was immobilized by such pain that I wasn't sure my mind could even process what was happening. Dark clouds begin to knit together across the stormy skyline, lashing down relentless rain. Water and blood mixes together and spreads around us. The ice-cold droplets penetrate my clothes and skin so the numbness I feel inside my chest was now reflected on my physical self.

The man who was once a warrior lay there frail and childlike in my arms, blood pooling from all the bullet wounds scattered over his body. It wasn't mean to happen *like this*. Daischel was the oldest brother and next in line to be the boss, *The Don*. At eighteen I was only a mere boy, although after tonight any childhood innocence that once lingered had dissipated into pieces. Watching my older

1

brother die in my arms had shattered any other direction I thought my life would go in.

Dash takes his final breath, his cerulean eyes widen, meeting my emerald ones for a final time. Anger replaces grief as it pierces through every nerve of my body, rage taking over me.

I will avenge you, brother, that is a promise.

Even if it is the last thing I do.

Chapter One

Graduation Surprise
Nine Years Later

Eleni

"Get up, Jarrod." I nudge him impatiently.

"Ah, come on, El, five more minutes." He casually wraps his leg around me and carries on watching the Giants game.

"You said five minutes twenty minutes ago." Irritation begins to flood me. I'm going to miss the last party of the year just because Jarrod is being an ass. "I'm going to get dressed." I stand up, directly obscuring his view of the television.

"I'd rather you get *undressed*," he says, licking his lips slowly. Suddenly his phone beeps and he looks momentarily uncomfortable.

"Who was that?" I ask, frowning. Recently Jarrod's phone had been going off non-stop.

"Somebody who puts out," he replies, bursting into laughter.

3

"Fuck you, Jarrod," I shoot back as I stalk out of the room. Everything comes back to sex with Jarrod, and the fact that he wasn't *getting it.*

"Babe, I was kidding. Please come out. That was Larry on the phone, he's expecting us at the party," Jarrod says through the door.

I look at my reflection in the mirror and try to avoid the disappointment in my eyes. I knew our relationship was on the rocks a long time ago, but I still persisted with it. The tension between us was mounting daily, but I still *hoped* he would change. That in time he would grow out of his 'trust fund playboy' persona. I decide to put our relationship issues to one side, it was the last party of the year and I was going to enjoy myself no matter what.

"Are you ready, babe?" His voice echoes to the bedroom but I ignore it.

I decide to add red lipstick to complement my outfit. I had picked out something casual earlier, a leather pair of pants and a red crop top. I add matching lipstick and smile at myself.

Something good is coming, I can feel it.

***

Dante

"You wait here in case he shows, and I'll be blending in at the bar," I say, putting out my cigarette.

"Why do I have to wait in the car? This is a college party, Dante, lots of hot girls. What part of that don't you get?" Nico whines.

4

"I get the part that you will get distracted by some blonde and lose focus, whereas I just want to get the job done," I reply, irritated.

"I am just as professional as you, *paisan*," he responds in his most serious voice.

"This time say it like you actually believe it, Nico."

"Fine, fine, I'll wait in the fucking car. He's definitely here, right?"

"Yeah. Farook tracked him here. That piece of shit really thought he would get away with not paying us."

"Fucker. I want to snap every one of his fingers off."

"Not yet." *That part would come if he didn't pay up.*

I head into the bar. As I imagined, it's full of drunk college kids who can't hold their alcohol. However, Nico isn't wrong about the abundance of tail in here. I walk in and heads turn toward me suggestively, but tonight I have tunnel vision and just want to get paid. This *should be* a straightforward debt collection, but if things went off track I have my trusty brass knuckles and pistol, so they will get back on track quickly. I'm not a tolerant man at all and some snot-nosed college kid trying to fuck me over is definitely something I don't take well to. My phone beeps twice, *Sapphire again.* She is another issue that I keep putting to the back of my mind. I sit at the bar ready to order when a girl sits next to me and starts to speak to the barman.

"I was here first," I interject irritably. My

patience is already hanging by a thread tonight. She turns to face me, and I am somewhat surprised. In a sea of blondes, she's a very striking brunette. Her silky black hair frames her tanned face, and her blue eyes stare up shyly, like a deer in headlights. My very own Bambi. I have a distinct urge to push her hair away so I can see more of her half-covered face but think better of it. She flushes deep crimson as I feel her react to my piercing gaze. Her head barely comes to the middle of my chest and I can see her periwinkle orbs trying to look over my shoulder in an act of distraction.

***

Eleni

We walk to the party in silence. They are hosting it at a bar off campus. It wasn't far to get there, but with the amount of tension between Jarrod and I, it felt like hours. He stalks ahead of me, making a beeline for his jock buddies as soon as we arrive. I walk into the bar without him, refusing to make a scene.

A few moments later Jarrod walks in, speaking anxiously on his phone. His face drains in color with every second that passes. I turn around to speak to him, but a group of partygoers knock into me. When I turn back around, he's gone. *I need a drink.* I head up to the bar and the barman nods at me as to ask what I want to order.

"I was here first," a husky voice behind me says.

I turn around and my mouth opens and closes in

6

quick succession when I see where that voice came from. My blue eyes meet his emerald green ones and I feel a shiver of anticipation run down my spine. He was six-foot two of tanned perfection. Jet black hair, green eyes, and a body to die for. Wrapped up in an all-black outfit, he looked more polished than every man in here. There was an aura about him that had me feeling cautious. Although he did not look any more threatening than anyone else in here, there was something about him. Something wickedly alluring that has me pause in deep expectation. He looks down at me coolly, his eyebrow cocking at my reaction. He knows exactly what is going through my mind. He smirks wolfishly, showing off his pearly white teeth as he takes a drag of his cigarette. I watch as his eyes devour me, and I feel my cheeks flush in response.

"Anytime time today." The barman raps angrily, tapping his fingers on the bar in annoyance.

"She can go first," he says, making a swift motion with his hands.

"Nah-uh, you were here first," I reply, beckoning him to order.

"Jack Daniels. Neat," he says, putting his cigarette out. Intricate Latin tattoos weave up and down his arms as he takes his jacket off revealing a tight black V-neck.

Veni Vidi Vici read the one engraved on his chest.

"I came. I saw. I conquered," he replies coolly, following my gaze.

"What exactly did you conquer?" I ask, trying to project an air of confidence even though my voice was coming out in a whisper.

"*Everything,*" he replies with no hesitation.

"Interesting." I pull a strand of hair behind my ear in a bid to avoid looking directly at him. I feel like my whole face is on fire, his eyes are looking through me like an x-ray and I strangely feel naked under his gaze. "So, do you go to school around here?" I clear my throat to sound more neutral and less like a squealing thirteen-year-old with a crush.

"No, I'm not much of a school guy," he replies drily, lighting up another cigarette. "I'm looking for somebody." He glances down as his phone starts flashing.

A small pang of guilt about Jarrod, and jealousy about who this mysterious stranger was meeting erupts within me.

"I think I've found what I'm looking for," he replies, thumbing through his phone. "Are you own your own?" He drains the last of his drink.

"Kind of," I say, trying to act nonchalant, telling a half truth.

"You shouldn't be on your own at this time of night, it's dangerous," he replies in a low tone.

"I can handle myself," I say defiantly.

He takes a deep drag of his cigarette, not taking his eyes off me once and jumps off his stool. "Enjoy your night, *Bambina*," he whispers in my ear before rubbing his thumb down my cheek, sending a bolt of electricity down my spine. I gaze up at him not knowing how to reply, but within seconds he had vanished into the crowd.

"Who in the hell is that?" Renee's Southern drawl asks behind me.

I shrug, trying to mask my true feelings. "I have no idea; he was looking for somebody."

"I wish he were looking for me, he was *fine*. I thought for a second you traded Jarrod in for him,'" she says hopefully.

"Have you seen him?" I ask casually. I didn't want to tell her the truth and give her more ammunition to hate him. I'd had enough drama for one night.

"Nope and I wish you wouldn't either," she says, glaring at me and crossing her arms. "Let me guess, he started sulking again because he still hasn't got you in the sack."

I roll my eyes in defeat, Renee knows me too well.

"Eleni, how many times do we have to go through this? *Dump that loser.*" She enunciates her last few words to drive her point home.

"He has good qualities…" I reply, trying to steer the conversation in a different direction.

"Like what?"

"Well…"

"*Ha!* You can't even think of one nice thing to say about him. Told you."

"I'm going to find Jarrod, see you later, Ren."

I walk outside and see Jarrod hunched over his phone, he wasn't wearing his arrogant smile, I would say he even looks slightly scared.

"Where the hell have you been? How dare you treat me like this?" I seethe.

"Cut the drama," he snarls, his face ghostly white.

"Jarrod," I say, using a softer tone, "what's

wrong? Why are you so twitchy?"

"Nothing," he says, pinching the skin on the bridge of his nose. "Let's go, I'm beat."

"It's barely midnight—"

"Let's go *now!*" He doesn't even wait for my reply. I watch him storm out into the dark night.

Whatever was happening, I had an unbelievably bad feeling about it.

"Jarrod, slow down! I can't keep up in these heels!" I gingerly try to catch up to him, but he was halfway up the block.

"Eleni, hurry up! I haven't got time for this shit," he shouts, still walking away from me.

"Go screw yourself, Jarrod. In fact, I don't think I want to see you again after tonight."

"Fine, whatever. Can we just get out of here now and you can have your bitchfit later?"

"That is no way to speak to a lady now, is it, Jarrod?" a voice says out of the darkness.

"Did you really think you could outrun us?" another voice joins in.

That voice…it was so familiar; I don't have to wonder who it is for too long as two men step out from behind Jarrod. The first voice I heard was a tall, blond man. Although it was dark, his face stood out menacingly. His smirk was wicked, and his dark brown eyes gleam with malice. I look at the man standing beside him and my heart drops. It was *him*. The man from the bar. He gives me a curt nod and smiles broadly at the terrified look on my face. He pulls a packet of cigarettes out of his pocket, and as he lifts them, I see a gleam of metal. A gun is nested in the waistband of his jeans.

Who is he?

How did they know Jarrod?

What were they going to do us?

"Did you really think we would let your one hundred grand debt slide?" the blond says to Jarrod.

I look at Jarrod in shock, his mouth has turned into an 'o' shape and beads of sweat start to formulate on his forehead.

"What is he talking about, Jarrod?" I say in a small voice. I forget the sheer terror of the situation in that moment and both men stare at me.

"Who do we have here then?" the blond man asks, licking his lips.

"I'm nobody," I say, moving back cautiously.

"We'll see about that," the dark-haired man from the bar says, looking at me.

His face is impassive so I can't tell what he's thinking, I can only feel his green eyes burning through me. Whatever he was thinking it didn't look good for either of us.

Chapter Two

Collateral Damage

Dante

Bambi from the bar is Jarrod's girlfriend?

I watch her face recoil in horror when she sees me beside Nico. I keep my face impassive, while hers floods in recognition. I can see the way Nico is staring at her and I feel irritation build within me. This was a pretty unfortunate situation for her to be in, but a debt is a debt. I had a plan, and nobody was getting in the way of it. I was going to get my money one way or another.

***

Eleni

"Your boyfriend has a fondness for gambling and strippers," the dark-haired man continues as he keeps his eyes on me. He enunciates every syllable in the word *boyfriend* as if he were mocking me for dating Jarrod. "Very *expensive* strippers, I might add." He looks like he's enjoying the look of revulsion on my face.

"Jarrod, are you fucking kidding me?" I scream at him.

He doesn't even react; his eyes seem to glaze over in horror and keep flicking between the two men as if he were waiting for something.

Finally, he says in a low voice, "I just need a few more days, my trust fund will be coming through."

The blond man steps forward, taking a knife out and running it along Jarrod's face until a thin line of blood appears and starts to drip down his cheek. I involuntarily gasp and he smiles at me barbarically.

"A few more days? What do you think, Dante?" the blond man asks, taking the knife away and turning toward the dark-haired man, who is apparently called Dante. Dante doesn't seem to agree with Jarrod's compromise. He grinds his cigarette out slowly, looking at Jarrod coldly. His face is white with fury and I find it hard to believe that this is the same man I was talking to freely not so long ago.

"I think your time is up and you're going to pay me in *money* or in *blood*," he says icily.

Jarrod pauses for a minute, absorbing what had just been said and the implications behind Dante's message. Out of nowhere he turns around and sprints off into the distance.

"That son of a bitch! Nico, get him!" Nico runs after Jarrod and they both disappear into the night.

Dante walks over to me and locks his arms

tightly around my waist so I can't get away, his mouth leaning hard against the back of my head. "Your boyfriend is a dead man," he whispers furiously into my ear. My heart thumps so hard I think I will pass out.

A few minutes later I tense up as a shadow runs toward us, and Nico's figure appears under the streetlamp.

He's panting slightly. "That—piece—of shit—got—away."

Dante lets go of me with such force that I fall to the ground. "Are you fucking kidding me, Nic? He owes us one hundred grand. Padrone is going to go crazy."

Who was Padrone? Their boss? What happens now?

As I stand, I take a quick look around at my surroundings. There is a big apartment complex down the end of this block. If I could just make it down there, I could get help. I could escape.

Nico and Dante are conversing aggressively in Italian, they aren't even paying any attention to me. If I just back away slowly, then I can make a run for it. Heels or not, I would have to run fast. Nico was already out of breath so I could definitely outrun him, I wasn't sure about Dante, but it was worth a try, right? My eyes scan the distance from here to the apartment complex, and as if he knew what I was contemplating, Nico turns around and looks at me dead in the eye.

"Don't even think about it." He taps me on the nose and smiles at me knowingly, a smile that doesn't reach his eyes, a smile that does not hold any comfort but promised threat. "I believe you are what is called collateral damage. I'll bring the car around." Nico disappears off into the night again, leaving me standing next to Dante.

Some of my fear has worn off, to be replaced by anger. "What does he mean by collateral damage?" I say indignantly.

Dante smirks at me and lights a cigarette. "You'll soon find out."

"Jarrod is nothing to do with me, he's not even my boyfriend. You just heard us break up!' I say, my voice almost cracking with the amount of emotion I am trying to suppress.

"Yeah, like we were really paying attention to your conversation," Dante replies, rolling his eyes.

An hour ago I thought he was sexy and mysterious, now I am terrified into oblivion. I want to punch him in his arrogant face but hold back because I know what is in the waistband of his jeans.

He walks over to me and takes a long drag of his cigarette. "He gives me what is mine and he gets what is his."

"You can't be serious?" I reply, exasperated.

I'm screwed, Jarrod is long gone. *What if he never comes back? What will happen to me?*

"Deadly serious," Nico interjects, appearing from the shadows driving a black Jeep. He exits the car and opens the back door.

"Get in."

"No!" I shout, looking around to see if there's anybody in the vicinity that could have heard me, but the streets are empty.

Nico rolls his eyes at me. "Why have you got to be so fucking difficult?" He pulls a gun out from his back pocket and points it squarely at my chest. "Get in the fucking car now," he says, gritting his teeth and jabbing me hard with the gun.

The coldness of the metal renders me almost speechless and I can feel tears begin to fill my eyes. "Who are you?" I manage to push out as my voice trembles.

"You'll see," Nico replies, pushing the gun harder into my skin.

Dante makes a signal at Nico to remove the gun which he grudgingly does, but not without rolling his eyes. "Get in," Dante says softly, his eyes imploring me not to provoke Nico.

I inhale deeply and get into the car.

"That wasn't so hard, was it, Princess?" Nico smiles menacingly before slamming the door.

I bite my lip to stop myself from exploding with tears.

***

Dante

When I open the car door, she isn't awake. Her face is smudged with makeup where she clearly cried herself to sleep. However, that is the least of my problems. I carry her out of the car, her arms wrapping around my neck reflexively. She smells faintly like lavender and coconut, a scent that refuses to leave my senses for the next few hours. I tell Nico to find somewhere discreet to put her while I decide what our next move is.

Twenty minutes later, we enter the penthouse in silence. *Nobody* enjoys giving Padrone bad news. I watch Nico fidget with his lighter nervously, he knows what is coming too. We approach his desk cautiously; we didn't even have to tell him we failed to acquire the money. I can tell he has already figured it out from our body language.

He put his hands together. "This is the part where you're meant to present me with one hundred thousand dollars. Your pockets look empty, boys," he says in a cool voice.

"He got away," Nico mutters quietly.

"Dad, we'll sort it," I reply in irritation.

Tonight has been a bust from start to finish. Not only had I spent all night at some shitty bar, but we had not gotten paid. I need to think about what I'm going to do with his girl. I smirk to myself. There were many things I would like to do her, but that was beside the point. *Business before pleasure always*.

"His girlfriend is downstairs. If he wants to see her again then he needs to pay up. His family are not exactly short of cash, are they?" I reply, watching my father's eyes bore into me.

I watch on as *'the great Padrone'* as he was known to outsiders taps his fingers impatiently, "I'm leaving this one to you, Dante." He stands up. "Remember, you're the Don now. One wrong move and the other families will sense weakness from us." He points at both of us. "Make this right!" He stomps out of the office.

"Well, that was fun," Nico sighs, rolling his

eyes.

"Time to pay a little visit to Farook to find out where our friend Jarrod is hiding."

We take the penthouse lift to the top level. Farook is sitting in front of two screens idly pulling a strand of his dreadlocks in concentration.

"Farook, anything?" I pull out a swivel chair and sit next to him.

"He's vanished into thin air, none of his cards have been used. I have sent people round to his dormitory and it's empty, although his belongings and car are still there."

"Fuck." I bang my fist down on the table. This was not good.

"Any information on the girlfriend?" Nico asks, sitting on one of the tables.

"She's clean. Eleni Danielson, twenty-one. She's a medical student, just graduated. She's been with our man on and off for a while. She lives on campus with another girl, Renee Williams, but she's leaving for Georgia later today. No parents, they're retired in Greece. She's on her own. He really is a piece of shit. He likes to get very personal with the strippers, if you get what I mean," he says, giving me a knowing look.

"Who gives a shit what kind of man he is?" Nico replies, lighting up a cigarette.

"When you have daughters, you will understand where I'm coming from," Farook says, reclining back on his chair.

"Fuck that, me and Dante are bachelors for life," Nico says, taking a long drag of his cigarette.

"Farook, if there are any updates on Jarrod's'

movements, call me, *capiche*?'

"Will do, Capo," Farook replies, turning back toward the computer screen.

"Where is she?" I ask Nico.

"I put her in the basement," Nico replies.

"Really, Nico? What the fuck is wrong with you?" I reply, agitated. I need her on our side if I were to ever find out where Jarrod is, even though she might not know where he is per se, *she knew him*.

"Well, she's not exactly a fucking guest, is she?" he replies, exhaling harshly.

"I'm going to pay her a visit and see if I can get some information out of her, she might know some of his hangouts."

Nico snorts. "What makes you think she'll tell you?"

"I can be very persuasive when I want to be," I say, cocking my eyebrow at him. "She might open up now she's had a few hours to think about her situation."

"And if she doesn't?"

"She *will*." I say it with such finality that Nico only nods at me slowly. Cousins or not, he knows when I mean business.

Chapter Three

Omertà

Eleni

I must have fallen asleep in the back of the Jeep because when I wake up, I'm on a dusty mattress in a cupboard-sized room. There is a tiny window at the far edge of the room. I stand on the mattress to reach the ledge. I can't see much out of the window, apart from the fact it was daylight. Even if I could open the window, what was waiting for me outside? I slowly sink down the wall in frustration as panic begins to consume me. I put my head on my knees in defeat and slow, silent tears begin to drop. I was never getting out of here. I don't know how long I continued, but I feel a draft as the door opens and a dark figure stands in the doorway.

Dante.

He walks toward me and peers down at me in disgust, like my act of weakness repulses him,

"Stop crying," he says, extending his arm to pull

me up.

I don't move, I just give him, or at least attempt to give him an icy stare. I can barely see from the puffiness of my eyes; he sighs in exasperation at my stubbornness.

"Fine, I guess we're going to have to do it the old-fashioned way then." He bends down and roughly pulls me up to my feet.

"Get off me!" I say angrily, pushing him away and backing myself as far against the damp wall as I can get.

"Just tell me where he is and you're free to go." He walks toward me and places either of his arms against where I'm standing, leaning into me.

"What is wrong with you? I don't know where he is! If I knew, I would have told you. Do you think I would rather be here?" I say, pushing him away.

He looks down in surprise that I would have dared to even do that. I pull my hand back from his taut chest, quickly realizing that I had left it there a touch too long. He slams his hand against the wall, making me jump, but doesn't say anything.

"My parents have probably called the cops by now," I say, looking at him without blinking.

"Eleni...Eleni, do I look *stupid*? Do you not think that I haven't already had my men do a background check on you before coming here? I know *everything*. Your parents aren't even on this continent and your roommate is leaving for Georgia in about two hours. *Nobody* knows you're here." He smiles coldly, enjoying the look of shock on my face.

"You're not going *anywhere* until I get my money, one way or another, so you can sulk all you want, sweetheart. You're staying *right here* until Jarrod pays up." He pauses for a moment. "Because I'm feeling generous, I'll move you to a nicer room. I can't be fairer that that."

I give him my worst look and he laughs at me, his emerald eyes twinkling in amusement. A thin chink of light from the window shines on him, highlighting his Romanic features. If he weren't such a monster, he would be very handsome.

He smirks as if he knows *exactly* what I'm thinking. He moves even closer and puts both hands up on either side of me, trapping me within his arms. "It looks like you've got a thing for bad boys, huh?" He runs his forefinger down my arm, and I feel like I have been electrocuted, the intoxicating scent of nicotine and cologne making me feel slightly dizzy. I feel him staring at me, but I try to avoid his gaze until I no longer avoid it.

***

Dante

I am surprised when she pushes me away, no woman or man would dare put their hands on Dante Dischanel. I am momentarily amused by her defiance, but she will learn. I am supposed to be finding out information about Jarrod but that seems to have slipped from my agenda. Standing so close to her, I can almost feel the cogs of her mind turning in turmoil, between hate, fear, and attraction. *I will have her.* I decide it almost on the spot. Dante Dischanel always gets what he wants. My reputation is infallible. This innocent little Bambi didn't know what she has gotten herself into, she will play my game and enjoy every second of it.

***

Eleni

I gaze at him with as much dignity as I can muster. "Who are you and your men?" He looks at me for a moment and smiles so coldly that I feel an icy chill radiate off him.

"You'll find out soon enough."

Before I can probe him any further, I hear light footsteps and a woman walks in. She is an inch or two taller than me with red wavy hair and tanned skin. Her gaze hardens when she sees how close Dante and I are standing. He, on the other hand, pays little interest to her. His face remains impassive and his green eyes stay fixated on me.

"What do you want, Sapphire?" he drawls in a bored voice.

His reaction seems to deeply offend her. She looks at me, then looks at him, putting two and two together and getting five. Her eyes narrow darkly, leading me to believe this was his girlfriend. He sighs in exasperation and lights a cigarette. I expect him to move closer to Sapphire to placate her, but he stays next to me, which seems to piss Sapphire off even more.

She folds her arms and taps her foot in anger.

"I've been calling you all night, we had *plans*." She enunciates every syllable to confirm that he was *hers*.

"Did you forget who you are talking to? Or would you like me to remind you?" He shoots her a hard look and I watch her flush with shame, knowing she has overstepped the mark. I don't know Dante well, but that one look was worth a million words. *Don't fuck with me or I will end you.*

It seems to have the desired effect as she backs down immediately. "I was worried," she manages to stammer, bowing to him apologetically to show her remorse.

"Whatever," he replies, taking another drag of the cigarette to signal the end of the conversation.

He turns toward me and smiles coldly. "This is Eleni. She is helping me with some *business*."

She shoots me a look of pure contempt while Dante's back is turned. "Farook is looking for you, he has some information that he says will interest you." She folds her arms and smiles at him to show she's redeeming herself.

"Good." He takes one final drag and puts out his cigarette. I feel relief as he walks past me toward the door. He pauses before he leaves the room. "Sapphire, move Eleni into one of the deluxe suites." He then walks straight out of the room without glancing back.

She folds her arms and stares at me in loathing and I mirror her. She needn't worry, I wouldn't touch him if he were the last man on this earth.

***

Dante

I walk in the room at the same time as Nico, who smirks at me, bemused.

"Did Sapphire find you?" He bursts out into laughter, a deep throaty laugh that made me smirk despite my mild irritation. Nico is the closest thing I had to a brother after Dash died. Even though Nico is only my cousin, I consider him my brother in blood and in arms.

"Yeah," I reply noncommittally, not wanting to discuss Sapphire. Nico found it a great source of amusement, I, however, did not. "Farook, what's the 411?" I ask, pouring Jack Daniels into a tumbler.

A little early for drinking, but whatever. It had been a long night; Eleni perplexes me. She isn't like the normal broads I was used to meeting, who dropped their panties without me having to flash so much as a smile. I'd give her a couple of days of settling before she caves. I will make her beg for me; they always give into me in the end. I could do with a new plaything to amuse me for a while, the things that I will do to her will have her asking for more and more. I can't wait to make her submit to me.

Farook sighs, interrupting my interesting train of thought. "You're not going to like this...he's fled the country."

I throw the tumbler against the wall. "Are you *fucking* kidding me?" This truly kills the interesting thoughts I was having about Eleni.

"He's smart. He chartered a private plan from an

airfield last night and had them delete the flight plan. He's basically a ghost."

"So, to conclude, we haven't got a shot in hell at getting him back, that's what Farook is saying," Nico replies, pulling a chair out, his legs stretching out on the desk.

"What does the girl know? Did you find out anything?" Farook asks, tapping his fingers on the counter.

"Bring her in here, now, Sapphire moved her upstairs." I light a cigarette while Nico springs up to retrieve Eleni.

A few minutes later they walk in, Nico holding her arm tightly and pushing her hard in front of me. I can see he's hurting her, and I raise my eyebrows at him. This amount of force wasn't needed yet. "Sorry, Princess, I thought you liked the rough stuff." He smooths her arm where he had grabbed her roughly, but she slaps his hand away, glaring at him before turning her back on him and facing me.

***

Eleni

"What do you want from me? I have told you one million times I don't know where he is."

"We know you don't, he's fled the country," Dante replies, taking a drag of his cigarette. He stares down at me, looking for a tell in my expression that I was lying. As if I knew all along that Jarrod was planning this. "Any idea where he might be?" He tries to keep his voice neutral, but his eyes betray his true emotions. I can feel the anger radiating off him. Jarrod was long gone, and Dante wasn't going to get a cent back from him.

"I told you, I don't know where he is. What is going to happen to me now?"

"Nothing you're going to like." Nico guffaws loudly.

"Shut up, Nico, I need to think about this." Dante pulls out a chair and stares at me, composing his thoughts. His penetrating gaze reminds me of how close we were earlier. It makes me feel uncomfortable watching the emerald of his eyes pierce me, so I look away.

"You can't just keep me here forever, I'm not your hostage. I have rights, you know," I say, trying to sound authoritative.

This seems to have the opposite effect of my intention as they all start laughing, not a warm laughter but a cold, menacing one.

"We don't care about the law, sweetheart, I thought that everything that has happened in the last day would have shown you that," the third man in the room says slowly. He wears a similar black suit to Dante's and has long platinum white dreadlocks that reach his shoulders. When he speaks his various gold teeth gleam in the light.

Dante rolls his eyes at my apparent naivety. "We don't live by rules society tells us to, why should we be puppets strung along by crooked men with briefcases? We are governed by ourselves and make our own rules and laws. We infiltrate the hierarchy of each level of the society to our advantage. The only rule we live by is the sacred oath of Omertà."

"That doesn't even make sense. What is Omertà?" I ask, taken aback at his explanation.

"The Mafia code of silence. Snitches end up in ditches, if you get my drift," he replies, taking one last drag of his cigarette before putting it out.

"Mafia?" I say slowly, swallowing hard. "Please, I won't tell *anyone* about this, I swear. Just let me go." I feel my voice beginning to waver because the harsh reality of being potentially stuck here with these animals forever was starting to terrify me.

"Of course, you won't, darling," the third man says sarcastically. "She's heard too much now. Do you want us to finish her or what?"

"Good idea, she can take a nice nap at the bottom of the river. She won't rat then," Nico chimes in and winks at me. I hate his smug face; I know, given half the chance, Nico would definitely kill me here and now.

"Work for me," Dante says slowly.

"What?" I ask, confused, trying to figure out what he means.

"You have two choices, only one of them ends with you living. Work for me, pay off Jarrod's debt, and you're free to go," Dante says, looking at me square in the eye.

Farook and Nico exchange looks, momentarily shocked by Dante's act of mercy, but bow their heads in agreement once Dante locks eyes with them.

"Work for *you*?" I ask, ignoring the other choice of impending death. "Doing what?"

A small smile creeps over Nico's face and my

heart sinks. "You're a pretty girl, I'm sure we can think of *something* you'll be good at." Nico's smile deepens as he begins to lick his lips salaciously.

"What do you mean?" I say in a small voice, my heart starting to thump heavily.

"Maybe I should demonstrate to you exactly what I mean." Nico strokes my arm slowly and I wrench his hands off.

"I am not working as *that*." I feel my voice start to trail off as my temper rises.

"Nico, shut up," Dante says forcefully. He gives Nico such a chilling look that Nico's face pales and he looks down at the floor. "Take Farook down to the docks and check out the new shipments. Make yourself fucking useful for once."

Nico nods slowly and they both leave.

"I'm not going to be a whore for you and your men, so don't even go there," I say, looking him square in the eye.

He moves toward me quickly, making me jump, and pushes the hair out of my face. "I think we can find something a bit more befitting of you, besides, I don't like to share."

Share? What does he mean by that? Just the way he's staring at me sends the hairs on the back of my neck standing on end.

"Farook says you're a medical student.' He pulls out two chairs and indicates for me to sit opposite him. He crosses his legs and yawns slightly, his shirt rising an inch or two so I can see his tanned, perfectly sculpted torso, then I see the silver gun tucked in his waistband and my mind seems to flicker from desire to terror. I can sense the wanting in his eyes and body language, but I look away and focus over his shoulder, so I don't have to stare directly at him.

"Yes, in theory I am a doctor. I just need to finish off my surgical residency, then I will be fully qualified," I say, finding a spot on the wall over his shoulder to concentrate on.

"You will patch my men up, tending bullet wounds and other injuries during the day. At night, you will work as a hostess in one of my clubs."

"I told you I'm *not* working as a whore!" I reply hotly, bringing my gaze back to him.

"Nothing like that, just serving drinks and booking VIP tables. The tips are good, you'll be making back that money in no time. I guess you'll have to stay with Sapphire for now until I find you somewhere else."

"No way!" I say, putting my hands up in protest.

"I can see she has made quite an impression on you."

Like a rattlesnake eyeing its prey.

He picks up the phone and starts dialing. "Zosha, it's Dante. Come and see me at my office when your shift is done."

Who is Zosha? Another Sapphire? He probably has a rotation of women on call for his needs.

"I'll speak to Zosha tomorrow, for now get some sleep. You're working for me now; you're going to need it."

"What if I don't want to work for you?" I say in a whisper, half knowing the answer already.

He stands up, towering over me as he leans in slowly, encroaching every inch of my personal space. Taking my face into his hands, stroking my cheek, he says, "You either work for me or you die. Pick your poison, Eleni."

Chapter Four

The Big Bad Wolf

Eleni

So, I either play his game or die?

I lay awake all night contemplating my options. If I didn't know Dante had money before, I did now. The room was beyond extravagant, adorned with gold decorations, marble floors, and to top it off, silk bedsheets. If I weren't in such a shitty situation, I would have enjoyed basking in luxury.

Dante, or I'm guessing one of his subordinates, had left some clothes on the bed, brand new clothes with the tags on. I didn't touch them. He already thought I was his property. This would probably give him more of an ego boost. I shower and change back into my old clothes, albeit taking the new underwear that had been left out, that was the only part of his charity I was willing to take. *Work for me or die*, those were the last words he said to me before walking out and leaving me there. One of his men came in shortly after and escorted me back to the room after Dante was done 'talking' to me. I didn't bother looking out the window for an escape this time, we were so high up I would have to be Spiderman to find a way out.

I pace for a while. Raw energy piles up inside of me every time I move. I need to get out of here. I gingerly approach the door, half expecting it to be locked, but it's open. I feel a volt of electricity run up my spine. *This is my chance.* I walk out of the room, half expecting Nico or Dante to wave a gun in my face, but the hallway is empty, I look down and see the same man who escorted me to my room last night sprawled out on an armchair outside of the room. His jacket hangs over the arm of the chair. I slowly move forward, not even daring to breathe in case I wake him, and grab his jacket. I put it on, hiding my hair in the interior so I look like one of Dante's men from behind in case someone spots me from afar.

I approach another long corridor, and next to it is the penthouse lift and a fire escape. There is no way I am getting in the lift; I approach the double doors leading to the fire escape and tear down the stairs three at a time. By the time I get to the bottom I feel like my lungs are on fire. I open another set of doors and then I am outside. I exhale deeply; I escaped. *Freedom.*

I run, faster than I will ever probably run in my life. I trip and fall, scraping my face on the sidewalk, and when I touch my cheek, blood seeps onto my hands. I don't think too much about it because all I can think about is getting as far away as I can. I discarded my heels at the penthouse, knowing they were going to slow me down…something I instantly regret once my feet touch the cold concrete. I wait until I get a couple of blocks further down then collapse against a wall. I realize I am still wearing the guard's jacket; I check the pockets and find a roll of hundred dollar bills. *Happy days*. I walk another block up the street and hail a cab.

"You okay, lady?" The driver turns around, taking in my apparent distressed condition.

I catch myself in the mirror, shiny face, eyeliner smudged to hell, and my hair looks like I have been dragged through a hedge backward. "Yeah, I'm good, just put your foot down."

He grunts and turns back around. there must be around five thousand dollars in here, I muse to myself. I could be on a flight home in a couple of hours, I just need my passport. I decide to skip going to the authorities, what Dante told me last night didn't exactly fill me with confidence. I was better off leaving the country altogether. I get out of the cab and give the guy a hundred dollar bill. "Keep the change." I feel in a generous mood, I just need to grab my passport and I am out of here.

I walk toward the dorm; it's silent. This is the second day of summer break, there's not a soul in sight. Renee would be in Georgia now; I really need to call her when I get back to Greece and explain everything. I put my key in the lock and turn it, the room is dark and silent. I feel at the wall for the light switch and brightness illuminates the room.

"Hello, Eleni." That familiar voice is like ice

dripping down my spine. I stop breathing for a minute and slowly turn around.

It was *him*.

He's laid out on my bed with his hands behind his head and his gun laying ominously on my old teddy bear. "Going somewhere?" he asks in a low tone, smirking at the sheer terror etched on my face. I note that he hasn't raised his voice once. I can feel the rage radiating off him. Even though he's smiling, the smile doesn't reach his eyes. His jawline is firmly set, and his eyes are cold and dark, like the sea when the sun disappears, and a storm is bubbling in the skyline.

"How—did—?"

Then everything went dark as my legs buckle underneath me from shock.

Please let it all be a nightmare.

My eyes are closed but I am very much awake now. I pray that everything that had happened in the last twenty-four hours had been a nightmare.

"Get up." I feel a foot prod my arm, not hard, but with enough force to make a point.

I open my eyes and Dante's face is hovering above me, smoking a cigarette. He leans down even further and blows the smoke in my face. "I said get up. Now."

I shoot him a look of pure contempt and pull myself up. He stands up at the same time as me, so we are almost chest to chest even though I am smaller than him in height. The top of my head only meets the middle of his muscular chest.

He turns around and puts the cigarette out on my desk. *Son of a bitch.* He reads my mind and smiles

35

boldly. I can feel goosebumps erupt like wildfire at the back of my neck. "What are you playing at?" He uses his low tone again. Dante was one of those few people who don't have to raise their voice to get their point across. The lower his intonation, the higher level of his anger.

At this point I was just as angry as he was. "Why is it so hard to understand that I don't want to be your prisoner? None of this is my fault," I scream.

"It's harder to understand that you prefer to be dead. Didn't I make my terms clear to you last night? Pay off the debt and you're free to go."

"You can't make me do something against my will," I say through gritted teeth.

"I think I can, and I *will*," he says, smiling slowly.

"It's against the law," I say, knowing that makes zero difference to him and his distorted views.

"The law? If you want to go to the police, go ahead, they're in our pockets anyway. I'll drive you my damn self." He laughs coldly and folds his arms in victory. "I'm untouchable, so cut your bullshit games and deal with it."

"I would rather die than be your prisoner." The words come out before I could even process what I was saying.

He stares at me coldly. "Is that what you really want?"

Is it?

I look at the floor, wishing it would swallow me whole. "No, it isn't."

"Good, because if you ever try to pull a stunt like that again, I will kill you without hesitation." He grabs me by the neck and holds on tight for a few seconds before he releases me, and I choke in fresh air.

***

Dante

I should have already killed her.

She has already caused me so many problems. My hands wrap around her delicate neck until I feel her begin to choke. Anger won't solve this, I need to salvage this in a way that will keep her alive. Nobody knows she left apart from Zeek, and I don't think Zeek would be telling *anybody* that he let some college girl get the better of him. If Nico knew, he would be shooting up the place like a Goddamn mob movie. No, it was better I deal with this one on my own. I resort back to my normal tone because she's looking at the floor and I'm sure she is about to start crying. I don't need this shit right now. I want to make this transition as smooth as possible, but she needs to stop being so fucking disobedient.

"Where are you taking me?" Her voice shakes a fraction, but she isn't crying. I can see her trying to keep it together as she distracts herself by sitting on the bed and playing with the fabric on her quilt.

"To your new place."

She looks at me in horror. "Not with Sapphire?"

"No." I chuckle at the look on her face. "Zosha, you'll be staying with her for now."

She looks at me awkwardly for a minute and

I *know* she wants something.

***

Eleni

I'm not leaving until I have a shower or change of clothes. I feel wrecked and I'm not going to turn up at some random girl's house looking like hell. "I want a shower and a change of clothes. My *own* clothes." I fold my arms and look at him. His face is impassive, so I'm not sure what he's thinking.

"Fine, don't be long. Nobody knows we're gone." He pulls my suitcase off the top of my wardrobe and indicates for me to pack while he sits on my bed.

"Why does nobody know I left?" I frown, knowing him, I would have thought half of New York would be out looking for me.

"Because I want to keep it between you and me." I look at him, startled by this.

"This is the only time I will show you mercy, try this again—" He stares at me stonily and the intention is clear. He takes a drag of his cigarette. "Zeek wants his jacket back and he says if any cash is missing, he'll know about it."

I sigh loudly. "I took a hundred-dollar bill for cab fare."

He looks at me, stunned. "You're getting chased by the Mafia and you hail a cab?" He rolls his head back and laughs. He's smiling properly this time, not the cold, menacing smirk that he normally has painted on.

"Whatever." I pull my towel from the hook on the back of the door. "I need to get undressed, so…" I indicate with my hand for him to leave.

"No fucking way am I leaving you on your own."

"You're beyond annoying," I say, walking into the bathroom and slamming the door with force.

I jump in the shower and let the hot water wash away my tension, my face stinging where I hurt myself. I look at myself in the mirror and don't even recognize the girl whose biggest fear two days ago was whether she would break up with her boyfriend. My lips are dry from dehydration and my eyes painfully puffy. I cover myself as best as I can with my towel and walk back in. He's on his cell and looks at me when I enter, ending the call.

I put my hands on my hips. "I need to get dressed."

"So, get dressed," he says lazily as he moves his eyes up and down, taking in my dripping body with just a towel separating me from nudity.

"I'm not getting dressed in front of you!" I reply in hot indignation, I could get dressed in the bathroom, but I wanted access to my closet.

"You're not the *first* girl I have seen naked. You haven't got anything I've not seen before." He smiles at me, his eyes traveling up and down my body, making my face heat up as he licks his lips slightly. I know exactly what he is thinking.

"You're not seeing me naked," I reply haughtily.

He stands up suddenly and I move back because I'm not sure what he'll do. He moves close to me and runs his hand lightly up my thigh, I feel myself unintentionally squirm with anticipation. He leans down to my ear and softly growls, "Are you sure you're not tempted?"

I try to avoid his gaze, but he tilts my chin up with his finger and our eyes meet, static exploding in the air. Even though I infinitely despise him, I can't understand the tension that clouds me every time he's in close vicinity. Actually, I can understand it, but I don't want to. Curiosity for dangerous things only leads to dangerous situations.

"What happened to your face?" he asks, thumbing my cut.

"I fell down while I was running," I reply, tightening my towel. Something about the way he is looking at me makes me feel very vulnerable and it isn't just the fact that I am nearly naked standing in front of him. His eyes seem to look right through me. He notices my awkwardness and turns around toward my dressing table, looking through my creams. *What the hell is he doing?* He turns around and places one hand on my face firmly, and with the other he starts to dab at where I fell delicately with a cotton bud. I realize I've been holding my breath this whole time and I start to gently exhale before I pass out. He smiles at me in satisfaction, knowing that I'm affected by him being so close. He finishes what he is doing and tosses the bud in the trash, then walks over to the window with his back to me.

***

Dark Temptation

Dante

"I'm averting my eyes for your modesty," I say as I turn around and face the wall.

And my own fucking sanity. When I touch her, she looked up at me with those huge Bambi eyes. They evoked some kind of involuntarily twinge of gentleness within me that I shook off immediately. Any emotion, even just a chink of feeling, will leave you susceptible to weakness, and that is one thing I never want. I look up from my revolving thoughts and see her reflection in the window. She is standing there in her bra and panties, raking through her wardrobe packing. I smirk to myself. My instinct was right. She has a banging body. Everything is in perfect proportion. I imagine her body underneath mine, her lean legs woven tightly around my torso as my body dominates hers.

"I'm ready." Her voice interrupts my X-rated thoughts. I turn around and thankfully she is fully dressed.

***

Eleni

When he turns around, there is a strange look on his face. I take one glance at the room that has been my home for four years and I feel sadness echo within me.

"You know the score. Once we leave here, there will be no more repeats of this. If you want to live, you will honor the deal we made. *I own you,*" he

41

says forcefully, emphasizing those three words.

I nod slowly and he exits. In that very moment I know my life belongs to him. There is no going back, no escape. If I want to live, this is what I have to do. *At least I'm still alive.* That is the only consolation I can come up with. My heart begins to wildly pound again but there was no use in my emotions clouding this, it has been done. I walk outside, letting the air cool me down.

"Zosh, I'll be at your place in twenty." He turns around and narrows his eyes at me. I don't know whether he can tell I am upset or not, but he doesn't acknowledge anything. "Get in." He indicates behind me and there is the most beautiful car I have ever seen.

My jaw practically hits the ground, and he laughs at my reaction.

"Show off," I say, rolling my eyes and walking to the passenger side. He unlocks the door for me, and I enter the luxury vehicle. I turn toward him and he puts his shades on and takes down the roof off the car.

"Okay, now I'm showing off." He winks at me and lights a cigarette.

We start driving and I'm filled with a sense of restlessness.

"Is Zosha your girlfriend?" I blurt out.

He looks at me, surprised. "No, Zosha works at my club. I don't mix business and pleasure," he says, taking a drag of his cigarette as we pull up to a set of red traffic lights.

Most of the day is gone at this point and there is a golden hue appearing in the sky where the sun will be setting over the city.

"What about Sapphire?" I ask, knowing I'm probably overstepping the line but not caring.

He exhales deeply and throws his cigarette outside the car. He looks agitated by the thought of Sapphire, which makes me feel relieved for some reason.

"What about Jarrod? I didn't peg you to be with such a loser."

I open and close my mouth and realize I can't answer the question. I doubt Dante will empathize with my situation. He is a man just like Jarrod, after all, and probably worse. I know this type; he would play games and dispose of you when you have served your purpose.

"Are you not going to answer the question?" He eyes me but I remain tightlipped.

***

Dante

I look at her as she avoids my question. *What is she hiding?*

She rolls her eyes and look in the other direction.

I smirk at her evasiveness; she would be a fairly good asset. If she ever got arrested nobody could ever break her once she put her walls up.

"So, you like asking questions but not answering them?"

"Pretty much," she replies, tilting her head at me as if daring me to challenge her. I am half irritated, half impressed. She is really something else. If she knew the things that I am capable of, she wouldn't dare talk to me like that. I'm sure she has an idea, but that was just the tip of the iceberg. "So, are you ready to start paying off this debt?"

"Well, I haven't got much choice, have I?" she snipes and her back slides down the car seat slightly in defeat.

***

Eleni

"I guess it's poetic justice."

"What is?" He stares at me, perplexed.

"*Dante's Inferno*, the book. I am literally going to be living in your hell."

"You better get used to it, sweetheart, you ain't seen nothing yet. We're here now." He pulls up in front of an apartment complex and takes his key out of the ignition.

He gets out of the car and I follow him at a funeral march pace, lugging my suitcase and rucksack of clothes behind me.

We go up in the elevator, not saying a word. I feel my nerves sending me into overdrive. Dante swipes a card, and the door opens. *Why does he have a card to this apartment?* I walk in after him. The outside is deceiving because the inside is huge. I look around and I suddenly feel inadequate being in such luxurious surroundings.

"Zosha, where are you?" Dante is back to his normal, agitated self. He probably just wants to get rid of me and I feel a little bubble of disappointment rising. He is the only familiar thing I know. If he leaves, I'm going to be completely on my own. I roll my eyes internally. If I was going to miss *him,* I knew I had hit rock bottom.

"All right already, keep your hair on, boss."

Zosha, I assume, comes out of one of the rooms. She is tall with glowing brown skin and long blonde hair. Her dazzling smile almost blinds me—a friendly smile—which is something I haven't seen in a while. She gives me an enthusiastic wave and I immediately feel at ease.

"Zosha, this is Eleni. She will be staying with you until further notice. During the day she will work with Chang at the warehouse, and at night she will be a hostess under you at Escada. She doesn't go anywhere alone; she will be under your supervision. She is either with you or Chang, she doesn't go *anywhere else* unless I say so. Got it?"

He looks at me while he is speaking to Zosha. I can detect the subtle threat he is making. "Zosha has brought you some clothes for when you work at the club. Anything else you may need, she will go with you to get it. You don't go anywhere on your own, am I clear?"

"Crystal," I reply, gritting my teeth in irritation.

"Good, I'll be in touch," he says, giving me one of his famous looks.

His phone rings and he answers. "Yeah, Nico, I'm on my way. I had something to take care of." He looks at me again as if to say *don't mention this ever* and gives me a curt nod before he walks out. Suddenly I'm left here with a stranger. I look up at her shyly and she flashes me a million-megawatt smile.

"Don't look so bewildered, I don't bite." She laughs, seeing my reaction. "I heard you had a run in with Sapphire." She lights a cigarette. "Don't worry, we're all not as crazy as that bitch."

I giggle at her bluntness and immediately know that we will get on, she has made me feel more at ease than I've been in the last forty-eight hours.

"Run in would be an understatement. I don't think she likes me very much." I shrug, not giving a damn about Sapphire, she was the last thing I was worried about.

"How did you get mixed up with Dante, if you don't mind me asking?"

I sigh and start to fiddle with the strap of my rucksack. "My boyfriend—well, ex-boyfriend—ran up a one hundred grand debt and split. It's fallen on me to pick up the pieces. I need to pay up or else."

She takes a sharp intake of breath and looks up at me sadly. "I know what *else* means. That boy better run. Nobody crosses the Dischanels, and when they do, it's not pretty. I know it's probably not any consolation, but you're lucky to be alive right now."

"Nico wanted to kill me," I say, remembering the other night and Nico putting a gun against my chest. I put my hand there, just remembering the feel of the metal on my bare skin. "Dante stopped him."

And he stopped me from getting killed today probably too.

Zosha rolls her eyes. "Nico is very trigger happy; Dante keeps him in check."

"Dante is a really good guy…just don't piss him off." She giggles at me, seeing my reaction. "I'm guessing you already have?" she asks quizzically.

I shrug, not wanting to go into it, and she senses my need not to delve any further.

"Honestly, Dante got me out of a tight jam. I had a—" She pauses for a second, composing herself.

"I had a tough childhood; I was in and out of foster homes. When I was sixteen, I met this guy, Jay…" Her voice tails off and starts to wobble. "I thought he loved me, but he started to ask me to do things for him. *Favors* for him and his friends…"

My heart twinges in my chest as she carries on.

"When I didn't do what he wanted, he would beat me. Soon after he put me on the streets and I wasn't just doing favors for his friends but for anyone, anytime, anywhere. He tried to put me to work in one of Dante's father's clubs to get more clients. When Dante found out what he was doing, I never heard from Jay again. Dante gave me a job, a place to stay, and a future I never thought I'd have. He gave me hope. I will always be grateful to him. I'm not saying he's an angel, but he had my back when I had nobody else."

I put my arm around her. "I'm so sorry you had to go through that." Even though we barely knew each other, our circumstances had bonded us as we both revealed parts of our past and present we wanted to forget.

"It's fine, the past is the past." She folds her arms, gaining composure. "Ground rules: You don't go anywhere without me. I'm not getting myself in trouble with Dante for anything in the world and you better believe it! Let's talk Escada. Dress to impress and flirt a lot. As long as you remember that you'll make plenty of tips. Some of the girls do extras…"

I looked at her blankly. "Extras? Like what?"

She laughs at my naivety. "As in going the extra mile for your customers."

I look at her, horrified, which makes her laugh even more.

"No way! No fucking way! I will not be doing *that*."

She shrugs. "Some of the girls swear by it."

Not me.

She leads me into a big bedroom, decorated in royal purple. "This is your room. Pretty nice, right? These are some outfits I picked out for you to wear. Try them on and let's see if they work. There is a bathroom through there—" She pulls out a chair and starts texting someone while I go off and change.

Outfits? I had seen more material on a washcloth.

"Zosha…are you sure these are for me?"

"Yeah, why?"

"They're a little…fleshy."

"If you want to make them tips you got to show some skin, Grandma!" I can hear her laughing. I look at myself in the mirror.

It's sink or swim time, Eleni.

Chapter Five

Dark Side Of The Moon
One Month Later

Eleni

A month had passed since I started working for Dante. Nobody was more surprised than me that I lasted that long. On many occasions I did contemplate trying to escape again, but what was the point? He would definitely track me down again, and the consequences would be worse this time around. My life had become surreal in such a short amount of time. During the days I worked with another surgeon called Chang at the warehouses who taught me the ropes. Mainly I was patching up Dante's men. At night I worked with Zosha at the club and the other girls welcomed me as she had. I did well on the tips front although I never did any extras. I hardly saw Dante, he always went through Zosha or Chang when he checked in, which was okay by me. The less I saw of him was a bonus.

"Penny for your thoughts?" Zosha interrupts me, carrying a tray.

"Cruella is here, guess whose arm she's hanging off?"

I roll my eyes. "Has Dante thrown her a bone yet?" We laugh like it's the funniest thing ever. My friendship with Zosha made me yearn for Renee.

"I'll take these up to her ladyship, talk to you later."

***

Dante

"I'm surprised Sapphire has let you out of her sight for so long," Nico remarks while checking out a young blonde in front of him.

"Are you talking to me or checking her out?" I ask, mildly irritated because he was right. Every time I turned around her dark eyes were watching me.

"I'm multitasking, paisan," he replies, draining his glass and turning his full attention on me.

"Like I've told you, and especially her, it was a one-time thing."

He rolls his eyes.

"Okay, maybe it happened more than once, but the same terms apply."

"You try telling her that," Nico replies, ordering another round of Jack Daniels.

I already had told her on numerous occasions, but Sapphire didn't understand no, which was a big fucking problem for me.

"I thought we couldn't sleep with any of the girls who worked for the firm."

"Well, you can't because you're a fucking animal, and everyone would be getting knocked up. Being Capo, I have certain privileges, but saying that, don't hit it unless you can quit it."

"They really need to put that in the bible somewhere," Nico muses while eye-fucking some brunette in the corner. He really was an animal, which is why I had him on a short leash.

"Oh, look who's coming over here." He smiles at me innocently.

"Don't fucking leave or I will shoot you."

I hear the clatter of Sapphire's heels and smell the scent of Armani Code. Before I know it, she's in my ear.

"Baby, I was just thinking about me and you," she whispers seductively in my ear.

She puts her elbow on the table and rests her head on it. I'm not fooled. This is a trick to push out her cleavage. I'd seen it all before and now it's boring as fuck. I could feel my patience begin to wane and temper flare. "Knock it off, Sapphire, there is no *we*. There is me and there is you. *Separately*. I am your Capo, nothing more, nothing less. Go home before you embarrass yourself anymore." I look at her and she is stunned by my dismissal. She folds her arms at me like a petulant child. I ignore her and turn away. "Nico, we will speak later." With that I put my glass on the table and leave.

***

Eleni

I find myself walking up to the rooftop, which is my favorite place. I come up here frequently to escape all the noise downstairs, not to mention my own head. It was the only place that I felt free. I look up at the moon which is half covered by the dark clouds of the night.

Will I ever get out of this mess?

"What are you doing up here?" A voice nearly makes me jump out of my skin.

I know that voice.

I turn around and see Dante. He's standing against the wall, his face darkened in anger. I could tell he was really pissed off by the way his jaw was set into a firm line.

"I just come up here to think sometimes, I wasn't planning the great escape," I reply, rolling my eyes and turning back toward the sky.

He walks over to me and stands by the opposite wall. "I never said you were, but thanks for the reassurance." He lights a cigarette, staring at me intently. "I've been getting good reports from Chang and Zosha. How are you getting on, Eleni?"

I shrug nonchalantly. "Fine."

It will be a lot better if you just let me go.

"I heard that." He smirks at me, taking a long drag of his cigarette.

I look at him in surprise. "What?"

He tilts his head back and laughs, and all his previous annoyance disappears. "What you just said in your head."

Now I'm really confused. "How?" I turn my body toward him, intrigued. He moves closer, and I back myself against the wall slightly. He scares me, and I don't mean that I find him intimidating—well, I do. But I feel scared because my heart starts to beat a little faster and I can feel my hands clamming up when he's close to me. I bite my lip and try to look away, but he moves closer and runs his finger down my forearm and back up again. He pulls the dark strands of hair away from my face, so he is looking at me unobscured.

"Why are you so scared? If I wanted to hurt you, I would have."

He walks closer to me and bends down so his mouth is against my ear. "I can feel your body tense up as I move closer; your lips aren't moving, but your body is speaking to me loud and clear." He moves back slightly and leans his hands on either side of me against the wall. "If you want to fuck me then just ask, *Bambina*, there is no need to be shy," he whispers, his fingers tracing the plunging neckline of my dress between my breasts.

"I think you're mistaking me for Sapphire. I don't do sloppy seconds," I say, removing his hand, which was lingering too close to my comfort.

I watch as his smirk falters, and for the first time in a long time I feel *satisfaction.*

***

53

Dante

I am taken back by her rebuke.

She is rejecting *me?*

I can have any woman.

Apart from her.

I shrug it off and just concentrate on Bambi's eyes smiling at me in victory, like she has finally won a round against me. I smirk to myself, once I was done with her, she would be begging me for more, enjoying every second of it. "Not many people would dare talk to me like that," I say, bringing my face closer to hers. Enjoying her shift of body language now I had moved closer to her, I know she wants me, and when she does finally give in, the satisfaction will be worth the chase.

"I'm so sorry, your highness." She mock curtsies while smirking then suddenly I can hear a noise coming closer. I turn around, as she does at the same time.

"What the hell is that?" She looks at me in terror. "It sounds like—"

"*Gunshots!* Eleni, get down!"

***

Eleni

I wake up and I'm in a strange bed. All I can feel is my body aching. A face appears in front of me. I glance down and she's wearing a nurse's uniform, then it dawns on me I'm in a hospital.

"You're awake. How are you feeling?" the petite

nurse with braids asks.

"Like I have been hit by a bus," I groan.

She chuckles. "You're incredibly lucky, you were shot twice. Both superficial wounds, no long-term damage done. We have given you a few stitches, but apart from that you are good to go. Do you remember how it happened?"

"I don't remember much; I was talking, then…" My voice trails off as I try to piece together what happened.

"That's good, dear, you're starting to put it together," she says, tapping on my IV drip. "The detective will be coming to see you shortly and then you're free to leave."

"Detective?" I pull my head up, my heart starts racing. If Dante finds out I've been talking to the police…I gulp. If I talk, he will he kill me.

Before I can even start to protest, a man in a sharp suit enters. He is around six foot with dark features and even darker piercing eyes.

"Miss Danielson, good to see you are conscious. I'm Detective Fonseca, NYPD. What can you tell me about the events at Escada nightclub last night?" He gets out his notepad and sits on the chair next to my bed.

"Not much, it's still a little fuzzy," I say in a low voice, hoping he will back off if I put on the little girl lost routine.

"What do you know about Dante Dischanel, Miss Danielson?" He ignores my reluctance and stares at me square in the eye.

"He owns Escada, that's about it." I look him back in the eye without blinking.

"Are you aware of him being involved in any criminal activities which may have contributed to the shooting at Escada?"

"No, why would you think the shooting is linked to something else? It was random, I was just an innocent bystander."

His eyebrows raise slightly like he is saying *as if.*

"I'm leaving my card here, Miss Danielson. Do not hesitate to call me should you remember anything." He gets up and leaves, and I exhale deeply and lay my head back down on the pillow.

***

Detective Fonseca

He walks out of the room slowly, mentally making a reminder to himself to find out every last piece of information he can about Eleni Danielson.

She's clearly got caught up in something she can't get out of, young and naïve, that always gets them in the end. He'd been trying to bust Dante Dischanel for a long time, but every lead he ever had went cold, witnesses disappeared or ended up dead. Maybe this girl would be the break he needed to destroy the Dischanel underground empire for good. He vowed to make it his mission to get her to talk, no matter what he had to do. Ten years in the organized crime unit had taught him you can't play clean if you want to win. He will nail this son of a bitch, no matter how long it takes.

Dark Temptation

***

Eleni

I could have told him everything and it would all be over...why didn't I?

It could have been easy. I could have been safe, but after everything Dante had said and did, I know it wouldn't be that easy, in fact, it would be *impossible*.

I'm contemplating all of this in my head when I hear something. *"Pssst."* I look up and a doctor enters the room with a surgical mask. I look at him, confused, as if to say *why are you whispering?* Then he pulls the mask down and it's Farook.

"Am I hallucinating or is that you, Farook?" I say faintly.

"It's me," he says in a low voice. "The Feds are everywhere; I need to get you out of here without being seen. Dante is outside in a black Mercedes. How are you feeling?"

I note the change of tone in him since we first met, he even seems, dare I say it, friendlier.

"Okay, I guess," I say hesitantly.

He puts a bag down on the bed. Fresh change of clothes. Get dressed and meet him outside."

I look at Farook timidly. "Is he...pissed off?"

Farook smiles, his gold teeth shining under the bright hospital lights. "Dante is always pissed off. I thought you knew that by now."

Farook and I walk up the block in silence. He discards his fake uniform, and we stand on the corner. I hear a car approach. I turn around and

Dante is there.

"Get in," he says quietly.

Farook gives me a nod, getting in another car driven by Zeek, and I get in Dante's car. We drive off. I'm guessing it's around evening, I look around, taking in the surroundings.

I can sense him looking at me. I know he wants to say something but is hesitating. After a while he speaks. "I'm guessing you didn't say anything to that detective."

"Of course not, I barely spoke," I say, rolling my eyes at him.

"I'm sorry you got caught up in this," he says in a low voice.

I finally turn around to face him and his face looks hollow.

"Are you expressing some form of concern, Dante? It almost seems like you have a heart," I say sarcastically.

"I wouldn't go that far." He smirks.

"I'm going to find the people who did this, and when I do…"

He doesn't finish the sentence, but the message is clear.

I look out of the window. "Where the hell are we? This isn't the way to Zosha's," I ask, confused.

"We're not going to Zosha's, we're going to my place."

I look at him, still confused, and I'm beginning to get a bad idea about this.

"Seeing as we're still working on the identity of the attackers, I want you to stay with me for a while."

"Why can't I stay where I am?"

"It's the safest option, and I don't want Zosha in any danger in case they decide on further retribution. I want you with me and protected."

"I can take care of myself," I reply, mildly irritated. This was the last thing I needed.

"So you said when we first met. Not many girls can take two bullets and still be cocky," he says as we approach red traffic lights. "This is happening, end of discussion. I have already moved some of your clothes over from Zosha's."

I stay silent, seething inside. "Whatever." He was right, there was no point arguing because he would win. "What about Sapphire?" I ask, looking him dead in the eye.

"What about her?"

"I'm not living with her." I fold my arms.

"You won't have to; she doesn't live there," he says crisply.

"*Does she stay over*?"

"No," he replies, ending the conversation.

He pulls us up in front of a huge penthouse tower which is probably bigger than my high school.

"It's just me and you."

I inhale deeply.

That's what I'm afraid of.

Chapter Six

The Heat

We walk into this huge apartment and it's even grander than it is on the outside. He leads me up a huge spiral staircase to what I'm guessing is the master bedroom. Lavish isn't even the word I would describe it. I was no longer surprised anymore, clearly Dante was interested in the finer things in life, and with all the money he must have, why the hell not?

"This is my room, but it's going to be yours tonight."

I turn around to him, confused. *Is he saying what I think he is?*

He laughs at my reaction. "Get your head out of the gutter. What I'm saying is your room isn't ready yet. Nico used to live here, so naturally we had to burn everything in that room," he says with a smirk. "Nobody else has lived here since, and I didn't plan on that changing until now." He sits on the edge of the bed and lights a cigarette. "I'll take the couch tonight, that is what I meant, however..." He pats on the bed seductively. "I'm open to other suggestions."

"I wasn't shot in the head, Dante. I'll pass," I reply, not as convincingly as I wanted it to sound.

He smirks back at me, noticing the lack of conviction in my voice. "I'll leave you to get settled in." He walks out, closes the door, and I'm left standing there in his bedroom.

I sit on the huge bed and look at myself in the mirror, taking in my slightly battered appearance, and take a deep breath. I see Zosha has packed a bag for me, and I rifle through and pull out my toothbrush and nightwear. I start to get changed and realize it was going to be tricky.

"Fuck," I curse in pain, trying to take my top off, but it gets stuck on the stitches, and if I move an inch more I'm going to rip them out.

"Eleni?" Dante walks in the door and sees me half dressed, and a small smile appears on his face.

"Is all this for me? You shouldn't have."

***

Dante

I walk in and I see her half out of her clothes. The thread from her stitch has snagged on the material and I can tell it's causing her pain.

"Don't just stand there, help me," she says irritably.

I walk over and extract her from her top carefully. I can tell she's embarrassed because she looks over my shoulder. The reflection I saw of her in her dormitory doesn't do her any justice. Up close she is better. The curve of her hips and breasts finished off by a tight waist. I can feel the beast in me rumble hungrily as that familiar feeling of want rises inside. Every time she looks up at me with those huge Bambi eyes, I just want to fuck her until she can't see straight.

***

Eleni

He walks in fresh from the shower, partially dressed in boxers but topless. His body is dripping slightly as he moves closer and swiftly untangles me without missing a beat, I avoid looking at him, but his gaze never wavers from my body. Even though it was late night in New York, *the heat* inside was beyond anything I ever experienced. He grabs the tank on my bed and negotiates my arms through the sleeves. I was expecting him to be rough and yank my arms like a doll, but his touch is gentle, and I try not to jump every time he makes contact with my skin. I look into the mirror's reflection and I can see the hunger in his eyes as his hands move over my torso. I try my best not to touch him, afraid of what might happen if I do. I don't trust myself around him. The V of his abdomen is tempting to look at and I spend my time trying not to think about where that V leads…

"This must be unusual for you?" I ask, looking at him.

"Huh?" he replies as we look at each other properly for the first time.

"You're putting clothes on a woman rather than taking them off." I snort, and he rolls his eyes back at me.

"There is a first time for everything. You're all done." He walks out of the room without a second glance and closes the door.

I brush my teeth, then climb into bed, patting down the pillow and lying flat. The pillows have his faint scent, and without thinking I inhale them, imagining it was him who was next to me. I must have fallen asleep at some point because I'm back at Escada on the roof and suddenly the gunmen are back. There are more of them coming from every direction. I turn to my left—Dante is gone and I'm on my own as they get closer to me and now firing, I can feel every bullet hitting me...

"Eleni wake up!"

I jump up and see Dante standing by my side looking mildly irritated, his arms crossed, and his hair is disheveled from where he has jumped out of bed.

"It felt so real. I was back at Escada," I say, clutching my chest.

He flicks on the lampshade and stands over me.

"I thought you could handle this. Not so tough now, are you?"

He walks around and sits next to me on the bed. "Nothing will happen to you while you're with me," he says quietly.

"Hundreds of armed men surround this place, camouflaged; this place is a fortress. Nobody will ever penetrate these walls. Go to sleep, Eleni."

"Stay with me." It comes out as a whisper and I see the surprise in his eyes.

"Not like that…just until I go to sleep, please." I look up at him and he rolls his eyes in annoyance.

"Eleni—"

"Please, Dante," I say, looking up at him, and he sighs in exasperation.

"Don't tell anybody about this, I don't want people to start thinking I'm running a fucking babysitting business."

"You're all heart, Dante."

"Yeah, yeah."

He climbs over me and lays down on the other side of the bed, folding his hands behind his head. He turns toward me with a look of amusement on his face. "Has anyone ever told you that you are extremely high maintenance?"

"Nope," I reply, and turn myself around, so I am directly facing him with only a tiny space between our bodies.

"So…" I start to speak, then he interrupts.

"No, it's my turn with the questions. What were you doing with Jarrod? I thought someone like you might have better taste." I can see he's genuinely curious about it, with perhaps a twinge of, dare I say, *jealousy* in the question.

"He wasn't always like that. Actually, by the sounds of it, I hardly knew him anyway." I turn on my back and look up at the ceiling. "We broke up because I knew it wasn't right between us. I knew for a long time but thought it would get better. He wasn't happy because I wouldn't sleep with him."

"What do you mean? Why wouldn't you sleep with him?" Dante turns to look at me, confused, but I avoid his gaze and I won't look at him because this conversation is going to become uncomfortable.

"Because…" I say slowly, "I didn't want to waste my first time on him." I stare up at the ceiling, feeling my face flush. I look at him from the side and I can tell I have taken him by surprise. He composes his expression but doesn't say anything. "Say something."

***

Dante

I wasn't expecting *that*.

I stare at her in fascination while she turns her face away from my gaze. Even though she isn't looking at me I can feel her awkwardness. She's right though; she is *too good* for Jarrod. She needs a proper man to break her in. I never considered being with a virgin. It was too innocent for me to contemplate, considering the caliber of women I normally attract.

"Tell me about the Dischanel family. How did it start?" she asks, interrupting my thoughts.

"It started during Prohibition. My great-grandfather immigrated here from Sicily, and the generations after that just continued on."

"Is this always what you wanted?" She turns to face me, her face fills with curiosity.

"There was never a choice, this was always my destiny after my brother died. I needed to continue on to survive. These are not my men; they are my family; we've gone through a lot."

"I'm sorry to hear that," she replies delicately.

"I would die for my men and they would do the same for me," I say with finality, ignoring her reference to Dash.

"The older Caporegimes are from my father's reign, but the street soldiers including Nico, Zeek, Sapphire, and Farook belong to my regime."

"What does Sapphire do?"

"Narcotics—distribution and organization of our product. She's good at keeping the suppliers happy. I thought I told you I was asking the qu—"

I look over at her and she's fast asleep, her arms under her head, and a dreamy expression on her face. Just as it was getting interesting.

***

Hours later I wake up and see daylight is streaming through the window. I jump up, surprised that I have slept through the night. Normally I can barely sleep three hours straight. I look to my left and Eleni is still sleeping. She is facing the other side and her hair is sprawled over the pillow like black silk. I can't have any repeats of last night, I don't even remember the last time I slept next to someone I had sex with, let alone sleeping next to someone I hadn't. Last night had complicated things. After her revelation, it should make me want to stay away, but it seems to have had the opposite effect on me.

Chapter Seven

Sweet Little Lies

Eleni

I wake up and the sun is shining through the curtains, and all the fear from my nightmare suddenly seems to have evaporated. I think of Dante and what I shared with him and I groan inwardly. *How can I face him?*

I walk into the kitchen. Before I have a chance to say anymore, he walks out wearing a towel. There is a maid preparing breakfast and she bows deeply to me when I enter which makes me feel awkward. I stutter out a good morning, thankful that it isn't just me and him.

"How's the arm?" The maid pours coffee into two cups. I nod at her in thanks and she leaves the room. He looks at me for a response, his eyes drinking in every part of me.

"Yeah, it's fine," I say, tucking my hair behind my ear.

67

"Anymore nightmares?"

"Nope…" I can't seem to stop staring at him, my eyes following the water dripping off his six pack down his abdomen.

"Why are you avoiding my gaze?" Snapping me out of my thoughts, he looks squarely at me and senses my discomfort.

"You can look but you can't touch." He chuckles.

He knows exactly what is on my mind…he can read me so well—in fact, too well. He moves closer, but I stay exactly where I am.

"I have a few requests for you."

He snorts but indicates for me to proceed.

"Since I took a bullet for you and didn't rat you out…" I start carefully.

"I'm not waiving the debt, so don't even think about it," he interjects, annoyed.

"Why don't you wait for me to finish instead of interrupting?" I snap. "I know you wouldn't, which is why I wasn't going to ask that. What I do want is my independence back. I don't want to be babysat by Chang and Zosha anymore. I want my cell phone too."

"Why don't I throw in a Porsche too?" he replies sarcastically.

"Sure, why not?" I match the tone of his voice and he stares at me for a second.

His phone rings and he leaves the room to take the call. He walks back in a few minutes later, and this time he is clothed. I feel half relieved because I can look at him properly now without trying to keep my eyes from straying, and half disappointed

68

because no matter how much of a jackass he is, unfortunately he is also pretty Goddamn hot.

"Fine, all those things you wanted are granted, but if you try to pull any stunts…"

"You'll kill me, I get it."

He pulls out his phone. "Nico, bring Eleni's cell phone when you come here. It's in the safe at the penthouse."

"Happy now, Bambi?" he says in a mocking tone.

"Bambi?" I ask, confused.

"Doe eyes," he replies, looking straight into my blue orbs without blinking.

I stare at him for a second, sensing the shift in atmosphere. "Well, I'm going to have a shower now." I walk out feeling confused.

***

Dante

Nico hands over the phone to me. "I take it Sapphire has some stiff competition. When she finds out Eleni is staying here, she's going to hit the roof." He smiles, taking great amusement in the situation.

"I don't give a fuck; Sapphire knows the score. How many times does she want me to tell her that I don't want her? Back to our mystery shooter," I say, turning the conversation back to business.

"Intel suggests it was the Salvatore Family," Nico says.

"No way, they're small fry," I reply

dismissively.

"Not since Lorenzo Salvatore has become Don. The Arabs are bankrolling the Salvatore family. They're cleaning up nicely in Eastern Europe with weapons and narcotics."

I'm taken back by this revelation, so I just sit there, stunned, while Nico carries on.

"If they topple our regime, they will control the narcotics flow over the United States, as well as gaining some of our powerful contacts and allies within the judicial system," he says matter-of-factly.

"Cocky son of a bitch," I reply, lighting up a cigarette. I make a throat slitting signal across my neck. "Finish him."

Nico nods and goes into the office to make some more enquiries about Lorenzo while I sit by the window and contemplate our next move.

Eleni walks in freshly dressed and made up, there is a flush in her cheeks from her smile.

"I'm going out for a while, has Nico left?"

"No, he's making some calls next door. Out where?"

"Out," she replies, her smile dropping, replaced by irritation.

"Where? With whom?" I enunciate every word to make it clear I want answers.

"What happened to you giving me independence?" Her hands are clenched in annoyance. I can tell that is not the only thing she wants to say, but she restrains herself.

"Whoever shot you is still on the loose, until they have been eliminated, you are still vulnerable."

I'm trying to keep you safe.

Those are the words I don't say, and I see the anger in her face drop.

"I understand," she says in a low voice. "But I need to get out of here for a while, otherwise it all just keeps rattling around in my head."

"Where are you going exactly?"

"To East River Plaza, to see Renee, my roommate. She's back from Georgia."

"Do you want Zeek to take you there? He's outside waiting for me."

"No, I'll be fine. I'll call you if I have any problems. Nico put all the numbers in my phone."

"Your room will be ready when you get back," I say to her.

"Great." She leaves and my eyebrows furrow in distrust.

"What was that about?" Nico says walking in.

"Nothing."

"Where has she gone?"

"To the mall, tell Zeek to tail her."

"You don't trust her?"

"I don't trust *anybody*."

***

Eleni

The first thing I had done when Dante gave me back my cell was called Renee, not the police like I first imagined, or my parents. *What is the point?* I'm in his world now, and nothing could save me but paying off the debt. Living together was going to prove a huge test to my resolve, especially after last night. But right now, all I wanted to do was see my best friend again and pretend like I was just a regular twenty-one-year-old. I decided against telling Renee anything, I didn't want her dragged into this.

"Eleni!" Renee runs across the mall and gives me a huge hug. "Where in the hell have you been? I've been calling you like crazy!"

"I explained about my cell issues." I'm glad she's hugging me and can't see my face because I'm telling her so many lies that I don't know where one lie starts and where the others end.

She pulls away and looks me straight in the eye, and I think she has caught on. "Tell me you've dumped Jarrod," she says, and I am immediately mollified she believes my lies.

"Well, he's definitely out of the picture," I say carefully, not wanting to reveal too much.

"What would you say if I told you I have met my soulmate?"

I look at her, shocked. She never said anything on the phone about this.

"What? Who is he?" I say, surprised.

"His name is Aiden." Her face goes a little dreamy when she says his name and I am surprised at her reaction because I have never seen Renee ever act like this about a guy.

"How did you meet him?"

"It was on my first day back from vacation. I was walking up to campus and he helped me with my bags. The rest is history. He's here today, I want you to meet him," she says excitedly.

"Sure, I'd love to." Her smile gets a little wider

and I feel happy she has found someone.

We take the escalator up to the food court and she stands in front of me, gabbling on about this amazing guy. She shouts his name when we get to the top of the escalator, but I can't see anything as she is obscuring my view. She moves out of the way and I take a sharp intake of breath when I see who is at the top of the escalator.

Detective Fonseca. Aiden is Detective Fonseca.

Time freezes as I stand in front of the detective. He pretends he doesn't know me at all, and I go along with the façade. When Renee introduces us, he even throws in a handshake for good measure.

"Hi," I say stiffly, frowning at him in displeasure.

"How wonderful to meet you, Eleni," He smiles at me like a predator who has just caught his prey.

Renee turns and faces him. "How was your day, honey?" She nuzzles into him and it physically makes me sick.

"Aiden's a cop," she explains, looking flush with pride. "He spends all day catching the bad guys." Fonseca looks directly over her head and smiles at me, a knowing smile that makes my stomach churn.

"What is it you do, Eleni?" he asks in a polite voice.

"I work in a club," I say pointedly.

"That must be interesting. I'm sure you have many exciting stories." A small smirk plays on his face.

"Not really," I say blandly.

This is making me feel extremely uncomfortable. He's using Renee to get to me, but how could I tell her without revealing everything else? Detective Fonseca is enjoying my discomfort and the raging war in my head. *He wants this.* In his mind he has leverage against me, and the only way he will back off is if I tell him about Dante. I need to get out of here to figure this out.

"Renee, I have got to start work soon, I forgot I'm on an early shift. Can we catch up another time?"

"Sure, what a shame you guys didn't get to know each other better," she says sadly, completely oblivious to the game of cat and mouse Fonseca is trying to play with me.

"See you soon," I say, giving her a quick hug goodbye.

"Bye, Eleni," he says, waving at me again with a cold smile that sends shivers down my spine.

***

Sapphire

Eleni rushes out of the food court, running down the escalator two stairs at a time. Clearly ruffled and terrified, so terrified she doesn't notice Sapphire watching her from a distance with a small smirk on her face. Sapphire's thumb flicks through the pictures that she has taken of Eleni with a police detective and imagining how Dante will react when he sees them. She'll probably be dead by nightfall, Sapphire smirks to herself as she hits send without a second thought. There was only one woman that was meant to be in his life, and it was her.

Always.

***

Dante

I hear her footsteps approach and my fists clench a little tighter. My phone is still clamped in my hand with Sapphire's photo of Fonseca and Eleni still ingrained in my mind. I don't even care that Sapphire had taken it upon herself to follow Eleni, her instinct was right. She betrayed me, and I rage consumes me. Farook stood opposite me silently smoking, his gun gleaming in the waistband of his jeans. We're waiting for Zeek to report back to confirm Sapphire's photos, but it doesn't look good for Eleni.

We know what to do with rats.

She walks in and her face looks pale and drawn. "Hey," she says quietly.

"Did you have a nice time with Detective Fonseca?" I ask in a low voice.

I watch her face grow even paler. "How—?" She clears her throat, panicking. "It's not what you think—I can explain." Her voice starts to falter.

***

Eleni

How the fuck does he know about Fonseca? I go back to his place ready to tell him my dilemma and

75

he already knows. He's talking to me in that low voice again, and that means one thing: *He's angry*. His face is set in a firm line and Farook looks menacingly at me. I know what is in his back pocket and I feel myself swallowing the lump in my throat so all my emotions don't spill out.

"This should be good," Farook exhales cigarette smoke and folds his arms in anticipation.

"Fonseca is Renee's new boyfriend. I swear I didn't know." My voice is shaking now so my words come out like a whisper.

"So, it's all a big *coincidence*." Dante rolls his eyes like I'm acting.

"How would I have known he was going to be there? I haven't had my cell phone for weeks," I say, regaining my composure. I look at him square in the eye to show him I am not lying.

"You could have spoken to him at the hospital."

"Farook was right there outside the door, he would have known if I had said something."

"She has a point; Fonseca didn't spend long in there," Farook says quietly.

"If I were a police informant, I wouldn't fucking come back here, would I?" I say, getting worked up.

"If you're so innocent, why didn't you call me from the mall?"

"Because I knew you would jump to conclusions, just like this." I fold my arms in anger and he looks at me with matching contempt.

Farook's phone rings and he listens for a while, then hangs up, looking awkward. "Zeek confirmed that Eleni split as soon as Fonseca arrived. He said she looked shocked when she saw him. Also, Dre mentioned that Sapphire was not happy when she found out Eleni was staying here, so she may have engineered that photo for her own reasons."

They both go quiet and I look at them, waiting for acknowledgement that I was right.

"Do you fucking believe me now?" I scream at him but his face remains impassive. "How many people do you have following me, Dante?"

"Just Zeek for protection, I didn't want you to go somewhere on your own unguarded. Sapphire wasn't supposed to be there."

"I will talk to her. She overstepped the mark, and she will be punished accordingly." He looks me in the eyes as if that is consolation.

"I want an apology," I say, meeting his gaze.

He snickers at me. "I wouldn't fucking hold my breath."

Suddenly something snaps inside of me, and I slap him, hard. As soon as I do it, I drop my hand, seeing the line of fury etched upon his face. He grabs me by the arm, hard, like he is going to snap it. I feel pain shock my system, but then he drops it after a couple of seconds as if it were made of fire. Farook moves closer to act, but Dante motions him back with his hand. He looks like he is going to say something, but he doesn't. I walk away, slamming the bedroom door in frustration and sliding down the door in defeat.

***

Dante

My face is stinging from her slap. In any other scenario I probably would have shot someone who put their hands on me like that, but I held back. She was hurt so she retaliated, the natural order of human reaction. This was strike one, next time I wouldn't be so timid.

"Capo," Farook says, glancing away.

I know he is wondering what the fuck is going on and why I let her get away with doing that.

I didn't know myself yet, my automatic reaction was to hurt her back, but something inside of me couldn't go through with it. Seeing the pain on her face shocked me out of it. I didn't want to be the animal she thought I was. My phone rings and it's Nico. "I have some information about Salvatore's warehouses. Come and meet me at our spot for drinks."

It's the best fucking idea I have heard all day.

Chapter Eight

Criminal Attraction

Dante

Before I meet Nico, I want to deal with Sapphire first and put this whole fucking fiasco to bed. I ask Sapphire to meet me at the compound while Nico waits for me outside. I want to make this as quick and to the point as possible. Her eyes light up when she sees me, and she thinks that her little plan has worked.

"Sapphire."

"Yes, baby," she says, playing with my tie and hanging off my neck like a weight.

"I know what you did." I look at her, but she avoids my gaze and starts to unbutton my shirt. I grab her hand to make her look up.

"I gave you proof of her betrayal. Snitches end up dead, I caught her red handed." Her flirty tone has gone, and I can feel the anger in her voice.

"You're right about snitches." I light a cigarette

and look at her, excellent poker face as always. She is looking up at me with wide eyes like I am about to tell her something that she doesn't already know.

"Eleni isn't a snitch, though. She left as soon as Fonseca arrived, which you already know. Zeek was tailing her and confirmed her story. She didn't know Fonseca was going to be there and you know that, but you still sent me the photos. Why? You knew how I would react."

Sapphire switches back to her sweetheart act. "Babe, I'm just looking out for you. I don't trust her," she whines.

"I don't need you to look out for me," I say sternly.

She looks affronted and starts sniffing slightly, as if to indicate she is about to cry but she won't, she's made of steel.

"What would have happened if Zeek had never told me the truth? I would have killed someone innocent for nothing."

"Whatever." Sapphire lights up her own cigarette and exhales the smoke with a bored expression on her face. "She's trying to get in between us. Can you not see that?" she rages.

"There is no fucking us. How many times do I have to tell you? We slept together a few times, that's it. Cross me again and it will be you who will be dead. From now on you report to Nico. I don't want to hear or see you."

Her eyes turn dark and I see her cheeks flush, not in embarrassment but in *anger*. I walk out leaving her standing there seething.

Later that night, Nico and I drink whisky at one

of my rooftop bars in the city. We sit high up in the mirrored VIP section; this was normally the time we would pick out the best-looking girls from the club to take home. They couldn't see us up here, but we could see them. However, tonight is about business and making sure we exact revenge. Any act of weakness on my part would come with dangerous repercussions if I didn't act against Lorenzo. Zeek and Farook join us, the alcohol pouring down my throat dulls the ache in my cheek and distracts the thoughts running through my mind.

"Sounds like you had a rough day, Capo?" Nico mimics getting slapped and they all fall about laughing.

"Man, Dre says Sapphire was on some crazy shit today. I was glad I wasn't there," Zeek adds, lighting a cigarette.

"Are we sure Salvatore is our man?" I change the subject, sick to death of hearing about Sapphire.

"Definitely, I have a little informant in the Salvatore family that confirmed it."

"How do you know the info is legit? What's in it for her if she is your informant?" I say shrewdly.

"An Italian stallion with an even bigger Italian sausage," Nico says, as subtle as a sledgehammer.

We all roll our eyes while Nico signals for another round from the pretty waitress.

"Is there anyone you're *not* sticking it to, Nic?" Zeek asks, half irritated, half in admiration.

"It ain't easy being sleazy." He points and winks back.

"What does she want in return?" Zeek asks.

"What she wants and what she gets are two

different things, smash and pass as always. When I'm done with her, she won't hear from me again. If my tip is right, we raid his hideout tonight and wipe him off our list once and for all. We have all the ammo and men already organized. What do you say, Dante?"

I nod; this is a perfect outlet for my frustration.

Farook and Zeek start making arrangements about getaway cars while Nico gets on the phone to his informant to double confirm addresses.

A hand snakes around my waist and I jump up in surprise.

Arianna, one of my usual girls, appears behind me. "How's tricks, Dante? It's been a while," she says, full of subtext.

"All good, sugar," I reply, my eyes drawn to her barely there dress.

"How about you and I catch up tonight? It's been a while."

"I'm busy tonight," I reply.

"Okay, how about *now*?" she asks, twirling a piece of hair around her finger and looking at me seductively.

A few hours later, I'm walking into one of the Salvatore warehouses. I don't know what it is, but I have a bad feeling about this. It's quiet. *Too quiet.* I look at Nico and his forehead creases, and I can tell his thoughts mirror mine. Before I even know what is happening, I hear ammunition ring out, deafening me, then all I feel is pain.

***

Dark Temptation

Eleni

I lay in bed tossing and turning, I can't sleep. I know it's either incredibly early in the morning or late at night. I didn't hear Dante come in, so I assume he's either at work or he's out. I hear footsteps creak on the floorboards, and I jump up, but then everything goes silent. I pull open my door and peek down the hall, but nothing is there. Farther down the corridor there is a light on, however. I gulp down any fear I'm feeling and push the door open. I exhale as I realize it's only Dante. Then I realize he's bleeding a lot. His face is badly bruised, and there is so much blood coming from his shoulder because he's been shot. He holds his shoulder and mutters something about being ambushed, and somebody called Lorenzo Salvatore, but he can't seem to put a coherent sentence together.

"Dante," I say softly. "We need to get you to a hospital."

"No fucking way. Hospitals equal questions, and questions equal Feds. I've got it under control," he says, breathing hard. Clenched in his hand are a bundle of bandages and a bottle of vodka.

"You can't be serious, Dante! You'll bleed out if you don't get medical attention."

"Then let me fucking die!" he says, groaning in pain.

I rush to my room, grabbing everything that could be of use, and run back in.

"What the fuck is all of that?" he says, rolling his eyes.

"Improvisation."

"Why are there tampons there?" He looks at me, horrified.

"To soak up the blood."

He groans again. "I'd rather fucking die."

"Just shut up and let me work."

"Great bedside manner you have," he says through gritted teeth.

"If you don't shut up, I'm going to shove this bandage in your mouth."

"Fine."

"Strip," I say slowly, and he looks at me like I'm crazy.

"I need to access the wound. Lose the shirt."

He pulls off what is left of his shirt and I examine him quickly.

"You're lucky."

"Lucky?" He looks at me again like I'm insane.

"It hasn't hit any major arteries or blood vessels. Like I said, you're *lucky*."

I pour some vodka on a bandage. "I'm going to sterilize the wound; this may hurt."

I lean across him and we are chest to chest, I feel my skin on his. I wipe the wound with alcohol to sterilize it, and I feel him inhale with pain, but he never utters a word. The bullet was on the surface, so I manage to pick most of it out with tweezers, Chang would have to do the rest tomorrow in a hospital setting. I siphon the last of the blood with the tampon and stitch him up with floss…a little amateur but it would have to do for now. "All done. Make sure Chang takes a proper look at that tomorrow."

"Thanks," he says quietly, patting his arm gingerly as the color starts to return to his face.

He looks at me while I'm tidying all the stuff away. "It's funny, I'm the one who got shot but your heart was racing just as fast as mine."

"I don't know what you mean," I say, avoiding his gaze. "Goodnight, Dante." I head out without glancing back once, my heart still beating even when I am in the safe confines of my own bed.

***

Dante

I wake up and check my arm. I don't feel the agony I felt last night, it's more of a dull ache. I get up and knock on the door to Eleni's room but I don't hear an answer. Maybe she's still asleep. I push the door slightly and her bed is empty but the door to the en-suite bathroom is open and steam is piling out. I sit down on the bed and listen as she goes through four verses of Rihanna's *Wild Thoughts*. Jesus, she really can't fucking sing.

She walks in and doesn't notice me at first but then as she bends down to dry her hair and flicks it back up, she catches my eye. Her eyes widen in shock. "Have you ever heard of knocking?" I snicker at her while she folds her arms in annoyance.

***

85

Eleni

When I see him in the mirror I nearly jump out of my skin.

"I did knock. You couldn't hear me over your singing, and I do use that term very loosely."

Shit. I felt myself flush a little at this information.

I take in his casual appearance. "Dante, you're not wearing black, is it some kind of holiday?"

He is wearing faded ripped denim jeans and a white Billionaire Boys Club sweater.

"Ha, you've got jokes, Rihanna."

"How's the arm?" I gently roll up the sleeve of his shirt to check the wound, which looks clean.

"Better. I'm going to have Chang to check it out now. Thanks," he says, looking down and moving a piece of wet hair clinging to my face.

I look up at him in trepidation and suddenly there is thick electricity hanging in the air. There are indeed a lot of things I want to say to him, want to ask him, but sometimes you don't need words. He slowly moves closer, giving me every indication of what he is going to do next, and rubs my lip as if asking my permission to kiss me. I nod and he bends down slightly, so we're face to face. He kisses me slowly at first, then he starts to pick up the pace as he pushes his body closer to mine. Now there is only a towel and few pieces of clothing separating our bodies.

I wrap my arms around his neck and run my hands through his thick dark locks, my body becoming awash with heat at his touch. It was never like this with Jarrod, I have never felt such raw passion that makes me lose focus. He nudges me towards the edge of the bed and pushes me down slowly. At this point I am very aware my towel is hanging on for dear life, but I don't care. *I want him.* The intensity increases between us and the kisses become more desperate, his hand runs up my inner thigh, moving higher and higher. Just as he pulls open my legs roughly and settles in between them, I hear the door slam and Nico's voice vaguely in the background. My whole body is tense with anticipation as I mentally implore him to leave, but Nico's voice becomes clearer as he comes closer and closer to where we are.

"Farook and Zeek are on their way. I forgot to ask you what happened with that little blonde Arianna from the club last night. Did you fuck her?"

We both stop in our tracks and I push him off me and stand up. His expression is impassive as he watches me firmly tuck my towel into place.

"Don't let the door hit you on the way out," I say, turning on my heel, walking into the bathroom, and slamming the door.

***

Dante

Excellent fucking timing, Nico.

I watch her face crumple as Nico's words sink in. I don't say anything, and I let her walk out as I curse my cousin's stupidity. I join Nico in the office where he's lighting a cigarette and pouring Jack

Daniels into a tumbler.

"It's ten in the morning," I say irritably.

"I'm here for a good time, not a long time," he replies.

"What's rattled your cage, sunshine?" He looks up at me, taking in how pissed off I am.

"Almost being assassinated tends to have that effect on me," I say, lighting up a cigarette.

"I still can't figure out how we got hit so hard. It was like they *knew* we were coming."

"What are the casualties so far?" I absentmindedly flick the lighter on and off.

"Heavy."

Nico's phone rings and he answers, his face becoming perplexed.

"They knew we were coming last night; it looks like we have a rat in our crew."

"Who?" I say, my temper rising.

"I don't know yet. We need to start pulling phone records and checking bank accounts."

Nobody betrayed me and lived to tell the tale. When I found out who it was, they would need dental records to formally identify them. I trust my men with my life, they are my brothers, my family, but when they betray me things get ugly. A very painful execution to the traitor would be the best lesson for what happens when you commit treason in Dante Dischanel's family.

"Promote Ra and Ajax, the more bodies the better. Call your informant back. I want a name. Whoever this motherfucker is, I want them dead. Not a quick death, one that is slow and painful."

"I'm on it," Nico replies, draining the last of the

liquid from the tumbler.

"More importantly, I want to find out who fucking shot me last night so I can return the favor threefold."

***

Eleni

I throw on my work scrubs. Why am I so worked up? It's not like he's my boyfriend or even close. I walk in the living room and see Dante and Nico talking in low voices. They stop when I approach. Nico gives me a large smile.

"Princess, long time no see."

"Yeah, time flies when you have a gun to my chest."

"That was the past, I think we can both move on from that."

I snort at him and look at Dante, who is clicking away on his phone.

"Farook will take you to and from work today," he says, still not making an eye contact.

"Sure," I say, glaring at him.

Nico looks back and forth at us, sensing the atmosphere. His phone rings and he walks off.

Dante finally looks at me, taking in my glare. "What?"

"Nothing."

He frowns at me for a second and then Farook appears and I leave.

***

Dante

"What have you done this time?" Nico says, interrupting my thoughts.

"Nothing," I say, shrugging.

"So, Arianna… what happened? Did you seal the deal?"

"No," I reply, rolling my eyes.

"What, are you fucking crazy?" He looks horrified. "Dante, it was an open fucking goal. What is wrong with you?"

"I wasn't into it; we had the warehouse attack to plan."

"*Wasn't into it*? We didn't do the attack until hours later. You had more than enough time. The Dante I know would have smashed. There is something up with you, *paisan*," he says, looking at me, confused.

"Maybe I'm just not as much as an animal as you are."

"Clearly not, because I would have hit that until she couldn't walk." He snorts.

***

Eleni

Farook and I drive in silence, his eyes flicking between me and the road. "Are you okay?"

"Yeah," I say even though I'm not, because I feel like a bubble of sadness is welling up inside me and

I don't know why.

We get closer and closer to the compound and as we drive past a drugstore, I remember I used up most of my tampons last night. "I need to get some things, can we stop?"

Farook sighs. "Okay but make it quick. Dante is waiting for me and he is not a patient man."

He parks and I mill about in the aisles, looking at makeup and other shit. Dante could wait forever as far as I cared. I bump into someone and drop what I'm holding. I apologize distractedly as I pick up the items that were now scattered on the floor.

"Hello, Eleni."

I know that voice.

I look up and Detective Fonseca is looking down at me with those dark eyes and I feel my heart start to beat a little quicker.

"I'm glad I ran into you," he says, crouching down to my height. "I hope I didn't scare you the other day. Renee was worried when you just left like that."

I stand up, leaving him crouching down.

"I don't want to scare you, Eleni, I'm one of the good guys. Dante Dischanel is an extremely dangerous man and I want to help you, but you have to help yourself first by talking to me."

"You're using her to get to me, aren't you?" I say quietly.

"Like I said, Dante is a dangerous man. I can help you but first you need to talk to me."

"I think I can judge for myself who the real danger is," I say, glaring at him.

He draws himself up to his full height. "Don't

say I didn't warn you," he whispers menacingly, and I feel the chill of his threat run down my spine.

My heart thumps in my chest as I look at his cold dark eyes burning into me. "Eleni." Farook interrupts me and he looks at Detective Fonseca coldly. "Is everything okay?"

"Yes, Detective Fonseca was just leaving."

"I'll be seeing you soon, Eleni." He glares at me one last time, then leaves.

"What the fuck was that about?" Farrok's asks, crossing his arms angrily.

I shrug. "He just appeared out of nowhere."

"What did he say to you?"

"He's using my friend as leverage; he wants me to give up Dante."

"He said all of that?"

"No, but he implied it."

Farook sighs in exasperation. "Dante is not going to be happy about this."

Chapter Nine

Law And Disorder

Dante

"He *what*?" I look at Farook incredulously.

"He was waiting for her in the drugstore, well, not *waiting*. As far as I know, nobody was following us, but he seemed to expect her."

"So, he's using her friend to get to me?" I say, not liking the situation.

"What did she say to him?" Nico asks, narrowing his eyes.

"Nothing much, from the looks of it he was getting really pissed off."

"Has Eleni told her friend?"

"No, she knows she can't tell her anything."

"What now?"

"Keep an eye on him. He sees Eleni as the key to bring me down. Let's not give him any more opportunities to do that."

They both nod.

"Ra and Ajax, how is that going?"

"Good, Sapphire isn't around today, though."

"What?"

"Women's problems."

I roll my eyes. "She's your problem now, keep her on a tight leash."

"Yeah, thanks for that. All I need is Sapphire busting my balls." I smirk at him, relieved she is finally out of my hair.

"Are you going to keep Eleni around after she finishes paying the debt?"

"I don't know."

"It will be useful to have a doctor around after last night."

"I guess so," I comment impassively.

***

Eleni

"El!" I turn around and Zosha is standing in the doorway of Chang's room. I feel myself smile as she gives me a huge hug. "I've missed my roommate, girl, and then some! How is life living with the boss?"

I shrug noncommittally. *If you only knew.*

"You must be pleased about Sapphire, right?"

"What about her?" I ask, confused.

She laughs out loud. "How can you be living with the boss and you don't know what is going on?"

"It's not like we sit around all day having pillow fights and braiding hair. What happened?"

"He demoted her after what she tried to do to you. She reports to Nico only. Dante told her he doesn't want to see her ass anymore. Not that they were even an item, only in her head," Zosha says, smirking at the look on my face.

"As I said to you, *never* piss Dante off. Oh well," she says with a smile. "See you later!" She skips off, reveling in happiness at Sapphire's misery.

Several hours later I'm back at Dante's place. I collapse on the couch and put a pillow on top of my head. *I am so tired.* Dante seemed to get out of that warehouse ambush a lot easier than some of the other guys I had treated today.

Talking of, he walks in dressed in his usual black apparel. He sits on the edge of one of the armchairs and looks down directly at me. "I heard you had a run in with Fonseca today."

"Yep." I turn around and lean forward so my elbows are resting on the couch and I'm looking up at him.

"You haven't told your friend anything?" he warns.

"No, I don't want to put her in a worse situation. Like she would believe me anyway. Would you?"

"Probably not. What else did Fonseca say?"

"He told me you were a dangerous man," I say in a mocking tone.

"Haven't you heard I am?"

"I prefer to base my opinions on my own experiences."

"So, what is your opinion of me?"

"Do you really care that much what I think?"

He shrugs and I take the opportunity to probe

him about Sapphire. "I heard you and Sapphire broke up. Too bad, Dante, your ego must be missing that boost."

He moves closer to me and pats my head like an adult comforting a child. "We never broke up because we were never together, she just amused me when I was bored. If I want another toy, I just click my fingers and four other women will jump. Is that what you wanted to hear?" he says smugly.

"Like I care, Dante, I was just making conversation." I stand up to leave, feeling embarrassed, but his arm blocks me.

"Eleni, I didn't realize you were so jealous." Now he's laughing at me and I'm the one who looks like an ass.

I slap his hand away and stand up. "I don't think so." I try to walk away but his arm is still blocking me.

"That's not what you were saying earlier. I distinctly remember how much you wanted me," he says as his eyes twinkle in amusement.

"Shut up," I say, trying to shut down any memories of this morning and turning to leave but he pulls me into his arms and starts kissing me. He lifts me up like I'm weightless and my legs wrap around his muscular torso. He places me on the cabinet as his mouth finds the sensitive part of my neck and he starts to suck hard, sending spasms of pleasure within me. Without thinking, I unbutton his shirt and shrug off my own top. His hands release me from the lace enclave of my bra and his mouth moves lower down to my breasts. I moan as he bites my lower lip before he moves down, his teeth scraping against my delicate rosebuds as I moan from his touch. He frees himself and I watch his pants drop to the floor as my hands explore his tight chest. I drag my tongue down his jawline as he begins to growl in my ear, his erection pushing against my stomach. He lets out a guttural groan of anticipation.

"Is this what we call an 'in-house doctor service'?"

Zeek and Nico are standing there in the doorway, both are smirking broadly as Nico brazenly checks me out over Dante's head, looking impressed.

"*Che due coglioni!* Haven't you heard of knocking before?" Dante says angrily, turning his back on me to give me some modesty while I pull my bra and top on.

"We did knock, you were clearly busy and couldn't hear us," Nico says, still smirking.

Dante pulls on his pants and shirt, cursing in Italian while Nico and Zeek start smoking in the hallway.

Ring ring.

Someone's cell phone is ringing. Mine.

Zeek chucks it at me, giving me a knowing smile, making sure I understand that he saw *everything* despite Dante trying to shield me.

"Hello," I say, trying to compose myself.

"Eleni! Its Renee."

"Hi Renee." Dante's face darkens as I say her name and Zeek and Nico turn around to face me, their faces stony.

"Aiden says you bumped into him today, what a coincidence, huh? I thought you didn't like him at first, but Aiden says that you really hit it off."

"Yeah sure…" My voice trails off and Dante is mouthing at me, asking what she is saying.

"You never mentioned you had a boyfriend, Eleni."

"Huh? Boyfriend?" I see Dante's eyebrows rise and Zeek and Nico start snickering.

"Aiden mentioned that you said you were seeing someone, and he thought it would be fun if we all we went out on a double date. We could all get to know each other. Don't you think that's a great idea? He's off tomorrow, can you make it?"

"Sounds like…fun. I'll call you back and let you know," I say faintly and hang up.

"What was that about?" Dante says slowly, taking in the expression on my face.

"Fonseca has told Renee you're my boyfriend. He wants to go on a double date tomorrow."

"That cocky son of a bitch, what did you say to her?"

"I said I would let her know, but we can't do this," I say, glaring at him.

"Why not?" he says, looking at me.

"How can I say to Renee that we're together when we're not? I'm not lying to her again. It's not fair to keep dragging her into this."

"Eleni, stop being so fucking naïve. She's already in this," he says, rolling his eyes. "This is not some high school bullshit; this guy is trying to put me in jail. He's trying to get to you. If you don't show up it looks like you're scared, and he'll try harder. Who knows what he'll do to your friend next?"

I'm still glaring at him and he puts his hand on my shoulder.

"If we show up together, he will know you're mine and he can't get to you. When he knows, he'll leave her out of this because she won't benefit him," he says in a softer tone.

"Yours?" I look at him, trying to ignore the butterflies building in me.

"As in a part of my family. We have to do this; I need you to do this," he says, his voice much harder than before, making clear that no is not an option.

"Fine."

"Good. Call her back. Eight o'clock at Havana Nights. One of my other clubs, we're going to do this on my turf to make a point."

I nod and call Renee back to confirm. Every time I talk to her my conscience squeezes because I keep lying to her repeatedly.

***

Dante

"Isn't this giving Fonseca what he wants?" Nico asks, confused.

"What Fonseca wants is for me to panic and hide. This way I'm putting everything out in the open. Anything he wants to ask Eleni, he can ask while I'm there. I want him to know he can't intimidate her."

"Why Havana nights? Do you really want police scum on your property?"

"Because it's low-key. I don't want any bullshit

going down like what happened at Escada. I want everyone surrounding the place tomorrow, but nobody comes in unless there are specific instructions. The only people I want in there are Nico and Farook, with Ajax as my driver."

"Sounds like a date for you and Eleni." Nico and Zeek smirk at each other.

"It's not a date," I reply, rolling my eyes.

"What the fuck was all of that out there then?" Nico asks.

I look up at Nico and he looks away sheepishly. I wasn't in the mood to crack jokes. I had Salvatore and Fonseca both to contend with now.

They both leave and I hear the door slam.

Eleni pops her head around the door. "It's confirmed."

"Great, we need to work out what we're going to say to him."

"About what?" She looks at me with curiosity.

"About us. He'll try and catch us out."

"We met at a party and lived happily ever after," she says sarcastically.

"There are no happily ever afters in my world, Bambi, I only live for the moment." I trace my fingers around her lips, noticing they are slightly bruised from earlier. I try to read her because I want to continue on where we left from.

"Why don't you call Arianna and live for the moment with her?" She frowns at me, clearly still very pissed off despite what happened earlier.

"I couldn't sleep with Arianna because there is somebody else I want more." I walk out and leave her standing there, shocked.

100

Twenty-four hours later, I am pulling up to a deserted warehouse in Brooklyn, New York. Farook and Nico are on either side of me both wearing grim faces, we know what I have to do. Betrayal has its price. *Pain*. I make my way down the rickety stairs, dust falling from the floorboards until I see the rat who nearly got me killed. I pick up an axe and a pair of pliers, not knowing which one would be my tool of decoration today. Ajax stands by the chair with a pair of knuckle dusters on, having warmed up our guest nicely for me. I can barely recognize the face, which is a plus already.

"I'll take it from here," I say as Ajax pulls off the knuckle dusters.

He bows deeply and moves to the back of the room to watch me work.

"Tell me why."

"I didn't—I don't know what you're talking about," Andre replies, his voice ragged.

"You've been taking money from Lorenzo Salvatore; I've seen who you've been speaking to and I know about the payments."

Andre goes silent, knowing there isn't anything else he can do to prevent this.

"How did he make a contact with you?" I say, punching him hard.

"I don't know," he says, looking down.

"Wrong fucking answer."

I pick up the pliers, deciding to start with them first. "Where do you want me to start, Andre?"

He looks at me, his eyes widening in fear as his body starts to shiver. I decide to start small, pulling off each nail on his right hand, his screams echoing across the basement as Nico, Ajax, and Farook stoically watch on. I continue methodically before moving to the left hand, then motion over Nico and Farook for the second part. For the next event he will need to be held down as the pain will be unimaginable. His muffled screams go on for hours until I'm content that my job is done. I don't normally like to get so graphically violent, but this was a good lesson for the rest of the men who watched on, they needed to see what happens when you betray the boss.

I pick up the axe and swing. There was a loud thud as his head drops and I'm satisfied that the message has been clearly received.

***

Eleni

My hands shake as I apply mascara. Dread fills my stomach as I think of Fonseca's dark eyes burning through me.

"Eleni, hurry the fuck up!" Dante's words boom through the door and I can hear his hands tapping impatiently.

I put the finishing touches to my lipstick and take a deep breath.

It's showtime.

I yank open the door expecting to see Dante waiting for me, but he's downstairs. I follow the voices down the stairway and Dante, Zeek, and another man stare up at me. They all stop talking.

"Damn!" exclaims the other man, who I haven't

seen before this night. He doesn't take his eyes off me until Dante turns around and gives him a death stare. When Dante's back is turned he gives me a small, shy smile.

"Ajax, bring the car around," Dante says sharply.

Ajax, which is apparently his name, walks out the room and gives me one last look before he exits.

I mock bow to Dante. "Are you ready, Sire?"

"Cut the shit, Eleni. Does everyone know what the plan is?"

"Yes, we're all good to go."

"Remember, I want to keep this low-key; we're still reeling from Salvatore's attack and I don't want to draw any extra attention to us. Fonseca already has enough ammunition to want to destroy us, let's not give him anymore. Let's get this bullshit over with." He walks out and leaves me behind to follow. I can tell he is on edge but masking it.

I silently pray that this evening goes well but I don't hold much faith. This has to be the most surreal situation, or at least one of them, that I have ever been in. Dante sits next to me, his arm casually draped around me and his hand resting on my knee. Detective Fonseca sits opposite us, his eyes scanning like lasers, trying to pick up one thread he can pull to expose this lie. Renee is the only one not aware of the game and sits there in ignorant bliss.

"This is an amazing club; how do you get so many well-known singers to play here?"

"I have connections," Dante says quietly.

He locks eyes with Fonseca, and they have a mini stare out contest. I sip my champagne and pretend not to notice the building tension.

"Connections like Lorenzo Salvatore, you mean?" Detective Fonseca says, smiling.

Dante looks back at him blankly. "Who?"

"It was so romantic how you guys met at a party," Renee remarks, ignoring Fonseca's last comment.

I nod and smile, looking at Dante, and he pulls me closer as we try to maintain the illusion.

"I wouldn't call getting shot romantic," Fonseca says darkly.

"What are you talking about, Aiden?" He ignores her, and she turns to me.

"Eleni, what does he mean?" she says in an unsure voice.

"It's really not what it sounds like, Renee." I try to act nonchalant as my voice trails off.

Detective Fonseca starts laughing. "Let's just say Eleni's boyfriend likes to use her as his shield for when his enemies want to shoot him."

Renee gasps and I feel Dante's body stiffen next to me. "That is defamation of character, Detective." Dante finishes his drink and stands up.

"I am the law, Dischanel. You won't be able to bribe yourself out of this one. I am going to put you away if it's the last thing I do." Fonseca stands up too and the tension reaches boiling point.

Dante walks around to him and grabs him by the neck, I turn around quickly and jump in between them, as I know Fonseca would love to throw Dante in jail for any reason.

"He's not worth it, Dante." I face him and put my hands on his chest to calm him. I can feel the adrenaline running through him.

"Get out of my club," he says, turning white with fury.

"With pleasure," Fonseca hisses back.

He stalks out but Renee remains there, her eyes brimming with tears. "Eleni, come with us. We can help you. Whatever you have gotten yourself into, we can get you out of it. I didn't realize he was a criminal," she whispers, horrified.

"Renee, he's the one you need to watch out for, can't you see what he's doing? All of this is a game. He's using you to get to me," I plead.

"Oh Eleni, Aiden is right. You are in too deep." She looks at me sadly and walks off. I feel my heart shatter inside.

"Why the fuck did you get in my way?" Dante blasts me with anger once they're gone.

"Do you want to spend the night in jail? Because that's where that was going. Can't you see he wanted you to fall in his trap so he could arrest you? Now I've got Renee involved in all of this because of you!" I scream back, throwing a glass at him, which just narrowly misses his ear.

"Your BFF is the least of my problems. I've got Feds on my doorstep and rivals trying to kill me!"

"Screw you!" I say in disgust as I walk down the stairs.

Ajax is waiting outside of the car smoking a cigarette. He sees my face and opens the door without saying a word. I swallow the lump in my throat and wait for Dante to get in the car. The journey goes on wordlessly. Every now and then I see Ajax's face in the rear-view mirror. He looks at me with concerned eyes but looks away when Dante catches him. As soon as we get back to the house, I walk into my room and slam the door. I don't even get undressed or take my makeup off, I just lay where I am with all the weight of the world on me.

I wake up several hours later and everything is in total darkness, I change and take my make up off and lay back in bed, but I still can't sleep. I walk out to the balcony and swing the patio doors open. The cool air sends a welcomed breeze as I sit on one of the sun loungers looking up into the darkened night sky.

"Eleni, what are you doing? It's three a.m."

I turn around and Dante is standing by the door in his boxers, wiping his eyes.

"Did I wake you?" I frown. I was so quiet; how did he hear me?

"When you opened the door, you set off the sensor alarm," he says, yawning.

"Oh, I'm sorry, I didn't realize. I couldn't sleep." I turn back toward the sky, hoping he will leave. Instead, he walks closer and sits next to me.

"Why can't you sleep?"

I put my knees underneath my chin and ignore him.

"Eleni, I'm…"

I turn around to face him and he looks me straight in the eye. "You're going to make me say a word I don't say often…I'm sorry. I shouldn't have snapped at you," he says with sincerity, and my iciness starts to thaw.

"Did Dante Dischanel just admit he was wrong? Wow," I mock. "I'm sorry I woke you." It's so quiet it's almost a whisper.

"You didn't, I'm too wound up to sleep anyway."

"Is Fonseca going to leave me alone?"

"I don't know." He shrugs.

"I thought you had the answers to everything."

He clears his throat. "Eleni, I've been thinking…"

I look up at him and my heart starts to thump a little harder.

"You saved my ass tonight; I would have been in jail if it weren't for you. I want you to join the family properly."

I'm taken back. *I never expected this.*

He sees my face. "Think about it, you don't have to give me an answer right now. I could do with someone like you in my corner," He says softly.

"Okay, I'll think about it," I say slowly.

He smiles at me and the pale moonlight illuminates his emerald eyes.

"I guess I should get some sleep," I say, standing up.

"Or…" He stands up and looks at me.

"Or what?"

"Or this." He kisses me slowly, his eyes brimming with lust. "I want you, Eleni."

He looks at my face, searching for an answer.

I kiss him back passionately. *"I want you too."*

He smiles down at me as he pushes me down on the sun lounger, whispering soft Italian words in my ear.

***

Dante

The alarm blares in the background and my heartrate quickens. According to my security screen, it says the intruder is out on the balcony. Last night I told Zeek and the rest of the men to hit the rest of Lorenzo's warehouses. Nico's informant had given us a few addresses around New York, so this was perfect retribution for me getting shot. But was someone in my apartment now? Was this blowback from the latest attack? I fasten my hand around my pistol and walk slowly toward the doors but then take a breath when I realize it's only Eleni. I yank open the doors and she turns around.

"Eleni, what are you doing? It's three a.m." Tiredness finally catches up with me as I wipe my eyes. She gives me a monosyllabic answer and turns back around, clearly pissed off. I reflect on a couple of hours ago and I realize I may have overreacted slightly. If she didn't pull me off Fonseca, I would probably be in jail right now. Right where he wants me. Her hair blows slightly in the wind and I feel like I need to say something to stop the uncomfortable tension. I find myself apologizing to her and saying something I did not expect. "I want you to join the family properly." It was something I had been thinking of for a while but didn't know how to say. She looks at me for a second, clearly shocked, and my eyes take in her beautiful body in her shorts and bra top.

My body responds to her as I move closer and my lips find her soft ones. I push her down on the sun lounger and she kisses me back slowly. I'm not used to this, her inexperience. I am trying my best to be gentle but it's not something I am accustomed to. When her Bambi eyes look up at me, though, it's something I'm willing to try.

I find myself whispering things to her that I never thought I would say out loud to someone as I stroke her softly. "I want you to tell me to stop if you don't want to do this," I breathe in her ear, praying she doesn't tell me stop.

"Take me, Dante." She moans in my ear the words I have been waiting to hear since the day I met her.

Chapter Ten

Connected

Eleni

He carries me wordlessly to the bedroom and throws me on the bed, just hard enough to let me know he is in control. He climbs on top of me, balancing his weight on his elbows, and he begins to kiss me, slower, then harder. He whispers my name in between kisses, and though it is dark, through the stretch of moonlight that is shining in, I can see his face staring down at me hungrily with a primal stare. He unclips my bra and I feel my nipples pebble in anticipation as he roughly sucks them, then swirls them with his tongue, causing me to moan slightly.

I feel him gently starting to tug my panties off and suddenly I feel a little nervous at being so naked and vulnerable. I tense up a little. He notices and strokes my hair. "Are you sure you want to do this, Eleni?"

"Yes," I say as he smiles at me hungrily, and pulls them off in one swift move, throwing them over his shoulders.

He removes his own boxers and frees himself. Even though it's dark I can tell he is packing. My mouth drops as I take in his size and he smirks at me, clearly used to that reaction.

"Don't worry, I'm going to take care of you."

He starts kissing me again harder, this time working his way down from my mouth to my neck, and then he's at my chest, kissing and biting on the sensitive parts until I find myself moaning out loud. He stops and looks down at me, amused. "Bambi, we're just getting started."

He continues kissing my chest with deft movements as my hands run through his soft locks, arching my back to give him more access to my flesh. He moves down even further, his mouth sucking and biting my abdomen as my body vibrates with pleasure. I stifle a giggle as his tongue tickles my naval ring, then he goes lower, and suddenly his tongue is sliding over my inner thighs. "*Cazzo,* Eleni, I need to taste you." I nod fervently, my hands clawing his back as his head moves lower, encasing me in ecstasy.

I feel him insert two fingers inside me and I gasp as he begins to work me hard and slow. I'm soaking wet at this point and trying to close my legs because he's driving me insane. He pushes them further apart with his knees and drags his tongue down to meet his fingers and they all work in sync together. I feel euphoria build within me.

"Dante!" I scream as I feel waves of pleasure

enrapture every nerve in my body. He moves back up and smiles down at me, taking in my flustered appearance. "I think you're ready for me now."

His hand rakes through the bedside cabinet for protection, grabbing a box and taking a condom out. He rips the wrapper with his bare teeth. He leans over me carefully and puts his hands over mine, positioning himself. I inhale slightly, he senses my nerves and bends down to kiss me hard before he starts to thrust. I feel myself gasp a little as I adjust to the feeling of him inside of me. He carries on thrusting until his groans become more intense as he nears his climax.

***

Dante

I'm working my way inside of her walls and she feels so tight I want to explode. With every thrust her body grows less and less tense as she starts to take me in inch by inch. Every time I look into her Bambi eyes, I know she belongs to me. My hips circle hers one last time and I feel her gasp as her virginity is officially gone. I look up and her face is flush with pleasure.

I pull out of her slowly and discard the used condom. "Are you okay?" I ask in a low voice.

"I'm fine." She smiles back at me shyly, pushing her hair out of her face.

How can she be so shy when I have explored every part of her body?

She lays down on her pillow and looks at me. I

return her gaze, not even remembering the last time I stayed this long with somebody after sleeping with them. I must have fallen asleep because when I look over, her head is turned the other way and she is fast asleep. I get up and take a piss and check my phone quickly to see if I've missed anything. I contemplate whether to go back and sleep next to her or to sleep elsewhere but I decide I'll sleep next to her tonight for one night only.

I lay back down, putting my hands underneath my head, and she rolls back on her side and puts her chin on my chest.

"Hey," she whispers to me.

"Hey yourself."

She opens her eyes and looks at me dead in the eye. "I'm not tired."

Just those three words make me hard instantly. She pulls herself on top of me and starts to kiss me, her body grinding slowly. She breaks the kiss and smiles at me mischievously, then she moves down. I think she wants to switch positions, but she keeps going lower until I feel her hot breath on my cock. I look down at her, surprised, because I wasn't expecting this. Her tongue swirls around me as I hit the back of her throat and I see sweat beads pooling on her forehead as her face begins to redden in sheer effort. I help her out by putting my hand on top of hers and begin to stroke my member slowly, watching it disappear in and out of her mouth. I feel myself reach my peak as my body begins to tighten. "Eleni, I'm c—" I don't finish the sentence but feel myself explode as she swallows every last drop.

***

Eleni

I've never done anything like this before so I'm just improvising. I can tell by the way he groans and how his body tenses that I'm doing something right. I can feel his surprise as he hits the back of my throat. He puts his hand over my small fist as I start to stroke him, causing electricity to run through my mouth and limbs. Finally, he climaxes in my mouth and I see the look of sheer ecstasy on his face.

"I can't take it anymore," he groans, pulling me up and flipping me over so I am on my stomach. I feel his hands digging into my hips as he starts to work me from behind and I can feel him thrusting deep inside me. My hands clench the sheets as he thrusts slowly. Suddenly he stops and pushes me on my back. He works his way down my jawline and chest with kisses and gently starts nibbling on my breasts while his fingers work me underneath.

"I can't wait anymore." I squirm under him.

He pushes himself up so he is leaning on the headboard and pulls me on top of him. He leans over to the cabinet and rips another condom packet open.

"Now we're ready, ride me, *Bambina*."

I don't need any further encouragement.

***

Dante

I watch her as she rides me slow, then speeds up, then slows back down again. I was mesmerized watching her perfect little body bounce up and down. I know I'm close to climaxing, so I pull her body close to mine. I grab her ass hard as her nails dig into my shoulder. Her petite body shudders as she arches her body back farther and we both come together, panting away.

She leans down and kisses me slowly, then puts her head on my chest. I just concentrate on the rhythmic sound of her breathing as she finally drifts off to sleep, my heart and mind racing furiously as I try to validate what I have done. Even though we have only spent one night together, the feeling of being inside her is addictive. I know I have to cut it off before it becomes a problem for me. Every touch is intoxicating and I am a man with enough vices without adding another one.

Chapter Eleven

Caught Slipping

"Dante."

"Mhm."

"Dante, get up, man."

"What?"

I open my eyes and Farook and Nico are looming over me, smirking. I also notice I am wearing nothing. I remember now. I woke up before sunrise and slept on the couch. I didn't want to wake up next to Eleni and have to have an awkward conversation about last night.

Nico interrupts my thoughts. "What's going on here?" Nico chucks my boxers at me after he picks them out of the rest of our clothes that were littered on the floor. "Why—" Nico doesn't finish his sentence.

I turn around and Eleni walks out of my room wearing my shirt and rubbing her eyes. When she sees Nico and Farook standing there, she freezes in embarrassment. They look at her, then they look at me, and their smiles widen.

"Oh, we see." Farook snorts while trying to contain himself.

"Stop fucking staring like idiots and get out of here."

That wiped the smiles off their faces. They amble out of the room toward my office. I quickly pull on my boxers and face her. She's leaning on the wall, shyly playing with her hair.

"Morning," she says in a low voice.

"Morning," I reply. I can hardly look her in the eye.

In the cold light of day, I know last night was a mistake. I let my attraction to her get the better of me and now I found myself in a difficult situation. Sure, I wanted her. I could easily pick her up right now and throw her down for round two, or was it round three or four by now? But no, I need to control myself and start thinking with my brain, not my cock for once.

"Dante—" she starts but her voice trails off.

I know exactly what she's going to say because it's a conversation I've heard dozens of times with the same generic answer said back each time. But Eleni is different. She lives with me, for a start. I need to break it to her gently that this wouldn't be going any further than last night. "Ajax is waiting for you downstairs. He'll take you to work when you're ready."

Her forehead creases in confusion and I can see she is affronted with my coldness.

"Okay." She glares at me and walks out of the room, slamming the bedroom door behind her.

It was better to stop this now before she becomes more of a distraction to me.

***

Eleni

I rip his shirt off and throw it on the floor. I can still feel the heat of his body on mine like it was embedded in my skin. I jump in the shower, trying to scrub every inch of him off me, aware that Ajax is waiting for me downstairs. I bite my lip to stifle the sting in my throat. The Dante from last night is gone, replaced by the Dante I first met. The icy gleam in his eyes told me everything I need to know. I quickly dress, hardly noticing what I was even wearing, and yank open the bedroom door. Nico, Farook, and Dante—now showered and clothed—were standing outside talking. They all turned toward me. I can feel Dante's emerald eyes burning through me like a laser beam, but I ignore him.

"Morning, Princess, did you sleep well?" Nico takes a drag of his cigarette and smirks at me with a knowing look. Dante frowns at him, then Nico drops his smile and starts conversing quietly with Farook.

"Nico, do something useful and pay your informant a visit. Take Farook with you."

They both walk out, and the apartment is silent. Thick tension hangs in the air and I try to avoid looking at him, but I feel his gaze burning into me.

"Let's go for dinner tonight, I'll pick you up

around eight."

"Dinner?" I look at him, perplexed. Did I read the earlier conversation wrong or did he change his mind?

"Yeah, I want to talk to you about last night."

"Last night?" I say slowly.

"What I asked you last night, about joining the family."

And just like that I deflate again. "Oh okay, eight sounds fine," I say in what I hope is a normal voice.

"Good, see you tonight." He walks out of the room without looking back once, leaving me feeling confused all over again.

***

Dante

"Zeek is on his way." Farook breaks my train of thought as he and Nico walk in my office.

"I thought you were going to Staten Island. Did you fucking fly down there?" I say, swiveling around to face them in my chair.

"I can't get through to her, the line us dead. I never meet her unless she agrees on time and location," Nico replies distractedly.

"Did Zeek have any success last night?"

"Not as much as you clearly did," Farook replies with a wink.

"So…details," Nico replies with a smile, breaking out of his distraction.

"Are you a sixteen-year-old girl?" I roll my eyes at him.

"Well, while we're waiting for Zeek, you might as well keep us entertained. How was it?"

"Fine," I say airily, wanting to end the conversation.

"It must have felt good getting one over on Jarrod and banging his girlfriend."

"She never slept with him," I reply, lighting a cigarette.

Nico was a persistent son of a bitch and I knew he wouldn't let up. "Bullshit, how do you know that?" he says cynically.

"She was a virgin." I look up at him and Farook and their mouths gape open.

Nico looks dumbstruck for a moment. "Do they even exist? Holy shit."

"Can we shut the fuck up about this now?" I say irritably.

"Don't be shy with the details, Dante, you have got me all curious and shit," Nico says in anticipation.

"Nico, I'm going to throw you out the fucking window, and you can shut up as well, Farook."

"I'm not even saying anything!" Farook replies in indignation.

"You're still listening, though!"

"One last question. How did it feel? Was it crazy weird?"

I don't say anything but they both stare at me in silence, awaiting my answer. "No, it was good...and this is the last fucking time I'm going to talk about it."

Nico stays silent for a second and I think he's finally shut up. "It looks like I've been wasting my time with strippers." He and Farook both start laughing raucously, and I ignore them because I don't want to think about Eleni or last night.

Zeek walks in looking like hell and collapses into the chair next to me.

"Fun night?" I ask sarcastically.

He rolls his eyes at me. "We've hit every Goddamn Salvatore safehouse and nothing."

"Lorenzo is in hiding, that's good," Nico muses while putting his feet up on my desk. I cock my eyebrow at him, and he takes them down.

"It's not good enough," I reply heatedly. I'm not even angry at Lorenzo, I am angry at myself because I did the one thing that I shouldn't have last night.

"What about Fonseca?"

Zeek interrupts my thoughts and I snap out of thinking about Eleni.

"He knows what buttons to push. I was this close to knocking him the fuck out yesterday, but Eleni stopped me, otherwise we would have been having this conversation through a glass window in jail."

Nico and Farook smirk knowingly and Zeek looks bewildered. "What?" he asks, confused.

"Let's say you're not the only one who had an eventful night, if you get what I mean."

Farook and Nico explode with laughter as Zeek looks at me, then finally realizes.

"Damn, Dante, so you're playing doctor with the actual doctor. You've got good taste. I gotta hand it to you, she is pretty Goddamn—"

I look at him and he stops talking immediately. "Back to Fonseca.' I drop my tone and they know I mean business. "He's trying to build a case against me, so I need my lawyers ready. Farook, you know what to do."

Farook nods and leaves the room already on his phone, ready to spring into action.

"Nico, get Sapphire to make sure none of our shipments have been tampered with. Salvatore might be trying to set up a blockade against us as retribution."

"That might be a problem." He rolls his eyes and lights up a cigarette.

"Why?"

"Sapphire is hardly around. She clocks in and out but she's like a ghost."

I frown, concerned, because I know Sapphire is the most unsubtle person ever. She thrives on attention. "Something isn't right. She's hardly what you'd call low key."

"Maybe she's heartbroken because she isn't getting the vitamin D anymore." Zeek and Nico both crack up laughing but I can't ignore the uneasiness in the back of my mind.

***

Eleni

Did I regret last night?

Yes.

No.

Mostly no. The way he looked at me last night, it felt like it meant something but now, we were back to sub-zero temperature Dante. I know he regrets last night. I feel his rejection twinge in my chest because I was starting to fall for someone who didn't exist, last night's Dante has disappeared into the night. The elevator to the parking lot opens and I recognize Ajax from the other night. He's leaning on the car smoking a cigarette, his eyes are blue like Dante's but less intense and more boyish.

I smile at him and he blushes slightly.

"Hey."

"Hey yourself," I reply, enjoying his nervousness. "We met the other night, right?"

"Like I could forget." He says those words with such forcefulness that I'm the one left blushing now.

Chapter Twelve

The Point Of No Return

"So…Eleni, interesting name by the way."

We're sitting in a blacked-out Jeep making small talk. This is the first time we've been alone together, and dare I say it, I'm a little nervous.

"I guess I could say the same about you, A-JAX?' I look at him and he smiles at me.

"It's actually pronounced AYAX, like the Dutch soccer team."

I look at him blankly. I know nothing about American sports, let alone anything European.

"You're Dutch?" I peer at him, recognizing the slight twang in his accent.

He nods at me, smiling. "I need to work on my New York accent a little more, I think."

"I like it, it makes you different."

He looks at me as if to say something but changes his mind.

***

Dark Temptation

Ajax

Jesus Christ.

This girl is going to get me into trouble. Was she Dante's girl or not? The look he gave me last night when he caught me staring was enough to confirm something is going on there. Although, seeing the tension between them last night, it seemed highly likely that they were together. She refused to look at him the whole journey home and I could see she had been crying. I remember the three words Zeek told me when I was initiated: *Never Cross Dante.* For the last three years, I had been doing fine on that part until now. I watch her tuck her ebony hair beneath her ear and smile at me shyly before she looks out of the window. Clearly, she was a woman of paradoxes, demure but confident, sharp but vulnerable.

***

Eleni

I watch his pensive sea-blue eyes as they bore into me. Unlike Dante's emerald glare, Ajax's orbs were a warm blue sky on a sunny day. They promised comfort and compassion instead of punishment. His cheeks were flushed slightly as I wondered what was going through his head. He was attractive in a completely opposite way to Dante. Ajax favored ripped jeans and muscle tees instead of Dante's fitted attire of expensive watches and sharp suits.

His tanned six-foot frame is adorned with intricate tribal tattoos and piercings in his nose, lip, and eyebrow. I can't help but watch with interest as his lip ring slides against his tongue every time he speaks, in fact, it made me shiver a little on the inside. *What is wrong with me?* I had just slept with Dante less then twenty-four hours ago and now I'm thinking of Ajax and how that lip ring would feel against my mouth. Now my cheeks were the ones flaming. I turn my head to look out the window so I don't have to look at him or think about Dante's face flashing through my mind like angry thunderbolts.

***

Nico

Dial tone again.

I click my tongue in irritation, half knowing that my informant in the Salvatore Family has been made. Not only had I lost our one inside woman in the Salvatore Family, but I had lost a damn good lay as well. Ah well, plenty of girls to make up for it but only one came to the top of my list.

Zosha.

I know she fucking hates me but there is a thin line between hate and lust, right? Or is it love and hate? Not that I knew anything about love or wanted to. Every time any woman would say those words to me and expect an answer, my eyes would roll in irritation. I don't want to wife you, I just want to fuck you and then I'm on to the next one.

But Zosha is something different. She knows me, she knows my world. I looked forward to coming to her apartment after a job and fucking all the adrenaline out. She got me on a level that no other woman had, but when she started getting attached and talking about feelings and commitment, she had to go. Late at night when I wanted to vent and talk to someone, did I regret it? *Maybe.* Until I found another plaything to distract me.

"Nico? Are you fucking listening? Or shall we just sit here in silence like fuckwits?"

Dante's sharp voice broke through my train of thought. He had been in a shitty mood all day. I knew it was because of Eleni, even if he didn't yet. *She had got to him.* Who would have thought it? Dante and the Virgin. Like I said, who would have fucking thought it? I laugh to myself inwardly, because If I said this out loud Dante would probably send me through a window.

"Yeah, I think she's been made. No answer." I light up a cigarette and watch Dante rapidly start cursing to himself in a mixture of English and Italian swear words.

"We've hit all his warehouses, that will smoke him out. He won't want to lose any more money," Zeek replies and that seems to calm Dante down.

"It's Friday night and we're in a strip club with alcohol, let's fucking making the most of it," I say, changing the subject and knocking my whisky back in one gulp.

"Simple things amuse simple minds," Farook replies, smirking at me, sipping primly on his Coke.
Pussy.

"Fuck off, Mr. Boring. Shouldn't you be getting home now? It's getting late, and widdle Farook has a curfew. Ilayda will be out looking for you as it's nearly dark."

Everyone laughs, including Farook.

"She probably will," he replies, draining the rest of his Coke and giving us a mock salute to indicate he is done for tonight.

"Blondes or brunettes?" I ask Zeek and Dante.

"Neither. I'm meeting Eleni."

Zeek and I raise our eyebrows at Dante.

"Oh, Dante has a date, Zeek."

We both smirk and Dante rolls his eyes at us. "It's not a date and I don't have to explain shit to you."

"Dante doesn't need burgers when he has prime steak at home."

"He's getting priority doctor services," I chime in, and Zeek and I both explode in laughter as we watch Dante frown in annoyance.

He looks at his watch. "I'm going to be late. Padrone is back from Sicily tomorrow. We'll meet at the penthouse."

He exits, leaving me and Zeek standing there.

"More for us. I'll take the redhead," Zeek says, watching her grind across the pole with ease.

I beckon the rest of the girls over. I'll take one for the team, Dante, I smirk to myself.

***

Karlie

Several hours later Nico has left with a dozen girls while Zeek hangs back to speak to the redhead he's had his eye on all night. Unlike Nico, Zeek is shyer and a little more reserved. It would be easy for him to take her home and one night her in typical Nico fashion, but Zeek is a little more smitten then he realizes. "I want to take you on a date," he says coyly.

"You what?" She looks at him in shock.

"You know, a date. I want to get to know you properly," he says sheepishly.

She smiles at him, he isn't her usual type. He is a little too *deer in the headlights* for her. He will do for now until she finds someone else with a little more power. Karlie Anderson had been dealt some shitty cards in life, and she didn't see herself grinding on a pole for the rest of her life. She has *big plans*.

***

Eleni

I jump in the shower, letting the heat relax some of my tense muscles, I was running late to meet Dante. Would he even show up? Knowing what Dante was like, he would probably style some excuse to avoid the conversation I wanted to have. I hear my phone chime away distantly and run out to answer in case it is him.

"Hello," I say, grabbing the receiver, nearly out

of breath.

"Eleni?" The voice at the end of the receiver says nervously, but it isn't Dante…

"Renee?"

"We always said we would never fight over a guy and look at us now."

I don't say anything.

"Eleni, your boyfriend, he's dangerous…"

"He's not as dangerous as yours." I roll my eyes, knowing she won't acknowledge it. "What do you want, Renee? I think you need to look a little closer at Aiden before you start questioning my judgment."

"Can we talk, please? I miss you, El."

"I—"

I hear the door slam. Shit, it was Dante.

"I'll call you, okay?" I hang up the phone. I'm confused but I can't tell Dante about this, not yet anyway.

"Hey." He walks in and I clutch at my towel, forgetting I'm half dressed. He smirks suggestively, looking at me up and down, taking in my appearance.

"Who was that on the phone?"

"Wrong number."

***

Dante

She's lying.

It was done so smoothly that anyone else wouldn't have noticed but everyone has a tell and I know Eleni's. Every time she is unsure about something, she tucks her hair behind her ear.

Who was that on the phone?

I know I'll find out one way or the other, but right now I don't give a shit. I see the water dripping off her and it's making me hard thinking about the body underneath that towel.

"So, dinner?" I say flatly, my appetite vanished, seeing her barely dressed. "Even though you're clearly running late." I smirk at her.

"I thought you would cancel on me."

"I never cancel on business or pleasure."

"Which one am I?" she says, raising her eyebrow at me.

Does she know what she's doing right now? Playing with fire.

"Depends on what you want to do tonight," I say, crossing my arms, making my intentions clear.

"Well, seeing as we're late for dinner…how about we skip to dessert?"

"That is the best suggestion I've had all fucking day."

I walk toward her and kiss her hard on the mouth, pulling off her towel. She stands there shyly for a second, feeling exposed and trying to cover herself up with her arms. "Don't, you're perfect, and I mean it," I say, running my forefinger from her lips to her navel. She relaxes instantly and smiles back at me. I kiss her again, this time savoring every second of her touch. I told myself I needed to stop this, and I would…

After tonight.

She wraps her arms around me, her wet body against my clothes sending me into overdrive. I start to undress but she slaps my hands away because she wants to do it herself, unbuttoning my shirt effortlessly, not breaking our kiss once. Bambi is a quick learner, or maybe I was just a good teacher. She gets to my belt buckle and frees me, gasping a little as she feels my erection press against her urgently. She looks up at me and all I can see in her eyes is fire.

Chapter Thirteen

Broken Rules

Dante

I pull her up me and she wraps her legs around my waist. I can feel her heat rubbing up against my groin and it's turning me on endlessly. I carry her into the bedroom, kicking the door open in the process. Our kisses are becoming more rampant as the anticipation between us heightens.

I place her on my bedroom cabinet, pulling her toward me as my fingers enter and start to explore her. One, two, three. She moans as I enter the last one in and I feel her body shudder and start to saturate with wetness as I move deeper inside of her. I dip my head to her neck and start to kiss down it slowly with small butterfly kisses until my mouth finds her nipples. They're already pebbled in hardness and I graze them with my teeth before sensuously sucking them, teasing her by alternating between rough and slow as my fingers make circles within her.

"Dante," she moans as I bite her nipple gently while squeezing the other one. "I need you now." Her eyes roll back in pleasure.

I stop kissing her and she frowns at me. "Condom," I explain as I remove my fingers.

"I'm on the pill," she replies.

I look at her, frowning at this revelation. "But you're—you were—"

"I know." She tucks her hair behind her ears in embarrassment. "It helps with my period. I didn't want to mention it as it was our first time…"

"And you didn't know if I was clean or not." I finish her sentence, laughing, and she looks back at me awkwardly.

"I'm clean, regular check-ups, and I always glove up, so we're good, baby. This is going to be even better, being inside of you with nothing to hold me back." I move closer and kiss her harder. She reciprocates with the same enthusiasm, biting my lip, then sucking it slowly, eliciting a deep growl from me. I pull her body closer and see she has made a moisture mark on the cabinet. She is so wet for me and it turns me on even more.

"*Cazzo*, Eleni, I can't wait anymore," I growl as a guttural moan starts to escape my body.

***

Eleni

Dante pulls me even closer, his face molded into pure, primal lust. He grabs my hips tightly to position himself and opens my legs wider as he fiercely slides inside me. I gasp a little as waves of euphoria hit me as he enters me alongside a little pain as my walls adjust to his size. He breaks the kiss and I look at him, confused.

"I can't go slow," he says, leaning his forehead against mine. He meets my gaze. "I want to fuck you hard."

I nod at him, unable to even speak as I hold on to the edge of the cabinet while he begins to relentlessly pound into me. I can feel my back hitting the wall behind me, but I don't care about that right now as the pleasure is overriding any pain I feel. I can feel he's holding back but I want him to unleash everything on me.

"Harder," I instruct, and he smirks at me, quickening the pace. I lean my head back, submerged in bliss as he starts to suck at my neck gently. I reciprocate and start to kiss the nape of his neck as he rasps heavily in my ear. He thrusts harder and I feel my body explode in a million fireworks as rapture overwhelms my senses. A few thrusts later he reaches his climax and I feel hot liquid fill me. I have dark grooves on my hips where he has held me so tight, but I don't care, it was worth it.

He strokes his thumb across my face and kisses me lightly. "Are you okay, Bambi?"

"Why do you keep calling me that?" I say, panting slightly.

"Because of your eyes, they do something to me. They're hypnotizing."

"Well, judging by what just happened, I'm not

complaining."

"You were amazing," he says, kissing me harder, and I feel something pressing against my thigh. I look at him again and a wolfish smile is building, his eyes darkening in seduction. I kiss him back with vigor and he picks me up as if I were weightless and carries me to the bed.

***

Dante

I wasn't expecting that.

She's driving me wild. Every time I'm inside her it just gets better, which is bad news for me long term, but tonight I give myself a pass to revel in temptation. I pick her up and gently lay her on the bed. Although I'm ready for round two, this is not going to be a quick fuck. I want to take my time with her. I lay on top of her and begin to kiss her slowly. Our tongues dance with each other, wrestling for dominance as she slowly bites the bottom of my lip hard. *Oh, you want to play, Bambina?* My fingers start to enter her slowly, circling inside of her as she arches her beautiful neck back in pleasure. I continue making come hither signs inside her as I feel her hips start to gyrate on them.

Her mouth kisses and sucks at my neck hungrily as her nails rake up and down my back.

"Dante, please," she begs as I push her firmly down, my fingers continuing to knead her. I move down to her stomach, kissing and sucking her torso gently, prolonging her torture. I move my head lower and tease her, kissing the apex of her thighs before I drag my tongue inside her and feel her melt in my mouth. My fingers join my tongue as they all work on her together. I watch her body start to drip. Her hands are pulling on my hair tightly and she is trying to close her legs as she can't take anymore.

"Dante, I can't—"

I pull her legs wider apart and push my head further down, feeling her knees start to shake as her body climaxes. I peek up at her and she's panting away, looking down at me, flushed with desire. She rolls on top of me, pinning my arms back and straddling me, her body dripping like Niagara Falls.

"My turn," she says, smirking at me as I watch her head move lower down and disappear. A thin sheen of sweat builds up as she takes me all the way down her throat, her tongue swirling around me gracefully. I thrust my hips forcefully as I feel the familiar sensation start to build within me.

***

Eleni

This is only the second time I have done this, but I think I'm doing it right, judging from Dante's groans. I start slow, then go fast, and alternate the pace. He strokes my hair and starts to pull a little, so I know it's working. Once I get into a rhythm, I take him deep in my throat and feel his body shudder.

"*Cazzo,* Eleni, what are you doing to me?" he growls as he pulls my hair harder. I put my hands on his thighs to steady myself as his hand starts to move up and down, stroking my throat. Finally, I feel his body jerk and hot liquid seeps in my mouth. I look up at him and lick my lips to show how good he tasted, and his eyes grow wider with excitement.

***

Dante

Shit.

Just seeing her do that instantly made me hard again. She's teasing me, and I fucking love it. I reach down and instantly find her soaking wet. I circle her lips and my fingers start to play with her and her body tenses as I gently stroke her clit with my thumb, then flick it as she gasps in excitement. I turn her around so I am behind her, and my cock brushes against her from the back while I continue playing with her front. I watch her body recline back and forth with double pleasure.

***

Eleni

I feel his fingers work their way down and stroke me softly, slowly entering me, then flicking my clit, sending thunderbolts across my body. He flips me onto my stomach and nuzzles me, slowly kissing the back of my neck. He pulls my legs apart from behind and settles himself in between them. Reaching his hand underneath, he strokes me from the front and slowly glides into me from behind, sending my body into overdrive. He positions his hands on my hips and begins to thrust hard, sending my body instinctively forward, but he holds me tightly in place.

He yanks my hair so the back of my head is on his shoulder and whispers in my ear, "Do you like that, baby?" He nibbles on my earlobe and licks the back of my neck. "Do you want me here?" He pushes one finger into me, and I start to breathe a little more heavily.

"Or here?" As he enters two more fingers in and starts to move them all in sync while thrusting into me from behind.

I gasp, not knowing which sensation to react to first. "You're so deep," I manage to gasp out.

I can feel him in my stomach, in my guts, everywhere. He laughs and moves his hands lower from my hips to grip my ass cheeks and starts to thrust again, this time harder. I don't know which sensation is more pressing, the pain or the pleasure. I can feel him pounding inside of me so deeply that it sends vibrations through my whole body. I feel a shiver run through me and I clutch the sheets, meeting my climax as the moisture drips down my thighs.

"You're mine," he growls into my ear. "*This belongs to me.*" He thrusts deeper. "Say it, Eleni." He pulls my head back onto his shoulder as he thrusts into me again, his fingers circling my clit as my body starts to jerk uncontrollably.

"*I'm yours*," I groan as he licks the side of my face.

***

Dante

I watch her body shudder as she reaches her climax, turning me on and making me hungry for my own, but I'm not ready yet, I'm not finished with her. I flip her over so I'm leaning against the headboard and she is on top of me. Her hair is slick with moisture and her mouth swollen from kisses. She's so wet that it doesn't take any effort. I feel her body contract as I hit every spot she has. She starts to ride slowly, rising then lowering herself on top of me. Harder, then slower. She doesn't break eye contact with me, so for a second I'm hypnotized as she encloses me in her tight walls.

"Dante." She starts to moan as her body arches back.

I can feel myself on the verge of my own climax and I lean forward into her, the familiar scent of lavender intoxicating me. Given a chance, I would spend all my nights wrapped up tightly inside of her, but that isn't an option.

"You feel so incredible," I say as I suck her neck hard. She starts to slow down the pace as she bounces gently on my cock. I take her by the chin and kiss her slowly. She kisses me back delicately, leaning her forehead against mine as her body continues to grind on me. Both our bodies are drenched in each other's juices and sweat. She doesn't say anything and neither do I, but I hold her gaze and she holds mine. We both know, as if by invisible force, something has shifted. I grip my hands underneath her ass because I know I'm close. She starts to ride me again but slower, flicking her eyes up at me seductively.

"Oh, Dante…" I feel her body start to clench, she is ready to come and so am I. I pull her closer and we climax at the same time. I feel her hands pulling at my hair as I release myself inside of her. We don't say anything for a few seconds, just stare at each other. She smiles at me, pushing her hair back, and kisses me demurely on the lips. I lay back so she is on top of me, lying flat, and run my hands through her damp hair.

"Say something," she says, looking down on me, stroking the side of my face.

What the fuck am I supposed to say? That we had a connection? That I was starting to feel things that I shouldn't? That something as meaningless as sex has turned out to be more than I ever bargained for?

That she is breaking ever rule I ever had.

Chapter Fourteen

When All Is Said And Done

Dante

"What do you want me to say?" I wrap a piece of her ebony hair around my finger as she looks up at me.

I'm not going to lie; she is making me feel a little exposed as her periwinkle orbs stare down at me.

"Tell me a secret." She rolls off and settles next to me, so we are face to face. I lift my arm so she lays her head in the nook. I bring her closer and she drapes one of her legs over me.

"I've got you right where I want you." She smiles at me.

"No shit," I reply. *Because if you told me I would be lying here in bed with some broad and not throwing her out after fucking her I would have told you that you were crazy.*

"A secret? I never wanted to be this man. I had a

brother, and this was meant to be his destiny."

***

Eleni

I watch him as he trails off and takes a breath. Clearly this was a hard subject for him, so I don't say anything. He seems so vulnerable right now and I'm honestly a little shocked. I never thought of Dante as someone who would have any chink of weakness. He always seems so resilient and strong, almost deadened to emotion.

"He was killed when I was eighteen. I had to take over or we would have been finished." He says the rest mechanically over my shoulder rather than looking me in the face. "I wasn't ready for this, but my dad was pretty insistent."

"What about your mom?" I ask quietly.

"She's been dead since I was three, revenge attack on my father that went wrong. She was pregnant with my little sister."

I look at him in shock, but he still avoids eye contact.

"I'm—"

"Sorry? You don't have to be. Shit, Eleni, are you actually feeling bad for big bad Dante Dischanel?" he says, laughing.

"Hmm, I wouldn't go that far."

He pulls me even closer, so we are almost nose to nose, his legs wrap around me like a vice, holding me tighter.

"There is something about you and I can't seem

to figure it out," he says, stroking my cheek.

"The fact that I don't fall at your feet like all the other girls?"

"Perhaps…"

Is this just sex to you? Is what I really want to say to him, because the way he's touching me makes it seem like I mean more to him than a quick lay. But I say nothing because I don't want to ruin it. My eyes are growing tired now. I look up at him and his are already closed. He looks so peaceful asleep. I place my hand over his chest and listen to his heart beating rhythmically, matching mine as I finally fall into my own sleep in his arms.

***

Dante

I wake up in the middle of the night and Eleni is burrowed in my chest. I can feel her body heat against mine. I remember last night and try to rationalize my feelings.

We were caught in the moment.

I told her about those things because she caught me off guard.

I had reasons to validate my behavior.

Didn't I?

I watch her sleep before I drift off into my own uneasy sleep and keep my body wrapped around her just for tonight.

***

Dark Temptation

Eleni

My eyes flicker open as daylight shines brightly through the window. Once they adjust to the bright sunshine, my hand automatically goes out to pat the pillow beside me, but it is empty. I lift my head up and feel a soreness underneath me from last night's session. I half smile remembering last night's antics, and half wince knowing I will feel it all day, every time I so much as clenched a muscle. The door opens and Dante walks in wearing his boxers, talking on the phone. We catch each other's eye, and he ends the call.

"Who was that?" I ask casually.

"Nico. He's waiting outside for me. It's your day off, right? Ajax will come over later. I don't want you here alone."

"Okay," I reply, looking him square in the eye.

"We never got a chance to speak about you joining the family. Have you thought about it yet?"

"Not yet."

"I want an answer soon, Eleni. This will be a good opportunity for you to work with Chang—"

"And get shot?" I fold my arms in anger. He's acting like last night never happened.

"There is more to being in this family than getting shot. I thought you would have realized that by now." He glares at me and I stare right back.

Checkmate.

The coldness in him has returned and there is a different person standing in front of me compared to the one whose arms I slept in last night. Once again, he leaves me feeling stupid and used.

His eyes remain dark and impassive and his tone mechanical. "Rosa will fix you breakfast when you're ready to get up." He turns on his heel and walks out of the room, leaving me sitting there like a fool. Anger surges within me and I follow him into the bathroom. I walk in and see his naked silhouette in the shower. I open the door and he stands there in shock.

"What are you doing?" I see that glint in his eye again as he takes in my naked form but I'm not in the mood for his games.

"What are *you* doing?" I repeat the same question to him. "Why are you acting like last night never happened? Am I just a piece of ass to you, Dante?"

He says nothing.

"Answer me!" We both stand there getting drenched, the only sound is the water beating down harshly on our skins.

"I can't be what you want me to be," he replies in a low voice, pushing his hair back from his eyes and leaning against the shower pane.

"What are you talking about?" I reply, not letting him get out of this with some bullshit excuse.

"Didn't you slap the shit out of me the other day? Didn't you have to physically restrain me from beating up a cop? What kind of fucking person does that tell you that I am?"

I can feel my emotions start to rise as steam clouds the windows and my eyes threaten to brim with tears. The pain I feel physically is nothing compared to the searing pain of rejection in my heart.

"You know my lifestyle. I don't have time for girlfriends or romantic notions."

"What does that mean? I want you to tell me instead of hiding behind words."

He moves closer and grabs my face roughly, his own face is etched with anger, and for a second I think he's going to hurt me, but he grabs my legs and lifts me up and pushes me against the tiles entwining my hands with his and lifting them above my head.

"It means when I'm here, I'm here, and when I'm not, then I'm not." He's almost shouting now as the water is so loud and the steam is clouding around us, tension thick in the air.

He moves closer and I can feel my body ache for him despite his callous behavior. His hardness presses against me, telling me he wants me too, and I can tell from the look in his eyes he wants this right here, right now. He kisses me roughly, pushing me back against the tiles. His hands grip my ass tightly as his cock grazes against me, sending ripples of excitement around my body. He moves his lips down, kissing my neck, and his tongue caresses my chest.

My nipples start to pebble in anticipation as moistness ignites within me as well as the familiar ache he left from last time. He starts to thrust slowly and our bodies rock back and forth, hitting the concrete hardness of the tiles. He moves his head down and I feel the familiar sensation of his tongue and his fingers working inside of me, and I lean back as the hot water falls on me. He pushes his head even deeper inside of me and I feel my eyes roll back in euphoria as his tongue hits every spot.

My body shakes with pleasure as I drip on him, but he continues his assault of sensations. I come again, and he finally releases me. He works his way back up, leaving his fingers firmly in place, slowly circling my clit. Just when I think I can't take much more, he takes my nipples in his mouth again, grazing his teeth against them hard. He enters me with no warning and my body reclines in shock as my walls adjust to his size. He pulls out and kisses me hard on the mouth without even looking at me before entering me again. This time I'm more prepared, my body feels more pleasure than pain. There is no intimacy in his movements or actions. It's like he's going through the motions. This is different from last night; he is different. He seems robotic, his movements mechanical like he's proving a point to himself. To him, this is just fucking, nothing more. I won't be used as a toy for his amusement.

"No!" I push him away and he drops me, looking surprised.

"You can't just pick me up and drop me when you want, Dante. I want it all or nothing."

"This is all I can give you, take it or leave it," he says flatly, folding his arms in defiance. My heart shatters in my chest as I finally realize I can't claim his heart because he doesn't have one. I walk out of the shower, my absence giving him the answer to his question.

***

Dark Temptation

Dante

I see the fire in her eyes and I suddenly get hard, I want her right now. The water is dripping down her body and it's making me hot as fuck, but I need her to know this is all it will ever be, and last night was a one-off. I lift her up, grabbing her tight little ass, and push her hard against the tiles, stretching her hands over her head with mine on top. "When I'm here, then I'm here, and when I'm not, then I'm not," I shout over the top of the sound of the water. Her body is wrapped tightly against mine and I can feel she is wet despite her being clearly furious at me. No more Mr. nice guy, this is going to be sex as it should be and no in between. I kiss her hard on the mouth, waiting for her to push me away, but she doesn't. I feel myself start to harden a little more as she pulls me closer, gripping her hands through my hair. The heat from her body and the shower is pushing the tension between us to breaking point. I leave her lips and move down to her chest, sucking and biting the shit out of her nipples as I hear her sweet little moans in my ear. *You ain't seen nothing yet.*

I bend down, putting her legs over my shoulders, *she knows* what's coming next. I work my fingers in her first, then I dive in roughly, roughly kissing her slit, then sucking her clit mercilessly until I feel her drip down in my mouth again and again. Her legs are shaking, and I smirk to myself as I leave my fingers in there to stretch her out for what is about to come next. I pull her legs back around my waist as I work my way back up and bite her nipples hard, grazing her delicate pink buds between my teeth.

I thrust into her and I feel her gasp as she takes me inside and I can feel her walls tightening around me. She's so fucking tight and I love it. Normally, I would have continued the foreplay a little more, but this is not about sex, this is about *fucking*. None of that intimacy laying in my arms bullshit. I pull out and kiss her roughly as a warning, then I'm ready to enter her again, and when I do, I feel her body gasp, this time in pleasure. She tries to make eye contact with me, but I continue to pound away mechanically. Suddenly she pushes me away, leaving me surprised.

"You can't just pick me up and drop me when you want, Dante. I want it all or nothing."

I stare back at her, half bemused in her confidence and half pissed that I was just about to climax, and she fucking spoilt it. "This is all I can give you, take it or leave it." I match her defiance, letting her know that I can't give her what she wants even if I wanted to.

I see the tears fill her eyes, her face crumpling as she walks out without glancing back once. I punch my hand on the shower pane, almost smashing the glass, and push my hair back in agitation. "This is all your fucking fault," I say, looking down at my rock-hard cock.

Chapter Fifteen

Exit Wounds

Eleni

I exit the shower, grabbing a towel on the way out, and I can feel the tears start to escape. I walk into my bedroom, slamming the door. I see my reflection in the mirror, and I don't even recognize myself. My eyes are blotchy from crying, my lips swollen from his hard kisses, and my hair completely wild from this morning's escapades. There is only one person I want to see, one person who will understand me, and I don't give a shit whether Dante forbids it or not. I hear the door slam and the elevator doors close as I take my phone out.

***

Dante

"Dante?" Nico snaps me out of my thoughts.

"The fuck is wrong with you?" He looks at me with a raised eyebrow.

"Nothing," I snap back, lighting a cigarette.

"You got laid last night, I can tell. Who—? Eleni! Again? Damn, I need to invest in a virgin. Who would have thought—"

I stare at him and he trails off, knowing I don't want to talk about it. I curse at my own stupidity to keep sleeping with her when we live under the same roof. I had given her false hope for something I could never deliver. At least she knows where we stand now. I saw her tears in the shower, although she tried to hide them from me. I know her well enough to read her emotions. The sex was amazing, and if we finished what we started in the shower, that would have been even better, but everything else that she wants I can't give her. We pull up wordlessly outside Padrone's penthouse and make our way into the building. Nico's eyes flick toward me to give him permission to speak, but I'm not in the mood. We get off at the elevator and make our way into my father's office. He looks well after his trip to Sicily; his dark skin and white hair contrast each other. He leans back on his chair as if waiting for us to speak.

"Well?" he says in his usual, clipped tone.

"Lorenzo is still MIA, but we have hit all of his clubs and warehouses. He can't attack us even if he wants to."

"Andre?"

"Taken care of. I think I made my point *graphically*."

"Good, what steps are you taking to track

Lorenzo down?"

"We have, or had an informant, but she seems to have, uh, disappeared," Nico replies sheepishly.

"Fonseca?"

"His files are sealed. He isn't FBI, he's just a regular cop."

"That doesn't mean he isn't being protected by someone. We're not the only family with contacts."

"Arman Rafiq, Salvatore's backer, wants a meeting with us."

"Why?" I ask suspiciously.

"Now Salvatore is indisposed, it's affecting his profits, so clearly he wants to meet with us so he can get his product out there."

"Can we trust him?"

"There is only one way to find out, get this meeting organized, if Rafiq switches sides, that gives us the monopoly over Salvatore. We need to find a way to do it without arousing Fonseca's suspicion or we find his price. Everyone has a price, even cops. Call Dre and have him find out as much as he can about Fonseca. See if he knows about this informant, whether she is down as missing or if she's been found dead. Cops on the Salvatore's payroll might have her body discovered somewhere else; it will delay the identification process."

Nico walks out clutching his phone and my father stares at me for a while.

"What?" I ask, rolling my eyes.

"You look tired, son."

"I've been busy while you were away."

"Are you sure that is all it is?"

"Meaning?" I fold my arms in anger, as he is

really starting to piss me off now.

"I thought it was down to the antics you were getting up to with that young girl."

My dad is too old school to drop the actual words he really wants to say. He knows we've been hooking up, and he is not pleased. I look at him, surprised. How the fuck did he even know? It's not like we we're doing it in public.

He looks at me shrewdly. I detect a half smirk on his face. "You insult my intelligence, Dante. I own New York. Do you think I would find it hard to work out what you get up to in my absence?"

"I don't know what you mean, Dad," I reply, brushing him off.

He rolls his eyes. "Keep your head in the game and don't act like a Goddamn *Stronzo*, that is all I'm saying, and I won't repeat it again." He opens his newspaper as a sign that I am dismissed. This is his way of telling me he disapproves of my behavior. Well, it was done now, so he could shove his disapproval where the sun don't shine. I stalk out of his office, slamming the door. Childish, I know, but I don't give a fuck anymore.

***

Eleni

I get dressed quickly and my heartbeat quickens, knowing I am going against everything Dante has forbidden me to do. I need to see Renee and warn her about Fonseca. Her life shouldn't be ruined because of my actions. I will be in trouble beyond my wildest imagination if he finds out. He wasn't around, so that was a good sign. I walk into the kitchen and see Ajax. I must look shocked because he grins.

"I can't say that was the reaction I was looking for." He laughs, and I blush in embarrassment.

"Casual Friday?" I ask, taking in his apparel, tight black jeans, Converse, and a sleeveless tank showing off his elaborate tattoo collection.

"I'm not on a job today, so I figured I didn't have to bring any weapons."

He laughs at my expression. "Kidding. Dante wanted me to stick around here today."

"Babysitting duties?"

"You've got it, sister," he says with a wink.

Shit. How am I going to get out of this? There is no way Ajax is going to let me out of his sight.

"Ow." I double over in mock pain.

"What's wrong?" He looks at me in alarm.

"Cramps, it's that time of the month." I sigh in pain.

"Oh…right." I have to contain my laughter as he looks away sheepishly.

"Can I have some time alone? Unless you want to stay here with me…" I do another sigh of pain, clasping my side for even more dramatic effect, and his eyes widen in repulsion.

"Nope! I'll be in the office. Give me a shout if you need anything." He practically runs out the room and I stifle my laughter at how easily he was deceived. I guess I learned that from Dante, I thought to myself.

I walk out of the house, being careful to avoid

any cameras, and slowly close the door.
Free at last but at what cost?

***

Nico

Ring.
Groan.
Ring.
I just went to sleep.
Ring.
Fuck off.

I fumble around looking for my phone, promising to break the neck of whichever jackass dares to ring me so early.

"What?"

"Nice phone manners, asshole." I hear Dre's deep voice on the other side of the line.

"Give me a break, I just went to sleep five minutes ago."

"Like I give a fuck." He laughs, and I laugh too because we can never stay mad at each other for too long.

"Sofie is dead, execution Sicilian style." I exhale deeply. It's official, she had been found out as our leak. I run my hands through my hair, figuring out our next step.

"Oh, and Fonseca can't be brought, he wants to bring Dante down at all costs. He hates the Mafia and anything to do with it, there is no way he's affiliated with any other families. Dante is going to have to ride this out. I don't know how he is going to swing this meeting with Rafiq. Fonseca will be watching like a hawk."

"Thanks for all the good news," I say sarcastically.

"You're welcome," he says before clicking off.

The bed covers move, and a long, tanned leg becomes uncovered.

"Baby, come back to bed," a voice purrs from under the covers as a blonde head of hair pops out.

Nadine? Nadia? Natasha? N-something from the club last night emerges out of my red silk covers and drapes herself over me, but I'm really not in the mood, and I know Dante is going to flip his shit when he finds out the latest news.

"Why are you so tense? Let Noelle help you, baby."

Noelle, that was it.

I'm about to protest then I think fuck it, we're both here and I feel myself getting aroused as she grinds herself on top of me, so why not? She moves her head down and flicks her eyes up at me every now and then to show she is about to go down on me. *Hurry up and cut out the fucking theatrics.* I must admit it's worth it when she finally gets down to it, she takes me so deep in her mouth I'm surprised she doesn't choke with my size. I pull her up before I am about to come because I don't want to waste it on a blow job. I push her down on the bed and pound her hard, the headboard shakes so much I think it is about to break the Goddamn wall. I watch her climax before I come shortly after and roll over.

"Nico, that was—"

"Yeah, I know," I reply reflexively, pulling my boxers on, already thinking about my next task.

"You're leaving?" She looks at me, dumbfounded.

"Well, actually, you are. I've got shit to do."

"You're throwing me out?" She looks enraged and I snicker at her.

"We're not exactly Romeo and Juliet, babe, I met you five hours ago, and I've fucked you in every way possible. What else is there to do?"

She throws a pillow at me and grabs her clothes from the floor before storming out.

"Fucking jerk!" she calls from the hallway before she slams the apartment door.

"You're welcome," I call back.

Shower first, then break the news to Dante.

I've already forgotten about the girl who left the apartment.

***

Dante

"Where are Nico and Zeek?"

Farook shrugs. "Things got pretty wild last night—"

I roll my eyes, imagining what has probably happened.

My phone rings. *Ajax* flashes up on the screen.

"Yeah?" I ask. He is not my favorite person. I didn't particularly want to leave him alone with Eleni after I saw the way he reacts around her, I know he likes her and that enrages me, but I shouldn't really give a shit because I can't have her anyway.

"Eleni is gone."

My heart skips a bit when I hear those three words.

Gone.

"What do you mean, gone?"

"Her stuff is still here, maybe she has gone to see someone?"

The secret phone call yesterday pops up in my mind and I know exactly who she has gone to see. Eleni is too sentimental, and I won't let that be my downfall. I feel the anger rise in me and fling the phone against the wall. It smashes into pieces as Farook looks on, shocked.

"Track her phone," I say to Farook.

Big mistake defying me, Eleni.

Big fucking mistake.

Chapter Sixteen

Black, White And Grey

"So…"

"So…"

I sit opposite Renee in a Starbucks a few blocks away from Dante's place. A tight knot in my stomach is forming as I wonder if Ajax has figured out if I'm gone or not.

"Eleni?"

"Hm?"

"I just said I don't want this guy to get between us."

"Which one?' I snort at her. Dante isn't an angel, but Detective Fonseca is worse, although she doesn't know it yet.

"What do you see in him?" She looks at me, aghast. "He's a gangster."

I roll my eyes at her. "Says who?"

"You know he is, Eleni, stop being so difficult about this. He is bad news. Why are you defending him?"

Dark Temptation

I don't owe him anything but talking about this with Renee feels wrong. I came here to warn her about Detective Fonseca, but she ignores me, and the subject keeps switching back to Dante. I want to confide in her about what has happened between Dante and I romantically, not about his other activities. However, I don't feel comfortable to tell her anything anymore. In fact, I don't feel comfortable around her anymore, period. Something has shifted and I felt like she wasn't even listening to me, she was just fishing for information.

"I didn't come here to talk about Dante." I change the subject, not wanting to delve into the *grey matter* of Dante Dischanel.

"I want to help you, Eleni, but you need to help me first. Help *us* first."

"Us?" I frown at her and my pulse quickens a little, this meeting is starting to unnerve me. Renee seems different and I think I just put my finger on why.

"If you cooperate with Aiden, he can get you away from Dante. He just needs some information—" She says it so breezily that it takes me a while to figure out what she really wants.

"Are you fucking kidding me? Is this why you called me the other night—to be your *informant?*"

I stand up, my eyes are blazing in fury. I thought she was my friend. I came here to talk to her, and she's trying to get me to do the one thing I would never do.

"You're just his puppet, aren't you? This was never about me and you, it was about him."

She rolls her eyes at me as if we're having a childish argument about what movie to see. "We're trying to help you get away from this monster, don't you see what he is capable of?"

I am so taken back by this that I laugh—not because I find it funny, but because Renee is pointing one finger at me, not knowing that Aiden Fonseca himself is an iron fist in a velvet glove.

"You need to help yourself before you start trying to help me," I scream. "He's the monster, he's only with you to get to me!"

She looks at me sadly, like I'm too stupid to understand her true intentions and pauses before she gets up and hugs me. I'm so taken back by this that I hug her back. I pull away, knowing that I will never see her again, and that I have lost the best friend I've ever had. I open the door of the coffee shop and start walking down the street. At some point I start crying, and I don't know why, but I can't stop the tears seeping from my eyes.

"I would be crying too if I were you, Eleni, you have no idea what you have done," a low, menacing voice from behind me says, and I jump around, expecting Dante, but it's Ajax. His normally sky-blue eyes have become icy and he looks pissed.

***

Dante

I tap on the desk impatiently while Farook contacts Ajax about Eleni's location.

I'm mad. Real mad, and I can feel heated anger bubbling inside me like a volcano ready to erupt. Nico walks in looking like hell. His lips are bruised, and his neck is purple.

Fucking liability, I think to myself irritably, despite knowing I was doing the same thing as him last night.

"Sofie is dead. They pulled her out of a river in Coney Island Creek tied to weights."

"Sending us a message I see, Lorenzo knows she was his leak, so he will come after us again," I say bitterly.

"Fonseca can't be brought; he hates you too much."

I smile to myself. *Fucking great, this day keeps getting better.*

"What?" Nico looks at me, confused by my lack of reaction.

Farook hangs the phone up. "Eleni is at a coffee shop a few blocks from your place."

Nico looks confused. "Yeah, and?"

"Fonseca's girl is there. Ajax has eyes on her, and he will retrieve her when she is alone."

Nico looks at me, alarmed. "Do you think…?"

"No, but if she does…I want to handle this myself. I'm going there now."

"No," Nico says, crossing his arms and crushing his cigarette. "There is too much heat on you right now for public confrontations, Dante."

"Besides, you need to meet with your lawyer. You need to work on your loopholes before Fonseca figures a way to use them against you," Farook replies nodding at Nico in agreement.

"Fine," I say, exasperated. "Tell Ajax to bring her to me."

I don't need to finish the rest of the sentence, there is a thin line between loyalty and treachery.

***

Eleni

"Ajax." My voice goes an octave higher as I register the fury on his face.

"How are your cramps?" He spits the words at me as if they were venom.

"I—" I stutter, trying to cobble an excuse together. "How did you know I was here?"

"Dante has a tracker in your phone," he says flatly, as if that was the most obvious thing in the world.

"He what? That is an invasion of my privacy." The words tumble out in anger.

"Privacy? Are you trying to hide the company that you are keeping?"

I feel the color drain from my face.

He smirks. "Not so clever now, are you?"

"I—"

A beep goes off in Ajax's hand and he looks puzzled for a second. I try to speak again but he puts his fingers to his lips. Ajax pulls my bag off my shoulder and I look at him in confusion. He roots around and pulls out a tiny device. He stamps it with his foot until there is nothing left.

"Listening device." He folds his arms and I comprehend for the first time what the

164

repercussions are for my petty act of revenge.

"How did you know?"

"This is a security sensor. It beeps if there are any recording devices in the vicinity."

I pause in horror. *The hug, she planted it on me.*

"Ajax, I'm sorry. If I knew—"

"Save it for the boss. He's not happy with either of us."

Shame washes over me as I realize I have not only fucked things up for myself, but I dragged Ajax into this too.

"I'll tell Dante it's my fault—"

He laughs at me coldly. "Since when does Dante listen to excuses? Get in the fucking car before you get into any more trouble." He pulls open the car door and nods. He enters from the other side and we have a wordless journey back to Dante's. I keep trying to speak to apologize but my mouth goes dry in trepidation of Dante's reaction.

***

Dante

I light up a cigarette and pour myself a whisky as Ilayda gives me options about Fonseca.

"Dante, it's not even five—"

"Are you my lawyer or my mother?" I continue pouring and watch her sigh in irritation.

She is about to continue when I see Eleni walk in, accompanied by a very pissed off looking Ajax.

"Ah, the wanderer returns," I say, crossing my legs and taking a deep drag of my cigarette.

Her eyes are red, and her face has gone pale. If she's hoping for the sympathy vote she's got the wrong fucking audience.

"I don't need your permission to go out, you're not the boss of me," she says in a small voice unconvincingly.

"Well, until this debt is paid off, I am very much the boss of you." She looks down in defeat and I feel myself getting more worked up even though this is victory for me.

"Why do you keep making stupid decisions, Eleni? Renee is in league with Fonseca, is it so hard for you to fucking understand that she is not your friend anymore?"

She flinches but keeps looking down.

"Are you playing double agent, Eleni? Are you trying to deceive me? Do you want Fonseca to lock me up?" I say in a calmer voice because I want fucking answers.

"No! I just—" She inhales deeply. "I thought she was my friend. I was trying to warn her about him." Her voice starts to waver and Ajax and I both laugh. She looks up, horrified, at Ajax.

Yes, sweetheart, he is as much a piece of shit as I am.

"Just because you're heartless, it doesn't mean that everyone else is," She spits back at me, and I see the sadness in her eyes has turned to anger.

"I'd rather be heartless rather than blind to what is in front of me. Ajax texted me about the listening device as soon as he found it."

"I didn't know. I swear to you I would never—"

"Dante, drop it."

I forget Ilayda is behind me for a second and she looks at me as if to say *enough*. I watch Eleni stare back at the floor again and her shoulders sag in defeat, but I can't drop it.

***

Eleni

I give the woman on Dante's left a small smile even though I feel like I'm going to cry. I appreciate her putting her neck out for me, whoever she is. I don't seem to have anyone in my corner anymore. Ajax shoots me a look of disdain to show me he definitely has not forgotten what I did.

"Enough, Ilayda, I never asked for your opinion," He barks, and I see the anger rising in his face again. She rolls her eyes and sits on the couch.

"If Ajax hadn't found that listening device, the Feds would have been carting me off to jail as we speak."

"I didn't expect that, I thought she was *my friend*. I didn't go to meet her to work against you. Not everything is as black and white as you think, Dante." I look up at him and meet his gaze firmly, noting the storm clouds in his green eyes.

"There is no such thing as a grey area, you are either loyal or you're not. You can't be best friends with the law and working for me." He enunciates the word *working* so I know what he really means. *Sleeping with him.* My mind flashes back to last night and I can't believe how much has changed in twenty-four hours. I know he's thinking the same thing too from how he's looking at me.

"I'm not going to see her again—ever." I attempt to make a peace offering.

"Damn fucking right, you won't. Ajax, take Zeek and find out where Sapphire is. Nobody seems to have a fucking clue, and I need to know what's happening with these Goddamn shipments." Ajax nods and walks out. Ilayda walks into another room on a call. It's just me and him standing here and I can feel friction building in the air like an invisible wall between us. He walks toward me and looks me straight in the eye. "Where do we go from here, Eleni?"

Chapter Seventeen

This Isn't A Fairytale.

"Ahem." A voice interrupts us, and I look up to see the tall brunette woman who was next to Dante earlier.

"We haven't been formally introduced. I am Ilayda Majeed, Dante's lawyer and Farook's wife."

I look at her in shock, and she giggles a little. "Keeping it in the family."

Dante rolls his eyes next to her. "Is this a business meeting or a fucking sleepover? Let's get to it. Eleni, this conversation isn't over, either." His eyes narrow to slits and he disappears into his office, slamming the door.

"It's going to be a long day when he's in this kind of mood." She sighs and follows Dante to his office, and I am left alone, contemplating the huge mess I have created.

***

Dante

"Dante, calm down." Farook looks over at me from my desk. He can see me getting worked up because things are getting out of control and I'm *always* in control. The Eleni situation is pissing me off, her juvenile act of revenge could have really taken a turn for the worse, and I knew it was my fucking fault. I know Padrone will flip when he hears about this. Ilayda walks in and she and Farook share a knowing marital gaze. She sits in front of me and starts talking slowly, like I am an unruly child who she needs to discipline.

"So far the DA's office has no discernible evidence which ties you to Sofie's death or the fire at Victorie. It's all circumstantial."

"So, I can meet with Rafiq without Fonseca putting his nose in?"

"I don't see why not. You didn't have anything to do with Sofie, but we don't know whether Salvatore's undercover cops could flip it. With Rafiq, you're both legitimate business owners. As long as you don't do anything stupid to draw attention to yourself, then you should be fine." She gives me a disapproving look and folds her arms.

"Like what?" I roll my eyes at her and look at Farook in annoyance that he told her.

"Let me see." She mock thinks. "Attempted public confrontations with Detective Fonseca's girlfriend, something along those stupid lines. I can't believe you would think of doing something so reckless, Dante. What were you thinking?"

I'm getting pissed off, but I know she's right, so

I just silently seethe.

"That is the reason why we have button men and soldiers as insulation, so these layers prevent anything being traced back to you."

"Thank you for this lesson in Mafia 101. Aside from the sarcasm, is it safe to meet him?"

"It's safe for now, but Fonseca won't let this go, so tread carefully."

"Farook, set up the meeting for Friday."

"Yes, Capo."

"Eleni is the only loose end in this. Do you trust her?"

"I don't trust anyone," I reply mechanically.

"Give her a break, she could have snitched multiple times but didn't. She *knows* she can't be friends with Fonseca's girl anymore, she's sorry," Farook interjects.

I roll my eyes at him and he shakes his head at me. "She's just a college kid, Dante, don't be so hard on her."

"When I was her age, I'd already made my bones." I clench my jaw defiantly.

"You were born into this life, she wasn't," he says it in a low voice and meets my gaze.

I snort at him. "You're too soft, always have been."

"That's true." Ilayda sighs and Farook throws her a look of annoyance.

"Have you asked her about joining the family? That way we know where her loyalty lies," Ilayda replies, toying with the pen in her hand.

"Yeah, I did. I don't think she wants this."

"Depends on what your definition of *this* is." She

throws me a knowing glare.

"What?" I lean my back on my desk and stare at her innocently.

She rolls her eyes at me. "She's not the first to be burned by Dante Dischanel and she won't be the last, I'm sure."

"Do I pay you to be my lawyer or my conscience?"

"You pay me because I'm fucking incredible at my job and I'm giving you this advice for free."

She has me there.

"I'll talk to her; I've been through this myself, remember." She clatters off, leaving Farook and me standing there.

"How do you put up with her?" I ask, annoyed.

"She's smart, beautiful, and fucking amazing in bed."

I roll my eyes at him and he winks at me.

***

Eleni

I lay face down on the bed, pissed off at myself.

She planted a wire on me. A wire! If Ajax hadn't have found it, I could have landed Dante in jail without even knowing it.

The door creaks open and my stomach ties in knots, expecting Dante at the doorway. I can just imagine his frosty eyes and furious glare, but it wasn't him. A blond head appears in the arch of the doorway. "How is our little runaway doing?" He smirks at me.

"Get lost, Nico."

"Touchy."

"You can't make me feel worse than I already do."

"You clearly don't know me, sweetheart." He walks in and leans on the wall, observing me with a devilish grin playing on his lips.

I turn on my front and look at him. "How mad is Dante?" I ask, dreading the answer.

"On a scale of one to ten, I would say a million. I'm sure you can make it up to him in many ways." He smirks as I blush furiously.

"Don't you have somewhere else to be?"

"No, I'm your chauffeur tonight. Dante wants you working at Escada, and I've been chosen to have the pleasure of escorting you there and back. Ruining my fucking night, that's for sure, I had plans." He sighs in irritation.

"I'm not supposed to work tonight," I reply, confused.

"Well, now you are, so fucking get dressed. I'll be waiting outside in one hour."

He leaves the room. I'm stunned. *He doesn't want me around, that's why he wants me at Escada tonight. I feel the knot in my stomach tighten.* I slowly start to get ready, swallowing the salty tears of shame that keep threatening to envelop me. Ilayda walks in just as I'm finishing my lipstick off.

"Hi."

"Hi," I reply sheepishly.

"We didn't get a chance to talk before."

"I'm sure Dante has filled you in about me," I say, sighing turning back to the mirror.

"Something like that…Dante is a complicated guy, but he'll get over it eventually."

I snort, knowing that isn't likely.

"I wanted to talk to you. Dante has asked you about joining the family?"

"Yeah, although I'm sure he'll be rescinding that offer pretty quickly."

"We all make errors in judgement, Eleni. Dante doesn't blame you…" She trails off and I look at her.

"Okay, he does a little, but he'll get over it. I know this isn't exactly how you planned your life…"

"No kidding, I just want my life to go back to normal." I feel the lump rising back in my throat.

I wish this never happened. I wish I'd never met him. This is not what I planned.

It was like she read my mind. "Not everything happens like it's supposed to."

"What are your plans after you pay back Dante?"

I shrug. "Start a residency and get a job, wait for things to go back to normal, I guess."

She chuckles and I frown at her.

"You've had an intense couple of months. Do you think that you could ever go back to normal? Sometimes we crave what eludes us.' She sighs at me almost sadly, and I feel there is more to this story than what she is saying.

I look at her. "How did you meet Farook?"

"It's not a pretty story."

"My life isn't exactly a fairy tale either," I say sarcastically.

She sits down on my comforter and starts tracing

the intricate pattern with her finger.

"I was born in Turkey, the black mountains of Afyonkarahisar, where they harvest the opium poppy. One day when I was sixteen, me and my brother were playing. We must have gotten lost because we ended up in the poppy fields.' She pauses for a second and tries to compose herself. "My mother warned us about playing in the fields…we must have been loud because trucks pull up in front of us. Men armed with weapons jumped out at us. They thought we were thieves. I thought they were going to kill me."

I'm silent now, listening to her, and I feel my heart beat a little quicker.

"What happened?" I ask, my throat dry.

"The leader got out, he introduced himself as Raz, but I knew who he was. He was known as *Afyon Kral*. The Opium King, the most feared drug lord in Turkey. He asked me how old I was and when I told him, he laughed for a long time and said he liked them young, then he grabbed me and threw me in the truck. My brother tried to stop him…but Raz's men shot him. I could hear his screams as we drove away." Silent tears were falling down her face now and I reach out to touch her hand, but it is ice cold.

"How did you get away?"

"I didn't. We drove to Ankara that night and got married."

I gasp in shock as she carries on in a flat voice like she is telling me what the weather will be.

"I learned incredibly early in our marriage that it was easier to comply with Raz. I still have the scars and cigarette burns from when I didn't." She lifts up her skirt and I can see faded marks on her inner thighs. "After two years of hell in Turkey, we moved to New York. Raz wanted to try his hand in the big boy leagues. By this point I was crushed in every way a person can be. My spirit, my body, my mind—everything. I was a shadow of the girl I once was."

"I can't imagine," I say in a small voice, trailing off because I can't think of one thing to say that might comfort her from reliving his.

"We were living in Manhattan at this point. I hardly saw Raz. He was either high or with one of his other girlfriends…not that I was complaining. One night I was sleeping and awoke to a man with a gun to my head, an assassin sent to kill Raz. It was Farook."

"That's how you met!"

"Yep, Raz had been trying to muscle into Dischanel territory and you know how that usually ends. When Farook realized I wasn't Raz, he froze. By this point I was over living if you could even call it that. I grabbed his gun and put it to my head. You can imagine this wasn't the simple scenario Farook had envisioned when he was sent to kill Raz.' She pauses and I beckon for her continue, in awe of what she is telling me.' He managed to wrestle the gun from me, and I cried and cried and told him everything Raz had done to me. I don't even know why I did; I think I just needed to say it out loud. It was like a release. Poor Farook, nineteen years old and being used as a sounding board for his target's wife."

"What did he say?"

"It wasn't what he said, it was what he did. He packed my things and took me to Dante's place."

"Of all people, Dante?"

"Yep, Dante wasn't in charge back then, but he and Farook were best friends from school. Dante's brother and his father were running things. Dante spoke to his father on behalf of Farook, and I was granted sanctuary within the Dischanel Family. Dominic knew I had inside information on Raz which he could use to trap him. He wasn't doing it out of the kindness of his heart."

"Dante actually helped you?" I ask, bewildered.

She snorts. "Not me, Farook...and it was more Dominic. Dante couldn't have given a rat's ass back then. Sapphire was the only other girl in the family at that time. I was living with her for about a week before I had enough and wanted to shoot her, so I moved in with Farook."

She smiles for the first time and I see a twinkle appear in her dark eyes. "I definitely cramped his style. Gone was the bachelor pad and the revolving door of girls. Farook knew he had to keep a low profile to hide me from Raz."

"So, were you guys...?"

"No! No way! That was the last thing on my mind. Farook was a perfect gentleman. He took the couch, and I took the bed...although I was having so many nightmares, he slept next to me on the floor sometimes."

"Did Raz find out where you were?"

"Naturally. Raz was no fool, he had heard whispers that the Dischanel Family wanted to take him out."

"What happened?"

"Raz tried to kill Dominic. Three weeks later, Raz was shot to death outside one of his nightclubs."

"Dominic killed him?"

"No, Dante did. That night he made his bones," she says darkly.

"What does that mean?" I ask, scared.

"It means Dante killed for the first time. Dante was officially third in command after Dominic and his brother. I was finally free of Raz's oppression, and for the first time in what felt like a lifetime I didn't have to look over my shoulder anymore. Farook bought me an airplane ticket and the next day I was back home."

"You must have been so happy."

"I thought I would be, but I wasn't." She gives me a knowing look.

"But you were home. Your nightmare was over."

"I was thrilled to come home to my parents, they thought I was dead. My brother was still alive. Raz hadn't killed him, only wounded him. It was strange being home in a place that was so familiar, but I felt like a stranger. I wasn't the sixteen-year-old who once roamed freely there. Every part of the house was a reminder of the girl who didn't exist anymore. It was a cruel reminder of the innocence I had lost. I could tell my family was upset too. I think on some level they would have preferred if I were dead. I didn't belong there anymore. I was a piece of the puzzle that didn't *fit* into place."

We both stayed silent as I let the horror of her

story sink in.

"What did you do?"

"I booked a flight back to New York and twenty-four hours later I was standing outside Farook's apartment."

"You never saw your family again?"

"Not until my first child was born. I needed to start my new life before I could revisit my old one."

"What did Farook say?"

She laughs. "He was a little shocked, to say the least. I don't think he banked on seeing me again. I don't think I realized how much I loved him until I was standing outside his door."

"Wow, I can't believe you guys ended up together after all that."

"Honey, that isn't even the whole story. When I turned up at his place, I was kind of nervous he would turn me away, but he didn't. We stayed up all night—"

I stifle a giggle and she rolls her eyes. "Not like that. Farook wanted to do things properly. He didn't want me as just a girlfriend. He wanted to make it official, but we had to get Dante on board. Farook knew Dante would see me as a distraction. I decided to practice law because I knew it would make me a useful asset to the family. Dante wasn't pleased at first that I was taking one of his wing men away but Farook made it clear he wasn't going to give me up, so Dante relented in the end. I spent years in night school getting my GED, then college and law school. After I graduated we got married. It was truly the happiest day of my life. It's been a long road but against all odds we made it, eight years and two daughters later, we're still standing. I practice in family law, so I can help other women who are in the same situation as me. I want to make a difference."

"But you represent Dante too?"

"Yeah, I practice a little criminal law too, but I only represent the Dischanel Family."

"How do you—"

"Practice law and stay married to a criminal? Not everything is as straightforward as it seems. I'm dealing with the hand that life has dealt me, which is what we all have to do in our own way. No journey or destination is going to be the same."

"I'm still reeling from your story."

She smiles at me. "Try living it. If in your heart you believe that you can have a normal life, then I wish you nothing but the best. But from my own experience, normal doesn't exist. Your life as you once knew it *doesn't* exist. The old Eleni isn't here anymore. People that you thought were your friends—" She trails off and my chest pangs, thinking of Renee's deceit. "Don't let your emotions cloud your judgment, you can build an excellent life for yourself in this family.'

"What do you mean, my emotions?"

"I mean Dante. I know there is something going on, I'm not stupid."

I sigh. "Is it that obvious?"

"I've known Dante for a while, and when he's really mad about something, there is usually an underlying reason why. I know this is the last thing you want to hear, but he's a good guy."

"Debatable."

"I know he's a dick sometimes."

"All the time."

"Like I said, it's your decision, but if you really want a future with Dante, you need to think of the lifestyle that comes along with it. Being in love with a man with a target on his back, late nights, canceled dates, constantly worrying whether they're safe, what they're doing and who they are with. Do you trust him? Can you sleep at night when he's not around? Not knowing where he is and who he might be with? Is he really worth it? Those are the questions you need to ask yourself, Eleni, before even getting involved with one of these guys."

I sigh, rubbing my head. "I never thought about it in that context, and I don't think I will need to. He said we can't be together. Besides, after today—"

She shrugs. "What Dante says and what he does are two different things, but this isn't about Dante, it's about you. I hope you make the right choice based on you, not anyone else."

She leaves the room and I stand still with the weight of the world on my shoulders.

Chapter Eighteen

Side-Effects

Eleni

My head is still reeling from talking to Ilayda, but it's so busy in Escada tonight I barely have time to think. I'm supposed to be working with Zosha tonight, but I can't seem to find her anywhere. I see Farook and Dre standing at the bar talking, so I interject, "Hey, have you seen Zosha?"

"She's gone in the back, we need more tequila," Dre replies, checking his phone. "I've got a meeting with the big man, see you later." Dre walks off, leaving me standing there with Farook.

"So, you met my wife?"

"I did. I never figured you would even have a wife."

"I'm a man of many surprises."

"Clearly."

"Have you made up your mind up about Dante's offer?"

"Not yet."

"Tick tock." He walks away, leaving me standing there even more confused than before.

***

Nico

Eleni barely speaks to me on the way here, she doesn't even take the bait for any of jokes about her sleeping with Dante. Disappointing. I was fucking bored out of my skull until I saw Zosha. As soon as she caught my eye, she disappears into the storeroom, and like a predator hunting prey, I followed her.

"Are you hiding from me, Z?"

"Don't call me that."

"It's my nickname for you."

"Nicknames are affectionate. You don't hold any affection in you."

"You're breaking my heart, baby, with that talk."

"You don't have one."

She turns her back on me, looking for bottles. I grab her wrist and pull her back into my arms.

"Look at me."

"No."

I kiss her hard, but she doesn't respond.

"You always do this, Nico. I can't keep running back to you." She looks at me with her huge eyes, but I don't feel any guilt. When I want something, I take it.

"I want you. I miss this, I miss coming home to you at night. I miss fucking you."

Her body starts to relax, and I know I almost have her.

"I miss this." My hand works her way underneath her dress to the lace on her underwear and I feel her body start to melt as I stroke her thigh before working my fingers through the lace.

"Nico—" Her voice is starting to wane; the fight is going out of her.

I kiss her again, and she responds this time, her hands are undoing my belt and she giggles. She finds me hard. "No changes in this department, baby." She opens the buttons of my shirt and starts to stroke the wolf tattoo on my chest.

"I missed him."

"He missed you too." I nuzzle her roughly and pull up her dress. I can't wait anymore, so I rip her panties in half, and she looks at me like I'm crazy but I don't give a shit. We are tongue fucking now and my fingers are massaging her clit as I feel her start to drip on me. She moves down and takes me in her mouth, and I feel my eyes roll back a little but right now I just want to fuck instead. I pull her up and start pounding the shit out of her, her walls tighten around me like she was made for my dick. Halfway through, I forget about a condom and I curse myself.

"I told you I'm on the pill."

I don't care about that shit, I know Zosha wants a baby, and I'm not taking that risk, so I pull out and relieve myself on her thigh. I snort at her annoyance that I ruined her dress but she's smiling at me all the same. *I know what's coming next.* She moves herself down slowly, gazing up at me as she takes me in her mouth and I let her finish what she started earlier. I push myself further, so she takes me deep, her tongue swirling and flicking all around me like she's doing tongue aerobics. I feel that familiar clench and I release all down her sweet little throat then I hear…

"Oh my God!" We both turn around and Eleni is standing there with her mouth wide open.

"I know I'm big, babe, but there's really no need for that reaction." I smirk at her as I pull up my pants.

"Nico, get out." Zosha wipes her mouth and gives me the look so I make myself scarce.

***

Eleni

What the hell did I just see?
"Zosha—"

"Save it, Nico and I have a past that we sometimes revisit." She looks at me with her arms crossed.

"You're too good for him," I say, horrified by what I have just witnessed.

Nico, of all people, the biggest jerk I have ever met.

"Thanks."

There is an uneasy silence building.

"Everyone knows you're fucking Dante, so drop the Saint Eleni act. A little cliché, don't you think, banging the boss?" she says spitefully.

I'm hurt for a second at how cruel she's being to

me. "At least he doesn't bang everything with a pulse. Nico is so sleazy."

"Doesn't he? Wow, you really think Dante will be your knight in shining armor? He will fuck you over just like he does with every other sappy girl who thinks he's going to be Prince Charming."

I want to say something back, but I can't, my eyes are getting misty again and I piss myself off with my sensitivity level.

"Dante needs more Cristal, take it up to the penthouse if it isn't too much trouble for little miss perfect." She stalks off, leaving me standing there bewildered.

I thought she was my friend.

Renee was supposed to be your friend too, look how that ended up.

Dante doesn't want me in the way I want him to, Zosha hates me, Ajax hates me even more. I don't fit into this life so where do I fit?

I walk out of the storage room in a daze and collect the Cristal and head upstairs to the penthouse. The first face I see is naturally Dante's. He seems in a better mood. His face is lit up by his smile and he and Dre are joking about something. I feel relieved he seems to have gotten over my earlier indiscretion. I scan the rest of the room and Ajax is there with a brunette draped over him, and I feel a little, dare I say, jealous. He catches me looking at him and holds my gaze, but I look away. I still feel hot shame when I think how much I got him into trouble today with my stupidity. I make small talk with a few of Dante's men and one of the few other girls in Dante's regime, Ra. I look around to see where Dante has disappeared to because he isn't talking to Dre anymore, then I see him with a girl. She's sitting on his lap, her hand stroking his dark hair, and I see his hand resting on his thigh, circling it as it moves up higher. She whispers to him and he gives her a small nod as she starts to kiss his neck. He catches my eye and our gazes lock, sending a spasm of pain to my chest.

"Eleni?" I stand there motionless, holding a bucket of ice. Its coldness was nothing like the numbness I felt in my chest. The blonde that he unwrapped himself from grabs the champagne bottle out of my hands.

"About time."

He ignores her. "I thought you were downstairs."

"I didn't know I was meant to be working tonight at all."

"We were short staffed. I didn't think you would mind after earlier," he says meaningfully.

I ignore his little dig. "Zosha said you wanted Cristal; I'm just following orders, boss." I enunciate the words and his eyebrows raise but he doesn't react.

"How are things at the bar?" he says flatly.

"Nothing I can't handle." I fold my arms and there is a dead silence between us, like an invisible force sitting in between us.

"You didn't bring glasses." I forgot about the blonde bimbo who was now interjecting herself in the conversation.

"You've got legs," I snap back, watching Dante's mouth curl into a satisfied smirk.

"I know you didn't just talk to me like that!" She

walks toward me threateningly, but Dante blocks her.

"Both of you shut the fuck up," he says quietly and we both eye him in indignation.

"Get back to work, Kimber."

"I finish at two." She winks at him and flounces off.

"What?" He looks at my reaction, I can feel the repulsion written over my face.

"Nothing, I just thought you had better taste."

His eyes narrow and glitter dangerously as a warning that a line has been crossed. I hold my breath waiting for him to react, but he doesn't.

"Cut the fucking attitude and get back to the bar, my business is not your business."

We stand there for a second, both angrily eyeing each other before I walk off. I run down the spiral suitcase from the penthouse to the club, feeling tears begin to attack my eyes.

***

Dante

"What was that about?" Nico interrupted my thoughts.

"Don't ask," I reply irritably, lighting a cigarette.

"That bad, huh? Eleni didn't mention anything about me, did she?" I watch him try to act nonchalant.

"No, why would she?" I looked at him, searching his face for answers.

"She may have caught me in the storeroom with

188

Zosha…" He trails off and winks at me.

"For fuck's sake, Nico, are you an animal?"

"Affirmative, Capo." He guffaws and shrugs at me.

"Make sure you take Eleni home after her shift, no detours."

"What do you mean?' he asks innocently.

"Cut the bullshit, I've known you since you were six. Take her straight to my place, you won't be taking anyone else home tonight."

"Fine." He sighs sullenly like a petulant child.

"If I'm taking Eleni home, then I guess you have other plans?"

"Something like that."

I don't say anything, I just think of Kimber's long limbs wrapped around my body, crushing all the pressure I felt about this meeting with Rafiq.

"I need to loosen up." I reply, feeling anything but loose.

"I don't know about loosen up, but she won't be walking tomorrow." He smirks at me crudely. "What about Eleni?"

"What about her?" I reply, my tone showing the conversation was closed.

He looks at me but doesn't say anything back.

Damn, she has really got under his skin were the words burning through Nico Dischanel's mind.

***

Eleni

I'm not going to be that girl who cries in a club. I

leaned my head back to try and force the tears back in, but my throat burned mercilessly.

"What has a girl got to do to get a drink around here?"

I turned around and Ra was standing there leaning over the bar, looking mildly irritated.

"Sorry." I mumble feeble apology and watch as she looks at me in disapproval. Boy, I can tell why she was the only girl in Dante's team of men. Her glare was enough to make me look away. She had shocking red hair, half of it plaited back and the rest wild. Multiple piercings adorned her eyebrow and she had two on either side of her lip.

"Are you okay?" she asks as the tumbler in my hand smashes to pieces.

"Yeah, I'm fine," I reply, sweeping the debris away and getting another glass.

"You can't kid a kidder. Don't let that skank get to you." She looks at me knowingly and I feel her dark eyes pierce through me.

"Which one?" We both laugh, and it feels like a lifetime since I have smiled.

"They're all smash and pass girls, a dime in a dozen. I wouldn't worry about it too much," she says as I pour her a drink.

"Wow, Ra, are you being nice to me?"

She smiles sympathetically and something clicks.

Does everyone know about Dante and me?

She cocks her eyebrow at me as if to say, *yes, we do*.

She lights a cigarette and downs the tumbler, signaling me for a refill.

"I'm not crying over—"

Again, she raises her eyebrow at me as if to say, *yeah right.*

"It's not only that, I feel like I don't belong here."

"Sure, you've made some pretty bad choices, Eleni…"

"Thanks, Ra, I feel so much better." I roll my eyes at her.

"That doesn't mean anything, that was then, this is now. Sometimes you gotta bite the bullet. You've had a rough time here. Not everyone would still be standing after everything that has happened to you."

"I guess so."

"Have you decided what you're going to do about your dilemma?"

"I think I just made my mind up," I say, pouring her another round.

***

Dante

I zip up my pants and throw my shirt on. I'm meeting Rafiq in less than five hours and I feel anything but relaxed.

"I'm leaving," I say, grabbing my keys from the table.

"How about another round?" Kimber lays on her side, lighting up a cigarette, looking up at me seductively.

"I got bored during the second. I'm out."

"Well, don't fucking come back." She stands on

her knees, outraged at me.

I kiss her hard on her mouth to prove a point. "You don't mean that."

She misses the point and tries to wrap her hands around my neck, but I stop her and walk out of the door, trying to block out the regret that was beginning to claw at me.

***

Eleni

I wake up early and walk around the apartment silently. Although the sunshine lights up the room, I feel *cold* inside. I try to avoid the obvious fact that Dante slept somewhere else with someone else last night. I make myself a coffee and am sitting in the kitchen when I hear the door slam. Dante walks in wearing last night's clothes and we both look at each other, knowing where he has been.

"You're up early," he comments, leaning against the wall.

"You're in late." I cock my head, mimicking his action.

"I'm going to bed." He yawns and starts to turn around.

"If you want me to leave, just say it. I'm sick of the cold shoulder."

"I think it's the other way around." He turns back and folds his arms indignantly.

"Huh?"

"I asked you to join the family and you declined. I'm not going to beg you to change your mind."

"I never said no, I said I'll think about it."

"I know you won't, you want to be normal," he says sarcastically.

"Normal is overrated and it isn't what I want anymore." He looks at me, perplexed.

"What are you saying, Eleni?" he asks, frowning.

"I'm saying I'm ready join the family and prove my loyalty to you."

He walks toward me now and I stand up, so he's looking directly at me. "Are you sure about this? This is a one-way door, Eleni, you can't turn back."

"I'm sure I want this," I say firmly.

"This doesn't change anything between us, you know that?"

"I know," I say, returning his steady gaze.

He walks a little closer and pulls a strand of hair hanging over my eyes behind my ears. "I meant what I said about us, I can only offer you something purely physical, take it or leave it."

"I understand." Even though I know we both can't give each other what we want, I swallow nervously because I feel on edge being so close to him. His body is within arm's reach of mine and I can feel myself reacting to him.

"Good." He smirks at me and sits down on one of the kitchen stools.

"Were you with Kimber last night?" The words spill out before I can even stop them.

"Does it change anything?"

"No."

My heart continues to thump in my chest. I don't know whether I'm making the right decision or where it will even take me but when I looked inside myself this is the only place I want to be. The old Eleni was gone and the new version of me has stepped out of the flames.

Chapter Nineteen

The Last Temptation

Eleni

"So where were you last night?"

He chuckles. "Wouldn't you like to know."

I roll my eyes at him at his lack of answer.

"I was hungry, and I needed to be fed, take from that what you will."

"Whatever. What happens to Jarrod's debt?"

"It's done."

"Why?"

"Because you're in the family now of your own volition, you don't owe me anything."

"Where do I fit into this setup?"

"Nothing changes, you work with Chang during the day and Escada at night."

"I'm not working at Escada anymore." I meet his steely gaze with my own and he frowns.

"Since when do you call the shots?"

I grab his cheek mockingly. "Since the day we

met."

He pulls my hand away firmly. "Why don't you want to work at Escada? Did someone do something to you?" I can feel him getting worked up, his palm against my warm one.

"What is the point of me being there? It's not me."

"Is this about Kimber?"

"No, Dante, bang who you want."

"Thanks for the permission." He snorts at me but doesn't let go of my hand.

"Contrary to popular belief the world does not revolve around you, Dante. I've just had enough of working there."

"You're a bad liar, I know when you're upset."

"Ironic."

He catches my eye, knowing exactly what I mean.

"Whatever, Eleni, if you don't want to work there, fine. I'll find you something else to do."

He lets go of me and runs his hands through his silky black hair.

"I'm going for a shower. I have this meeting with Rafiq today."

He pulls off his shirt and starts to unbutton his pants. and for some reason I look away even though it's nothing I haven't seen or experienced before.

"Good luck…" I trail off, still trying to keep my eyes off him.

"You can give me some good luck right now."

He moves closer and places my hand on the V of his abdomen, slowly pushing down, and my pulse begins to race. His tongue moves slowly down my neck, sucking and biting. He looks at me with those devilish eyes and I feel my self-control waning as his lips move on mine. He places me on the countertop, feverishly undressing me with ease. His hardness pushes against me and I work him with my hands until he reaches his peak. His fingers inside of me are like rain to my desert, and my hips grind against him as if he were inside of me. He pulls me closer, ready to gain entry, but then I see the bruises from last night on his neck, and everything comes crashing back to reality.

"We can't keep doing this." I push him away and he stands over me, exhaling deeply.

"I know."

"Maybe I should move out."

He looks stunned for a second. "Do you want to move out?"

"Do you want me to want you to want me to move out?" I try to inject some humor into the situation.

"We should have some boundaries; we both need our own space to figure this out."

"I guess we need distance so we both know where we stand."

He stretches his arms, giving me a preview of what I just missed—his arms and abs sculpted to perfection within his olive skin.

"I'll call you when my meeting's done, we need to figure this out."

"You can't. I threw away my phone after the whole Fonseca thing."

"Good idea. I'll have Ajax pick you up a new one."

"Wow, Dante, was that a compliment?" I say in mock surprise.

"A small one."

"You can go on assignment with Ajax later today, it'll give you a taste of what is to come."

"Sounds terrifying."

He smirks at me but says nothing. "You might want to cover up the love bites before your big meeting."

He puts his hand to his neck and rolls his eyes. "Is that why you stopped?"

I shrug. "I guess you'll never know."

He walks away and I hear the shower start up. Every inch of me wants to follow him in there but I don't. I sit on the counter and lean back, wondering if he will ever stop having an effect on me.

***

Ajax

I snort as Eleni walks in dressed in what she thinks is a camouflage outfit. Tight leather pants, a matching tank, and big dark sunglasses.

Not that I'm complaining about the leather pants or the tank top, today was temptation enough without having her assets to deal with as well.

She really is the perfect package.

"Are you auditioning for *Charlie's Angels*?"

"Ha-ha, so funny, Ajax. I didn't' know what to wear. Should I change?"

"No, you look—I mean, it's fine, let's go."

"Before we go…I just want to say how sorry I am about before." Her lips quivers and I want to pull her closer.

"It's fine." I roll my eyes.

"Friends?" she asks, her eyes hopeful.

Friends. My heart sinks a little at hearing that word.

"Sure, no friendship bracelets though."

She giggles and kisses my cheek as she walks out, leaving me blushing like a fourteen-year-old with a crush.

"Where are we going?" Her head bends forward in my car as she searches for music on the radio.

"You'll see. I hear you're officially part of the fold?"

"Yep." She leans back and turns her body to me, pushing her glasses up so her blue eyes meet mine.

"What made you decide?"

She shrugs. "Resistance is futile. I could never go back to my own life anyway. Too much shit has happened."

"Did Dante's charm clinch it?" I say it lightly, not wanting to press hard on this.

"Not even close." She side-steps the question but doesn't avoid my gaze.

"I probably shouldn't ask but are you two a thing?" I switch my gaze between her and the road, not wanting to appear too keen for an answer.

"Again, not even close,' she says flatly. "I told him I should move out soon, it's for the best.'

We come up to traffic lights and I stop and give her my full attention. "So, you're single?"

She pushes her hair behind her ears and blushes

slightly. "I guess I am."

"Good to know."

"Why is that?" She smirks at me.

"Maybe one day you'll find out."

"Here is me thinking you're all serious and stoic. You've taken me by surprise."

"Oh, that is just the least of what I'm capable of." I let my eyes take in her body and they return to meet her own gaze and she is definitely blushing. I know she feels the heat between us. If Dante knew about this I would be fucked. Girlfriend or not, I know what is Dante's remained Dante's no matter what.

But at this moment, I couldn't care less.

***

Eleni

Jesus, if I had known the conversation we were about to have I would have not bothered to wear any blusher. I felt my cheeks burn with Ajax's eyes.

I don't know what to reply to his admission, so I say nothing. He glances at me every now and then and I occasionally stare back, trying to navigate this frisson of tension. He pulls up to a hotel and I raise my eyebrow at him. "This better not be what I think it is."

He chuckles. "Unfortunately, not. Sapphire has given us a tip that Lorenzo is hiding out here."

"Lorenzo?" I feel fear building up in my chest, knowing he was behind me getting shot at Escada.

"Nothing will happen to you, I promise." He looks at me earnestly, picking up on my terror.

"How does Sapphire know he's here? I thought she was MIA," I ask, clearing my throat, trying to get the feeling of fear out of my voice.

"Sapphire always has an ace up her sleeve." He smiles at me and I roll my eyes.

"Say no more."

We drive into a parking facility across the road from the hotel and Ajax gets out a wire and places it into his ear.

"All we have to do is give them a signal when we see him, and they will move in. We're just here to do surveillance, not the dirty work."

We both sit on the hood of the Range Rover and Ajax puts his hand on top of mine because he can sense my nerves.

"It will be fine, I'm here."

Suddenly we spot a car parking in front of the hotel and a figure appears outside the doors. I'm guessing it is Lorenzo who is flanked by three burly men. Ajax spoke quickly into the receiver of his wire and another blacked out Rover appears. Gunshots ring out like fireworks and Ajax grabs me, pushing me to the ground as they continue. His strong arms push me into his chest, shielding me from the chaos.

"I've got you" he says as I feel my body shake against his.

The gunshots halt and Ajax's phone rings as confirmation that they have Lorenzo, and his men are dead. He pulls me up and I run into his arms, still shaking from what I witnessed.

"Sorry," I mumble, pulling away from him.

"Don't be," he says, pulling me back toward him. He strokes my face gently.

My heart beats faster as I stand on the edge of temptation.

Chapter Twenty

Indecent Proposal

Eleni

I stay in his arms for what feels like a lifetime. I can feel his strong shoulders enveloping me, the black ink of his tattoos straining against the fabric of his white shirt.

"Are you okay?" he whispers into my hair, and the sound of his husky voice sends shivers down my spine.

"I'm fine." I pull away slowly, trying to recapture my composure.

"Let's get out of here." He pulls open the car door and I hop in.

We share a wordless journey home with occasional half glances at each other. I feel uneasy at this attraction I am beginning to feel for this inked stranger. With Dante it was an instantaneous attraction, but this was different, a *slow burn*. The more time I spend with Ajax, the more I begin to pull toward him. *But at what cost?* We remain silent until we pull up outside the penthouse. He squeezes my hand before we get out of the car. Is this a reassuring touch or is he trying to affirm the chemistry that is building between us?

***

Dante

"Dad?"

"Hm?" He turns around, distracted, like he just saw a ghost, his hands fumbling on his tie, so I fasten it for him.

"I was just thinking about your brother." He says the words in a low tone.

"I miss him too." I concentrate on his tie to avoid meeting his gaze.

"I don't say this a lot, but I am proud of you, Daischel's shoes were big ones to fill."

"You're telling me." I snort as he pats my arm gently like if he wants to say something more.

"What's with the fanfare, Dad? I'm worried."

"You're an excellent Caporegime, and you'll be an even better Padrone when I step down."

"Dad, stop. You have more mileage in you than half of my men."

"I may just want a quiet life in my senior years."

"Yeah right. When have we ever had a quiet life?"

We exchange smiles and he rests his arm on my shoulder. "True, but I won't rest until Amaury Vasquez is dead. I want to avenge my firstborn son."

"I promise you, Dad, we will."

He pulls me in his arms, and I feel like a child again, unburdening all my fears and grief on the one person in this world who understands me well enough to take it all away.

"Gentlemen." Arman Rafiq stands there, a small man but a powerful presence. His grey hair is styled back like a lion's mane, highlighting his stoic features.

"Arman, good to see you again." My dad leads the meeting, pouring us each a glass of whisky. Next to Arman I'm guessing is his daughter. Our eyes meet, and she gives me a half smile, looking up at me with her large dark eyes before introducing herself as Jameela.

Even when I look away, I can still feel her gaze on me, and when I would catch her eye, she wouldn't look away shyly. No, she wanted me to know she was looking at me. How fucking bold is she? We engage in small talk for a while, before Arman brings up the subject that we all want to talk about.

"As you know we were working with the Salvatore Family for a while, however we are keen to cut out the middleman and come straight to you as your feud with them is having a knock-on effect on our exports. I know you have the right political influences that could improve our trade. What do you say to that?"

My father nods at my reply.

"Sounds good, we just need to look at the profit margins. As you say, we have a heavy political influence, which means we take an extra cut out of any contracts we take out as an insurance policy, to prevent any legal disparities from rising. I also want a guarantee you won't do business with anyone else. If you double cross us I will find out about it. You produce the product, and we control the distribution."

"What percentage are you suggesting for this arrangement?" Arman looks at me shrewdly, his dark eyes narrowing, trying to deconstruct my words.

"Sixty-forty to us."

"Absurd." He bangs his fist on the table and I see Jameela's eyes widen in panic.

"I just told you the reasons why, we need to pay off the law so nobody gets caught, or do you want your men picked up on the borders and put in jail cells?"

"Lorenzo and I had an equal partnership."

"Lorenzo is in a cell downstairs. You can renew your partnership if you want but I doubt you will turn out much profit, as we have absorbed his operation from Brooklyn all the way to Long Island. It would be a shame for you to lose out on such a lucrative deal as well as some pretty powerful connections, however, we wish you all the best."

My dad gives me a curt nod to commemorate my smooth delivery and I see a panicked look cross Rafiq's face. *Jackpot.*

"Let's not be hasty, Baba." Jameela's silky voice cuts in and Arman sighs in exasperation.

"Dominic, let us old heads talk," he says as she gives him a small nod.

206

My dad leads him to his office, and they disappear before the door shuts with a thud.

"You're a talented negotiator," I say to her.

"I'm talented at a lot of things," she says, smiling back at me provocatively, her dark skin contrasting against her pearly white teeth.

"Subtlety not being one, I guess." I sigh in exasperation. *Flattery will get you nowhere.*

"I'm not afraid to go the *extra mile* when I see something I like." She mimics me and leans on the bar, lighting a cigarette.

"Careful, if you play with fire you will get burned." I put her cigarette out and walk away, watching her stand there stunned.

***

Nico

We've got him.

"I'll be there in an hour, let Dante know."

Click.

"I've got to jet; I'll be back tonight if I get the time."

"Don't bother, this won't be happening again."

I see Zosha's reflection in the bedroom mirror while I am getting dressed and her mouth is set in a firm line.

"You always say that," I reply, pulling my shirt on.

"This time I mean it." Her voice is cold, and I can feel her gaze burning into me in the mirror, but I ignore it because I don't need her shit right now.

"I'm through with you."

"Sure, until next time." *Always with the fucking games.*

"Not this time."

"Is this because of Eleni?" I turn around to face her, resting my hand on her knee and pushing it slowly up her silky thigh.

"No! Her taste in men is almost as bad as mine." She pushes my hands off and covers herself up to her neck like the comforter is a magical barrier.

"You're hurting my feelings now, baby." I smirk at her.

"You don't have any, that's the fucking problem, Nico! You're dead inside! I've known you for years and I still don't even know anything about you."

For some reason this touches a nerve and I feel myself starting to get worked up. That is not a good sign. "Don't fucking start this shit again. You know who I am, and I will never change that for anyone."

"Not even the girl you love?"

"The girl I what? Where the fuck did you get that idea from?" I feel my neck beginning to burn with heat.

Love? What the fuck is that, anyway?

"I know you do," she hits back at me, sensing my weakness.

"No strings attached, you agreed."

"This could be more if you just let me in," she says softly.

"If you want my body, it's yours. If you want my heart, think again. I don't have one."

She stares back at me, her eyes brimming with tears, and I get up and walk out.

Dark Temptation

I don't need this, not fucking today when we have captured Lorenzo Salvatore.

***

Dante

I throw water in his face to rouse him. Zeek and the others had already had one round with him, but he refuses to break. He thinks he's a tough motherfucker—we'll see about that.

"Lorenzo fucking Salvatore. I don't believe we've had the pleasure of meeting."

"Dante Dischanel. if it isn't the Prince of New York," he says sarcastically.

"I'm the king, and don't you fucking forget it."

"That's what you think." He smiles broadly at me and I'm disconcerted by his confidence.

"You're going to tell me how you got one of my crew to turn against me."

"Which one?" he says smirking.

I take out the hammer in my pocket and smash it against his hand, his screams echoing around the cell.

"You will never break me, Dischanel, never."

"Sounds like a challenge," I say as I take the hammer to the other hand, breaking a couple more fingers.

"Never," he says as his face pales.

"Is that a fact? I'm thinking of decorating the cell. Red is my choice of color. I think you can help." I switch on the drill saw and see his face whiten further as I put on my plastic overalls.

209

A few hours later, Nico and I are sitting in my office, Nico clearly dealing with a hangover.

"Nico, stop fucking yawning." Both of us are sitting in my office looking equally pissed off.

"I didn't sleep last night," he grunts back.

"Well, stop fucking everything with a pulse."

"I'm here for a good time, not a long time," he says, slouching on the leather sofa.

I lean back in the chair on tenterhooks, wondering about this meeting, Arman and my father have been in there for hours thrashing a deal out.

"I'm going to find out where Sapphire is. This bitch never answers her phone, then she just turns up out of nowhere with the catch of the century." Nico gets up, looking irritated.

"Rather you than me." He gives me a 'fuck you' stare and walks out while I tap irritably on the table.

My phone vibrates.

Penthouse.

I drive to my father's penthouse and he is in the office clutching a tumbler.

"Well, is he in?"

"Partially," he says, not looking at me.

"What the fuck does that mean?"

"Language, Durante!"

"You only call me by my full name when something is up! Did Rafiq try and pull a fast one? I will fuck—"

"No, he has agreed to the deal in principle," he says, sighing.

"Okay, so that's a good thing, right?"

"He wants something in return for us getting an extra cut."

"Like what?" I'm not mistaking this, my father is avoiding my gaze and instead looking directly over my shoulder.

"He wants…"

"Dad, spit it out!" I feel my heart rate begin to accelerate.

"He wants you to marry his daughter."

"He what?" My glass shatters to the floor as I feel rage start to build.

"It's not a bad deal, Dante."

"Are you out of your mind, Dad?" I look at him incredulously.

"Listen to me. She may not be your first selection of a bride but think of the business we can garner in the Middle East. Rafiq's connections are vast, spreading from China to Russia. You would be doubling the Dischanel fortune, Jameela is a very wealthy woman in her own right. She has an extensive portfolio in the oil business, not to mention she's attractive and smart. I believe it was her who made the suggestion."

"I don't give a shit if she's a Victoria's Secret model and part time NASA pilot. This is not happening."

"Dante—"

"Dad, don't Dante me like we're having a petty argument, this is my life! I'm not signing it away to some stranger. I don't even want to get married period!"

"It's not a big deal."

"Then you fucking marry her!"

"Your attitude is not welcome, Dante!"

"Neither is this offer!"

We both stare each other square in the eye at a standstill.

"Why does she want to marry me? Is she crazy? I met her for all of an hour."

"Because you have your father's looks." My dad smiles at me, trying to soften me up.

I know him too well.

"It's not funny, Dad, we have to talk to him again."

"Dante, I've been talking to him for four hours. It's this or nothing."

"I don't want to lose out on this deal, Dad."

"Then don't. You know what you have to do."

Chapter Twenty-One

You, Me, And Him

Eleni

I stifle a yawn, still tired from yesterday's adventure.

"Am I that boring?" Chang jokes, watching me rub my eyes.

"No, not all. Dante had me on assignment yesterday."

"I heard, and you thought Disneyland was the most magical place on earth." He chuckles.

"It just keeps on getting better." I shrug at him, still confused with my own predicament.

"Do you mind if I clock off early? I have anniversary plans with the wife."

"Sure, go ahead," I say, waving him out.

I hear the door shut and lean back in the recliner, closing my eyes for a few seconds. When I open them, a face is standing over me and a pair of emerald eyes are looking down on me.

"Jesus, Dante, you almost gave me a freaking heart attack." I say, jumping up and clutching my chest.

"What can I say, I'm good at sneaking up on people."

"So, I see." I try to calm down the frantic beating of my heart.

"What are you looking so pensive about?"

"Nothing." I look away, pushing the image of Ajax far from my mind. "How was your meeting?"

I see a look of darkness pass his eyes so quickly that if I didn't know him well, I would have missed it.

"Fine. Rafiq's daughter seems interested in working with us." He says it tonelessly but there is something hidden behind his bland tone.

"I bet she is. I doubt that's the only thing she's interested in." I snort at him.

"Meaning?" He cocks his head to one side, playing dumb. "Is Eleni a little jealous?"

"Not in the slightest."

He walks toward me, the gap between us getting slimmer, and my heart rate starts to race again.

"I've missed you in my bed, it hasn't been the same without you there," he says, rubbing his thumb across my cheek.

"Well, you were in Kimber's yesterday, so you can't have missed me that much." I glare at him, he isn't going to smooth talk his way out of this.

"Sometimes you have got to take scraps if you can't get the main meal." He smirks at me and I roll my eyes.

"Was that meant to be compliment? Because it

sucked."

"Stop playing games, Eleni, I know you still want me." He pushes my hair back and tilts my chin up. I see the intent in his eyes, so I do my best to avoid his gaze. Like a snake charmer he was drawing me in. His gaze so hypnotic it's hard not to look at him. *Yes, I want him, but do I need him?* I knew him too well; this would only end in tears. My tears, my heartbreak again. I wouldn't feed him even though I was starving for his touch.

"I want it all or nothing," I say firmly, taking his hand off my chin.

"What if I gave you all of my good parts?" he says, licking his lips.

"What if I told you to get out?" I reply, stepping back from him.

"You're full of charm today" he says, sighing in defeat.

"I learned from the master," I say, cocking an eyebrow at him.

"Real cute. Did you have fun on your assignment?" he asks, leaning on my desk.

"I guess. What happens next to Lorenzo?"

"Don't worry your pretty little head about it. Do you still want to move out?" He lights a cigarette.

"Sure, why not? There is nothing keeping me at your place, is there?"

"I don't know," he says, exhaling smoke. "Is there?"

I don't say anything, and we stare at each for a second, neither wanting to be the first to break. "I made myself clear to you. If you want to stay, then stay, but don't be under any illusions about me and you. I'm not your Prince Charming."

"I never asked you to be Prince Charming."

"You don't have to; I know you, Eleni. You think that you're going to be the girl to change me, to save me from myself, but you're wrong. You're not the first to think that and you won't be the last either."

"You're the last person I want to save right now," I reply, pushing past him, not wanting to admit that he's right and deep down I want to be the one.

"I'll be out late tonight, don't wait up." The last three words are delivered like small daggers to my chest before he walks out, leaving me as confused as I was before he walked in.

***

Sabrina

"Where is my husband?" Her corkscrew curls shake in anger as the two men in front of her stand with their heads bowed.

"One minute he was at the entrance and the next he was gone." Rodrigo sighs deeply, trying to explain how they had lost their boss in the blink of an eye as well as the men who were guarding him.

"So, you have no idea where he is?" Her dark eyes beam in anger.

"Sabrina, we will find Lorenzo. You have my word. I don't want you to worry about this." Malachi tried his best to be somber, but Sabrina looked disinterested.

"I stopped worrying about what Lorenzo did a long time ago, you think I don't know who he has been with?" They both look at each other, stunned that the *Capomafiosa* knew about her philandering husband.

"I strongly advise—" Rodrigo starts but Sabrina cut him off.

"I said find her."

"You don't call the shots, you're a woman." Malachi looks at her, horrified that she didn't know her place.

"Well, you better get with the program or you'll be the next one to go missing."

Malachi opens and shuts his mouth a couple of times before sighing in resignation.

Suddenly a dark figure appears from the shadows.

"Stop sneaking up on me like that, Romeo," Sabrina says angrily, chiding her little brother.

Although he wasn't so little, six-foot tall Romeo Sanchez had dark eyes and an even darker soul. Born and bred on the streets of Bogota, Colombia, he was nicknamed 'the alchemist' for developing and selling his own narcotics and distributing them all over South America. "Forget about the girl, we need to go after Dante and send him a message."

"How are we meant to do that?" Rodrigo says, looking irritated at being given advice from some little squirt. Rodrigo D'Anda was a *Consigliere, a* respected advisor to the Salvatore family, as was his father and his father before him.

"I know one of the champagne girls at Dante's club, she has a big mouth in more ways than one, may I add."

"Gross but continue." Sabrina replies as her brother smirks arrogantly.

"They were celebrating the capture of somebody last night; it doesn't take rocket science to figure out that they have Lorenzo."

"How are we going to get into Dischanel's compound?" Malachi says, rolling his eyes.

"We're not going to get *in*, Lorenzo is coming *out*."

"How?" Malachi leaned against the wall, watching Romeo's dark eyes brighten dangerously.

"We're going to force his hand by taking something that belongs to him. I have a little surveillance job for you boys."

***

Karlie

Elsewhere at Escada, Karlie returns backstage after another scintillating night on the poles. She was due to see Zeek later but that didn't cheer her up much either. For someone who did such a dangerous job, he seems so soft. He wasn't as ruthless as the other men he worked with; he lacks any killer instinct, any surmountable ambition.

"You have a visitor in the Chardonnay room," Stan barks.

"I'm finished for the night, Stan," she snipes irritably back at her boss.

"He's willing to pay double."

Well, I won't say no to that.

218

She walks into the room and sees a dark silhouette; her heart starts to pound slightly. He steps out of the shadows and it is the same man she has seen three nights in a row, with the same look of lust in his eyes he has had every night he has seen her working the pole.

"Allow me to introduce myself, I'm Aiden Fonseca. I think you and I have a lot to talk about."

"You do?" She smirks at him.

"I think I have an arrangement that would benefit both of us."

"Start talking," she replies as he pulls out a large wad of hundred dollar bills from his pocket and her eyes light up.

***

Dante

"You're late," Dad tuts as I walk in his office for our meeting.

"You're lucky I came at all," I reply, pouring myself a whisky.

"Perhaps if you weren't so distracted by other things then you wouldn't be late."

"Meaning?"

"Meaning leave Eleni alone, she does not belong in our world—"

"My business—"

"Is *our* business." He finishes my sentence but not the way I would.

I open my mouth and he glares at me; I know I won't win this. Maybe he is right, Eleni is a scab that I keep picking and every time I do one of us bleeds. I don't want to hurt her anymore or see her face crumple like it had done when I hurt her. I needed to leave her alone so we could both coexist without complications.

"Dante, it is just a formality."

"Huh?" I'm confused as he breaks into my thoughts.

"Just because she's married doesn't mean you have to be, you can be free to pursue other avenues. Nobody is asking you to take a vow of chastity."

"No, just one of marriage!" I light up another cigarette, having already gone through a whole pack yesterday thinking of ways to escape this situation.

"Son, there is money to be made here." I watch him try to reason with me using every trick of persuasion from the Dominic Dischanel playbook.

"Yeah, from my misery," I reply flatly.

"Business is business."

I was about to reply when Nico walks in and stares at us, sensing the atmosphere.

"What's going on?"

"Another regular day. Oh, and your uncle is trying to force me into an arranged marriage."

"What?" Nico says, aghast at the thought of losing his favorite cousin and wingman.

"Rafiq won't agree to the deal unless Dante agrees to an engagement with his daughter."

"Fuck, that is messed up." Nico looks at me, horrified.

"He doesn't have to change his lifestyle, after a few months when the alliance is finalized, he can do what he wants. It's only a piece of paper," Dominic replies.

"I guess so, still, rather you then me." Nico chuckles.

"Why can't Nico marry her? He's as much a Dischanel as I am."

"What? No! I'm too much of a hoe to be a housewife. Make sure you tell all your side bitches you're not available anymore and send them all to me," he says with a wink.

"You're so fucking helpful right now."

"You know me, cousin, a problem shared is a problem halved." He smirks at me. "I'll meet you downstairs. Let's pay Salvatore another visit, hopefully after your last one it he's loosened *his* tongue."

I sigh, exasperated. Did I really expect Nico to go against my father's opinion? I felt like the walls were closing in on me, there was no escape.

"Dante?"

"What?"

"Don't lose focus so late in the game. Jameela knows this life and understands how to conduct business."

"So what?"

"I want you to carefully think. Dante, this decision could shape your whole future."

That is what I'm afraid of.

I walk out and barely remember driving to my destination, the crushing weight of expectation is grinding down on me. Can I really marry a total stranger? Have her living with me? *With Eleni?* Jesus, how would Eleni even react? Me walking down the aisle with someone when I told her that I couldn't even have a regular relationship with her? I felt impending dread at the decision I was going to have to make.

***

Nico

"Where is the Capo?" Farook asks, leaning against his car.

"I don't think he'll be joining us today."

"The meeting went that bad, huh?" Farook asks, cleaning his Ray-Bans with his jacket sleeve.

"Only if you're Dante. Rafiq wants an engagement between Dante and his daughter to cement the business alliance."

"The fuck? That's practically extortion, Dante won't agree to that!" Farook runs his hands through is dreads in disbelief.

"But Padrone will, he says it's a good investment."

"A man should not sacrifice his heart for money," Farook says solemnly.

"Okay, William fucking Shakespeare," I say, rolling my eyes at Farook's passionate stance. "Padrone says it's a piece of paper, Dante can still do his own thing with his ding a ling." I chuckle as Farook tuts loudly.

"Marriage should be a commitment, a holy vow, not a business deal," he says, outraged.

"Jesus, Farook, is this a fucking sermon? Get your head out of your ass."

"Why am I even speaking to you about this? Your idea of commitment is screwing the same girl twice."

"Don't hate the player, hate the game."

"You're an asshole."

"So I've heard."

"You gotta pay the cost to be the boss," I reply, lighting a cigarette as Farook looks pensively into the distance, both of us wondering where Dante's decision will lead.

***

Ajax

I wait in the parking lot for Eleni's arrival, leaning against the hood trying to act nonchalant but failing.

Shit, why am I so nervous?

I know I stepped over my boundaries yesterday, but I can't help it.

I want her.

If Dante knew this, he wouldn't be trusting me to chauffeur her around everywhere. He sounded distracted on the phone, but I know better than to poke my nose in Dante's affairs.

If he even had an inkling about what I was thinking right now, I would be dead.

My phone trills and I get a message from Zeek telling me to pack a bag because we're going to Staten Island for an assignment just as Eleni walks out of the building.

"Hey," she says, tucking her hair behind her ear.

"Surprised to see me?"

"A little, but happy, nonetheless." She beams at me and I can't help but smile back at her too.

Why does she have this effect on me?

"Change of plan. I need to pick up a bag from my place first, then I'll take you to Dante's—your place."

"Just call it Dante's, I'll be gone soon."

"You will?" I get a little excited by this news. Surely this means they're not a thing."

"Yeah, I need my own place. What about you? Do you live with somebody?"

I know what she's hinting at, but I play it cool.

"Yeah, with Zeek, who is hung up on some stripper right now, and it's driving me crazy."

"What's wrong with that?"

"It's so unlike Zeek. I've known him since we were teenagers. He's never acted like this, he's completely head over heels with her."

"What about you, Ajax? Are you hung up on anyone?" Our eyes meet as we approach red traffic lights.

"No, I don't really have time, I guess I am a—"

"Smash and pass kind of guy?"

"Yeah wait—where did you hear that?" I frown at her half embarrassed, half amused.

"Nico." She smiles at me knowingly.

"I see." I nod, not surprised at all.

"So, you're looking for Miss Right Now?" she says, playing with the radio, trying to find a station.

I put my hand on her knee and she jumps a little.

"No, I'm looking for Mrs. Right."

"Any idea where she might be?" she says

quietly, our eyes burning into each other.

"I think I have a good idea," I say, watching her face flush as the lights go to green.

***

Eleni

The tension between us is at a boiling point as I enter his apartment. I sit down on the couch primly as he starts packing in the next room. There is a tiny crack in the door, and I can see his silhouette moving from the wardrobe to the bed where his bag is. The sound of the shower follows. I try to distract myself by walking around the living room. I see my reflection in the mirror and what a blushing mess I am. I begin reapplying my lipstick and flattening my hair to try and distract myself. When I look up again, I see the reflection of him getting changed in the mirror wearing just a towel. Ink adorns his tanned, chiseled torso, his muscular abdomen leading down to the V sign near his pelvis. He pulls on his boxers, looks up, and catches my eye.

Shit. Shit. Shit.

He pulls the door open, leaning against it casually.

"I, uh, um, it was the reflection," I finish weakly.

How the fuck am I going to explain this?

He walks toward me and doesn't say anything as he looks down at me, his eyes fill with desire, and all that stands between us are a few layers of fabric.

***

Ajax

I catch her looking at me in the reflection of the mirror and can read the lust in her eyes. Thinking of all the ways I would make her mine sends electric shots of longing all through my body, but just as quickly, cold realization hits me. *Every step toward Eleni is a step away from my loyalty to this family, to Dante.* But I still keep walking until I'm in front of her. We both stare at each other in anticipation at an impasse neither of us know how to cross.

Chapter Twenty-Two

Caught Up

Eleni

He moves toward me and pulls me into his arms, his body is still damp from the shower as my own pool of wetness starts to form.

"Eleni," he growls in my ear as I feel his faint stubble rub against my neck. I can't but help let out a little gasp at the shots of excitement that were exploding all over my body.

He's barely touching me and I'm already melting. He pulls me further into him until he is *so close* to my face that I can see the moisture building on his lips. There is fire in his eyes as his lips move nearer and I am ready for his lips to devour mine.

Cough.

"Am I interrupting something?" Zeek stands in the center of the room leaning against the door. He looks pissed off staring at a partially clothed Ajax standing dangerously close to me.

"I'm just getting dressed," Ajax mumbles, moving back.

"Well, you're not doing a good job of it," Zeek says, seething at Ajax's attempted lie.

"Nice to see you again, Eleni, this time with your clothes on," Zeek says, looking between us with his eyes narrowed. I blush thinking about Zeek seeing me half-dressed when I was making out with Dante, clearly he's trying to make a point.

"Zeek," Ajax says firmly.

"Ajax," he replies with the same tone.

"I need a drink," I say, walking into the kitchen and closing the door behind me.

***

Ajax

"Are you out of your mind?" Zeek explodes as soon as Eleni closes the door.

"What?" I reply, walking into my bedroom to continue getting dressed.

"You know what." Zeek follows me. "Do you want to make it to your next birthday? Because what I just saw in there tells me otherwise."

"Nothing happened."

"It was about to."

I didn't say anything because trying to lie to Zeek is like lying to myself. I run my hands through my hair. Nothing happened, but I wanted it to, I *want* it to.

"Have you…you know?"

"No, nothing like that."

"You're living dangerously, Ajax."

"Don't I always?"

"Yeah, and where has that got you in the past?"

I roll my eyes at him. "Says someone who is dating a stripper."

"She isn't my Capo's...whatever she is," he snipes back.

"Do you share her tips?" I say acidly, watching his face darken in anger.

"I'm going to pick up Ra, I will be back in an hour. Try to keep your clothes on, *Wesley.*"

He walks out, slamming the door. I can tell I pissed him off because he calls me by my real name.

"Are you okay?" I walk into the kitchen and Eleni is perched on one of the stools.

"Yeah," she says, looking up at me sheepishly.

"I'm sorry about Zeek, he shouldn't have said that."

"It's fine, he probably came in at the right time."

"I thought it was pretty shitty timing, actually."

We both laugh and it breaks up some of the pent-up tension between us.

"You don't look like a Wesley," she says in a teasing tone.

"So, you overheard Zeek. Now you know why I go by Ajax."

"Well, I never thought your real name was Ajax. Where did it come from?"

"I grew up in Amsterdam and played for a team there for a while called Ajax. I got injured and caught up in a few things, so I had to leave Holland. I kept the name as a reminder of home."

"Caught up?"

"Long story," I reply, leaning my hand on the wall above her. The distance between us is closing in again and I feel that familiar tension building between us.

"Aren't they all?"

"I might tell you one day," I say, wiping an eyelash off her face.

"You owe me a wish," she remarks.

"Do you believe in that?"

"Maybe I'm waiting for the right person to prove that wishes do come true."

"Anyone in mind?"

"Perhaps."

"Eleni, you and Dante...is it really over?" I ask the question that has been on my mind for a while. I need to know before this goes any further. I don't want to start something with her knowing she is still pining for my boss.

She sighs. "It never really started, it's not like there's much to get over."

"You know what the best way of getting over someone is?"

"What?" she asks, puzzled.

"Getting under someone else." I smile at her mischievously and she leans in closer to me, so close I can see the blue of her eyes and the tips of her mascara-laden lashes.

My phone trills and I am reminded of Zeek's warning.

"Let's get you home before Zeek gives us detention."

She laughs. I grab her hand, and we walk out. I

make sure to let it go as soon as we leave even though I didn't want to.

***

Zeek slams the door of the car, not quite believing what he just saw.

Is Ajax insane? Did he not know what Dante would do if he found out what almost happened?

He exhales deeply, at least he had one good thing going in his life. *Karlie.* She's a keeper. He pulls out his phone to dial her number, but she doesn't pick up. I guess she's busy, but not as busy as Ajax, he thinks darkly.

***

Detective Fonseca

Ring.

"Shut that thing off," a husky voice interjects.

Karlie hits the reject button and switches her phone off.

"That's more like it."

"How long have we got before she's home?"

"A little while yet," he says, checking the digital clock next to him. Renee isn't due home for another hour. Plenty of time for his favorite redhead.

"I should go now." She starts getting dressed but he stops her.

"You know what you have to do"

She bites her lip uncomfortably. "I don't think I

can. If he finds out…" She doesn't finish the sentence because if Zeek ever finds out about any of this, she would be dead, no doubt about it.

"I thought you wanted us to be together." He says it so flawlessly that anyone would think he was being genuine.

"I do." she says, wanting to be with this man so much, the perfect Alpha.

"Then you do this little thing for me and I'll give you everything you ever wanted. We can start a new life together anywhere you want."

"Anywhere, Aiden?"

"*Anywhere*." Aiden Fonseca smiles at her as she starts kissing his chest slowly and he knows he's got her right where he wants her.

After all, you can never win if you don't play a little dirty. Dante Dischanel was going to find that out the hard way.

***

Snap. Snap. Snap.

I take photo after photo of the brunette and the tattooed guy who led her out of the apartment. This is ludicrous, I thought. I am a Goddamn Consigliere being treated like an errand boy.

"This wouldn't happen under Lorenzo," I fume to Malachi, who is sitting next to me.

"Well, Lorenzo is locked up; he can't help you now. I told him about that crazy bitch he was hanging around with, she was too dangerous for her own good, but no, he never could resist a pretty face."

"They weren't even pretty most of the time either," I reply, and he laughs.

"Why are we taking pictures of this girl? Who is she?" I say, pointing to her. I wonder if the guy in front of her is her boyfriend from the coy looks he's giving her.

"I don't know, but she lives with Dischanel. Romeo thinks she will be useful. I'm not complaining, she's a hot little thing," Malachi says, zooming in.

"What does he want with her?"

"Whatever it is, it can't be good."

***

Dante

"What is wrong with you?' It's like you're not even here."

Kimber's whiny voice interrupts my thoughts and I see her looking up from under me. She tries to stroke my face and I push her hand away. Intimacy is not what I need right now. I just want to find a vent for my frustration, and she's it.

"Nothing," I reply, my mouth covering hers to shut her up. I try to find my rhythm as I mechanically continue pounding her, her body starts to shake under me as she starts clawing at my back. I come to my own belated climax, but I don't feel any better than I did before I arrived here. My body might be here, but my mind isn't. Wherever I am, it's not with Kimber. I know who I want lying underneath me right now and it's *not her*. I get off her and light a cigarette, leaning on the headboard.

"Dante, baby, talk to me. Why are you so distant?"

"I'm not."

"If you don't want this, then tell me now." Her grey eyes burn into mine.

"I want what I want, when I want it, and nothing more than that, *ever*."

"You're a piece of shit."

"Somebody's late to the party." I smirk and she moves to slap me, but I grab her wrist—not hard, but hard enough to show I could hurt her if she continues.

"I hate you." She pushes past me and slams the bathroom door.

Join the club, sweetheart.

I drive back to my apartment still in a haze. It's late, and all the lights are out. Eleni must be asleep. I can't help but look into her room and she is huddled in a little ball in her bed. All I can see is her hair spilling over the pillow like black silk. I try to leave but my legs don't move. *I wish I were lying next to her.*

"Dante, is that you?" I see movement under the covers and her head emerges.

"Yeah, it's me. I just got in."

"Oh, is something wrong?"

"No, I'm going to bed now. Sorry I woke you."

"Dante? What's wrong? You have a weird look on your face," she says, squinting at me in the darkness.

"I'm good, go back to sleep," I say, leaning

against the door.

"I need to pee anyway." She gets up and walks past me. I grab her hand and pull her toward me, so we are chest to chest.

"Dante, what the hell is wrong with you?" She looks up at me, as perplexed at my behavior as I am.

"Nothing, ignore me. I've been drinking.' Even though I'm sober as a judge right now and still holding her hand in mine, I let her hand go. I watch her walk away before retreating into my office and pouring myself a generous tumbler of whisky. I pick my phone up. "Dad, I've made my mind up."

One day later I'm standing in the penthouse watching my father toast my engagement, the gnawing feeling in my chest that I have made the wrong decision seeming to grow with each breath. But it's *too late* to go back on it now.

"I'm pleased to announce a deal has been brokered with Arman and I that will merge both the Dischanel and Rafiq families together forever. I would also like to take this time to toast to Dante and Jameela's engagement. Let us all lift our glasses up to celebrate the happy couple. *Salut Chindon.*"

One hundred years, I think as my heart sinks further.

I bring the glass up to my lips, but I don't sip, this is something I don't want to toast to. My chest feels heavy carrying the weight of something I don't want. In the cold light of day, I feel stone cold sober. Every time I look up, I see Jameela's huge dark eyes staring up at me like I'm a juicy bug that got caught up in her web. *Cazzo, what the hell have I got myself into?*

Dad carries on with his speech and I feel all eyes on me.

"Dante, are you sure about this?" Farook whispers to me in a low voice, his dark, brooding eyes filled with concern.

"Yeah," I reply, not wanting to discuss it anymore.

"This is a big step. I mean, fuck, Dante, you've never even had a girlfriend before and now you're making a sacred vow." I turn cold inside at those two words.

"I need to do it for the family, you remember what life was like after Dash died. The uncertainty, not knowing if we would even survive the war. I can't put my father through that again. If we merge with Rafiq—we will be untouchable."

"But Dante, this is not business, this is your life."

"Sometimes you have to take one for the team," I reply, draining my glass and ordering a double whisky. I can't go through this night sober. I thought being sober would make me feel better—it didn't.

"Real romantic, Dante. It's your life but please think about this clearly."

Does he not know that this has consumed my mind like poison since I agreed? That this is all I have thought about for days on end? I can't deny Jameela is attractive, but she isn't…she isn't what I want. She isn't the person who comes to my mind deep in the night, the face that floods my subconsciousness with all sorts of feelings I won't even acknowledge in my waking state of mind.

My dad turns to me. "What date were you thinking for the wedding, son?"

"*Neveruary*, something along those lines," I reply acidly.

"I'm thinking a spring wedding." He completely ignores me and turns his head back to his neighbor.

"I feel like we should hold a memorial for your little black book," Nico says in a somber whisper.

"Not now," I say, shooting him a look of disdain. I can feel the room start to close in on me as I unbutton the top buttons of my collar trying to ventilate myself.

"I never thought you would go ahead with this."

"Neither did I but it's the right thing."

"The right thing done for the wrong reason is still the wrong thing," Farook intercedes.

"Do you have a book of fucking quotes that you carry around with you?" Nico replies, rolling his eyes.

"Marry her but on your terms, none of that death do us part mumbo jumbo. Remember, she is the one who is married, *not* you."

"Sound advice from someone who considers sleeping with two sisters acceptable behavior," Farook fires back at Nico.

"Don't forget the mom as well." Nico winks at Farook, who looks at him in disgust.

"Dante might end up falling for her, you never know."

"As if! That is the last thing I want. This is just *business*."

"Business or not, she's going to want something from you. I don't think she'll expect you to play *Clue* with her every night."

"So what? Dropping her the pipe every once in a while does not constitute as love. She can have it but that's all she's getting from me."

"What a charmer you are, Dante," Farook says, shaking his head.

"I know, right." I rub my eyes, I forgot to shave today, and I didn't even realize.

"Are you going for a dark, brooding look?" Farook mocks.

"It's called an *I have to marry a stranger, fucking help me* look."

They both laugh and I join in because I have no energy for anything else.

"I can't believe you're getting married, man; shit, I would rather be dead," Nico says, taking a long drag of cigarette.

"Thanks, Nico, I really appreciate that positivity."

"You should start wearing black to mourn the end of your life as you know it. Shit, Sapphire will freak when she finds out."

"Where is Sapphire?" My mind tries to click back to the last time I saw her.

"Fuck knows. She calls and checks in, but I don't see her. At least I don't have to put up with her crazy ass bullshit."

"It is unlike Sapphire to be so quiet." Have I been so distracted that I haven't noticed Sapphire's absence and complete withdrawal from the family?

I walk outside, feeling the cool breeze on my

back. Nico and Farook look at me, concerned. Behind Nico's jokes I feel his eyes look at me, slightly worried at my decision. It even has me double taking at my own impulsiveness and need to please my father. To be the perfect son replacing the favorite who was taken before his rightful time. We talk for a few minutes before Dad comes out. If he asks me about this wedding one more Goddamn time, I'm going to take a swing at him.

"Jameela is here, she wants to spend some time with you."

"Why?" I look at him, repulsed.

"Because you are about to get married and she wants to get to know her groom," he replies, looking exasperated.

"Where is she?" I look around, but I can't see her.

"She was just here a second ago, I'm sure she hasn't gotten far. Stop with the stick up the ass behavior, Dante, it does not suit you." He walks away, leaving me pissed off.

Farook looks at me shrewdly. "I told you, she wants more than…" He points at my groin. "That."

"We'll leave you to have some one-on-one time with your bride-to-be. Remember, Dante, no sex before marriage." Nico snorts. They both explode in laughter and walk off, leaving me standing there watching all the walls collapse, closing me in.

***

Eleni

"Who's next?" I put on surgical gloves as I wait for Chang to check the list.

"It looks like nobody. Let's take five."

"Sure," I reply, pulling off the gloves and tidying the room.

I hear a knock at the door and turn around, surprised. I thought there were no more patients. A very tall, tanned brunette walks in. I'm a little in awe of her beauty and she knows it. She stares at me appraisingly, as if sizing me up, before she speaks.

"Excuse me, I'm looking for someone, I think I may have gotten lost," she says in a very polished British accent, but I can tell it is not her first language.

"Dr. Chang will be here shortly, please wait outside."

"Oh no, I'm not here to see the doctor."

"Who exactly are you looking for?"

"My fiancé, *Dante Dischanel.*"

Chapter Twenty-Three

Nothing Breaks Like A Heart

"I'm sorry, *what?"* My ears start ringing like there was a screeching whistle running through my head.

"My *F-I-A-N-C-É".* She repeats the words and rolls her eyes like I'm slow.

I take a hard look at her and my stomach can't help but twist at her obvious beauty, dark silky hair which makes her brown eyes pop, offset with a golden tan. I can tell she comes from money by the way she dresses and the opulent jewelry she wears. My eyes move to her left hand and I notice a huge sparkling rock there, sinking my heart completely. I wonder if she knows what I'm thinking? Is my face betraying my emotions? She is smiling at me in a way that another woman gloats when she knows she has claimed a victory.

"Dante doesn't have a fiancée." The words tumble out of my mouth and I don't know why I'm so insistent on making this point for a man that isn't

241

even mine.

"He does now." She smiles at me and I want to punch her stupid face.

"Since when?"

"It's recent, very recent." She giggles and flicks her hair, purposely flashing her ring finger.

Blood seems to pump around my head, sending a million thoughts a mile around my brain. *Dante is marrying her. Maybe this is what he wanted all along, someone beautiful, rich, and classy. Someone who knows about the finer things in life, not me. He picked out a ring, he got down on one knee, and proposed. Does he love her?*

My mind is racing, I feel pain pierce me like someone is continually stabbing me in the gut.

"Who exactly are you?" She eyes me with suspicion.

"I work here, clearly." She doesn't have to know anything. I marginally recover, not allowing her to take my pride. Whatever is left of it, anyway.

"Aww, that's so cute, you have a doctor outfit and everything," she coos mockingly.

"Yeah, because I'm a doctor. What exactly is your job?"

"Being engaged to your boss is my job," she says in a thinly veiled jab.

"I guess feminism is officially dead," I reply back sarcastically, and I give her my own fake smile.

The door bangs and I hear Dante's voice, "There you are—" He walks in the room and spots me behind the door and all the color vanishes from his cheeks as we stare at each other.

"Babe, I was just having a look around and I found Elisa."

"Eleni," we both correct her, and I notice his voice sounds strained.

"Congratulations, Dante, you sure have yourself a prize." I smile at him as he looks ashen faced.

"Thanks," he says, looking away. He can't even meet my eyes, but I keep my glare fixed on him.

"Maybe one day you'll meet your own Prince Charming," she says wrapping her arms around Dante and kisses him. I feel a stab of pain hit me, but I don't let my smile drop.

He unwraps her arms from around him immediately. "I'll meet you upstairs. Wait for me in my office."

"Okay, sweetie, and remind me to add Elena to our wedding invite list."

I don't even correct her this time and neither does he, we just silently look at each other because there are no words to even describe the situation. She walks out and I wait for the sound of her Louboutins to disappear before I start talking.

"Anything else you forgot to mention, *sweetie*?" I say acidly.

"It's not something I'm exactly shouting from the rooftops."

"What?" I look at him perplexed, and for the first time I notice the greyish tinge to his skin and the circles under his eyes.

"I'm only marrying her to secure the deal with Rafiq," he says in a bland voice. "This is the only term he wouldn't negotiate. Trust me, I *tried*." He runs his hands through his hair, looking defeated.

"You're getting married for *business*? You got down on one knee and proposed with a huge rock for *business?*" I look at him incredulously, not believing what I'm hearing.

"What? I never proposed. Did she tell you that? Do I look like I do romantic fucking proposals? Whatever she told you is bullshit. She picked out her own ring and my father paid for it. This is all for show. We need this deal. Working with Arman can open so many doors for us."

"Are you convincing me or yourself?"

He looks at me for a second, silenced. "Why does it matter, anyway? I'm not the marrying kind, you know I'm not about that life." He smirks and lights a cigarette.

"Well, I guess you are now," I reply and his smile falters.

"It doesn't mean anything, just another piece of paper."

"Keep saying that to yourself, maybe one day you'll believe it. I'll let you get back to your *sweetie.*" I turn around and pretend to start tidying up my desk because I can feel that familiar itch in my throat rising.

"Eleni?"

"What?"

"I think what you said was right—it's—best you start looking for your own apartment. I don't think we should live together anymore—us—you know it was never a good idea."

"Sure," I reply, and I let myself go once I'm sure he's gone, sliding myself down the door, lamenting a lost love that never was.

Dark Temptation

***

Dante

I feel like I'm having some sort of panic attack as I walk out of the room. I lean my forehead on the door, and I hear Eleni on the other side sliding against the door. *What the fuck am I doing?* How am I supposed to go through with this wedding? It's not just a piece of paper like I keep trying to reason to myself. I was trying to contain myself, but I feel panic rising to the surface, and seeing Eleni, feeling her on the other side of this door, was a painful reminder of the decision I made.

There is no going back.

I trudge to my office, hoping Jameela isn't there, but I see her sitting in my chair with her legs on my desk.

"Don't you have somewhere to be?" I ask irritably.

"I want to be with *you,* hence why we're getting married."

"We're getting married for purely business-related reasons. I don't want *you*. I don't want anyone."

"I wouldn't say that is strictly true," she says, narrowing her eyes. "That girl, something is going on. Whatever it is, *it's done*."

I laugh at her. "You're giving *me* orders? There's nothing going on."

"There better not be, otherwise Daddy won't be happy."

I roll my eyes at her. "I don't know what your

expectations are of this marriage, but I wouldn't aim high. I'm not husband material and I don't plan on being that *ever.*"

"Not yet, but you will be."

I look at her. Is she fucking stupid? I don't want her. I couldn't be making it clearer, and she's just completely ignoring my pointed words. "You do your thing and I'll do mine," I say to make myself as clear as fucking daylight.

"That is what you think, Dante Dischanel."

She stares me down and I return her gaze, but she looks at me, unwavering.

Shit.

This wasn't going to be as straightforward as I thought.

***

Eleni

"Ra, I really don't want to go out tonight," I whine.

"Eleni, girl, stop it."

"Do you want to spend the night listening to Dante and his fiancée testing the bed springs?"

"No!" I reply horrified. Dante wouldn't be that callous to bring Jameela here, *would he?*

"I'm not even listening to your excuses, Eleni, I'm coming there soon be ready or else."

She hangs up, leaving me bewildered. Maybe she's right. I need to get this out of my system. Maybe I need to get Dante out of my system. *Forever.* Ra had spotted me having a tearful moment in Chang's office and put two and two together. She was adamant that we were going out tonight and that was final.

"And just where do you think you're going dressed like that?"

I reach out to grab my jacket and turn around to see Dante with only a towel wrapped around him leaning against the wall. I can see the flecks of water dripping off him where he is freshly showered. He looks like a little boy with his hair wet and tousled.

"Out."

"We've been over this before, Eleni, you tell me where you go."

"Why? I won't be here much longer." I lean against the door and fold my arms.

"That doesn't mean I don't—"

"You don't what?"

He sighs and adjusts his towel, and my eyes can't help but wander down to what his towel is hiding. He smirks at me and comes toward me with that famous Dante glint in his eye.

"Dante, put some pants on," I say, covering my eyes.

"Are you bossing me around in my house?" he growls, looming over me, standing so close I can feel his moisture dripping all over me.

"Make the most of it, I'll be gone soon," I say, pushing back to create distance between us.

He runs his hands through his hair, and I see his face drop. He looks like he has the weight of the world on his shoulders, so I walk forward and embrace him tightly. I feel him tense before he relaxes against me. We don't say anything, and I unwrap myself from those taut arms that I spent so many nights in.

"What was that for?"

I shrug. "It was goodbye, I guess. I don't want us to end on a bad note. We've been through a lot."

"*Never say never,*" he replies, looking me in the eye.

"I think we can safely say *never*," I reply quickly, trying to make this as painless as possible. My chest is starting to ache now and before I know it the tears will start burning in my throat awaiting release.

"Well, I don't." He takes my chin in his hands and I know what he's going to do next. He lifts me up as if I were weightless and places me on the kitchen countertop. He kisses me roughly, *hungrily,* like an inmate who is about to devour his last meal. His hands wander two fingers at a time up my thigh until they reach the top. I jump as I feel him begin to close in on the place I want him most and I wriggle my hips so he can pull off my underwear, but he simply rips them in half. I look at him half irritated, half turned on, his deft fingers entering me. Dante knows every inch of my body and exactly where every spot of mine is. I lean back as he pulls down my bra and his teeth bite my nipples hard and then suck softly before he kisses me fiercely.

***

Dark Temptation

Dante

She moves her hips for me to remove her underwear but, fuck it, I can't wait, so I just rip them off. She looks at me like I'm crazy, but she doesn't say anything because within a couple of seconds my fingers are consuming her. One, two, three at a time work in sync inside of her, lapping up all her wetness. I inhale her deeply, taking in her sweet scent and kissing her hard. Releasing her soft breasts from her bra, I bite, suck, and kiss away until I feel her breathing start to heighten.

I lean back on the countertop as she drops to her knees in front of me. I fling my towel off, watching as her small hands pump away at my hardness until I feel myself on the brink of eruption. Her tongue moves to me and she takes me so deep and I stroke her throat helping her take me deeper. *"Cazzo, Eleni, what are you doing to me?"* I ask her, wondering how she was so fucking good at this. I watch as her eyes flick up and down to see what my reactions are. I feel the familiar sensation of climax begin to overcome me but no, not like this. I want to be buried deep inside her. I pick her up like she is weightless and lay her flat on the counter, pushing her legs open roughly, and let my mouth and tongue do all the talking that I can't seem to do as I feel her completely surrender as her nails drag down my back and run through my wet hair.

***

Eleni

I drop to my knees in front of me, my body already coming alive with anticipation. He flings his towel off, showing my *favorite part* of him. I automatically reach for him and start to pump his cock in my hand before my tongue reaches for him licking the tip of his sensitivity making him groan.

He speaks in rapid Italian that I can't understand but I can feel from the way his body is clenching, whatever he is saying is probably a compliment. He leans back, engrossed in pleasure as I let my tongue lap around him. I take him so deep I think I'm going to choke as he pulls my hair hard, his actions telling me I'm doing this right.

"Not yet." He pulls out and picks me up like I'm weightless and lays me down flat. I miss this, the weight of his body on top of mine and the heat of his breath on my lower body making me squirm.

"It's not over." He kisses the apex of my thighs and swishes his tongue around my heat. "Until I say it is." With that he parts my legs and enters me forcefully, beginning to pound me with dominant prowess. Each time he thrusts, I feel like he's stretching me to infinity. We switch positions and I ride him slowly as he sucks my neck softly, then pinches my nipples. His mouth swishes them around, then bites them. I feel my walls start to tighten and he throws me down underneath him, sensing my need to come. He enters me fast and we climax at the same time. I feel his hot liquid engulf me and he stays buried inside me for a second. His head rests on my chest as I stroke his dark hair, which is still damp from his shower. He rolls off me after a few minutes and we lay there for a second, both panting away.

"You're marrying someone else."

"I know," he groans.

"Why—"

"You don't understand," he says, standing up in annoyance.

"No, I don't understand anything about you," I fire back.

His eyes soften for a second. "It's business only, I don't want her. If you believe anything believe that."

"Who do you want?" I say quietly, looking up at him.

"You know I can't answer that," he says slowly, his thumb stroking my cheek. "My father has already accepted Rafiq's offer, I can't pull out now."

"You have a choice," I say, tracing the tattoo on his chest with my forefinger.

"I don't, you know my father. He will go fucking crazy."

"I didn't realize Daddy still pulled the strings for you at twenty-seven."

"Shut up, Eleni! You don't understand anything." This triggers him because he jumps off the countertop and grabs his towel, wrapping it around him.

"I understand that you're a child who can't take control of his own life."

I watch his face contort with fury and his eyes darken.

Did I go too far?

Fuck it, it was over for real this time. We both knew it, despite what just happened. I knew deep down we could never go forward because we didn't work.

***

Dante

"Not interrupting anything, am I?"

Nico swans in and I feel his eyes sweep over the scene, taking in Eleni's disheveled appearance and her lipstick, which has found its way onto my face and chest.

"Nothing," I say, glaring at him. He smiles back at me, knowing exactly what went down here.

"Panties," he says, pointing at the floor.

"Nico, shut up." I roll my eyes as Eleni flushes slightly.

"What? I'm being helpful." He shrugs innocently.

"However, as they have been ripped in half, Eleni might not have much use for them."

"Nico, go fuck yourself," she replies, pushing him out of the way and entering her room before slamming the door.

"You're a piece of shit," I say, punching him on the shoulder.

"Says the guy who just fucked his un-fiancée over the kitchen counter, while his real-life fiancée is waiting downstairs."

"I don't want her, and everybody fucking knows

it but her."

"So, what are you going to do?"

"Nothing. I made my bed and now I'm going to fucking lie in it."

Eleni emerges freshly made up and I assume with new underwear on. She ignores me and walks to the door.

"Since when do you not say goodbye?" Nico asks.

"Since Dante let his Daddy rule him," she says, and glares at me with such intensity I feel myself get slightly ruffled.

"I hope you're wearing fresh panties," Nico calls out, chuckling as the door slams.

"Nico, shut the fuck up before I throw you out this window."

"Bro, don't take this out on me, this is all on you. Deal with it."

I leave the room, slamming the door, trying to get my head right before Jameela arrives.

Chapter Twenty-Four

Watching You, Watching Me

"What?" I ask innocently as Ra glares at me from the hood of her car.

"Something is up with you," she says, narrowing her eyes.

"No, what are you talking about?" I reply, looking away. Nico already knows what happened upstairs and I don't want anyone else knowing.

"You've had sex, I feel it!" she replies, laughing at my embarrassment.

"Shhh! Don't make a big deal of it, okay?" I speak in a low voice as we both get in the car.

"Please tell me it wasn't with Dante."

"Well, it wasn't Chris Hemsworth."

"He's engaged!"

"Well, tell his dick that, because it has a mind of its own. It's not going to happen again; he wants me to move out."

"Is this a good thing or a bad thing?"

"I just don't really want to think about it, I'd

rather just—"

"Drink?"

"Uh huh."

"That can be arranged."

We pull up outside a club and the queue is huge. I shrug at Ra and she winks at me and puts up a finger to wait a second. I stand awkwardly at the back of the queue, looking at all the excited clusters of girls waiting to go in. I remember a time I was one of them, and my only concern was whether I would be carded or not. Now all I could think of is that I have fallen for someone who I should at point blank have no attachments to, somebody who is not only dangerous to me on every emotional and spiritual level, but somebody who is simply *dangerous*. He's a gangster, a thug, a mobster, but most of all, he's about to marry someone else and that is what kills me the most.

"Have you got a light, *Princesa*?" I turn around to see a lightly tanned dark-haired guy leaning up against the wall. He cocks his eyebrow, waiting for a reply.

"Uh no, I don't smoke."

"Good choice. I hear it's bad for you."

"Then why do you do it?" *Jeez, what was up with this guy?*

He shrugs at me. "Because I like *bad* things."

"Well, your pickup line is pretty bad, so you must be in heaven right now."

He smirks at me. "You're feisty, I like it, *Princesa*." He moves from the wall and walks off.

"Eleni!" Ra beckons me to join her in front of

the queue as we make our way under the VIP curtain. We dance for a little and I finally feel I am letting go. "What do you want do drink?" I ask, shouting over the noise.

"Jack and Coke, make it triple measures."

I make my way to the bar, and as I imagine, the queue is huge.

"You just can't stay away from me, huh?" a familiar voice calls out.

"You!" I reply with an eyeroll. The smoking weirdo from outside is at the bar.

"It must be your lucky day, *Princesa*." He winks at me, looking down, and I can feel him take in every inch of me with his hungry eyes.

"Or I need to start hanging out at better places?"

"That one hurt. How about you buy me a drink and you tell me all about him?"

"I don't know what you're talking about," I reply icily.

"You can't be called Romeo and not know these things, *Princesa.* I know you've been hurt; I can tell." The words trill off his tongue and he licks his lips, drawing my attention to his mouth.

Okay, I admit he was pretty hot.

He is tall with curly dark hair and matching mocha skin, his eyes, unlike Dante's defiant emerald ones, were almost black, and every time I catch his gaze I shiver a little.

"One drink. What do you say?"

"Sorry, I'm with someone. See you," I reply, brushing him off and disappearing into the busy crowd.

I eventually find Ra on the dance floor and my

heart sinks as I notice who is next to her.

"What is *she* doing here?" I exclaim angrily. Zosha and I both look at each other, then round on Ra, who sucks on her straw sheepishly.

"Shoot, did I forget to mention that I had invited both of you? Damn, looks like we're just going to have to enjoy the night then."

"Ra!" we both say in unison.

"Why are you letting Nico and Dante come between your relationship? You can sure as hell know they would never let either of you come between theirs. Talking of Dante, I promised I would collect a debt off the very man who owns this club, which is soon to be Dante's. Play nice, guys!" She runs off, not even giving either of us an opportunity to reply as we eye each other in absolute disdain.

"If you think I would listen to anything you have to say you must be out of your Goddamn mind!" I round on her.

"Like Saint Eleni listens to anybody!" she fires back.

"You're the one in the wrong! I was trying to give you some good advice," I spit back.

"I don't need your advice, I'm a grown ass woman!" she says, folding her arms.

"A grown ass woman who keeps running back to a little boy!" *There is no way she is going to win this argument*, I thought as I breathe hard through my nostrils.

"That's rich, coming from you! The girl who hates Dante so much she ended up in his sheets, the same Eleni who thinks she's so perfect she can change Dante." She moves closer, her face set in anger. "All you are to him is a piece of ass and you know it! Don't try to pretend you're better than me because you're not. If I'm pathetic, then so are you, little girl!"

I stand there seething, knowing she has won that argument. "Screw you!" I scream as her words wound me like razors.

"Screw you too!" she screams back as people begin to turn around, waiting for us to get into a proper altercation. Zosha gives me a cold look before disappearing into the dark crowd.

Everybody resumes dancing again now the two crazy bitches have stopped killing everybody's vibe. I pick up my phone and furiously start to dial Ra's number, getting ready to unleash my anger on her before the red bar alerts me I'm at 1% then switches off.

Fuck.

"We meet again, *Princesa.*" I turn around and see Romeo standing in front of me, his dark eyes drinking me all over again. "It's a sign," he says, nodding slowly, smiling a slow, wicked smile like a hunter eyeing its prey.

"That we're in the same place?" I roll my eyes, seriously pissed off.

"How about we have that drink, *Princesa*? You're alone, I'm alone, why not?"

I was about to say I'm not alone, but actually I was.

"Sure, why not?" I reply tonelessly.

What's the worst that can happen?

We walk over to the bar and he makes a two

signal and beckons me to sit down. When he walks over he's holding a bottle of champagne on ice.

"Uh, wow," I reply, taken back by the gesture.

"Only the very best for a *Princesa,*" he replies.

We toast and he watches as I drink from the champagne flute, a small smile playing on his lips. A few minutes pass and I start to feel a strange sensation come over me. "So…" My speech is slightly slurred.

Huh? What is happening right now?

"Is there something wrong, *Princesa*?" He smirks as he drinks his own champagne.

"This tastes weird," I manage to string out, my voice sounding very unlike my own as my tongue sticks to the roof of my mouth.

"It's the best there is, *Princesa*, only the finest champagne for the most beautiful girl in this club."

Why are the lights so bright in here? They seem to blind me every time I blink.

Romeo puts his arms around me and walks me out of the club onto veranda. I look down and there's a huge drop to the bottom of the building. His hand rests on my back forcefully, and for a second I think he's going to push me. Suddenly he turns around, facing me, and starts to stroke my face. "I have big plans for you. What was once his will now be mine."

Terror begins to gnaw at me, but everything seems to move in slow motion. I try to move but my legs feel like they're stuck in quicksand. When I try to speak the words don't come out the way they should. I have to try and get somebody's attention, but Romeo is one step ahead of me. He reaches across and wraps me in a bear hug like we are long lost lovers. It probably looks romantic to onlookers but to me it is terrifying.

"Don't fight it, I've got you and I'm never letting go." He holds me tighter, his tongue flicking across my neck as he inhales my hair.

"What have you done to me?" I manage to croak out.

"You'll soon find out, *Princesa*."

***

Hours later Bane walks into the dark room, regretting ever taking this gig. *What a shithole*, he muses, taking in the derelict surroundings of the house downtown they would be staying in for now. It looks like a fucking crime scene and it probably will end up being one. He pauses as he walks in and sees the girl sprawled out, still unconscious, Romeo looming over her stroking her cheek and muttering to her gently in Spanish.

Fucking weirdo. Bane rolls his eyes at the incredulous sight. Romeo is meant to be some big shot Colombian drug lord and here he is pawing at this girl like a lovestruck teenager.

He clears his throat, hoping that Romeo will stop what he is doing. "Is she awake yet?"

"No, she's reliving old memories right now. The next stage will be hallucinations, all of her deepest desires projected into a dream-like reality." He turns to face Bane with a slightly maniacal look on his face. "She won't even realize it's not real."

"I guess that is why they call you the alchemist,"

Bane replies, unimpressed.

"Indeed, putting my potions in motion."

Romeo smiles to himself at how far he has come, growing up in the streets of Bogota, Colombia had been hard work. He started selling drugs for cartels at fourteen before he finally started to experiment with his own strands of cocaine, heroin, and ecstasy. After that, his rank had significantly risen, and he became known as *el alquimista*. He was a part of Colombia's biggest cartel, his reputation for his concoctions was almost as famous as his temper was. He had killed twice as many people as a rookie than most of his captains did. Romeo wanted people to know he wasn't a man to be fucked with.

***

Eleni

The lights had dimmed and now it was time for their first dance. They both looked at each other shyly at how far they had come. Dante couldn't believe his eyes as he took in the pristine vision that was now his wife as she walked with him toward the dancefloor. Her white dress trailed effortlessly behind her like a princess. No, she was a queen, his queen.

"What's wrong?" he asks. His eyebrows crease in concern.

"I just—" I can't put my finger on it, it doesn't feel real. At the same time, my heart swells with emotion as Dante stands in front of me in his tux on our wedding day. I look around the room, taking in

all the familiar faces of the crew. Nico winks at me while leaning against the wall, talking to one of the waitresses.

Maybe this was real?

"What is it, baby?" Dante says, running his thumb across my face.

His touch against my skin, lighting me on fire, and seeing the gleam of his silver wedding band creates a lump up in my throat.

This must be real, right?

Dante twirled me around and dipped me low. "This is the most perfect day of my life." I look up at him as our smiles mirrored each other.

"It was always you; I want you to know that," he says, lifting me back up as we dance to the dulcet jazz saxophone.

"I wish I had known that at the time." I look up at him and closed my eyes, and for some reason my emotions seemed to relive every inch of pain Dante and I had gone through.

"If I had known then what I know now, I never would have let you go in the first place."

"Keep talking," I say as he pulls me closer and kisses me lightly.

"You're lucky there are people around here right now," He growls in my ear. "Tonight, it's going to go down."

"I can't wait," I moan into his mouth as I feel his own excitement rub up against my thigh.

"Just the two of us, baby." He kisses my forehead.

I bite my lip. Shit, this is going to be hard.

"I wouldn't quite say that" I reply, looking up at

him and stroking my stomach slowly, watching his eyes widen with disbelief.

"Are you—"

"Yes, Daddy, I am."

His face breaks out in a smile and applause ripples through the whole room, then everything starts to swirl.

***

"One more box, babe," a familiar voice calls out to me upstairs.

I have a look around and take in the large bedroom littered with boxes and clothes. I lean on the huge bed, slightly confused.

How did I get up here? Where am I?

"Babe—"

He walks in the room and smirks at me, the sunlight through the blinds gleaming against his lip ring.

Somebody is slacking." Ajax walks toward me and leans his knee beside me as he bends his head down to kiss me slowly. I feel his lip ring twirl lightly across my lips as one million and one butterflies explode inside of me.

He pulls away and I must look confused because he frowns at me. "What's wrong, babe? Are you okay?"

"Yeah, I'm fine." I look up in his adoring eyes and suddenly I am. He sits beside me and takes one of my hands to his face and kisses it. I notice with surprise there is an exceptionally large diamond ring on my left hand.

Are me and Ajax engaged?

"Like I told you, I want to be more than just your boyfriend, I want to be your husband." He leans toward me, cupping my chin in his hand.

This time he kisses me harder and a flurry of memories come through my mind. Dante and Jameela getting married and having children, Dante being shot dead by Lorenzo Salvatore, and Ajax being made head of the Dischanel Family. Ajax was like a beam of light in that montage. He healed me and put all the pieces of my heart back together when I thought I would fall apart.

"You're the best thing that ever happened to me," I murmur through his kisses that are flooding me with heat.

"I love you, Eleni, so much." He gets up and I look at him, missing the touch of his mouth, but I needn't worry as I hear my favorite sound of him unbuckling his belt. His shirt follows after that and I take in the picture-perfect sight of ink scattered across his taut body.

He put his knees on either side of me and lays me down slowly, stroking my hair as my mouth finds his neck, sinking into him, wanting to mark my territory.

"I fucking love you," I reply, pulling at his waistband as he smiles at me in enthusiasm, pulling his boxers off and throwing them over his shoulder.

"I want the neighbors to know what my fucking name is," he says, thrusting into me as he begins to pound hard and my eyes roll back in pleasure.

"Ajax!" I scream but the words don't leave my mouth as everything turned black and starts

to swirl again.

***

Ra arrives back at the bar, feeling like she has given Eleni and Zosha enough time to patch things up. "I'm back, hope you haven't killed each other!" Ra looks at Zosha and she stares back at her blankly.

"I thought Eleni was with you." Zosha speaks slowly and her eyes start to widen.

"I left her with you," Ra replies back. "Where the fuck is she?" Ra's voice goes up an octave as they both look around manically, as if Eleni will just materialize from thin air.

"It's been hours, I thought she was with you. We had an argument and I left her on the dance floor." Zosha's face pales as she realizes what she has done and the almighty consequences that will follow.

"How could you?" Ra bellows at her.

"I just—" Zosha starts crying, her shoulders shaking heavily.

"We have to make the call," Ra says stoically. They stare solemnly at each other, neither wanting to tell bad news to the one they feared the most.

***

Dante

"Are you going to answer that or what?" Nico asks me, as my phone continues to ring.

"Or what?" I reply, throwing it against the door as it clicks it off.

I decide against seeing Jameela tonight, my head is fucked up enough already. I'm not in the mood for her bullshit. *Cazzo,* Jameela was ruining my life already and were not even married yet. I put my hands behind my head in exasperation as she called for the umpteenth time.

"I'm so glad I don't have to deal with that bullshit."

"Yeah, because you're a piece of shit and nobody will put up with you." I smirk.

"Says the 'nice guy' who just fucked another woman a couple of hours ago, despite continually saying he doesn't want her."

I glare at him, but he doesn't back down. I can't get mad at him, especially when he's right. I hear a noise in the hallway, and I assume Eleni is back. Just thinking about her again gives me a hard on as I remember our earlier antics. Instead, Ra and Zosha walk in, both looking like they have seen ghosts. My eyes narrow, knowing immediately that something is up. I look at Nico and he suspects the same.

"What are you doing here?" I stand up and walk toward them with Nico close behind.

"I—"Zosha starts, then falters.

"Where is Eleni?" I ask, and they both look down, not wanting to meet my eyes.

My heart starts to race as blood begins to pump furiously around my body. *"Where is she?"* I scream as they both jump in terror.

Nico walks beside me and puts his arm on my

shoulder to calm me down.

Ra looks up, completely bewildered. "That is what we came here to tell you, we can't find her anywhere. She went missing at the club."

"We think somebody kidnapped her," Zosha says, her voice breaking as Nico stares at her in horror.

"Somebody better start fucking talking, right from the beginning," I say in a low whisper.

I promise bloody retribution on whoever has done this.

Chapter Twenty-Five

Romeo Must Die

"Start talking now." I enunciate the words in a low tone, but every syllable radiates the anger building up in me.

"I—we—" Zosha says, trying to put a sentence together. Her mouth opens and closes, seeing the look on my face.

"It was my fault, Capo,' Ra interjects while Zosha looks on, shocked. "I left her alone while I settled Milo's debt. I didn't realize how long I had been gone. I'm sorry and I take full responsibility."

"I don't give a fuck whose fault it is, and I know this isn't the truth." I watch Zosha crumple at those words, giving me a clear indicator on who was really at fault, not that it matters at this minute. I would punish them later, but now I needed to get Eleni back. "Find her now. I want CCTV, I want witnesses. I want fucking answers. Call every Goddamn one of my men and get them down here now."

Zosha and Ra hurry out, slamming the door behind them. I look at Nico, and his eyes have darkened in anger.

"Lorenzo retribution?" he says quietly.

"Yep, I just never thought they would take her."

"Lorenzo's people must have thought you and she...she does live here, so..." He trails off.

They thought she was my girlfriend, and now they had taken her to get to me. What they didn't know is that I will fucking kill all of them. "Tighten the security around him threefold. they're trying to throw us off Lorenzo, so it leaves him exposed. I want all of my captains here, especially Sapphire. Where is she?"

"I haven't seen her for days, I'll call her."

I frown. Something isn't sitting right with me, but I can't focus on that now. "Wherever Ajax is, find him and bring him here. I need my best ready to go."

"That won't be a problem." Nico half smirks.

"What?" I look at him blankly.

"Ajax will definitely be there, he digs Eleni."

"Say what?" I reply, starting to get irritated.

Nico rolls his eyes. "It's obvious. Every time he looks at her you can tell he wants to fuck her."

"Good for him," I reply drily. Why do I even care? I can't have her anyway, but that doesn't mean *I want him to* a small voice in my head says. "Call Farook and find out everything about Lorenzo's men, his family, his properties, even his favorite fucking color. I want to know *everything*."

"This is too bold for one of Lorenzo's capos to do on their own, someone else is involved. I don't think they'll hurt her, not yet anyway. Maybe they want a swap or a peace deal."

"They can want whatever they fucking want. I will slit the throat of whoever done this and put it on the top of this Goddamn building to show everyone what happens when you cross Dante Dischanel."

"We will get her back." Nico tries to placate me, but I am beyond reasoning or redemption, *all I can see is red.*

***

Eleni

"Hello?" My voice comes out as a bare whisper. *Thirsty. So thirsty.*

I crawl out of the dusty bed and panic starts to overwhelm me.

Where am I? What am I wearing? I look down to see that I have been dressed in a red leather crop top and matching skirt. This is bad, really bad. I try to search my memory for something. anything, but it was all so hazy.

Wherever I am, it's so derelict and dark that I can hardly make out which direction I'm going in. I manage to stumble to the kitchen and see a window. I try to open it, but it has been sealed shut.

"No way out, *Princesa.*"

That voice rings a familiar chord in my memory, and I whip my head around to see who it belongs to. "You!" I gasp as my memories start to flood back.

"Me." He smiles at me, a devilish smile that

sends shivers down my spine. His handsome features are diminished by the darkness in his eyes.

"You drugged me, why?" I look up at him in horror, not wanting to contemplate the situation I find myself in.

"At first this was all so simple. Dante takes something that belongs to us, so I take something that belongs to him. *You*. Do you like the outfit? I had my sister pick it out."

He's speaking so fast that I fail to comprehend what he is talking about. The maniacal excitement is pouring out of him.

"What has your sister got to do with Dante?" I look at him blankly, and he stares on, waiting for me to put pieces together which are proving impossible in my current state.

"My sister, Sabrina *Salvatore*." He smiles with that terrifying smirk, and it all makes sense.

"As in Lorenzo Salvatore?" I say quietly, taking in this bombshell.

"Is her husband—*ding ding ding,* we have a winner. I figured I'd snag you and swap you for him, but now…"

"Now what?" I say, panicking as he walks closer and strokes my cheek.

"Now I want you more than I want that piece of shit back. All he did was make her unhappy. He can stay in that cell forever; I have something better here. There is something about you, Princesa. I think you might be what I have been always looking for. *Eres Mia Princesa*." He kisses my hair, and I can feel him running his hands down my back, sending chills down my spine.

"You don't even know me," I stutter, trying to stay calm and backing away from him.

"I will give you things he never can. You will be my only, *por siempre mi Princesa*. Can he say the same thing?" He strokes my cheek and kisses my mouth lightly. I struggle against him, but he pulls my body into his and starts to claw at my clothes until I slap his hands away.

"You drugged me," I spat at him.

"That was for safety reasons, I needed to subdue you. It wasn't personal. Like I said, *Princesa,* I want you. Dante can have Lorenzo and I will take you."

"He won't let you."

"We'll see about that." He kisses me on the forehead and walks out.

Leaving me here, *trapped.*

***

Dante

"Zeek has gone to check out Lorenzo's other properties, so far no luck."

"Keep trying," I say flatly, knowing the longer this goes on, the less likely survival is. I hang up the phone and drag myself in the shower, letting the hot water drench me.

Washing all my sins away.

Not fucking likely.

I wipe the mirror, taking in my reflection and dark circles. I need to shave and get myself down to the compound. I will find her even if I have to do it

272

with my bare hands.

"Where have you been?" A voice appears out of nowhere, nearly making me cut myself with the razor.

"Don't fucking sneak up on me. Are you insane?" Jameela's reflection appears in the mirror.

"Well, maybe if you picked up your phone I wouldn't have to sneak up on you!" she replies, clearly pissed off.

"I'm busy," I reply coldly, my eyes indicating at the door.

"You have men, they can find *her*." She doesn't even say the name, she doesn't have to. It is as if Eleni is in the room, an invisible barrier standing between us.

"This is my war, not theirs. What kind of Capo would I be if I just sit here and watch?"

"This is not about that, Dante, and you know it."

"I don't need to explain myself to you."

She walks closer and I wait for her to explode, but she doesn't. "I just want to make you happy, please give me a chance." She looks up and kisses me, standing on her tiptoes, pressing her taut body against mine. Her hand snakes beneath my towel as she begins to stroke me slowly, I involuntarily respond to her, and I can feel myself gravitate toward her, but when I open my eyes, reality is shattered.

"I can't, I don't want you." I push her away roughly.

"You'll soon come around to my way of thinking." She kisses me again and walks out, leaving me there angry and horny.

I push Jameela out of my mind and get dressed, arriving at the compound ready for action. Everyone has been here for the last twelve hours looking for something, anything that will help find her. One of my oldest friends, Reign, arrived back from China last night and greets me warmly. "It's good to be back, Dante, but not in these circumstances. What can I do to help?"

"Maybe you and Nico can work together on this one, like old times."

We both turn around to look for Nico and I see him eyeing up a new girl I haven't seen before.

"That is my sister, Anara," Reign says, gritting his teeth.

"I don't think Nico knows that," I say, rolling my eyes.

"He will when I fucking break his legs. Dante, I know it's not the best time, but do you have any space for her in the regime?"

"Sure, we'll set her up with something."

"Away from Nico," he says darkly.

"Far away." I smirk, knowing distance is not relative with my dear cousin.

"I've got something." Farook comes running in wide-eyed like a mad man.

"We've had a hit on CCTV. The guy who took Eleni—his name is Romeo Sanchez."

"Button man?" I reply quizzically.

"No, this is where it gets complicated." Farook sighs.

"Romeo Sanchez, sister of *Sabrina Sanchez,* who is now *Sabrina Salvatore.*"

"So, she's calling the shots now?" I reply,

lighting my probably hundredth cigarette of the day.

"Yep."

"Instructions?"

"Romeo must die."

***

Nico

"Ahem."

No response.

*" Ahem. "*I clear my throat extra loudly to get her attention.

She finally looks up at me, her almond eyes accentuated by her dark lashes. "Do you need a doctor for that cough?" she asks sweetly.

Feisty, I like it.

So, Reign has a sister, he kept that quiet. She is his half-sister, so I shouldn't really feel guilty about pursuing her. After a few inquiries from Ra, I realized his sister had been engaged to one of the most dangerous men in China. She had only been here for a day, but time, distance, and space were all irrelevant to me. Ra had made it clear that I am not to even go there, but nothing is more tempting to me than being told not to do something.

As soon as I saw her, I knew I wanted her. Of course, Reign being Reign, would warn me that if I so much as looked in her direction he would snap my legs in two. Normally, I would back off, but the thought of it being *forbidden* makes it even worse. I skirted around her for the last day, like a shark circling its prey. Yes, *theoretically* Reign is my friend, and that would be crossing a line, but fuck it, if banging her is wrong, I don't want to be right. Every time I catch her chocolate eyes around the compound it was a prelude to what was going to happen next. I could imagine her sexy honey legs wrapped around me as I pounded her for days.

"So, *Anara"* Even her name is sexy, I like the way it rolls off my tongue like *she would* be doing soon if I played my cards right.

"Not interested."

Say what?

"I'm not interested in *you*, so save it." She rolls her eyes as if I'm some creep at a club trying to hit on her.

Does she not know who I am?

"I'm—"

"Nico Dischanel—I know. My brother told me all about you. *Your ways.*" She looks at me dead in the eye as if daring me to challenge her.

"I don't define myself by what others think of me, do you?" I say icily.

"Then maybe there is more to you than meets the eye," she replies, looking at me dead in the eye.

She walks away before I can even respond, leaving me stunned by her dismissal.

***

Dante

The heat of the water sends ripples of pain through my body, but it's a good pain. The kind of pain that I need to find Eleni and stay alert. It has been a whole day and nothing. Time seems to move slowly, like an invisible hourglass falling grain by grain. She was okay, I reasoned to myself, I need her to be okay. I hear the sliding of the shower door and a fresh breeze of air hits my back.

"Jameela, get out!"

I try to pass her, but she blocks me. She's standing there wearing nothing. *Cazzo,* I try to look away, but it's hard. Water drops down every curve of her golden-brown skin.

"Make me," she purrs, leaning her arm across me and moving closer until she is chest to chest with me. I throw her against the shower pane, kissing her hard as she wraps against me tightly. We carry on for a few minutes until I realize with horror what I'm about to do. "Jameela, I said no!" I push her away forcefully, grabbing my towel, and walking out. When I turn back her face is dark with anger.

***

Ajax

"You shouldn't be here." He sighs, looking at me.

"I'm coming with you."

"Zosha..."

"I'm not leaving until she is safe, and that is that."

"I can't argue with that logic." Farook calls me with Eleni's location and without a second's hesitation I jump in the car to get here. Zosha, who had overheard the conversation, insisted I take her with me, and with hesitation I did. I don't know what happened between them, but she was full of steely determination that she was coming. I haven't slept since Eleni had been taken. A fire burns hard within me that won't go away. I need to save her no matter what, she doesn't deserve to be caught up in this. I don't care how pissed off Dante would be if I get to her first. Eleni has left a mark on me and I know now that this is something special, not an average crush.

Eleni, I'm coming for you.

Chapter Twenty-Six

The Lair Of The Serpent

Ajax

"Why is it so quiet?" Zosha says breathlessly.

The silence is deafening and even I know this is not a good sign. I was supposed to wait for Dante, but I can't wait any longer. Nico, Farook, and Ra must be on their way here soon. *I hope.* Where the hell is Dante anyway?

Suddenly footsteps creak down the stairs.

"Well, well, well, the cavalry has arrived." Salvatore henchmen surround us, *we are fucked.*

"So, this is the best Dante Dischanel has to offer, a tattooed model and a stripper." Applause and jeering fill the room.

"Ajax…" I can feel the fear in Zosha's voice.

"Find Eleni and get out of here," I whisper out of the side of my mouth as I automatically start to feel for my weapon.

"But—" She looks at me as if to say *what about*

you? They will kill you!

"Go!" She runs and one of his men walks toward me, rolling his sleeves up, the Salvatore lion emblem stares at me as I stand ready to face my fate.

***

Eleni

I am falling again, and I don't want to. I know what's happening, and I hate it. My thoughts are blurry and hazy. I try to crawl away, but he stands on my hand.

"Looks like Dante finally found me, he's not as stupid as I thought. You, on the other hand, I'll have to leave here. I've given you a little something so you won't be able to tell him anything I don't want him to know until I am away from here." He leans forward, and I can almost see triple of him. He kisses my neck, and despite my haze of hallucination I feel repulsed. "You and me, *Princesa*, *eres mia*." He walks out, and I can't move or form any thoughts, it's like I'm slipping away, and then it's dark...

"Eleni!"

"Zosha?" *No, it can't be. I must be dreaming again.*

"Eleni! Get up!" She's pulling me up now and this time I know it's real.

"I can't move," I say, my voice thick with distortion.

"You have to, Ajax is downstairs alone, and

Dante is on his way. We need to get out before they find us first."

I manage to drag myself up and she holds on tight and starts running, my legs and brain trying to work in sync to get away.

***

Dante

"Damn it, Dante!" Nico looks at me as the speedometer hits triple figures. "What the fuck is wrong with you? Do you want to get arrested tonight?" he says, alarmed.

I let my foot off the gas and watch the speed drop. "I need to find her," I say in exasperation. Nothing else matters to me. I try to apply tunnel vision, but guilt seems to exist in the back of my mind. I don't want Jameela at all, but now this changes things.

"Dante?" Nico says in trepidation.

"Jameela and I nearly—" I trail off, but he looks at me in understanding.

"Shit happens, it's not like Eleni and you have anything going on."

"I shouldn't have done it; it was a bad business move."

"Let's just concentrate on getting her out of there and smashing Salvatore scum."

"Where is everyone?"

"Ajax and the others should be there."

"No, Farook and Ra are behind us."

"That fucking hero went there on his own."

281

I hit the gas pedal harder, I wouldn't let anyone else down tonight.

***

Ajax

The blows keep coming hard.

"He's dead, leave him. We need to prepare for Dante's arrival." I hear the sound of a gun cocking as they walk away.

I crawl to the next room, feeling the blood drip down my face. I hear a door creak. *Fuck.* I would be definitely dead this time if anyone spotted me.

"Ajax!" Eleni runs toward me and drops to her knees. She looks strange dressed up in a tiny red outfit with her hair bedraggled and makeup smudged.

"Did he touch you?" I whisper hoarsely. Anger seems to overtake me as my thumb circles her cheek.

"Not like that." Her eyes swim with tears. "What have they done to you?" Zosha looks on awkwardly behind us, witnessing our bloody reunion.

"You need to get out of here, I'll only slow you down."

"No!" they both whisper in unison.

"Go, I need to wait for the others. Just go." I kiss her forehead, leaving a bloody stain. I must be really fucking messed up.

They both leave and I finally collapse in pain, the blackness taking over as my eyes close.

Dark Temptation

***

Eleni

We head down to the basement and I feel my lungs thicken with the mustiness of the air. A door opens, and Romeo's men surround us. *There is no way out.*

"It must be my lucky day, two pretty girls all to myself." A thickset guy adorned with tattoos leers at us in excitement, his mouth filled with silver and gold teeth. Zosha nudges me to the door on the left, indicating we should run. "One, two, three…go!"

We both run out as gunfire explodes. Suddenly cold air hits me and relief washes over me.

"We're free!" I turn around to Zosha, but she's not there.

Where is she?

"Eleni!" Dante and Nico run toward me.

"Are you hurt?" Nico looks at my bleeding face, alarmed.

"It's Ajax's blood, he's hurt really bad," I say thickly, trying to breathe and talk in unison.

"Zosha is in there," I wheeze.

"She is?" He looks troubled for a minute. "It's okay, I'll find her."

Nico runs in the house as four more cars pull up; men follow him into the property, pulling their weapons out.

I feel really disorientated; Dante's talking but his words seem to echo in my ears like he is very far away. He pulls me close, tucking my head under his chin. "Tell me he didn't hurt you, tell me he didn't

283

touch you," he says with his eyes closed, his voice barely a whisper.

"No, he didn't."

I feel him sigh in relief. "I've got you, and I won't let anyone hurt you again. This is all my fault, Eleni. I dragged you into danger again." I feel him exhale against me in exhaustion.

I look up and stare him square in the eyes, feeling myself for the first time. "I love you, Dante."

He stares back at me, looking pained, and it is the last thing I remember as the darkness claims me. I hear him screaming as I fall.

Chapter Twenty-Seven

The Deepest Cut

"Dante?"

"Mhm."

"Dante?"

My eyes open to sunlight searing my eyes. When I look up, Farook is standing over me with one eyebrow creasing in concern.

"What time is it?" I yawn, rubbing my eyes, and feeling like the weight of the world is on my shoulders.

"It's mid-day, you've been here for two days."

He passes me a cup of coffee which I gladly drain. "What's the latest?" I nod my head over to where Eleni is lying less than a foot away from me, covered in wires. Oxygen pushes her chest up and down in rhythm. I swallow, looking at her in the cold light of day and remembering her sinking into my arms.

"Uh—" Farook pauses, looking at me.

"What?" I feel bile start to rise in my throat.

"Chang says that her toxicity screen is through the roof. Romeo drugged her up to her eyeballs and it's having some kind of side-effects on her red and white blood cells." He trails off, looking at my face.

"Fuck." I put my head in my hands, tugging against my newly acquired stubble.

"Dante—" he starts, but I ignore him.

"This is my fault. I brought her into this. I should have known better. If I'd just left her alone none of this would have happened." Everything I touch seems to crumble into ash, Eleni is just another casualty in my life of people that have got close to me.

Farook bows his head and sighs, pulling off the tie around his neck and throwing it on the vacant chair next to me.

"How did it go?" I ask him.

"Quiet," he says, unbuttoning his black shirt. "We tried to find her family and we drew a blank."

"She didn't have any, we were her family." My voice almost cracks on the last part. "I still can't believe it; this feels like a fucking nightmare," I say, putting my hands together at the back of my head.

However much I wanted to attend Zosha's funeral, I couldn't be seen out in the open. I was too much of a target. Even my father couldn't attend. Things were still raw in the streets of New York, and if I'm not careful, I will be in a hole right next to her.

"A nightmare that the Salvatore family will pay for dearly," Farook replied angrily.

"Now is the time for regrouping. I want everyone to hit the mattresses and lie low. I can't risk anymore casualties, not after last night. Where is Nico?"

"Taking it badly." Farook sighs. "He found Zosha, he feels responsible. He hasn't been right since; he needs to get it out of his system." He cocks his eyebrow at me, and I roll my eyes, well aware what he was implying.

"Ajax?"

"Critical condition. He looks black and blue."

"I should have gotten there sooner—"

"Nothing would have changed. We live by the sword and we die by it. We know what the risks are of living this life."

"Yeah, but I didn't expect it to end this way."

My eyes drift over to Eleni and my chest constricts.

***

Nico

I slouch down on the leather armchair, watching the girl in front of me gyrate in front of a pole. I watch as she gracefully works the pole, wearing hardly anything apart from a piece of string and a bra. I can feel my body reacting to her as my jeans start to constrict against the denim material. I know this is wrong, *very very wrong*. But this is who I am, *this* is my *default*. I don't want to feel anything. Blame courses through me like poison without an antidote, and the guilt is physically killing me like a blade to my flesh.

The blonde gets off the pole and sits on my lap

seductively. She whispers things I can't decipher, but her hands are telling me all I need to know as they snake down my pants, giving me the release I crave. I follow her into one of the private rooms and she pushes me down on the red velvet bed, pulling off the little she's wearing. I can see the swell of silicone in her breast and ass as it tips over my lap.

She kisses me deeply, stroking the wolf on my chest and I pull away, my memories flying to when Zosha's naked body would be up against me doing the same thing.

"No touching, just fucking."

"Suit yourself." She laughs as her hands and mouth work me and she sheaths me with protection. My mind barely registers as she gets on top of me, rising and falling in sync, her eyes roll to the back of her head as she impales herself on my length of steel.

"Jesus Christ," she screams as her acrylic nails claw the fuck out of me.

"Not quite," I say, gritting my teeth. I push her flat on her stomach and pummel her from behind, grabbing on to her hips as I thrust my anguish away. I feel her body explode as she shudders against me. I flip her on her back, continuing to pound against her as my own muscular body finally finds a release against her curvy, slick one. I roll over onto my back and pull off the condom, lighting a cigarette. I start to put on my boxers, but when I look up, I notice her on her knees in front of me, looking up hungrily.

"I'm not finished with you yet," she purrs.

Dark Temptation

***

Six Days Later

Dante

My body jolts awake as I try to register what is happening, then I realize I have fallen asleep on my couch, fully clothed. I stand up, yawning, the last week has been hell. Ajax has luckily pulled through and is on the mend, but Eleni is still in an induced coma. I have spent days and nights by her side. What has happened weighs heavily on my chest—it was my fault. If she had stopped fucking with me—literally and figuratively—then this would have never had happened. She would have been safe in school; she never would have met me; she might even have a nice doctor boyfriend now. My heart jolts as I think of an alternate reality where we never met. My mind switches to the last words she said to me, *"I love you, Dante,"* and my heart sinks. I know that was probably the chemicals in her body speaking, but those words pull heavily in my chest.

I grab my towel as I head into the shower. My face has a greyish tinge to it because I haven't slept, and my stubble ages me beyond my years. I quickly shave, slapping my cheeks with aftershave to wake myself. After I shower, I get out and dry myself. I feel exhaustion overcome me as I sit on the bed as my eyes start to droop. My body suddenly comes alive, as I feel a pair of hands drape over my shoulders and lips trace over my neck.

"Move," I reply, irritably, pushing her arms

away.

She sits in front of me, looking up reproachfully. "Dante, I'm worried about you."

I cock my eyebrow. "Don't be, I am not your concern."

"How is Eleni?" she says softly.

"You don't care." I snort at her.

"If you care, I care," she replies. "We're getting married, there should be no hard feelings. Like you said, there is nothing going on between you, right?"

"There is nothing going on between us either, Jameela," I reply back.

"That is not what your body was saying in the shower…"

She moves closer, her face inches from mine. I can feel her body heat as her thick lips start to nuzzle over my neck. "Just let me take care of you, you're so tired." Her arms start to massage me in a circular motion as she starts to kiss my chest, following the cord on my throat to my mouth.

I hesitate for a second, knowing how wrong this is, but I feel hypnotized, and exhaustion clouds my judgment like a billowing haze in front of my eyes. She senses my hesitation and begins to kiss me slowly. I bat her way, but she continues again and again until I don't have the energy to resist her. She dives into my mouth, her tongue twisting away at me as my arms start to automatically undress her. I can't stop what I am doing as my mind goes on autopilot. She pushes me flat on the bed, her dark head disappearing lower and lower until I feel her hot tongue on me. She pauses and unlatches her mouth, then she pushes me down on the bed. I feel her tightness envelop me as her taut body rocks against me. Her teeth graze against my neck, then everything stops making sense.

Ring.

Shut up.

Ring.

Stop fucking calling.

Ring.

I wake up, bleary eyed, trying to shut off the ringing sound that is irritating the hell out of me. "What?" I say, thick voiced, trying to register my surroundings. I feel like I haven't slept for days and as a result my mind is blank. I roll over, and to my horror I see an arm wrapped around me with a thick diamond on the left finger.

Fuck. Fuck. Fuck.

"Dante?" Farook's deep voice brings me back to my shocking reality.

"Yeah," I reply back, trying to keep my voice low so she doesn't hear me.

"Eleni is awake." My heart rises and sinks at the same time.

How can I explain this?

My best answer is not to and pretend it never happened. Maybe nothing happened between us and this could all be explained. I try to follow that narrative until I see several ripped foil wrappers scattered on the floor.

Not even just once.

I groan internally. What the fuck was I thinking?

I wasn't. I was just doing.

"I'll be there in an hour."

"Dante, you sound weird, are you okay?" The

291

genuine concern in Farook's voice is making me feel more guilty than I do now.

"Yeah, I'll see you in a while." Jameela nuzzles into my neck and I feel repulsion rise within me. I slowly climb out of the bed, doing the walk of shame like a cheap whore, in my own apartment no less.

Fucking dumb ass Dante.

I take the quickest shower in the history of my life and run out of the house, putting my foot on the gas until last night becomes a distant memory.

Chapter Twenty-Eight

Secrets

Nico

"Get up."

"Mhm."

"Get up, jackass!"

I feel a high heel prod me and I grab the ankle tight with one eye barely open.

"Do that again and I will remove your kneecaps," I say with my eyes closed.

"I'd like to see you try, bigshot," a familiar voice replies.

"Anara?" I say groggily.

"The one and only."

I finally open my eyes and I am laying in the middle of the compound wearing my only underwear and one shoe.

How the fuck did I get here? I don't even remember anything apart from being at the strip club.

"Always a pleasure to see you," I say, leaning on one elbow and winking at her.

"It clearly is." Her eyebrows raise at my bulging groin.

"I'm always ready for action, babe," I say, patting myself down as an invite.

"You have lipstick on your chest and smell like a whore. What an attractive prospect you are," she says, rolling her eyes and sipping from the plastic coffee cup in her hand.

"YOLO," I reply, slightly amused by her coolness as I pull myself off the floor.

"Didn't your girlfriend just *die?"*

***

Anara

The room temperature drops to sub-zero as Nico's face changes into a mask of fury. He stands up and comes toward me like thunder. Wrapping his hand around my throat, pushing me hard against the wall, he says, "Don't talk about shit you don't understand." He tightens his grip, almost choking me.

I put my hand on top of his, pulling his off. "Take your fucking hands off me." I can feel my own temper starting to rise, any man acting like this is a trigger after my ex. I can feel a million flashbacks hitting my emotions.

He drops his hands as if they are burning with heat and his face goes back to normal. "I shouldn't have done that," he says, raking his fingers through his hair in horror.

"Fuck you!" I spit at him.

"I'm sorry, Anara, I really am," he says in a low tone, looking at the floor.

"Whatever," I say, walking off. I look back at him and he's sliding down the wall. I can sense the defeat in him, and it makes me uneasy. I know what is going to happen next and I will regret it. I walk back and stand in front of him, extending my hand and pulling him up. He looks at me, bewildered.

"Take a shower and get dressed," I instruct him.

"Huh?" he says, confused.

"We've got plans."

He looks even more confused, but a couple of minutes later, I hear the shower running and I smirk at myself.

***

Dante

I walk into Eleni's room, wondering whether my face will betray me.

"Dante." Farook is in the doorway.

"Where is she?"

"Running a few tests, but her vitals seem promising. She seems almost normal, albeit a little anemic. I told her about Zosha so you didn't have to."

"Thanks." I lean casually against the wall.

"What's wrong with you?" Farook eyes me curiously. He knows me too well, I can't lie to my best friend of eleven years. He can read me like a book.

"I slept with Jameela," I say in a low undertone.

"What? Are you fucking kidding me?" Farook groans and holds his hands to his head.

"I wish I were," I say, linking my hands together at the back of my neck.

"Worst timing ever, Dante! What the hell were you thinking?" he says angrily.

"I wasn't, she just jumped on me. I couldn't stop her."

"You talk shit," he says, folding his arms.

"I'm serious, you know how wrecked I've been lately, I barely know what day it is."

"Jesus, Dante, what did I tell you about leading her on? You need to tell Eleni before she does."

"Jameela knows the score, besides nobody will find out, telling Eleni will only make it worse."

"Famous last words, Dante." Farook snorts.

Eleni walks in and I try to regain my composure.

"I'll leave you guys to it," he says, excusing himself and giving me a meaningful look.

"Eleni." I look down at her as she glances up awkwardly.

"Dante." There is a silence between us.

"All of this is my fault." I swallow slowly. "You were a casualty in my war, but I promise I won't let this go until I bring revenge on the Salvatore family."

"Zosha died because of me," she says sadly, her eyes welling up. "It's my fault." Slow, silent tears begin to drop.

"It's not." I sigh and slowly wipe one of her tears away with my thumb. "This is all on me. I don't want you to think about this now, you need to recover."

She moves closer and puts her head on my chest, enveloping me with her arms. "Chang says you stayed here every night." She looks up in expectation, like I am a prince from a fairy tale instead of the villain she doesn't know I am.

"I wanted to make sure you were okay."

"I am now," she says, looking up at me and leaning toward me with her eyes closed. "Dante, about what I said to you at Romeo's place…" She swallows hard, looking up at me with her Bambi eyes that make my chest constrict.

"It's okay, I know you didn't mean it," I say slowly.

"Yeah,' she says quietly, "I didn't." She stares at me for a second and I move forward, like I'm going to say something, but there aren't any words that can fit what I truly want to say.

"Dante." Chang walks in and Eleni and I spring apart.

"Uh sorry, I need to talk to you."

"It's not a problem, let's talk outside." I pull off my jacket and throw it on the armchair.

"I'll be back in a second," I say, following him out, trying to avoid the spectacular twinge in my chest.

***

Eleni

Something has shifted between us, I feel it.

Why would he spend every night here if I mean so little to him? I sit on the armchair where Dante's jacket is laid out as my body creaks in exhaustion. So much has happened and my heart aches as I think of Zosha. Dante's phone vibrates in his jacket. I should go to Chang's office and give it to him; it might be important. I pull out the phone and my stomach drops as I see the name Jameela.

When are you coming back home to give me a repeat performance of last night?

I feel my breathing start to heighten as my throat burns.

Every time I fall for his bullshit, he hurts me. I never learn.

Rage builds up as I hold onto the phone so hard grooves are created on my skin. Dante walks in and I smile at him, feeling the crease in my mouth start to quiver as I do so.

"Eleni, are you okay?" He looks at me, furrowing an eyebrow and my fixed smile.

Slap.

I don't know what comes over me, but my rage explodes and I slap him hard across the face.

"What the fuck are you doing?" he screams, his hand clutching his very red left side.

"I know about last night, you bastard. *You bastard*," I scream. I hit and punch him, knowing I'm really hurting him at all, as his muscular form deflects every attack. He pins my arms to my sides.

"Stop before you hurt yourself," he says calmly.

"Too late, I saw her message to you," I say angrily, still punching him, hurting myself more than him.

"Stop!" he bellows, grabbing my wrists forcefully. "I shouldn't have done it, and nobody regrets it more than I do."

"Why did you do it?" I ask as my voice begins to shake.

"I don't know, Eleni, it just happened."

"If I mean so little to you why were you here every night? Doesn't that mean something to you?"

"I felt responsible for what happened, it was my fault," he says in a robotic tone.

"Do you love her?" My voice cracks.

"No!" he says, repulsed.

"How could you be so cruel? I'm in a coma and you're getting laid. Real nice, Dante."

"I never said I was a saint."

"Then why?"

"It was an accident."

"What, she tripped and fell into your bed?"

"What do you want me to say, Eleni? I didn't intend it to happen. I do not want to marry her, nor do I want her in any other way. If I had a choice, she wouldn't be it."

"Then who would you be with?" I fold my arms, staring at his stormy green eyes. His face is still red on one side.

"My life is complicated, Eleni, you know that." He rolls his eyes, reaching for a cigarette in his jacket.

"Stop making excuses and answer the question." I take the lighter out of his hand and throw it to the other side of the room. Anger starts to rise in his face.

"You already know the answer," he says,

Sarah Amelle

retrieving the lighter and putting a cigarette in his mouth. "It doesn't mean shit, Eleni." He takes a long drag. "I can't be with you the way you want me to. You know how dangerous our lives are, there is no margin for error."

"Am I not worth the risk?" I ask, glaring at him in anger.

"You *are* the risk, and I never want anybody to be able to hurt you again, which is why this can never happen. We both know the score, there is nothing more to say."

I open my mouth and Zeek walks in. Sensing he has interrupted, he coughs lightly. "We need you at the warehouse."

"Let's go."

Zeek walks out and Dante turns toward me. "Ra will take you home, she's on her way. I have already signed the release papers from Chang."

"Is that all you're going to say to me?" I say.

"Looks like it," he replies and then he walks out.

I slam the door and walk over to the windowsill, watching him walk outside in deep conversation with Zeek. His eyes briefly look up at me, but he turns his gaze away quickly. My heart is thumping in anger, sadness, grief, and everything else. I hear footsteps approach.

"I heard you were awake."

I turn around to that familiar voice and am greeted by a pair of sky-blue eyes and a piercing smile. He smirks, walking toward me, and everything seems to go into slow motion...

Chapter Twenty-Nine

Chemistry

Ajax

I walk toward her, my body still aching from the beating I took.

For her.

But it was worth it.

"How are you?" I say, stroking her hair lightly.

"I'm…" She pauses. "Zosha is dead."

Her mouth starts to tremble, and I pull her close. "It wasn't your fault, it was just…a terrible accident."

She stares at me, taking in the full extent of my battering, and puts her hand to her mouth in horror.

"I'm okay, it looks worse than it is." I laugh and gasp at the pull in my ribs.

"You could have died, Ajax; I wouldn't have been able to bear it if anything had happened to you."

"Why not?" I ask, needing to know for sure

before this went any further, I grab her wrists and implore her to look in my eyes.

"Because—I care for you. I like you a lot, Ajax."

"How much?" I raise my eyebrows at her as my face inches closer.

I want her.

And even though most of my body is broken, there is one part of me that is *definitely* functioning.

"This much." Her lips hover against mine and I take my cue as she kisses me ferociously.

I kiss her back, slowing the pace. I really want to *savor* this moment. I have been waiting so long for this. She wraps her arms around me as I push her against the wall gently. Her arms grip the nape of my neck as she pushes herself against me, my hardness now evident like a denim tent.

Cough.

We pull apart automatically and I am half relieved to see Farook standing there, not Dante. His face tells me everything he is thinking. "Ra told me she couldn't take you home," he says in a polite voice to Eleni.

"I'll make sure she gets off okay."

I bet you do.

Farook didn't say it, but his eyebrow cocks, indicating his thoughts.

"Enjoy your night while you can," he mutters, exiting the room. He leaves me with no doubts of what would happen if Dante found out but fuck it. I want this too much to turn back now.

"So, you're going to take me home?" she asks, tracing my jawline.

"I could…or you can stay with me tonight and

we'll do whatever you like."

***

Eleni

I teeter on the edge of this decision as I feel my body start to respond to the possibility of this happening. Dante's image flicks through my mind, but I shut it off.

He doesn't want you.

Ajax does and you want him too.

It's simple, isn't it?

"I would like that very much," I say shyly. His blue eyes light up in excitement as he moves closer, pushing me back up against the wall, his hands over mine, extending them over my head.

"I'm going to make this a night you won't forget."

Judging by the hardness I feel against my thigh, I take his word for it.

***

Anara

"Batting cages?" Nico looks around, bemused.

"No shit, Sherlock. Since you're one of these Neanderthal Mafia jackasses who can't open up without holding a gun in their hand, I figured this is a good release for you. I'll just sit here while you get it out of your system." I take a seat on one of the deck chairs and pull on my shades.

"I have other ways of getting things out my system. I think you would find that much more enjoyable." He winks at me.

"Anara Cho doesn't do community penis."

"You're fucking rude." He grabs the bat and puts on the helmet.

"You're not even arguing, so you know I'm right."

"I'm Mr. Worldwide, baby," he says, hitting an incoming ball. "Shit." He watches it fly high.

"How does it feel?" I ask, looking at him and putting the shades on the bridge of my nose.

"Surprisingly—"

Strike.

"Good," He says, fastening his helmet.

This goes on for twenty minutes in silence, every time he hits the ball I can feel the tension and frustration easing out of him. I can't help but notice his bulging muscles push through his tee. Jesus. He wasn't the only one getting worked up. *Think unsexy thoughts, Anara*. Not about jumping him right here and now. I push my shades off, trying to blink my thoughts away.

"What the fuck are you doing? You look like you're having a seizure," he says, pulling his helmet off.

"Nothing, just something in my eye."

Step one to making someone not attracted to you, act like a raving lunatic.

"Feel better?" I ask, throwing him a bottle of water.

He drains half the bottle. "Yeah, a lot." He

throws the empty bottle in the trash can with perfect aim.

"You wanna talk about it?" I ask, trying to act casual.

"You tell me about Johnny, and I'll tell you anything you want."

I groan as he smiles at me.

He is so bad that he is good.

***

Eleni

After a forty-five-minute drive we are at Ajax's place and nerves suddenly get a hold of me. Dante is the only guy I've been with. What if I didn't know what to do? What if it was awkward? He seemed to sense my nervousness.

"Relax," he says, taking my hand and kissing it. "We don't have to do this if you don't want to."

But I do, I really do.

I don't answer but I kiss him deeply, pushing myself against him. He understands my body language and picks me up by my ass. I wrap my legs around his torso. He carries me upstairs, laying me down on his bed as he begins to strip off slowly. I watch in wonder as all of his tattoos start to come to life with every muscle movement until he's only wearing a pair of boxers, which show me exactly how much he wants me.

I smirk as he comes closer, undressing me slowly until I am only left with my bra and panties.

Thank God, Ra brought me clothes while I was in the hospital, at least I had matching underwear. Although, I don't think Ajax would have minded by the way he's looking at me right now, in fact he would probably prefer no underwear. He leans me back slowly, so that I'm lying flat on my back as he lays directly on top, kissing me.

"You are so beautiful," he groans, unclipping my bra and throwing it over his shoulder.

This feels different. With Dante it was fast and furious fucking, apart from the first time where it was such a blur I don't quite remember all the details, apart from how hot it was.

He buries his mouth on my chest, taking his time sucking and biting. The cold metal lip ring against my own flesh sends mini electric volts to my nerves. His head moves lower until I feel his fingers on the edge of my underwear, tugging and easing them off in one swift motion. His fingers begin to explore me as his mouth goes back to my chest, biting me slowly as my hands rake through his hair.

"Ajax," I whisper slowly as I feel so many waves of pleasure rise up in me that I don't know what exactly I am feeling.

He lifts himself off me and pulls his own underwear off as excitement ripples within me, knowing what's in store. He lays back on top of me, kissing me hard, his fingers intertwining with mine and keeping eye contact. His mouth isn't talking but his body is. So, this is what a slow burn is? It dawns on me this isn't just sex to him, this is more. Before I even have time to contemplate what he's doing to me, his eyes lock with mine.

"I want to taste you, Eleni," he says, looking down at me with pure lust in his eyes.

I nod fervently but he shakes his head. "Use your words, baby, tell me what you want me to do to you."

"I want you to taste me," I whisper as I grab his head and pull him in for a passionate kiss. I begin to bite his lip slowly, making him groan.

"I want you to taste me, *Daddy*," he says, smirking. The thought of Ajax dominating me sends a jolt of excitement running through me.

"I want you to taste me, *Daddy*," I repeat, watching his eyes darken in desire.

He pulls away and his head moves lower. I feel his hot breath on the place I want him most. His tongue enters, causing me to nearly jump through my skin, his metal mouth ring pulsing against my clit is sending me over the edge. My body shudders and arches, covering him in wetness.

"You fucking taste amazing," he says, kissing my thighs.

I tug on the back of his hair tightly to let him know he's blowing my fucking mind, and pull his head up gently, bringing him face to face with me. I flip over so I am on top, kissing his chest, and now he's stroking my hair. I trace all of his ink, one standing out the most.

Carpe Diem.

"Seize the day." He smiles, closing his eyes as I watch the beautiful crinkle of his smile. My hands start to work his huge length, getting him sufficiently hard until my mouth takes over.

Whoa, it looks like Ajax really does like to get

everything pierced.

He looks down on me and laughs. "It's supposed to heighten your sexual experience. You're welcome," he replies with a wink.

I giggle and take him in my mouth, feeling his body clench as he pulls my hair slightly.

"Eleni, you're fucking amazing." He groans as my hands cup his balls while I suck and stroke simultaneously, until I feel his body clench and his hot white liquid seeps down my throat.

***

Ajax

Fuck.

That was amazing, her body slides up and she straddles me, both of us slick with sweat. She kisses me deeply, both of us tasting each other. I feel myself start to get hard again and reach inside the bedside cabinet, ripping open a foil wrapper with my teeth, then start to sheath myself, ready for the grand finale. She pushes herself down on me, already wet as she rides me slowly, her hips rocking to my rhythm as I grab her beautiful ass and watch her eyes roll back, ready for an incoming orgasm.

"Jesus, Ajax," she moans softly.

"Not yet," I growl into her earlobe.

She grinds on top of me, biting down hard on my shoulder. I turn her around so she is on her stomach and slide in behind her. My hand caresses her from the front, watching her hands grip tightly on the sheets. She arches her body, eager for more, and I push in a little deeper, letting my thumb circle her clit as her head pushes back in ecstasy. I feel close to my own climax, but I want to prolong it as much as I can. I don't want this to end. I spank her ass lightly and feel her body jump in surprise. She turns to me and smirks, impressed with my daring. I do it again, but this this time I push her body down so she is lying flat on her stomach, my erection buried in between her cheeks as I kiss her lower back and thighs.

"I love your ass," I say, squeezing it softly. I feel her shake with pleasure underneath. I bite it softly with my teeth, pushing my finger inside slowly. "I'm going to fuck you in this exact spot next time. I promise you will love it, but not tonight, baby. I want to save that for when you're more used to my size."

***

Eleni

Goosebumps appear on my skin as he utters those words and still continues to kiss and bite me. I had never thought about that kind of sex before, but the way he describes it heightens my curiosity. I don't think I can wait anymore, my body is shuddering in anticipation, as if he knows what I'm thinking. He turns me around, stroking my face slowly. "Are you ready to come for *Daddy*?" He kisses me passionately and I nod in longing. Our eyes mirror one another's passion.

"Yes, *Daddy*," I whisper back hoarsely as my

body starts to shiver under him. I trace his jawline all the way down to his dimples, his piercing blue eyes never leaving my own periwinkle ones. Ajax's eyes are the keys to his soul, they come alive every time he smiles. They radiate warmth and compassion, unlike the stormy green ones that I have been used to seeing for so long. He pulls my hands over my head and intertwines his fingers with mine, sliding inside of me as my walls tighten against him. We kiss slowly as our hips start to work in sync. Every time I try to move faster he slows me down. He wants to make this last, I don't blame him.

***

Ajax

"Are you ready to come for Daddy?" I watch her squirm and nod fervently; her thighs already slick with moisture. Her body is so fucking tight, almost sending me into overdrive, but I slow her down every time I feel her start to accelerate the pace. I want to take my time with her, and I want to look into her eyes and watch her moan my name. I can't remember the last time I was into this kind of romantic shit, but Eleni is different. *I crave her touch. I crave her even more.* From the first time I saw her, I wanted her. I want to love her and fuck her in every way possible. I might have come on too strong about her ass, but with something that perfect, who would not want to hit that from behind? My balls tighten thinking how many positions I could make her scream in. I lean down and lick her nipples slowly, my lip ring dancing around them as I feel her start to tighten around me.

"Ajax!" she screams, clawing on me as she climaxes, her legs wrapping around my hips as I follow suit and collapse on top her, kissing her slowly. I smile down at her; she is truly the best I've ever had. I discard the condom and pull her into my chest, stroking her and kissing her until we fall into a deep sleep, our bodies still intertwined.

***

Dante

"What's up?" I ask as Farook climbs in the car.

I had been at the docks all day getting emergency ammunition. I know another hit is imminent unless steps are taken to put some kind of peace plan in place. I yawn loudly, thinking about where the fuck I'm going to sleep tonight. I'm not going to my place, that's for damn sure. Nico could crash at the compound while Eleni stays at his place. I wanted her in safe hands.

"All good," he replies, looking out of the window.

Am I being obtuse or is he avoiding my gaze?

"Did Eleni get off?"

"Huh?" he replies, looking at me, horrified.

"Did she get off home, idiot? Ra was supposed to pick her up."

He was definitely behaving oddly, what the fuck was his deal?

He mumbles something incoherently, then continues to stare out the window.

"What's going on, Farook?"

There is no mistaking this, my best friend is definitely keeping something from me, and I'm going to find out what the fuck is going on.

"Spit it out, Farook!" I reply in irritation.

"Don't get mad," he says, looking at me sideways.

"Have you met me before? When have I ever not gotten mad?" I reply back with an eye roll.

What the fuck is wrong with him?

"I went to the hospital to make sure Ra picked up Eleni, but she wasn't there."

"Why not?" For fuck's sake if I want something done it's better to do it my damn self.

"Ajax was there…" Farook trails off and I feel an odd feeling in my chest.

"Yeah, so what?" I reply back nonchalantly.

"Eleni and him…were…getting hot and heavy…" He doesn't looking at me.

I take a few moments to process it. I feel like tearing the steering wheel right out of the drive shaft.

"Dante?" Farook says uncertainly.

I screech on the brakes, doing a U-turn as a hundred horns honk at me. I speed up in the opposite direction until I hit a hundred and twenty miles per hour.

"Dante, what the fuck? What are you doing!" Farook says, looking at me like I am crazy.

"I've got *unfinished business*."

312

Chapter Thirty

Finders Keepers

Eleni

I wake up aching, feeling like I had done a twenty-four-hour marathon.

Who knew Ajax had that in him? He's a beast.

I smirk as I turn my head around on the pillow, half expecting to be greeted by his smile, but his side of the bed is empty.

"Ajax?" I call out, but I don't hear any reply.

I can't find any of my clothes, so I grab one of his shirts from the closet and clumsily do up the buttons in a hurry as I walk down the stairs of his apartment. I finally see him sitting on the pool table speaking on the phone in his boxers, clearly doing something business related by the way his eyebrows furrow in concentration. When he sees me his smile light ups, and he ends the phone call quickly.

"What are you doing up? I was going to make you breakfast in bed." He pulls me into his arms,

313

and I stand between his legs as his mouth brushes against mine. He kisses me slowly, just the way I like it.

"I felt restless and I didn't know where you were, *Daddy*," I say shyly, tracing his jawline with my finger. Just that word seems to send desire straight to his eyes as his licks his lips slowly.

"Restless, hmm? I think I have something to cure that. I don't think that shirt has ever looked as good on me as it does on you, but I think it would look better on the floor."

He takes my face in his hand, kissing me harder as I feel his hard groin against me through the material of his boxers. He pulls my shirt off hungrily, his eyes devouring me. I hesitate slightly, my hands trying to cover up as I stand there completely naked, but he pulls my hands away.

"You're perfect, you have no reason to hide anything."

He picks me up, his bare hands exploring my flesh, and lays me down on the pool table while tearing his boxers off and climbing on top of me. "I don't think I can ever get enough of you," he rasps as I wrap my legs around him. I pull him closer, our bodies joining as one. He moves his head lower, slowly biting down my neck as his mouth makes its way to my chest. He takes my nipple in his mouth, circling around it with his tongue slowly, making me shudder in anticipation. Before biting it, then sucking again, he repeats the process with the other one as slow sighs start to escape me. His hot mouth then makes its way down to my navel, his lip ring and my navel ring colliding together until it makes its way down to where I want it most. Collaborating with his fingers until I can feel myself pulling his hair and calling his name.

***

Ajax

I can feel how much she wants me as my tongue slowly works inside of her walls. I feel her nails scraping against the back of my neck, tugging my hair. She wants me as badly as I want her. I feel her climax in my mouth, the sweetest taste ever.

Now it's my turn.

I pick her up, pushing her against the wall as my hips start to move in sharp circles, frantically thrusting into her as I hit her G-spot.

"Ajax," she moans against me, her teeth scraping against my shoulder.

I grip her and start to thrust fiercely; I can feel that familiar feeling of arousal in my abdomen starting to rise as beads of sweat start to build up on my back "Come for Daddy," I growl in her ear as she begins to jerk.

"Ajax!" she screams out loud as I continue to thrust hard. She bounces up and down, taking in every inch of me. I watch her teeter on the edge before I feel her body shake against me. I continue to pound her until I feel my own climax wash over me and I kiss her feverishly as our sweat-soaked bodies lean against each other.

The only place I want to be.

***

Eleni

"That was amazing," I breathe out, my heart racing against my ribcage.

"Likewise." He smiles down at me, stroking my hair.

We don't say anything for a while, our bodies sweating as we try to get our breath back.

"I think it's time for a shower." I look up at him coyly and feel him automatically harden on top of me.

"As you wish." He carries me upstairs. we don't break our kiss the whole time, even though every part of my body aches right now.

I can't stop.

He places me down in the shower. The hot steam sets the mood as he starts to lather me with soap, washing me gently everywhere, including my hair. There is something deeply intimate about this I can't put my finger on, he's so gentle. We're not even speaking but his eyes are talking to me, saying things that maybe his mouth and mine can't.

I do the same back to him, watching in fascination as the water droplets run down his ink-filled body. Our bodies melt into each other as I massage shampoo in his hair and his muscular body leans back into me. His mouth passionately moves against mine and I feel his tongue work down my chest until I stop him.

***

316

Dark Temptation

Ajax

"What's wrong?" I look at her, perplexed as she stops me from going to my new favorite place.

"It's my turn." She smiles, and she pushes me against the wall.

I smirk against her as she kisses me hard, her dark head disappearing. I can loosely make out her silhouette below me as her hands and mouth envelop me, eliciting groans of pleasure. Her tongue wraps around my cock and I feel my body constrict as I pull her head closer. The familiar feeling of heat starts to build as I feel it hit the back of her throat. I can never get enough of her touch, her allure. My body shudders and I climax in her mouth, leaning back against the wall in exhaustion.

"Did you like that, *Daddy*?" she asks, her mouth kissing my neck, automatically making me horny again.

"*Daddy* likes everything you do," I say, pulling her up and wrapping her around my torso. I use my lower body to hold her against the shower and my arms to push hers above her head. I start thrusting into her roughly as her mouth finds mine and our tongues meet again.

I drop her hands and legs and turn her around, pushing her hands against the wall and smack her ass roughly, feeling a ripple of excitement come from her as the hot water runs down both of our bodies.

I push her legs apart with my knees, my hands grabbing her firm ass as my fingers enter her from the front and I thrust into her from behind. Her head lolls back at me as I suck her neck and ear as she moans. I thrust harder, pushing her almost nose to nose with the wall.

Fuck.

She's so tight; it's like she's made for me. I feel her petite body shudder underneath me as we both climax at near enough the same time, my body collapsing in exhaustion and wrapping my arms around her. I pull open the shower door, the cool air helping us breathe, and find a towel to wrap her in, carrying her to my bedroom.

We towel off in silence, our mouths occasionally finding each other. We nearly start another round, but I need energy.

"Breakfast?" I raise my eyebrow at her.

"Breakfast." She nods.

"Then round…?" I've lost count.

"Then team *no sleep*," she replies back, laughing.

I pull her over my shoulder and walk down the stairs.

"Well, someone woke up on the right side of the bed."

My heart sinks as I slowly turn around with Eleni still over my shoulder.

Shit.

Chapter Thirty-One

Dante's Inferno

Dante

"Just calm down, Dante," Farook says slowly, as if he's trying to talk somebody off a building. "Deep breaths." He demonstrates breathing and exhaling slowly.

"Farook, shut the fuck up or that will be your last breath."

"Can we at least slow down? I want to make it to twenty-eight," he says, looking alarmed at the speedometer.

"Nearly here anyway. I should have done this a long fucking time ago."

***

Anara

"So." Nico looks at me while lighting a cigarette.

319

"So." I mirror his actions and stare back at him until he looks away.

"You've got fucking balls." He smirks at me with his devilish smile and I feel a thousand butterflies inside of me.

Could I have picked a more dangerous person to be crazily attracted to?

Mafia playboy. Check.

Man whore. Check.

Emotionally unavailable, unstable, and fucked up in every way. Check.

Still interested? Double fucking check.

"Tell me about Johnny." He licks his lips, taking a sip of Jack Daniels. We are outside a bar somewhere in Connecticut. We had driven for hours, talking after the batting cages, until we settled for this place. This is starting to feel like a date, and I know I should not take him seriously, but I want to fix him. I want to put together all of the broken pieces and make him whole.

I want him. Period.

"What do you want to know?" I say, exhaling. This is not my favorite topic.

"What happened? How did you end up engaged to someone like that?"

"Reign had a business deal that went wrong. Johnny wanted him dead and he would have killed him, but I offered myself as collateral and negotiated Reign's life."

"Shit, you are sister of the year,' he says, appraising me as if I had passed some kind of test."

"I controlled part of the Triad, money and drug laundering for Johnny for a while, until I left."

"Why did you leave?"

"You've heard of Johnny's reputation, his barbaric nature. I wanted out; I couldn't live like that. I escaped on my wedding day and never looked back."

"Wedding day? Damn, you're cold." He smirks.

"If I stayed he would have killed me. I have never looked back."

"You're here now and Tran can't hurt you."

"I can look after myself." I stared back into his dark eyes, not wanting to fall for sweet words laced with poison.

"That's for fucking sure, you're nothing like anyone I have ever met." He looks away when I stare at him, and I get the feeling he never meant to say it out loud.

"Is that a good thing?" I say, cocking my eyebrow.

"I guess we'll find out."

"Tell me about Zosha." I lean back.

"No."

"I told you about Johnny," I reply irritably.

He sighs. "We knew each other for a while. I shouldn't have let it go on as long as I did. She got hurt, just like anyone who gets close to me does."

"Did you love her?"

"No." He says it with finality, so I dare not push him on it.

"What do you mean about people around you getting hurt?" I say it softly.

"My mother, my father, everyone I touch seems to end up dead or hurt."

"Tell me about them."

He sighs again and I think he's going to tell me to get lost, but then he starts talking and my heart clenches inside, thinking of all the pain he has gone through.

"I was born in Sicily. When I was five, I was playing hide and seek with my mother and the house came under attack from another Mafia family. My mother looked for me and got caught in the process. They killed her on the spot. My father told me he would be back, but he never returned. Everyone in that house died that day apart from me."

"It's not your fault, you were just a child." I reach out to touch his hand, and for a second our fingers intertwine. Our eyes lock and suddenly I get that familiar feeling of falling down the rabbit hole.

Ring.

Nico's phone interrupts us and both of our hands jump away from one another as if they were both on fire. I can hear Dante's voice barking down the line in Italian. Nico replies back in rapid Italian, drains his drink, and indicates for us to leave.

***

Nico

We ride silently in the car heading back into the city, I had never told that story before to anyone. I feel uncomfortable revealing part of myself that I had concealed for so long.

"That story…"

"I won't tell anyone."

322

"Good."

"Your hard ass reputation will not be besmirched."

"Even better." I chuckle.

We pull up at the compound and she looks at me dead in the eye.

"Well, I guess this is it."

"Yep, it is," I say, wanting her to get out of the car very quickly before my intentions get the better of me. Reign is my best friend and she is his sister. His incredibly beautiful, bad ass sister that I can't get out of my head.

Eleni

"Well?" the voice booms.

Ajax puts me down slowly as I watch his eyes take in our partially dressed forms.

"Zeek, give it a rest." Ajax rolls his eyes.

"Eleni, can you give us a second?" He nods at me slowly, indicating for me to leave.

***

Ajax

"What is wrong with you?"

"Lots, but you know that already," I say with an eyeroll.

"You're playing with fire, you fuckwit!" Zeek replies back, anger etched all over his face.

"Dante is marrying someone else, she's single. What's the big deal?"

"You know Dante won't see it like that. You think he'll give you his blessing? She was living with him, Ajax. When has Dante ever had a woman in his house?"

"Well, she's not living there anymore, so why does it matter?"

"Well, you won't be living anymore period, by the look of it. I hope her pussy was worth getting a bullet in your head."

"Fuck off, Zeek, seriously. You are not my father, and like you can talk. You're dating a stripper."

"A single stripper, not my boss's side piece."

"Zeek, I'm warning you," I say, my temper starting to flare.

"You're like my brother, but if you want to go down in flames, then that's your fucking problem. I'll be back in twenty, and we're driving out of the city to do a job. She better be gone."

He slams the door, leaving me frustrated and questioning myself again.

Will Dante even care? I think I already know the answer.

***

Eleni

The door slams as I leave, and I can hear Ajax and Zeek's raised voices. I walk into the bathroom, trying to locate my clothes from last night. When I look into the mirror I blush slightly looking at the bruises and bites on my neck and chest.

"You like my handiwork?" Ajax appears behind me, his hands wrapping around my waist, and his tongue leaving kisses on my neck like tattoos.

"Always." I lean into his kisses, putting my hands over his.

"Where are my clothes, Ajax?"

"You don't need clothes; this is a clothes-free zone." He pings the waistband of my underwear, pulling them down playfully. I lean back in ecstasy as those familiar fingers work me before stopping to un-clip my bra, freeing me.

"Ajax, what about Zeek?" I say breathlessly.

"I don't think he's into ménage à trois, and even if he is, I'm not sharing." He laughs as both his hands cup my breasts and I can feel his urgency digging into my back.

"You know what I mean," I say, playfully elbowing him.

"He'll be back in twenty minutes; we have a job."

"That's not a very long time," I pout.

"It's long enough. How many times can *Daddy* make you come in twenty minutes?"

Let's find out.

***

Nico

"Anara."

"What?"

"Thanks for today, and sorry for earlier," I say sheepishly.

"Did Nico Dischanel just apologize? Damn, did you receive some kind of head injury?"

"I mean it." I look at her and take her chin in my hand as my thumb caresses her cheek. I'm momentarily shocked by my actions, it's not something I have done before. She moves closer and our lips touch for a second.

"No." I push her off. I can't do this to her or myself right now.

"Why not?" she says, stroking my jawline and gazing into my eyes.

"You know why, all the seven hundred million reasons why I am no good for you."

"I'm not good either, but sometimes I want bad things," she says seductively.

"You're actually killing me," I groan, putting my head on the steering well.

"You're no fun." She kisses my cheek and leaves the car, staring at me fleetingly before she disappears inside.

She's getting too close to me, but I can't find it in me to push her away. Yet.

***

Dante

"Come out, come out, wherever you are." I almost take the door off the hinges as I storm in, not giving a fuck, with Farook trailing behind me.

I walk into the bedroom and Jameela is there in a lace baby doll outfit, clearly waiting for me.

"Dante?" she says, surprised, as Farook walks in

326

behind me.

"I'll wait outside. You better not fucking mention this to Ilayda," he says, huffing out, trying to cover his eyes.

"Pack your bags."

"What?" She looks at me like I'm crazy.

"Pack your shit and get out."

She pulls herself off the bed and walks closer, standing on her tiptoes to draw herself up to my height.

"What did you just say to me?"

"I said get the fuck out of my house; I don't want you here anymore."

"I am your fiancée," she screeches.

"You are nothing to me other than a deal that was forced down my throat by your father, who was desperate to get rid of you."

"You dare speak to me like that?" She goes to slap me, but I grab her wrist.

"Don't put your hands on me or I will fucking rip them off! Get out before I throw you out," I say, dropping her hand.

She starts swearing at me in rapid Arabic as I start emptying the closets for her, throwing things over my shoulder as she stands there screaming at me. Bras, panties, shoes, anything.

It all had to go.

"Move your fucking ass before I throw you out."

Her face turns into a mask of fury and she slaps me hard, causing my ears to ring as the sound reverberates in them. She turns her back to walk away in victory, but I yank her by her hair as she yells in pain. Her head is on my shoulder as she looks up at me in terror, her eyes filling with tears as my hand tightens around her throat.

"No fake tears, sweetheart."

"You piece of shit!" she says through my choke hold.

"Piece of shit? Coming right up."

I throw her against the wall, still holding her by her neck.

"You're going to leave here now and not come back, otherwise I'll show you what a piece of shit I really am."

She spits at me in defiance and it lands on my cheek. I slowly wipe it off with my handkerchief and smile back at her silently. *She's really done it now.*

I grab her by the arm, dragging her out of the room and into the living room. Both Nico and Farook are standing there, clearly shocked, but I ignore them as she tries to fight me.

"Get out of my fucking life and never come back."

"You'll regret this; you are nothing without me."

"I'm the motherfucking King and I will always be!" I say as I open up the door and toss her out of my apartment and my life.

For good.

Chapter Thirty-Two

The Writing's On The Wall

Nico

I watch as Dante throws Jameela out, I mean literally throws her out on her ass. I'm normally the aggressor in our devilish twosome, but tonight Dante is like a man possessed.

What has gotten into him?

He slams the door, the mask of fury on his face fading back to his normal features.

"I love it when the trash takes itself out."

"Dante, what the actual fuck is going on?"

"I'm no longer engaged," he says flatly.

"Yeah, I got that part. What and why is the question?"

"I want to live by my own rules, I'm sick of being told what to do. This whole thing was a fucking disaster, sleeping with her reinforced that.

"She had great legs, though," I interject while Farook rolls his eyes.

"I'm going to bed. That's a polite way of saying you don't have to go, but you need to get the fuck out of here." He walks off, slamming his bedroom door.

"Don't ask, just don't. He has not taken today well at all," Farook says, running his hands through his dreads.

"Today? What happened today?" I say in confusion.

"I caught Eleni and Ajax…you know…and when I told Dante, he drove straight here, and yeah, that's pretty much it."

"Eleni and Ajax? Who knew he had it in him? That motherfucker clearly doesn't want to reach his next birthday." I smirk.

Ajax is dead…*beyond dead*. Dante is probably drawing up a list of ways he would kill him.

"Where were you today?" Farook says, interrupting my gloating.

"Me? Just the usual," I reply, taking Anara out of the equation completely.

"Reign is looking for you."

"He is? Why? I mean, why do you think he would be?" *Shit, did he know?* Surely Anara wouldn't say anything, would she?"

"I don't know, Nico. If it were that important he would have called you," Farook says, side-eyeing me.

"Yeah, well, I'll guess I'll be hitting the road too," I say, leaving Farook looking confused.

Sometimes it's better to say nothing than say anything at all, and with my big mouth, I know I can't keep things inside. Especially if it's about

Anara, she's starting to do something to me. Something I didn't like. *Not one bit.*

***

Eleni

"I'll call you when I get there, I'm not really looking forward to a road trip with Zeek." Ajax rolls his eyes and I watch his eyebrow piercing rise up toward his forehead.

"You'll be fine, it's me he has the problem with," I say quietly, my insides squirming every time I thought of the way Zeek looked at me earlier.

"It's not you, it's just the circumstances. When Dante finds out, you know he won't be happy. Even though you're not with him anymore, he won't want anyone else to have you, not that I blame him." He smirks, leaning forward to kiss me.

"It will be fine." I lean my forehead against his and we stay there for a moment, knowing the impending storm that is ahead of us.

"As long as I have you, I can get through anything." He gives my knee a squeeze and kisses me hard, which I return back enthusiastically.

"I'm leaving now, or I won't be able to leave you ever." He groans, kissing me one more time before I get out the car and watch him leave.

I miss him already.

Ra texted me earlier to say Dante had organized me a new apartment to live in. She dropped off the keys to Ajax this morning, but I told him I was fine to go in on my own. I knew Zeek would be pissed if

I took up anymore of his time. I walk in feeling a little nervous, but I needn't be, it's gorgeously furnished. I don't like Dante, but I can't deny the man has great taste. I navigate toward the bedroom and give a small smile at the huge bed. Ajax and I will have a great time breaking this in, and that's the last thought I have before I fall into a dreamless sleep.

I wake up and its bright daylight. I can't believe I slept straight through one day into another. Exhaustion seems to run through me, and I know it's the side-effects of what I've been through. I strip and get into the shower, half smirking at the memories of my last shower. I walk out, drying myself off and wiping the steam from the mirror. Luckily for me, Dante, or I'm guessing Ra, has filled my wardrobe up. I search for something to wear as I towel myself off. I bend down to unwrap my hair turban and rough dry it the best I can. When I flip my hair back, my heart nearly skyrockets seeing who is in the mirror behind me.

***

Dante

She didn't even hear me walk in, proof why I can't trust her to live in another apartment block. That's precisely why I put her here, living right next to Nico, where I can keep an eye on her. The previous occupant wasn't thrilled to be given less than a day's notice, but he got over it. I watch in amusement as she bends forward, giving me a show of what I have been missing, and what Ajax has clearly gained in my absence. The thought leaves me bitter. She flips her hair up, spraying me with tiny droplets of water, as I take in the familiar smell of her lavender-scented hair.

"Dante!" she shrieks, the sound nearly deafening me.

"Yes, me," I say, amused, sitting on her unmade bed.

"What are you doing here?" she says, trying to cover up with her mini towel.

"I own the building," I say drily.

"It doesn't explain why you're in here; you can't just barge in when you feel like it," she says crossly, her eyebrows knitting together.

"You haven't got anything I haven't seen before. If memory serves me correct, I was the first to experience it," I say with a smirk.

"I would rather forget it. What do you want?" she says pointedly.

"I came to visit Nico; he lives next door."

"Nico lives next door?" she asks, horrified.

"Yeah, like I'm going to put you in an apartment on your own when you didn't even notice me walking in."

"I hope the walls are thick," she says with an eyeroll.

"For your sake or his?" I enunciate every word, leaving no illusion of what I'm talking about.

"Meaning?" She glares at me with insolence.

"I know who you were with yesterday and the night before. Ajax is one of my men, remember that."

"And I'm not your woman, remember that, *Capo*," she replies acerbically.

"Touché, Eleni, but you can't deny I'm better. Admit it, you know it's the truth." I smirk, watching her flush.

"Get over yourself, Dante."

"I'd rather get under someone else." I wait for a response, but I am disappointed at her lack of reaction.

"I don't want to fight anymore, Dante; I'm willing to be happy for you and Jameela. We should all move on."

"You don't need to be happy for me, I've called off the engagement."

***

Eleni

"What? Why?" I reply, my mouth gaping.

"Because I want to do what I want, not what somebody else thinks I should. I made a huge mistake thinking I could pull it off. It wasn't worth all of the money in the world."

"How did Dominic take it?"

"He'll get over it," he says quietly.

"Dominic's approval means a lot to you."

"How would you know?"

"I know you more than you care to think, Dante. We've gone through things most people don't experience in a lifetime. We've lived and almost died together."

He looks at me strangely for a second, as if he

wants to say something but decides against it. "So we have," he says slowly.

There is a long pause. There are too many things left unsaid and things that we're too late to say ever.

His phone rings and I'm grateful for the distraction.

"Yeah, I'm at your apartment, I told you I would come and pick you up."

I distinctly hear the voice on the other end of the line say *no, you didn't, we were supposed to meet at the compound.* I look at Dante shrewdly, but he avoids my gaze.

"I'll be there in ten."

"Looking for Nico, huh?' I say, cocking my eyebrow up at him.

"I'm leaving," he says, ignoring me.

"Wait, I'm coming. I need to pick something up from Chang."

"Fine," he says, taking a seat on my bed.

"Well, I need to get changed."

"So, get changed," he says, crossing his legs and smirking.

"Get out, Dante."

"I've seen it all before—"

"Out!"

He walks out and closes the door, leaving me confused as ever. Something is definitely up with him.

***

Dante

I definitely feel on edge.

So what?

I may have slightly lied about meeting Nico here, but so what?

I needed to see her.

She takes twenty minutes getting dressed and I barely register how agitated Nico sounded on the phone. I was preoccupied with my own distractions. We travel to the compound in silence, she barely looks at me and stares out the window.

Before we walk in, she steps in front of me. "You weren't looking for Nico, were you? Be honest, Dante, for once in your life."

She's got me there.

"I wanted to see you."

"Because?"

"I don't know, I just needed to."

"Because of Ajax?"

"Maybe."

"You only want me because someone else does. You told me yourself we could never be together."

"And we can't, but if I can't stay away from you, maybe it means I'm not meant too."

"That's your pride talking." She rolls her eyes.

"What if it isn't? What if it's because—"

"Dante, get in here!"

I pause and she looks up at me, waiting for me to finish, but I don't. This is not the right time.

"Dante!"

"I'm coming!" I reply irritably.

What could be so important?

I walk in the room, taking in Nico's shocked face and now I see why. Sapphire has returned, and she doesn't look like I remember her at all. She smiles at me serenely. I hear Eleni gasp from behind me as she enters the room.

"What stupid fucker knocked you up?" I say, snorting.

"I'm looking at him. Happy Father's Day, Dante," Sapphire replies, looking me dead in the eye as my smile freezes and Eleni looks at me in horror.

One month later and I still haven't recovered from the shock. Eleni left immediately without even looking at me, and she has avoided me since. Sapphire, on the other hand, has not left me alone, alluding to engagements as well as other ludicrous ideas that I would rather die than entertain.

"So, I'm going to be Uncle Nico?" Nico smirks while Farook titters next to him.

We're sitting in the penthouse brainstorming. After I ended the engagement I thought that it would destroyed our arrangement with Rafiq, but ultimately I had been able to salvage it. It wasn't the 60/40 deal I wanted, but I would rather lose money than lose myself in something that was doomed. The only problem I have seems to be Lorenzo. There is a part of me that doesn't know why I'm keeping him alive, but I know he's holding on to something important. Despite the amount of beatings I had inflicted on him he won't relent, and that smug smile is still plastered on his face. There are still so many holes in all the attacks that he has engineered against me and I need to know every single detail of how he's managed to penetrate my defenses before I kill him.

"You're going to be a *dead* Uncle Nico if you don't shut the fuck up," I reply hotly.

"You're the only one who can lose a fiancée and gain a Baby Mama in a month." Farook and Nico both laugh as I throw my tumbler against the wall.

If I thought the Jameela situation was bad, this was worse.

This cannot be happening. The baby is not mine.

I rake my mind, trying to think of the last time I slept with her. I always used protection with her, right? Or did I just expect her to make sure she took precautions?

Well, that worked out well.

I wasn't sure I wanted kids, a family, any of that. I definitely didn't want them with Sapphire, and when my father finds out, he's going to fucking kill me.

"Dante, say something, man," Nico interjects into my thoughts.

For once I am speechless.

"Carmelo arrived yesterday," Nico says sulkily.

Carmelo is our cousin from Palermo. Dad brought him in as extra muscle, much to Nico's disdain as well as my own. "Where is he?" I say, changing the subject, and trying to banish the sinking feeling from my chest.

"At the docks with Padrone. He's acting like his fucking shadow. When all of this Baby Mama drama is over, he needs to piss off back to Italy."

"Has Chang arranged the paternity test?" I ask in

a low voice.

"Yeah, it's all set up. If it's yours?"

"I'm not ready for that scenario, we'll cross that bridge when we get there," I say, sighing deeply.

Farook and Nico leave after a while, sensing my need to be alone. I make my way up to the penthouse roof, the only place I go when I need to get away. It holds so many memories, where me and my brother used to hide when our father was mad at us, where I had my first cigarette, and still use as my designated go to place. Where I come to be alone, the city seems to still and I am just with my own thoughts. I close my eyes, wishing my brother were alive, and my mind goes back to seven years ago, that fateful night he was killed. If I would have figured out who the mole was sooner he'd still be alive..

I should have stopped him. He was blinded by rage with no ammunition, yet he still went after Amaury Vasquez, my father's Consigliere who had turned rogue. I never saw him get shot, I just heard the gunshots, and in my head I knew they'd got him. I held him as he died, as the light faded from his eyes. The rain poured down on both of us, creating a bloody puddle, and at eighteen I knew my life would never be the same again. I feel the familiar burn of rage burn in the back of my throat, tinged with something else, which I blink back hurriedly.

"Dante?"

"Yeah," I say, disappointed that he found me so quickly.

"You know I figured out this was your hiding

place a long time ago, boy."

"Yeah, Dad, I know."

"What foolishness have you gotten yourself into now?" he replies. I can sense the anger in every intonation.

"It's not what you think."

"Sapphire is pregnant, I think it is exactly what I think."

"You know?"

"She came and told me."

"*Cazzo*," I curse. "I haven't seen her in months, I'm pretty sure it's not even mine."

"*Pretty sure?* What are you playing at, boy? How could you be so irresponsible? You tell me you want me to take you seriously, then you pull stupid shit like this?"

"Dad, just chill. I don't need this right now." I can feel my temper starting to rocket because everything he's saying is right.

"What if it's yours? You do realize this is a potential heir we're talking about? *Your heir.*"

"Dad, don't go there."

"You know what you have to do if the child is yours, step up and take responsibility for your actions."

He sweeps out leaving me standing there pissed off.

My phone rings and I hear Farook's voice in my ear.

"We have a problem."

Story of my fucking life.

Chapter Thirty-Three

Checkmate

Anara

"Are these shipments ready to go?"

"Yeah," I reply.

I'm not going to pretend I like Dre much, especially after all the shit he gave me before when Raphael got shot. I may have gotten a little trigger happy with a client who wouldn't pay up. Dre made a big deal of it and told Dante and Reign I didn't have the temperament to be on the streets.

"You're back on the roster starting tomorrow," he says in a way that makes it clear this wasn't his choice.

"I thought you didn't want me back out there," I reply slowly, trying to understand the shift.

"I don't, not with your temper. Let's just say I was overruled; you have a guardian angel looking out for you...*or not*," he says, rolling his eyes and walking away.

341

It has to be Nico...and without warning, my heart starts to bubble with an excitement that even the deep-rooted cynic within me can't ruin.

"You must be tired from running through my mind all day," a voice breaks into my thoughts, interrupting the Nico fantasy that seems to have swept me up.

"What?" I reply, turning around to see Carmelo standing behind me, eyeing me like I'm the special of the day. I have to admit he's hot, but the fact that I could pinpoint the genetic similarities in his and Nico's face definitely turned me off.

"My face is several inches higher than where you're looking, can my chest help you with anything?"

"Lots and lots, sexy."

"Charming, yet repulsive at the same time."

"When are you going to let me take you on a date?" He ignores me like I didn't say anything.

"The twelfth of never is good for me..."

"You play too much, Americana; I've been giving you signs all day."

"What a coincidence, I've been ignoring them all day."

"Feisty, just the way I like them."

"Annoying, just the way I don't like them. Piss off, Carmelo, I'm busy."

"You must have eye problems. I'm a catch."

I glare at him and he walks off. Prick, good looking prick, but still one all the same.

I continue with shipments, my mind occasionally slipping to Nico, and my jaw almost drops when he walks in.

"Hey, have you seen Carmelo?"

"He's somewhere around here. Dre told me I'm back on the streets. I'm guessing you had something to do with that."

"You're too valuable to be wasted here, we need bodies."

"Valuable?"

"Stop fishing for compliments, Anara," he says, rolling his eyes.

I walk closer until my face is only inches away from his. I see his face cloud in confusion, but I'm done playing games. I kiss him hard, and my hands wrap around his neck.

"Anara—" His voice is muffled. "Anara! Just stop!" He pulls me off him, looking incensed. "What the fuck was that about?" he demands.

"I like you and I know you like me too, what's the point in pretending anymore?"

"I—you're—Reign's sister."

"That never stopped you before."

"I just can't do this." He tries to back away, but I see his resolve waning.

"So, you like me?"

"I do, but you're my friend's sister. I do a lot of fucked up things, but this I won't do."

"What about what I want?" I reply, running my hand up his shirt until I can feel nothing but taut, rippling muscles.

"I'm not the kind of guy you should be with." He says it breathlessly as my finger works its way down his chest and starts to follow his treasure trail down.

"I'm not asking for a ring; we can just have fun."

My hand undoes his pants and slides down his boxers, his body tensing against me.

"No, this cannot happen." He pulls my hands out and zips up his pants, looking flustered.

"You can't deny there's chemistry between us, Nico."

"I can and I will."

"Look me in the eye and say you don't want me."

He stares at me for a second. "I don't want you."

I stand there shocked for a second, not expecting him to be so blunt.

"Anara, don't look at me like that."

I feel my eyes start to fill as the rejection starts to build up in me. I won't let him see me like this. I storm out, slamming the door behind me, leaving him there looking bewildered.

***

Dante

Chang is waiting for me in his office looking grave, and my heart drops, knowing this isn't good news.

"Dante, take a seat."

"This doesn't sound good."

"To carry out a prenatal paternity test, we either need fluid from the womb and placenta or blood from Sapphire."

"Yeah…"

Where was he heading with this?

"I did a quick examination of Sapphire it's not

good., she has high blood pressure so that rules out the traditional method and she didn't consent for me to take a blood sample. Bottom line, you're going to have to wait for the baby to be born to carry out a paternity test."

"Consent? Are you fucking kidding me?"

"Unfortunately, not."

"Can't we just--?"

"Dante, it's not happening."

"You've been shot, stabbed, and beaten. I'm sure three months of waiting won't kill you."

"I'd rather be all of the above than put up with Sapphire for three months."

"So, you're not ready for parenthood then?"

"No way! Definitely not with Sapphire, either."

"I'll keep you in my prayers."

"Much appreciated."

"Eleni hasn't seemed herself; I presume it's because of this—drama."

"I'll deal with it." Eleni hasn't even entered my mind.

"You'll be fine, Dante, you always are."

I exit Chang's office and go back to the examination room where Sapphire is waiting in a hospital gown. I can see her bump protruding slightly and a shiver runs down my spine.

"Did anyone think to let me know what the hell is going on?"

"You can get dressed; we're not doing a paternity test until the baby is born even if I have to fucking subpoena you to do it."

"So, we'll be spending a lot more time together, then?"

"Let me make this perfectly clear to you, Sapphire—this is not going to happen."

"It already did, babe, and you're looking at the result of it," she says, patting her stomach and smirking at me.

"Even if it is mine, I don't want to be with you. I will take care of my responsibility but that is as far as it goes."

"It looks like Eleni doesn't want to be with you, either. I hear she's with Ajax now." I can hear the venom in her words piercing me like glass.

"That has nothing to do with this."

"It must kill you that he is with her, kissing her, touching her, fucking her."

"Shut up, Sapphire." She smiles at me, knowing she got to me.

"As much as I would love to continue this, Lorenzo is expecting me."

"As in *Salvatore*?" I see a small flash of uncertainty run through her expression before her normal mask of candor appears.

"Is there any other?" I say irritably.

"I thought he would be dead by now. Why didn't you kill him when I gave you his location?"

"Because he hasn't told me everything I want to know. He's holding back."

"Holding back what?"

"If I knew, then I wouldn't need him to tell me!" She is really starting to piss me off now.

"I just thought you would have killed him already. What's wrong, Dante? Have you gone soft? Because the old Dante would have killed Lorenzo a long time ago." I can hear the sharpness in her voice.

"The old Dante made a lot of stupid decisions that I wouldn't make now, including you." Her face flushes crimson and I walk out, leaving her seething.

***

Nico

"I've been looking for you," I say begrudgingly.

I can't stand Carmelo, and the feeling is mutual. Our fathers were twins, Carmelo losing his Father in the same attack that I had lost my parents. Perhaps it could have been something that bonded us, but we both blamed each other for what happened despite neither of us being old enough to do anything at the time. Carmelo's father had been my Father's Consigliere—he should have known the attack was coming. Every time he saw Carmelo's face, it was a reminder of everything he lost.

"Now you've found me," Carmelo replies with a wink. His face is so smug and irritating. "How is my favorite cousin doing?" he says sarcastically.

"He will be better when you fuck off back to Palermo."

"Why would I do that when I am getting such a rousing welcome from Padrone? I am his favorite nephew after all."

"Favorite jackass, more like. Padrone told me we're having a meeting tonight, family only, so I guess that means you, although personally I couldn't give a shit whether you come or not."

"No can do cousin I have a date."

"With your left hand?"

"With *Anara*."

"Anara?" I say her name slowly as I start to feel a strange sensation overwhelm my body.

"Yeah, she's been giving me the eye all day."

"Are you sure it wasn't the finger? Because that I can relate to. This is the same Anara, as in Reign's sister?"

"She may be Reign's sister but I'm about to be her *Daddy*. I see the admiration in your eyes," he says smugly.

"It is repulsion, not admiration. When did this happen?" I say hotly.

"About five minutes ago. I've still got it, unlike your sorry ass. Don't wait up for me, *Stronzo*."

My heart thumps loudly in my chest and rage starts to fill me. Images of Carmelo and Anara seem to fill my brain and I punch the wall next to me, letting the physical pain mask my rage. I have stayed away from her since the batting cages because I was sensing my initial attraction to her growing into something else. I didn't want to hurt her, or for Reign to snap my legs or anything else, so I left it alone. I heard about what happened with one of her collections and it mildly amused me that I wasn't the only one who couldn't keep my temper. Despite Dre's hesitance, I got her back on the roster. It wasn't an act of romance; it was for work purposes only. Her asking Carmelo out is revenge and I can't stand it. Even when I try to make the right decision, I fuck things up.

Dark Temptation

***

Dante

"I'm late, I know." I look up to see Ajax skittering in with wet hair and a sheepish look on his face.

"Everyone has left," I say, enjoying how uncomfortable he looks coming face to face with me.

"What did I miss?" he asks, meeting my eye.

"This is Raheem, Dre's brother. He is traveling up from Miami visiting on a little project."

"I didn't even know he had a brother." Ajax holds his hand out and Dre shakes it.

"Yeah, we don't get on," he says, rolling his eyes.

"What project is Raheem doing?"

"Well, it will be something for both of you."

"Both of us?" I can see Ajax's face drop and I try to hold the smile out of my voice.

"Expansion. Originally I wanted to try Las Vegas, but that has been done too much. So my new plan is Miami."

"Miami," Ajax repeats slowly, his eyes telling me he's following my train of thought.

"I want you to go with Raheem to Miami, start the new business venture."

"I'm only a rookie, Dante, I wouldn't want to mess anything up."

"You're so humble, Ajax. I have the utmost trust in you. I know you would never betray me. *Right*?"

I watch as anger forms a shadow on his face. He

opens his mouth several times before deciding against saying anything.

"What's wrong, Ajax? Absence makes the heart grow fonder, right?"

I smirk, daring him to pick a fight. I could use something to take the brunt of my rage. The Miami expansion is something that has been in the works for a while. I planned on using it as a way to get rid of Carmelo for a couple of months, but this would be much more appropriate for Ajax. A perfect way for me to not have to acknowledge their relationship because there wouldn't be one.

"We're leaving tomorrow, so get your shit together." Raheem leaves the room and it's just the two of us. If looks could kill, I'd be dead.

"I know why you're doing this," he says, his voice small but shaking with anger.

"Doing what? You work for me and I'm sending you on a job."

"It's personal, Dante, don't try to bullshit me otherwise."

"If it is, what are you going to do about it?"

"You're a piece of shit. You told her you didn't want her, and she moved on."

"*To you*. Where is your loyalty?"

"We're not friends, I don't give a fuck what you think. You were engaged to someone else, now Sapphire is having your baby. Why do you care so much? You only want her because she is with someone else."

"Shut up, Ajax," I warn.

"I'm not going to Miami; you can go fuck yourself." I can see as soon as it comes out of his mouth he regrets it.

"So, you want to join Lorenzo in that cell? I don't take dissent well, Ajax."

"You're so scared of me that you want me in another state?"

"Scared? I think you forget who you're talking to. Will you be in Miami tomorrow or not?"

"Yes," he says, gritting his teeth.

I smirk. "Yes, *Capo*, you mean?"

"Yes, Capo," he repeats, his voice shaking with anger.

"I thought you would fight for her."

"I don't need to; I already have her." He smirks.

I feel like ice cold water has drenched me; he gives me a sardonic wave as he exits, reminding me of all the shit I have to deal with.

Chapter Thirty-Four

Bad To Worse

Eleni

"Hey you."

Ajax walks through the door and kisses me hard. I've almost gotten used to his lip ring and the sensations it gives me every time he kisses me.

He places his forehead against mine gently, and I can tell something is bothering him.

"What's wrong?"

"Dante is sending me to Miami for three months."

"What?" I feel the shock reverberate through me.

"Yep, on some project," he says tonelessly.

"He can't do that," I say, seething.

We both know that he can and will, everything is so new in our relationship I'm not sure that we can survive three months apart. He looks at me sadly, thinking the same.

"Eleni." He closes his eyes. "You didn't see how

he looked at me today, I don't think he will ever let up."

"He will," I say indignantly.

"I don't want you to be caught in the middle of a war that I won't win."

"What are you saying, Ajax?" I know exactly what he's trying to say.

"I'll call you from Miami and we'll find a way."

"You don't sound too sure about that, Ajax."

"He won't let us be together, ever. Maybe we should just quit while we're ahead."

"Quit?" I say, looking at him blankly.

***

Dante

"Penny for your thoughts?" Nico looks at me, inhaling a cigarette deeply.

"Lorenzo."

"What about him?"

"Something isn't adding up."

"Just fucking waste him already.'

"No, there's still something that isn't adding up."

"Is this about Sapphire? Maybe you're reflecting your issues from that onto Lorenzo."

"Thank you, Dr. Phil, for your expert opinion. Chang says we can't do a paternity test until the baby is born."

"That sucks."

"Tell me about it, she's already pissing me off."

"When is Carmelo going to Miami?" Nico suddenly asks with a slow smile building up.

"He's not, Ajax is."

"Why aren't you sending him?" he asks indignantly.

"Because my need to get rid of Ajax is stronger than my need to get rid of Carmelo. Where was he last night?"

"Out on a date," Nico replies, grinding his cigarette into ash.

"With whom?"

"Anara."

"Ouch. What do you think about that?"

"I don't care what either of them do," he replies hotly.

"Sure, so why is that little vein in your forehead about to burst?"

"Shut up! Says the person sending Ajax there just to get even."

"It's just business."

Suddenly we hear footsteps, both of us draw our guns immediately, then we see it's only Eleni.

"I wouldn't put that away just yet if I were you." I can see the anger on her face, and I know what this is about.

"On that note, I'm out." Nico waves his handkerchief at Eleni in mock surrender and leaves so it's just me and her standing there.

"Miami, Dante? *Miami?*"

"Ajax works for me, so I'm sending him on a job. Simple."

"It's not fucking simple; you have a thousand other men. Send them."

"Since when did I become answerable to you?"

"Since you started acting like a jerk."

354

"I don't need this," I reply, getting up and leaving her standing there. I grab my car keys and walk out of the penthouse as she follows me.

"Don't walk away from me, Dante, I'm not finished with you."

"But I am finished."

"Dante!"

She throws her shoe at me and it narrowly misses my ear, cascading noisily down the staircase.

I keep walking down and leave through the fire exit, the fresh air calming me ever so slightly until I hear Eleni clank down after me screaming insults. It begins to rain, changing quickly from gentle drops to hammering down heavily.

"Eleni, don't fucking start!"

"Why are you sending him to Miami?" She walks up and jabs me in the chest forcefully.

I push her against the wall. "Because I fucking can."

"I'm happy with him, why do you want to ruin my life?" she screams, and I can see fresh tears glint in her eyes.

I let her go and straighten up. "You really want to know why?"

It was now or never.

"Because—" I can't seem to say it; I kiss her hard on the mouth, pushing her against the glass doors. In this moment I feel alive. I can't articulate all the things I want to say to her, but the urgency of my kiss says everything I can't verbalize.

"You said you didn't want to be with me," she says, pushing me away.

"I lied to protect you, to protect myself, but I

can't lie anymore. Eleni, I am in l—"

"Dante!" Nico's voice echoes and I turn around, exasperated.

"Nico, this isn't a good time."

"Isn't that a shame."

Another voice from the shadows emerges, and I am face to face with Detective Aiden Fonseca.

"This is private property, get out."

"Not this time." He smiles wolfishly at me and my heartrate starts to quicken.

"Dante Dischanel, you are under arrest for crimes committed relating to the RICO act. You have the right to remain silent. Anything you say can and will be used against you in a court of law. You have the right to an attorney, and if you cannot afford one, one will be provided for you. Time to take a little trip downtown, Dischanel."

He roughly puts on the handcuffs and drags my resistant body down the path where there are four police cars waiting.

"Nico, call Franco and Ilayda."

"You'll be out in no time," he shouts, but I hear the doubt in his voice.

***

Eleni

"Do something, Nico!" I screech.

"Like what?" he replies, looking agitated.

Farook appears out of nowhere, looking equally as distracted.

"We have a problem, another problem."

"It can't be worse than this shit."

"Karlie is the leak."

"*Karlie?*"

"Zeek's girlfriend, the stripper."

"Are you fucking kidding me?"

"I guess he got to her at the beginning, she must have been spying on Zeek this whole time. He's going to be devastated."

"*Devastated?* I'm going to put my foot up his fucking ass, and then he can be devastated."

"Nico, calm down, we need to figure this out. Once they get warrants, we're fucked."

My heart starts to beat fast, trying to acknowledge everything that's happened and suddenly everything starts to go dark...

"Eleni?"

"Hmm."

I can make out Ra's shadowy figure above me.

"Where am I?"

"At Dante's place, you fainted."

"Why not my place?" I say, realizing I'm tucked up in my old bed.

"Nico's orders, it's safer for you here. Just rest, everything is being sorted as we speak."

"Will Dante be okay?"

"Of course, he's been through worse scraps than this."

Her voice did nothing to reassure me, as I could tell she was trying to convince herself more than anything.

"Is Ajax gone?"

"Yeah, he left earlier. It's better for him to get

out of here now before there are any indictments."

"Indictments?"

"You know, worst case scenario, but everything will be fine. Franco and Ilayda are on it."

She pulls the covers up to my chest and leaves the room wordlessly. I'm not sure what the time is, but it's still dark. Distant thunder rumbles outside, and I see intermittent flashes of lightning illuminate the sky.

I am still trying to process everything that happened last night.

Ajax.

I thought he would fight for me; I didn't expect him to let go so easily. Do I mean that little to him?

Dante.

I assume Dante is sending Ajax away for pure spite, but is there something else? The way he kissed me says something, it wasn't physically charged. I couldn't help but feel there is something else motivating it. I fall into a disturbed sleep, my mind conflicting all these scenarios as the storm raged outside.

A precursor of something else to come.

***

Dante

I stare at myself in the grainy mirror, orange clearly isn't my color. I had been here for what felt like hours. I knew Nico would have called Franco and Ilayda by now and one of them had to be working on getting me out. He was probably here in the station right now; I could imagine this was one of Fonseca's mind games. Keeping me isolated so I would be more inclined to talk. Dream the fuck on, buddy, because that would never happen.

"Having fun, Champ?" I hear the nasal tones of Fonseca echoing in the damp prison cell.

"Enjoy it while it lasts, Fonseca, because you know I'll be out soon," I mock.

"Not even your fancy lawyers can get you out of RICO. You made it so easy for me, Dante. I was right under your nose this whole time and you never noticed. You're getting careless, the old Dante would have picked this up before I even got close. Karlie tells me you're going to be a father soon?"

"Karlie?" I ask, trying to remember where I have heard that name from, it sounds familiar.

"Zeek's girlfriend and my side piece informant."

His eyes twinkle with malice as I process everything that's going on. "Like I said, Dante, this was happening right under your nose. She works in your club and was with one of your men, it was all so beautifully easy. She's not the brightest button out there, it was just saying the right things and extracting the information."

My mouth clenches in anger; all this fucking time Zeek's stripper girlfriend was a leak. How did he not see this? *How did I not see this?* Fury rips through me like a raging tornado. I put my hands through the bars and wind them around his neck. "You talk a real big game behind those bars because you have that gun in your pocket to protect you."

He says nothing but I can feel him reaching for his weapon.

"Sleep with one eye open, pig." I remove my hand and make a gun motion with my two fingers and push them against his temple.

"I don't need to, I'm untouchable, Dischanel."

"We'll see about that."

"Your lawyer is upstairs, bail is set at ten million dollars, which he has paid. Don't go anywhere soon because I'll be watching you like a fucking hawk until your court case."

He barks orders at a guard and my cell opens. I lean heavily against a wall. If I didn't get this whole mess fixed, I would be in front of a Grand Jury, and that only meant one thing for me: Prison for the long haul.

***

Karlie

The phone rings and Karlie's shaking hand picks up. "Aiden?" she says, her voice quivering.

"Yeah, it's me."

"Where are you? My bags are packed. We have to leave soon, Zeek must know by now and he'll find me here eventually."

"*About that…*" Her heart drops like a stone when she hears those words.

"Aiden? You said we we're going to start a new life together, you promised me that I wouldn't have to strip anymore if I was your informant."

"You are going to start a new life…in Witness Protection."

"What! No fucking way, Aiden, that is not what

we agreed."

"Well, it's a little late now," he says, bored.

"I'm not testifying then," she says in victory.

"Well, if you don't testify, then you're not protected. I'm in jail with Dante right now, I could pass him your location very easily."

"I thought you loved me…" Her voice starts to break.

"I love winning. A police car will be over to escort you to another safe house until we find somewhere more secure. If you even breathe a word about our little rendezvous, it will be the last words you say. You will testify against Dante and you will live under the Witness Protection program."

"But—" Before she even finishes her sentence, he hangs up.

She starts crying, realizing there was no going back, ever. She regrets everything she has ever done for Aiden Fonseca but it was too late.

***

Nico

"So, he's out?"

"He's getting out right now, Fonseca was doing as much as he could to delay it. The only sore point is Dante has to surrender his passport, as he is deemed too much of a flight risk," Farook replies, tugging at one of his dreads.

"I think a vacation is the last of Dante's concerns right now."

"What did we miss?" Carmelo and Anara waltz

in together and I narrow my eyes. *Were they together tonight?*

"I'm so glad you could join us; I hope I didn't interrupt your night," I say sarcastically.

Farook looks at me, perplexed, then at Anara and Carmelo, and opens his mouth to say something but thinks better of it.

"Well, it wasn't much of a night," he grumbled, giving Anara an irritated look.

"Let's go and see Padrone, Carmelo," Farook interjects, and they both leave together.

"Nothing happened." Her words tumble out like she has been bursting to say them out loud.

"I really couldn't care less, Anara. As you can see, I have other things to deal with at present."

"You do care, and don't pretend you don't. I shouldn't have gone out with Carmelo; it was a disaster. I spent half the night threatening to taser him if he didn't cut out being a jerk."

"Good for you."

"Nico—"

"Look, I entertained you because you're Reign's sister, I kind of felt sorry for you. Did you really think I would be interested in you? You're just a *kid*."

"I'm twenty-two," she spits out. I can see two pink blots on her cheeks where her anger is visibly rising.

"Exactly, a kid. I'm a savage, Anara. I don't do emotions or any of that other bullshit. Sure, we flirt a lot, but I do that with everyone. You're not that special. If you want to be with Carmelo, knock yourself out. You deserve each other." I say my last words laden with cruelty.

Before I know it a hard slap hits me across my face. Pain and surprise shoots through me, she looks at me, waiting for me to snap. Waiting for me to react, but I don't. I can see the tears falling from her eyes and that's more painful for me than the hard slap she inflicted. She runs out of the room, slamming the door as I sink into the armchair, hand on my throbbing cheek.

Chapter Thirty-Five

Revenge

Eleni

I feel someone stroking my hair, and it feels so good I don't want to open my eyes.

"This isn't the homecoming I had imagined."

I know that voice…

"Dante." My eyes flicker open.

"If I knew you would be waiting in bed for me, I would have come home sooner."

He climbs into the bed and starts to strip until he is only wearing his boxers.

"How did you get out so quick?"

"After all this time you still doubt me," he says, lying next to me.

"Well, it seems pretty serious."

"Yeah, it is." He exhales.

"Will everything be okay?"

"I sure fucking hope so, I didn't think you cared after last night."

"Well, just because you're a jerk doesn't mean I want to see you behind bars forever."

"Silver lining, I guess?"

"I'm glad you're okay, and that's about it. I'm still mad about last night."

"How mad?" He turns to face me, cocking his eyebrow, and slowly climbs over me so his head is under my neck.

"Dante…" I say, my voice coming out breathlessly.

He starts to work small butterfly kisses down my neck, and I try to keep the same energy of being as angry as I was with him last night. He moves down to my stomach and I can feel him start to pull down my underwear.

"Dante, no, and I mean it."

"Spoilsport."

He kisses the apex of my thighs and my eyes roll back, enjoying the sensation of feeling of his stubble on my thighs. He moves back up and lays on top of me so now we are face to face, I can feel his erection against my stomach, and it takes every inch of self-control to not indulge. He begins to kiss me slowly, biting down on my lip gently.

"I missed you," he says, his voice muffled as he moves down, biting my neck slowly.

"It takes going to jail for you to say that." I pull away and look him in the eye.

"Well, taking a piss next to where you sleep makes you appreciate the finer things."

"That is not a compliment."

"Well, it is…kind of. I really wish you would stop talking so we can—"

"No, incarceration aside, you moved my boyfriend to another state. Well, ex-boyfriend. He broke up with me because of you."

"I know you want me to say I'm sorry, but I'm not."

I push him off me and flip him over, so I am straddling him.

"Why aren't you sorry?"

"Because if he wanted you then he would have fought for you."

"You moved him to another state."

"So what?"

"You would have kept trying to break us up even if he didn't go."

"If I thought he was good enough for you I would give him my blessing."

"Like you're the right person to give anyone relationship advice, one ex-fiancée and one pregnant ex-girlfriend."

"It's not mine."

"Sure, Dante."

"I'm telling you I'm ready to fight for you, fight for us. Is that all you have to say?"

"It's your pride talking, you don't care about being with me. You made that clear."

"I tried hard to stay away from you, but I couldn't, and now I want to fight for you. I'll admit I was wrong so many times, but I want to make this work."

"Your words are weak"

"But my actions aren't."

He pulls me on top of him and kisses me fiercely, his hands running down the small of my back until they are planted firmly on my ass.

How can something I knew was so wrong feel so right?

What about Ajax? I try to garner the same anger I felt yesterday but it felt irrelevant, Ajax is the one who ended it without so much of a second thought to what I wanted. It was Miami, not the ends of the earth. We could have made it work.

If he wanted it to.

On the other hand, Dante had only been pushed into wanting to claim me because of Ajax. Did he really want me or was this him just trying to prove himself the ultimate winner? Is this nothing more than a pissing contest between Dante and Ajax?

"Dante, get off me. We're not doing this *again*."

"Eleni, you're killing me. I really need this right now."

"Use your left hand, I hear it's like being with a stranger."

"You're a hard ass."

"You're not exactly a paragon of good behavior."

He chortles to himself and starts stripping off. "I'm going for a shower, how about you join me?"

"I'll pass."

"You're heartless."

"And you're a jackass."

"I was being serious earlier, I'm ready to fight for you."

"You only want me because I didn't want you and I had somebody else. The novelty will wear off soon."

"No, it won't. I only want you, you're the only

thing I see in my future."

"And where does Sapphire and your pending charges fit in?"

"I can't do anything until I get a paternity test, but that baby is not mine."

"If it is?"

"It's not.'

"Dante, be serious. You have to consider the fact that it's a possibility. You and she were *together*," I say through gritted teeth.

"I'm not considering anything but the shower. I hope you will reconsider your original answer."

"Goodbye, Dante," I say, turning around and closing my eyes.

"You know where I am if you change your mind." His voice smolders in my ear as I feel him put one knee on the bed. His bare chest against my back sends chills up my spine.

When I feel his weight leave the bed, I breathe a sigh of relief. Being so close to him always had an effect on me that I couldn't quite put into words. The shower starts and runs for a while. He probably stays in there so long to wash all of his sins off, I muse. I must have fallen asleep because when I do the shower is off. I hear the door slowly open and I feel a weight on the other side of the bed.

"Cut it out, Dante," I say irritably as a finger strokes my leg all the way up to my thigh. He continues and his hand runs up the small of my back and starts to move around to the mounds of my breasts.

"I said cut it out—"

I turn around to tell Dante to get lost, but it isn't

Dante I'm looking at.

"Not who you were expecting, *Princesa*?"

I try to scream but the noise doesn't leave my mouth.

Romeo is back.

***

Ajax

"Are you going to be silent the whole plane ride?" Raheem says, breaking into my thoughts.

"There isn't much to say."

"I for one am glad it's you and not Carmelo I'm going with, that was the original plan."

"I bet it fucking was."

"Are you going to tell me what it was you did to piss Dante off?"

"It's a long story."

"We have two hours and fifty-two minutes; I would say we have time."

"I got together with someone he didn't approve of."

"I heard you got together with the boss's woman. You must have balls, kid."

"She isn't his woman; well, she was at one point. He was also engaged at the same time, it's kind of—"

"A long story."

"I broke it off with her and now I'm thinking why did I do that? I think I'm in love with her, I should have tried harder. I just didn't want her to get hurt anymore."

"Do you think she's going to get back together with Dante?"

"Well, I didn't until now, thanks for that."

"I'm just here for the reality check," Raheem replies, chortling.

"I shouldn't have given up so quickly. She's going to think I don't care about her, but I do."

"Then call her. We're not departing for another couple of minutes."

I get my phone out to call her and it rings before going through to voicemail.

"She must be super pissed if she's not answering."

"You'll get over it, the women in Miami are sensational."

"I don't want women, I want her."

"Think about it, Dante is letting you off lightly. Get away for a while and clear your head. If she's what you really want, New York is only a plane ride away."

"I've fucked up already, I let her go too easily. My last relationship burned me pretty bad."

"What happened?"

"Back in Holland, I got involved in some fucked up shit when my soccer career went south. Debts that I couldn't pay, which led me into this life. I fell for someone I shouldn't have. The mobster I was working for—his fiancée."

"So, this is a recurrent theme for you," Raheem says, ordering us two Jack Daniels from the extremely attractive and busty flight attendant.

"She also turned out to be an undercover government agent who nearly had me thrown in jail."

"Fuck."

"Yep, hence why I ended up here in America. Zeek's cousin hooked me up with a way out of Amsterdam and I haven't been back since. He used his connection with Dante to find me a job."

"You think this one is an undercover Fed?"

"Definitely not, but anytime things get a little heated with a woman, I think of Vanessa and how close she came to destroying my whole life."

"Damn."

"Why are we going to Miami, anyway?"

"Dante want us, well, *you* to persuade Alessandro Da Costa to part with his hotel. Dante thinks it will be good to have more legitimate businesses on the East Coast. This way it will be difficult for the Feds to infiltrate anything."

"Do you know of this Alessandro Da Costa?"

"Yeah, biggest balls in Miami, a real old school Mafia Don."

"What is the likelihood of him selling this hotel?"

"I guess you're about to find out."

Almost three hours later we are in Miami, the intense heat hits me as soon I step out of the airport and onto the busy streets.

"I miss New York already," I say, wiping my forehead and putting on dark shades.

"Are you kidding me? This is the best place on earth," Raheem replies, turning around to check out two bikini-clad girls walking past us. Twenty minutes later, we pull up to Da Costa's hotel and I can see why Dante wants this place. It is dripping in grandeur and opulence, and a real magnet for all the wealthy Dons of Miami. We make our way to the penthouse suite and I immediately make a beeline for the shower. I let the water run cold first, cooling myself down. My stomach clenches painfully as I think of Eleni and the way I left it.

"Hurry up, Casanova, we have a meeting in ten."

I put my head against the glass mirror and groan out loud. This is the last thing I want to do right now.

Ten minutes later, we are both washed and suited up, waiting outside Alessandro Da Costa's office. There is a large painting of him on the wall carrying a bloodied lion's head.

"No pressure then." Raheem smirks at me.

"Nobody seems to be here, I guess we should leave," I say, making a quick beeline for the door.

"Who's there?" a voice calls out.

"I'm here to see Alessandro Da Costa," I reply tentatively.

A female silhouette enters from the shadows and Raheem's jaw nearly hits the floor.

She is incredibly attractive with wavy honey hair and tanned skin. The type of girl you would see in a music video. The type you know is out of your league before you even speak to her.

"Mr. Da Costa is otherwise engaged; you may speak to me regarding your business arrangements."

"I don't think this something you can help with, sweetie; I've been sent here from New York to speak to him directly," I say, lighting up a cigarette.

"First, can you not smoke, the smell gets in my hair. Second, I am not your sweetie. If there is anything you need to discuss with my *father,* you can discuss it with me,'" she replies acerbically.

Raheem gives me an *oh shit* look and tries to conceal the smirk on his face.

"Your father?" I say, switching up my tone. I don't want to get on the wrong side of him by pissing off his daughter.

"Yeah, my father. Do you think because I'm a woman I'm stupid? I went to Stanford, for your information. I am not some Mafia dolly you can sit there and insult."

"Hey, I didn't mean—look, I'm here from my boss on strict instructions to speak to Mr. Da Costa only. Not because you're a woman or not smart, because that is what I was told to do," I say, exasperated, trying to fan down the fury in her face.

"Who is your boss?"

"Dante Dischanel."

"Figures." She snorts. "Where is the man himself then?"

"He's a little tied up with other business, sorry to disappoint you." I internally roll my eyes, I bet she wouldn't take this tone with precious Dante.

"Disappoint me? Dante Dischanel is an arrogant, self-centered asshole." Suddenly I feel myself warm up to her considerably more. "He's your boss, isn't this the point where you're supposed to defend him?" she says, raising her eyebrow.

"Just because he's my boss doesn't mean I have to like him."

She looks at me for a second, sizing me up as if maybe her first impression was off kilter.

"I have a message from my father. He says he's

not selling this hotel under any circumstances, and if Dante doesn't like that answer, he can go and fuck himself."

"I think I'll wait for him to say that to me."

"He'll be back tomorrow, but he won't be as polite about it as I was." She smirks and leaves the room.

"Don't even say a word," I say to Raheem, who starts laughing.

"We're fucked."

"Be positive."

"We're *super* fucked."

"That's the spirit."

***

Eleni

"You!"

"Me." He smiles at me unnervingly as he pins both of my arms down and climbs on top of me.

"I thought you were dead!" I say, trying to think back to that fateful night.

"No, *Princesa*, just waiting for the right moment to come back and get you."

"Dante is next door; he'll kill you."

"Dante is dead."

"What?"

"You think I would come here and not take necessary precautions? No, *Princesa*, I want everything to go to plan for our new life."

"Dante!" I scream at the top of my lungs.

"Dante!" he mimics and laughs.

374

"How did you even get in here?" I ask in horror.

"Jameela, she said it is a wedding present to Dante from her. I've been watching for a while. When he tossed her ass out of this apartment, I tracked her down and asked if she would be interested in vengeance. Too bad for her that she's dead now. I couldn't risk any kinks to my plan."

"Dante!" I scream again.

"You can scream forever, nobody is coming. You're mine now."

"No!" I fight against him, trying to squirm away from him.

His touch makes me feel physically sick.

"I was going to save this for later, but I can't wait." He starts trying to pull down my shorts roughly.

"No!" My heart begins to race as he gets more aggressive.

He undoes his belt buckle and pulls down his jeans and boxers.

"I am going to have you screaming my name, *Princesa*, I'm going to put a baby in you tonight."

I manage to get my knee free and kick him hard in the crotch. He doubles over in pain, and I push him off me and fall on the floor. I crawl to the door, but before I grab a hold of the handle, he has a hold of my leg and is pulling me back.

"Get off me!" I scream.

He's too strong as he drags me back on the floor and gets on top of me, his face is red with anger. Before I can even try to get off him he slaps me hard once, then again. I feel blood start to form in my mouth.

"If you wanted to play rough, *Princesa,* you should have said." He punches me hard and pain radiates across my body.

"Please let me go," I beg, my body drenched in pain.

"Never." He rips off my shorts and all that separates me from him are my underwear.

"You're going to have my baby, Eleni, and after this we're going to Vegas to get married. I'm a traditional man."

"I don't want you," I scream at him.

His hands are tugging at my underwear now and the horror of the situation is starting to dawn on me.

"Well, that's too fucking bad because there is nothing you can do about it."

Suddenly four shots ring out and I see Romeo keel over, smothered in bullet holes. I look up to see Dante...a bloodied mess...walking toward me, still shooting at Romeo until the bullets run out. I want to look away, but I can't. I need to make sure he was dead.

Dante kneels down beside me; his head is dripping with blood. "Did he hurt you?" he asks in a low voice, his face white with anger.

"Just a little, but he didn't—you know. You came just in time."

"Thank God for that." He exhales in relief.

"He said he killed you, I thought—" I get up on my knees, mirroring his position. "I thought you were dead." Silent tears begin to drip down as my heart thuds heavily in my chest.

"He just bashed my fucking head in a couple of times, it takes a lot more to kill this motherfucker than he thought. I just want to know how he got in here."

"Jameela." He said he found her after you dumped her, and she gave him the security codes.'

"That bitch."

"She's dead—he killed her."

"I can't say I'm disappointed."

"How can you be so blasé about this?" I say slowly as both of us are bleeding with a dead body next to us.

"Occupational hazard. I need to get you out of here so I can dispose of the body. You'll stay with Ra tonight and I'll send Chang too," he says, wiping the blood off my lip. "It looks like you'll need a couple of stitches."

"No, I want you to stay with me, Dante. *Please.*"

He looks at me for a second, then gets up and walks out of the room. A minute later he returns on the phone, talking in fast Italian and rolling his eyes a lot. "Carmelo, get your fucking ass here now; I don't care if you're entertaining triplets."

"So, you're going to stay with me?" I say hopefully.

"Yeah, but not here. this looks like a fucking crime scene and it's the last place I need to be right now with Fonseca on my case. We're going to your apartment. I'm going to get some clothes, you should get dressed too," he says, looking at me in my underwear.

Twenty minutes later we're at my place. Chang comes over and stitches Dante's head and tends to my bruising, promising us we were both lucky it wasn't worse. He gives me pain killers for my aching jaw before he leaves into the night. I look over and Dante is on the phone to Dominic, and I can tell it's not a pleasant conversation.

***

Dante

"Dad, I'm fine," I say thickly. My head is throbbing and the need to sleep is overwhelming.

"You're not fucking fine; how could you be so sloppy? Why didn't you change all of the security codes when that *Putanna* left?"

"The same *Putanna* you wanted me to marry, Dad."

"That's beside the point. You are my only heir left, Dante. I cannot outlive you. I will not lose another son because of recklessness."

"I'm nothing like Dash," I say hotly.

"What about Fonseca? Why didn't you notice that Zeek's girlfriend was the informant? I thought you kept a close eye on these things. Background checks, Dante? Come on, this is basic shit that you should know. Maybe if you weren't so wrapped up with fucking everything with a pulse you would know what's going on. You're losing your edge, boy. I am very disa—"

I slam the phone down, pissed off. He's saying all the things I know are true. Am I really losing my edge? It isn't something I want to contemplate with a raging headache. I make my way over to the couch and Eleni enters with a bottle of Jack Daniels and two tumblers.

"I think we've earned this," she says, pouring out two generous portions.

"You can say that again."

She lays down beside me and puts her head on my chest. We just sit there for what feels like hours in silence. My arm slouches over her shoulder and her fingers stroke my forearm. Despite everything that has happened, I never felt more at peace. I drain the rest of the tumbler and look down at her head on my chest.

"Eleni, I think I'm in love with you. I wasn't sure before, but after tonight it just reinforced everything that I felt was real. I know I've fucked up and done really shitty things, but do you think you can forgive me? Do you think you could give me another chance?" I pause for a second, waiting for her to respond, and after several uncomfortable seconds of possible rejection, I look down and realize that she's fast asleep.

Just my fucking luck.

Chapter Thirty-Six

The Calm Before The Storm

"That is fucked up," Nico exclaims as I recount last night's events to him minus the Eleni situation.

After I realized she was asleep, I carried her into bed and stayed awake all night watching her sleep like a fucking pussy.

Nobody could ever know about that part. Not even her.

"Padrone says I'm losing my edge, that I should have spotted all of this shit coming."

"How? You're not a fucking psychic. Who knew crazy Romeo and jilted Jameela would team up? What a fucking shame about Jameela, those legs were fucking insane."

"Really, Nico? *Really?*" I say, bewildered.

"What?" He shrugs. "Just because she's a demented bitch doesn't mean she can't have nice legs?"

"You're unbelievable."

"How is Eleni?"

"A little bruised and battered, but she'll survive. She's a tough cookie."

"So now Ajax is gone, are you two—"

"We're amicable."

"Amicable? Is that code for fucking?"

"Language, Nicolo," Padrone replies, looking at Nico disdainfully as he enters the room.

"On that note, I'm out," Nico exits, leaving Padrone and me standing there.

"Where do I start, son?" he says in exasperation.

"How about you don't. I have a long day ahead of me, Dad."

"You're going soft, Dante; you could have ended up dead last night."

"How was I supposed to know he was still alive? How was I supposed to know Jameela would do that?"

"The question is, Dante, why didn't you know? You told me you had men looking for Romeo, did you bother to check on the progress? Whether he was dead or alive? Did you think Jameela was just going to leave quietly after your temper tantrum the other night? No. Because you don't think, Dante, you just juggle knives blindly, trying to avoid them all."

"My sources told me Romeo was long gone."

"Your sources are clearly fucking wrong. One day I won't be here anymore, Dante. The question is are you going to live long enough to see it? How can I trust you when you can't even keep your own men in order? Zeek and the stripper? Explain to me how this evaded everybody's attention?"

"I don't preoccupy myself with my men's love

lives. if Zeek wants to bang stripper, that's up to him. How was anyone of us supposed to know she was an informant? Fonseca got to her after she started working for us, not before. This wouldn't have come up on a background check."

"You should have known," he says forcefully.

"How could I have known when Zeek didn't?" I slam my hand hard down on the desk in anger. I was really getting pissed off now.

"Zeek is not Caporegime, you are. How do you know he wasn't involved in this?"

"Because I trust him. If he wanted to sell me out, he could have done a lot more than this over the years. The stripper is Fonseca's key witness. If we can find her this whole RICO case goes away."

"You make it sound so easy, Dante, when you know for a fact it isn't. She is probably going into Witness Protection as we speak."

"I'll find a way to get to her. Zeek is on it, this is his redemption."

"You're distracted, Dante, and I know why."

"Well, let's see you get arrested and nearly killed in the same day and see how distracted you are."

"No, Dante, before that. Ever since you met that girl you have been distracted. Maybe if you weren't so busy playing doctors and nurses with her—"

"I don't know what you're talking about," I say, staring at him blankly.

"You're blinded by Eleni, and you're going to get yourself killed if you carry on like this." He grabs me by the shoulders and starts to shake me as if trying to shake sense into me.

"You're overreacting. Nothing is going on

there."

"So why did you stay over at her apartment last night?"

"I would appreciate if you didn't get your secretary Carmelo to spy on me. Nothing happened last night, she didn't want to be alone and neither did I. Nothing like *that* is going on."

"Why not start a ménage à trois? Maybe she and Sapphire could both be pregnant at the same time?"

"Shut up, Dad, that baby is not mine."

"And if it is?"

"Then I'll fucking deal with it."

"You'll do the honorable thing."

"Which is?"

"Marry her."

"Are you insane?" I ask, repulsed. "After what happened with the last girl you tried to pimp me out to, you're fucking out of your mind!"

"If that is your child, marrying her is the only way to legitimize your heir, Dante, and you know that."

"It's not going to happen," I repeat hotly, getting severely wound up.

"It's time to let Eleni go, Dante, she doesn't understand your life. She doesn't understand who you are, your responsibilities. Your legacy."

"Good, I don't want her to. I don't want some Mob wife, Dad."

"So, you want to marry Eleni? Is that what you're saying?"

"I never said that. All of this falls on me, it's nothing to do with Eleni. I take responsibility for all of this."

"I will say this for the last time, get your act together Dante, *or else.*"

He stares at me harshly for a second and leaves the room wordlessly, leaving me standing there riled up and ready to lash out.

Is he right? Am I losing my edge? Going soft?
Never, replies the indignant voice in my head.

***

Nico

"You know what you have to do, Zeek?"

"Yeah," he replies slowly.

His face is pale with dark circles under his eyes. I admit I wanted to kill him when I heard what happened, but now I feel a twinge of sympathy for him. She had obviously taken him for a ride. Not to mention sleeping with that creep Fonseca was enough to keep anyone up at night. "Dre has managed to track her down to an address they are temporarily using as a safe house. Once she moves, it will be impossible to find her. This is our one shot."

"How angry is Dante?"

"Pretty pissed…okay, majorly pissed…but hey, Romeo almost killing him is a great distraction now."

"I fucked up so bad," he groans.

"We've all been there—well, we haven't, but at least you can make it right."

"I wish I were more like you, Nico, heartless…I loved her, and she crushed me," he says thickly.

"Don't even think about fucking crying, Zeek, I'm warning you."

Something he says struck a deep chord in me.

Heartless.

Then I remember Anara's eyes welling up and I felt the awkward ache that I felt that day. She has avoided me since and made sure she was never at the compound when I was around.

Ah well.

It was probably for the best. This way she didn't get hurt and I didn't get my legs broken by Reign.

Three days later

"It's twelve, they're switching guard duty, so this is our time to strike."

I knew we had only three or four minutes until the new security came in to check on Karlie. This was the only time that she was unguarded.

"You know you have to do this, Zeek."

He nods at me, tucking the gun into the back of his jeans.

We walk in slowly; I nod to him while I wait at the door.

***

Zeek

My mouth is so dry that my tongue feels like granite, I have killed before plenty of times, but not like this. The cruelty of having to do this feels like a thunderbolt of pain, but then I think of the betrayal and my heart hardens a little. I haven't slept in days knowing that this is my final pitstop to redemption.

I walk into the room and can see her body under the mound of covers. I stroke a tendril of hair that has fallen over the pillow. She really is beautiful; I was willing to give her everything and this is what cuts me the most. I pick up my gun and plant it right in the middle of her head, the coldness of the gun must have roused her, because her eyes shoot open and I see fear imprinted on her face.

"Good night, Karlie." I pull the trigger as the only girl I ever loved is dead.

***

Nico

"It's done," I say into the receiver of the payphone.

The phone goes dead and I know Dante has gotten my message. Since his arrest, we have been going through bigger hoops to evade detection. Burner phones, payphones, and avoiding speaking on them altogether.

Zeek is slumped in the passenger seat next to me, lightly snoring. This has got him back into Dante's good graces. He'll get over it eventually.

I really could do with a pick me up tonight.

I drop Zeek off to his apartment and make my way to the club. I need a release tonight to distract myself from everything.

"Hey sugar, the usual?" Noelle sits on my lap and whispers in my ear seductively.

"Yeah, the usual." She walks me over to one of the private rooms and sits me in a chair.

She's writhing and grinding on me, but I can't seem to get there.

I close my eyes, trying to get myself in the mood, but it's not working.

"Something on your mind? I can fix that."

I open my eyes and Noelle is gone, replaced by Anara.

I watch her as she starts to strip slowly, her bra falling off slowly to show her tanned curves.

"I told you I could fix it," she purrs back at me.

She undoes my belt buckle and pants and I feel myself rise to the occasion. Her mouth feels so good on me that my eyes automatically close in ecstasy, but when I open them, Noelle has replaced Anara and I can't hide my disappointment.

"I can't do this," I say, pushing her off me and buttoning up my pants.

"What the fuck is wrong with you?" she asks irately.

"How long have you got?" I mumble, leaving the club.

What is wrong with me indeed?

Chapter Thirty-Seven

Red

Eleni

My black eye has started to fade from a dark violet to a pale yellow. A little concealer should cover most of the physical scars, but the mental ones still remain. Every time I close my eyes I see Romeo's face looming over me. Ra had been staying with me at night, at least when I woke up I wasn't on my own, and I knew Ra had a gun.

Just in case.

Dante and I haven't spoken since it happened. I wake up in bed alone with a comforter pulled over me. I don't actually remember getting into bed, but I must have because I don't see how else I got there. I thought he would call me, but clearly the other night was a one-off, an 'in the moment' kind of thing. Maybe we both need time to reflect on what had happened. The doorbell rings and I freeze for a moment. Every sound seems to trigger something in

388

me.

A flock of butterflies seems to have taken hold of my nerves as the door opens, expecting Dante, but it isn't him, it's Dominic. I can't say I'm not taken back; I don't think I have even had a conversation with him in all the time that I had been working for Dante.

"Come in, Ra isn't around right now." Surely he must be looking for her, why else would he be here?

"I've actually come to see you." I feel like he's x-raying me with his green eyes.

"Me? Why?" I have a bad feeling.

"I heard about what happened the other night. How are you feeling?"

"Better," I say slowly.

I feel awkward, I'm not sure why he's here. Dante or Ra could have given him an update.

What exactly did he want?

"You're probably wondering why I am here; I don't normally make personal house calls. I've come to talk to you about my son."

"What about him?" I can feel the edge in my voice already.

"What is going on between you and Dante?" I can hear the chill radiating in his voice, and it makes the hairs on the back of my neck stand up.

"Nothing is going on," I say honestly because there isn't.

"I don't believe that for one second, and I'm not happy with your relationship, whatever it may be. Dante is becoming reckless; his actions are not befitting a man of his status. You are a big distraction for him. he could have died last night saving you. In fact, how many times has he got hurt trying to save your life?"

I stand there for a second letting the words wash over me like poison. "I took a bullet for Dante, or are you forgetting that? The day Lorenzo shot me, or what about when Romeo kidnapped me so that you would give Lorenzo back to the Salvatores?"

"An eye for an eye makes the world blind, Eleni."

"Can you leave? I don't want you in my apartment."

"My apartment, all of this is mine. You are living in my world." His voice pierces me. He sighs for a second. "I don't want to be cruel, Eleni."

"Well, you're doing a good job of it," I fire back.

"What will you do when Sapphire has the baby?"

"It's not Dante's,' I say automatically, full of confidence I shouldn't have.

"What if it is his? Are you going to deny him the chance to become a father? How well do you really know him?"

"Does Dante know you're here?" I reply back icily.

"No, and we're going to keep it that way." He pulls out a piece of paper and writes something down and hands it to me.

"What is this?" I say, looking at a very long number.

"Do you like the look of that number or do you want a few more zeroes added on?"

"What are you talking about?"

"I want you out of my son's life, no matter the cost."

"What" I reply back, aghast, dropping the piece of paper.

"You have until the end of the day to get back to me with a number. I want you gone, Eleni."

"I'm not leaving and you're not paying me off," I screech.

"Eleni...this is not your world. Move on, finish school, meet a nice young man who can give you the life my son can't. I never ask twice, remember that." He pulls out a large envelope and leaves it on the table. "Either leave by choice or by force, the decision is yours."

He gives me another chilling stare and departs, leaving me standing there alone and shocked.

Twenty minutes later, Ra walks in and I recap the conversation as the envelope stares ominously at me from the coffee table.

"No way. I never thought Padrone would say something like that. He's so reserved usually," Ra says slowly, as if she's pausing to process the information.

"Well, he wasn't reserved when he was here. He told me Dante wants to have the baby with Sapphire...do you think he's right?"

"No way, and if Dante knew about this conversation, he would hit the roof. You need to speak to him now. Dante doesn't want a baby and he will never settle down. Once a bachelor, always a bachelor."

That is what I'm afraid of...

"Talk to him," she says, seeing my reaction. "Put your mind at ease. You're not going to get any peace of mind without having that conversation."

***

Dante

I tossed the burner cell phone into the river, making sure to snap the sim card first. I was taking no chances whatsoever.

My other cell rang, and I pick up hesitantly. This better not be Nico again.

"Yeah?"

"Blue or yellow?" a female voice asks.

"Sapphire?" I roll my eyes.

"Yes, babe. I'm at your apartment now, planning the nursery."

"You're what? Sapphire, get out now."

She clicks off and I resist the urge to rip the steering wheel off my car and instead do a U-turn. For fuck's sake, can I not catch a break today?

I drive so fast I'm surprised I'm not pulled over for speeding and run into the apartment. Carmelo has had the good sense to have all the floors reupholstered and cleaned to perfection. I see Sapphire sitting in Eleni's old room with a stash of baby catalogs and color charts.

"How did you get in here?"

"Carmelo gave me the key."

Fucker. Every time I think Carmelo could be labeled as partially decent, he makes a jackass move.

"Get out, Sapphire, I'm not in the mood."

"Padrone said you might say something like that."

"Padrone?" I say, confused.

"This is his idea. He wants to warm you up to your pending fatherhood."

"I should have known," I say, gritting my teeth.

"Come on, Dante," she says softly, her arms wrapping around me.

"No," I say, pushing her away.

"You can't deny we have chemistry, remember how good we used to be…all the things I used to do you that would make you scream." She kisses me hard on the lips, her nails raking at the back of my neck. "We're meant to be." She places my hand on her baby bump.

***

Eleni

"It's now or never, you ready?"

Ra pulls up in front of the penthouse. I see Dante's car parked out front, it looks like it's perfect timing for this conversation.

I exit Ra's car and make my way up to the top floor; the door is slightly ajar, so I walk in carefully and I can hear voices.

I follow the voices until I am facing the large mirror on the landing where I see two familiar reflections…

Sapphire and Dante kissing, with his hand placed on her bump, surrounded with baby magazines and catalogs.

I feel my heart shatter into a thousand pieces as a feeling of sickness overwhelms me. I quietly exit and run down the stairs two at a time. I need to get out of here. I run outside and Ra is still there, reapplying her lipstick in the rear-view mirror.

"Get me out of here," I say in a low voice.

The look on my face must say it all because she puts her foot on the gas pedal, no questions asked.

***

Dante

"Are you fucking kidding? Get off me!" I wrench her hands away and wipe my mouth. "What do I have to do to make you understand I don't want you? I've had enough of your games."

She doesn't say anything, but I can see searing anger build up in her face.

My phone rings, distracting me from my fury.

"What?"

"Lorenzo wants to talk to you, only you. Get down here."

"I'll be there in five, keep Lorenzo talking."

I put the phone down, leaving it on my dresser.

"I'm leaving, but by the time I come back I want all of this shit, including you, gone."

She stares at me but doesn't say a word. I walk out before my anger lifts through the roof. How dare my father involve himself in this? How could he go behind my back?

***

Anara

"Fuck." I kick the flat tire, cursing myself.

I knew I should carry a spare, but it takes all the space up in the boot of my car. Rain is starting to fall slowly but I can tell from the darkness of the sky a storm is coming. I pick up the phone to call someone. "Reign."

"Yeah."

"I need you to pick me up, I have a flat tire."

"Where are you?"

"Mariner's Harbor."

"Nico is not far away from you, I'll send him."

"What? Why can't you come?"

"Because I'm headed in the opposite direction. What's the problem with Nico?" I can hear the questioning in his voice, Reign is too overprotective for his own good.

"There is no problem."

I click off the call, pissed off, and kick the tire again.

Five minutes later Nico pulls up. I sit on the hood of the car.

He tries to make small talk, and I ignore him. The quicker he changes this tire, the quicker I can get out of here.

"Somebody can't take rejection." He smirks up at me with a wrench in his hand.

"I'm sure Carmelo's body will ease the pain."

The smirk is wiped off his face and I am immediately mollified.

"You said nothing happened between you," he says, gritting his teeth.

"A girl can change her mind." I smile back, taking deep satisfaction in his anger. He gets up quickly and puts his hands on either side of me. "Nico, what are you do— "

Before I finish my sentence, his mouth locks down hard on mine and he is kissing me like it's the last thing he'll ever do. The rain is starting to lash down harder, which doesn't seem to dampen his passion level, but then I remember what happened last time we kissed, and I slap him hard. "What do you think you are doing? Is this a game to you?" I say, pushing him hard.

"It isn't. I want you to promise me you'll stay away from Carmelo."

"This is all about fucking Carmelo?"

"He's not good for you, he's a piece of shit. Find someone better, preferably who's not related to me."

"Why do I care about what you want?" I screech.

"Because!" he screams back at me.

"Because what?"

Thunder cracks in the air and rain is falling so hard that we're both soaked to the bone.

"Because I can't stop fucking thinking about you and it's killing me."

"If that were true, you wouldn't have acted like that and said what you said."

"I was trying to push you away because everything I touch I fucking destroy, and I don't want to destroy you, Anara."

"You're just making excuses."

"I'm not. I care about you. I want you so fucking bad, but I can't have you. I'm not a good guy."

"What about what I want? I told you this doesn't have to be anything serious."

"You know that isn't true, Anara, I can see past your bad girl act," he says knowingly.

"Nico."

"What?"

"Just shut up and kiss me."

He pins me down on the hood of the car and we kiss for a long time until I feel the cold seeping into my skin. He puts me over his shoulder and carries me into his car, which is a lot bigger than mine, not to mention warmer. He lays me down on the backseat and we both start to undress with such speed that we would probably break a record. He leans over and presses a button and I feel the seats warm the coldness of my body.

"Heated seats, babe, for your pleasure."

His head slow disappears, and I feel his tongue and fingers slither inside of me, sending me into euphoria.

"Nico." I cry out as my knees begin to shake as that familiar sensation of climax overcomes me.

He pulls away suddenly. "I like this piercing, Anara," he says as his tongue flicks around the little earring on my clit.

"Nico, please, I can't wait," I whisper, barely able to keep it together as I'm teetering on the edge of climaxing for a second time.

"Can't wait for what?" he teases.

"Please." I squirm.

"Do you want me to make you come?'

"Yes!" I scream out.

"Yes, *sir*," he corrects me.

"Nico, please."

"What did I just say?"

"Please make me come, *sir*," I breathe out as his fingers circle my clit expertly.

"Your wish is my command," he says, pulling out a condom from one of the seat pockets.

He aligns himself on top of me, licking one of his fingers, then placing the other one in my mouth. "Taste how good you are, baby." I lick them clean and he smiles in approval. I feel him move down to my chest, sucking, nibbling, and biting as I get lost in all the sensations.

I lean back and wrap my legs around him as he begins to circle his hips, thrusting up to me. Our tongues fight for dominance as the windows start to steam up as we both move together in sync. His hard, muscular body drapes over me doing things I've only dreamed of as the storm rages on outside.

The drought is officially over.

Chapter Thirty-Eight

Love And War

Dante

I pull up outside the compound, ready to finally end this Lorenzo bullshit. This has dragged on for way too long. Either he tells me whatever he's been withholding, or I'm going to shoot him. I run downstairs to the basement where we keep all our special guests.

"Farook, what are you doing?" I say in surprise. Farook has his gun planted to a very fearful Lorenzo's head.

"You told me to waste him, so that's what I am doing," Farook replies, looking perplexed.

"I told you I was on my way."

"No, after that you texted me."

"I didn't message you." I feel my pocket for my phone, realizing I have left it on top of the dresser.

"Sapphire must have done it; I left my cell at the penthouse."

"Why would she do that?" A confused Farook pulls the gun away from a smirking Lorenzo.

"What the fuck are you smiling about?" I say irritably.

"You really are stupid, Dischanel."

"Keep talking and I might reconsider not shooting you," Farook replies, cocking the gun.

"Why would Sapphire, of all people, want me dead?" he mocks.

"She doesn't even know you," I reply slowly as a bad feeling starts to overcome me.

"Is it all starting to click into place, Dante? Sapphire has been my double agent for months. The warehouse fires, the attempted shooting at Escada. Those were all Sapphire's master strokes, she wanted to get you where it hurt you the most."

"You're lying," I say automatically, knowing there is a part of me that knows he's not.

"Why would I lie?"

"Because you're a piece of shit? Prove it," Farook says.

"For starters, she has a tattoo of an angel somewhere not so angelic."

Farook cocks his eyebrow at me for validation.

"Is that enough proof for you? Is it all clicking into place?"

"Why would she work with you? You're small fry," I say slowly.

"Because you dumped her, and she wanted revenge. All the bullshit I had to endure just to get her to start fessing up all the Dischanel secrets. It was worth it because I had you under my thumb and you didn't even know how. Hell hath no fury and all that."

"If she was your go-to, tell me why she gave up your location?"

"Because I underestimated what a crazy bitch she was," he says, visibly irritated.

"What does that mean?"

"She trapped me and tried to blackmail me into leaving my wife. When I didn't, she switched back to your side."

"What do you mean trapped?" I say, getting a horrible sense of foreboding.

"What do you think I fucking mean? She got pregnant. It was mine and I told her to get rid of it."

Farook makes a choking sound and we both look at each other.

"She refused to get rid of it, and next thing I know, I'm ambushed by your men. My reign is fucking over before it even started."

"The baby is *yours*?" I say, raking my hands through my hair.

"Yeah…wait. Did she try to pin it on you?" His laugher echoes around the cell.

"Why are you telling me this now and not before?"

"Because I thought I would get out of here to finish her myself, but clearly that isn't happening now. I know I'm a dead man, but I want my wife protected from that crazy bitch. I know she'll find a way to get to her. Promise me you'll protect her from Sapphire."

"Done,' I reply, taking the gun out of my pocket and shooting him in the forehead. He drops down dead and silence echoes around the cell. "Well, we didn't need him anymore."

"Dante…" Farook starts.

"I know."

"What do we do now?"

"We do what the man asked. Get Sabrina Salvatore down here."

"You want a Salvatore in here?" Farook asks me like I'm crazy.

"Yep, I have a plan."

***

Eleni

"No way, Eleni," Ra says, shocked as we enter the apartment.

I explain everything and she and I are both trying to absorb it.

"I saw it with my own eyes."

"Wow, I really thought he hated Sapphire."

"Maybe fatherhood has changed things." Even saying that word makes me feel sick.

"What do you want to do next?" she replies, looking at the unopened envelope.

"I need you to do something for me, Ra, can I trust you?"

She stares at me for a second and nods slowly.

***

Dante

"I think you were always the one, I just didn't know it until now."

"Really?" the female voice gushes in absolute joy.

"Really,' I say as I smile down at Sapphire. The words I'm saying repulse me. "I have a surprise for you."

"You do?" she squeals.

"One you won't forget." I smile at her.

"I can't wait. Just so you know, I always saw myself as a spring bride."

"Your surprise is here; I hope you like it."

I hear heels behind me and watch as Sapphire's face turns grey.

"I—You—Dante?"

"I don't believe introductions are necessary."

"You won't be making it to spring, honey," Sabrina replies in a thick Colombian accent. "You're good, Sapphire, but I'm *better*."

"Dante," she whimpers.

"Lorenzo told me everything, were there no depths your betrayal wouldn't sink to?"

"Dante…" Silent tears start to drop down her face.

"Save me the crocodile tears, Sapphire, I've had enough to last me a lifetime."

"Please, Dante, I can explain." She starts to weep noisily.

"You've made your bed, now lie in it, traitor."

"Is this a good time to discuss your affair with my husband?" Sabrina interjects, stroking one of her nails down Sapphire's cheek.

"I'll leave you to catch up," I say, exiting.

"Thanks, Dante."

"Dante!" Sapphire screams as I walk upstairs and close the door to the basement, deafening any noise.

***

Sabrina

Sabrina Salvatore stares disdainfully at the tramp who was sleeping with her husband—well, one of them, anyway. Her husband and brother were dead, but at least she had an alliance. Peace would exist between the two families for now until she had time to think of her next move. Her eyes drop down to Sapphire's small bump and her chest twinges in pain. Sabrina couldn't have children and it was probably one of the reasons why Lorenzo had lost interest in their marriage. Her eyes catch the baby bump again and an idea begins to formulate in her head as Sapphire begins to weep, asking for mercy. She snorts, having grown up with a Colombian drug lord as a father she didn't know the word.

***

Dante

It was necessary. My father's words rang in my ears.

Am I losing my edge?

If I were more focused, would I have seen Sapphire's betrayal?

Were all the signs there and I was too distracted to see? As for Sabrina, she was more than happy to negotiate a Dischanel/Salvatore alliance. Sapphire was the only bait I needed to draw the battle lines. Romeo's and Lorenzo's deaths were immaterial to Sabrina. She is now the head of the Salvatore family, her only threat would be Sapphire's unborn child. Lorenzo's heir. In love and war there are no compromises.

"Is it done?" Farook asks, lighting a cigarette and pouring us both large tumblers of Bourbon.

"Yep, two birds, one stone. Sapphire dealt with an alliance with the Salvatore family."

He hands me my cell, which was in Sapphire's handbag, and there is only one person I want to talk to right now.

"Do you still want me to swing by the warehouse?"

"No, have the night off."

"Someone's in a good mood. What are your plans tonight?"

"Celebrating with my girl."

"Your girl? So, it's official?"

"Not yet, but it will be. Everything has found a way of righting itself and I'm hoping this will too."

"Well, I approve, Dante."

"*Salut Chindon,*" I say, lifting my drink to his.

"*One hundred years*" Farook says as our glasses clink.

"Eleni?" I put the key in the apartment door but all the lights are switched off. I have tried to call her a dozen times but no answer. A little flare of panic builds within me, thinking of the last time she went missing. I know Romeo is dead but there is always someone else waiting in the shadows. I switch the lights on and something doesn't feel right here. I walk into her bedroom and I see the room has been stripped. Her clothes and belongings are gone, and her phone is on the bed. This doesn't seem the act of somebody who has been taken against their will. My mind starts racing as I try to figure out what has gone down here.

"Nico, meet me at Eleni's place and bring Ra and Anara."

"Why Anara?"

"Because I want the girls there."

"Why?"

"Because I fucking do."

"I'll have to find her first," he mumbles.

"Well, do it then. Jesus, Nico, what's up with you?"

***

Nico

"Nothing's wrong, Dante." I hang up and sigh as Anara lays against my chest.

"What is that about?" she asks, stroking my hair and looking up at me.

Eventually, we had made it back to my apartment after our little car adventure. Despite telling her and myself that was the last time it was going to happen, it then proceeded to happen five more times. I could kick myself at the unhealthy attachment I'm starting to feel for her. She is becoming my addiction, and each second I wasn't buried deep within her feels like a second wasted.

As if she could sense my inner struggle, she leans down and kisses me slowly. "Just relax, we can take it slow. I know you have issues." She snorts.

"Reign will kill me," I say, trying to break the kiss.

"I will kill you first if you don't finish what you started." She kisses me even harder and I can feel my erection pressing against her leg. I flip her so she is on top of me as my head lolls against the headboard, watching her work.

"Jesus, Anara." I sigh, feeling my eyes roll to the back of my head. Even if I wanted to leave, I can't. My mouth latches onto her rosebud nipples while the other hand slowly pinches the other breast, watching her experience the pain and pleasure.

"Nico, I'm so close." She sighs, bouncing against me as she meets my every thrust with matching urgency. I pull her closer as our tongues meet, fiercely fighting for dominance. Her hands rake at my back as her body finally arrives at her climax, followed by mine.

She falls flat on her back and I topple over her as we both try to catch our breaths. I am heading into unprecedented territory. Not only am I struggling with my own feelings for her, but I have to take into account how Reign will react to this. He'll jump to the worst conclusions and assume I'm using her. Am I? Or is she using me? I don't know how I have suddenly got caught up in something I have never wanted to happen, have actively fought against happening for a long time.

I will have to deal with the consequences of that when and if it happens, hopefully it will never happen. However, right now I have to put on my best poker face to see Dante and pretend that I haven't spent the last six hours screwing the girl who will be standing next to me.

Chapter Thirty-Nine

Never Say Never

Dante

"Finally,. I was about to send out a fucking search party," I say irritably.

Nico and Anara both walk in with blank stares. I look at Nico for some kind of explanation, but he doesn't meet my gaze.

"Eleni is gone," I say, looking for reactions on the faces of Anara and Ra.

"What do you mean gone?" Nico asks. "As in somebody took her? Lorenzo and Romeo are dead, nobody else would have done this."

"It looks like she left voluntarily," I say in a small voice as my chest begins to pang.

"But why?" Anara looks genuinely stumped and I rule her off my list of people that know anything about it.

She and Nico exchange secretive looks, and if I weren't as perceptive as I am, I would have missed

409

it. There is definitely *something* going on. If I were more invested I would have made it a point to investigate it further. Not that there would be anything to investigate, Nico knows she's off limits. Reign is one of my best friends and he is fiercely protective over his sister, but since when does Nico understand the word no? Another thing to worry about when I figure this Eleni situation out. I look around, narrowing my eyes for clues. Nico is looking out the window, distracted, with Anara sneaking looks at him when she thinks I'm not looking, and Ra is looking straight down, a sure sign of a guilty conscience.

"Ra, you're quiet today. Anything you want to add to the conversation?"

"No, Capo," she replies, her face deathly white.

"Anara, you can leave. Thanks for coming." Anara shoots Ra a worried look before bowing her head and leaving.

"What's going on?" Nico says slowly, sensing the sub-zero temperature in the room.

"Ra knows where Eleni is."

"Where is she?" Nico asks sharply, turning around to fully face her.

"I promised—" she says, bowing her head down.

"You promised?" Nico snarls. "You're a fucking Captain, the only promise you honor is to your Capo."

"Please, Dante, I can't," she says in a small voice.

"Why did she leave, Ra? Is there"—I pause as I say this part—"Someone else?"

"What? No, I would say it's probably the

opposite," she replies curtly, glaring at me.

"What are you talking about?" I say, exasperated.

"Ra, start fucking talking unless you want your new job to be scraping bodies from sidewalks."

"She saw you, Dante. Eleni saw you kissing Sapphire at your apartment," she says icily.

"What?" Nico cranes his neck to look at me. "You and Sapphire—"

"Sapphire is *dead*."

"What? " They both echo each other.

"I haven't had a chance to tell anyone yet, only Farook knows. Sapphire was a double agent for Lorenzo, she was sleeping with him. The baby was his, the rest is history."

"I don't understand," Ra says slowly.

"It means everything came down to Sapphire. Andre was the first to go over and Sapphire promised more men. Eleni getting shot, the warehouse fires, the ambush, all of it was her doing."

"Why didn't Lorenzo say anything?"

"Because when he told her to get rid of the baby, she threatened his wife. He knew he was going to die in that cell after the rest of the Salvatores didn't come for him. He told me his last request was that he wished his wife would be protected. We now have an alliance with the Salvatore Family. Where is Eleni? Why didn't she talk to me about her suspicions?"

"It wasn't just that…Dante, I really don't think I should tell you this part. You're not going to like it."

"I don't fucking like any of this, so tell me now unless you want me to shoot it out of you."

She winces for a second. "Padrone offered Eleni money to leave. He told her you wanted to be with Sapphire, and she was getting in the way of your happiness. He said that she was a distraction. Eleni came to your apartment to talk to you about it, but when she saw you with Sapphire, she figured it was true. There was no talking her around, she just wanted you to be happy. She didn't want to be a burden on your life." She trails off and looks at the floor.

Nico's mouth drops open and stares at me while I feel a hot, white fury overcome me.

"I'm sorry, Dante." Ra bows her head down.

"Get out," I say in a monotone voice. She leaves quickly with her head still lowered.

"Dante," Nico says in a small voice. I can tell he's not sure what to say to me.

All I can hear is white noise as my heart thumps heavily in my ears. "Leave," I say hoarsely.

Nico hesitates, as if to try and console me, but thinks better of it.

After the door shuts, I pick up a chair and throw it against the wall, picking up one of the legs and then smashing it until there was only small pieces of wood left. I continue this with most of the furniture. After a few hours, the anger in me only seems to have increased, so I do what I should have done hours ago and drive to my father's house. *She's gone* seems to flash through my mind like an electric shock that keeps piercing me in my ribs. I walk up the penthouse stairs two at a time, I'm too incensed to take the elevator. I yank open his office door, and my father is sitting at his desk with his spectacles on, reading the newspaper.

"I've heard about the Salvatore deal, well played, son."

"You bastard," I scream at him.

"What did you say, boy?" The atmosphere instantly shifts, and I can see the familiar lines of anger appear on his face.

"I know what you did, you tried to fucking pay her off."

"Dante." He sighs. "Don't be angry, I was doing what is—"

"Best? Telling her I wanted that fucking traitor Sapphire is what is best?"

"I didn't know that then, did I?" he replies in irritation. "Dante—"

"Shut up, Dad. Shut the fuck up. I cannot believe you, and you don't even feel bad about it."

"Feel bad about what? She was holding you back, and you were doing the same. She doesn't belong in this life; she will never adapt. Don't be selfish, Dante, it would have never worked."

Thump.

That is the last straw. I punch him square in the face, knocking him off his feet. A small part of me is questioning myself while the other part is victorious in pleasure. My father finally stands up, looking furious. "You put your hands on me? I will make you fucking regret it. I am the head of this family. Do you think you can fucking disrespect me because I made a decision? The right decision that you will thank—"

He stops mid-sentence for dramatic effect, I stare at him, waiting for him to continue, but he doesn't. He seems to pause mid-air as his face goes grey.

"Dad?" I say uncertainly.

"Dante," he says breathlessly as he grabs his chest and collapses.

***

Eleni

There have been several times that I almost walked out of the airport. Ra had tried to talk me out of this a dozen times, but my mind was made up. Now as I sit on the plane waiting to take off, my heart is beating so hard that I can hear the blood pounding in my ears. Like words, it whispered to me.

Dante. Dante. Dante.

It's better this way, I've made it easier for him. Although no amount of convincing myself would remove the pain I felt. They say what doesn't kill you makes you stronger. It strengthens you; it defines you, but not in this case. What doesn't kill you, weakens you. It makes you more susceptible to getting hurt again. I had fought for Dante before and lost. I couldn't surrender myself to him again, not after this. I would not watch him and Sapphire play happy families. It was time for me to walk away. Dante's face flashed a thousand times before me. As I thought of the old life I was leaving behind.

I choke back tears as the plane begins to ascend. It's better to break your own heart by leaving than for someone else to break it every day you're with them. This is the end of the long-drawn-out Dante and Eleni story..

Isn't it?

***

One Year Later

Nico

"Five more minutes," the voice under the cover purrs.

"I've got to leave now," I say breathlessly as I feel another wave of pleasure build up in my abdomen as I climax.

"Are you sure you want to leave, *Sir*?" she asks, licking her lips seductively.

"You're killing me, Anara, you know that." I stand up and pull on my boxers. I would have a shower when I get to my own apartment. There is no way Anara would let me have a 'PG-13' one here.

Cazzo, who knew I would find someone to match my infinitely high sex drive? This has been going on for a year, and every time I tried to say it was the last time, it never is. "Anara," I start, and she rolls her eyes.

"We can't do this anymore," she mimics the speech I have made a thousand times. "Too late, Nico, we both know you're not going to walk away from all of this." She wraps herself around me as I

415

try to avoid her naked form.

"You're a bad influence, you know that?" I say, looking down at her.

"I know," she says, standing up on her tiptoes to bite my lip.

"I'm leaving. I need to speak to Ra about a job I need her to do," I say, sighing and holding her at arm's length so she can stop trying to undress me. After Padrone's heart attack, I had been promoted to Dante's official second in command. I'm busier than usual, and with Dante's court case still pending, I'm picking up most of the slack.

Although Karlie is dead, Fonseca is still trying to pursue the case. Ilayda is pretty certain the District Attorney will drop it, he just needs a little *nudge* in the right direction. A nudge that would involve a briefcase of cash or a visit from a few men with bats, depending on how the District Attorney wants to play it.

"What job?" Anara asks curiously.

"I need to put a team together," I say, thinking of who would be my main go-to. Dante is supposed to do it, but we seem to have switched roles recently. Although he's busy with some of Padrone's duties, it was more of his other *activities* that I'm concerned about. There seems to be a permanent revolving door of women in Dante's bed and it's starting to affect his performance business-wise. Often bleary eyed and hungover, he isn't exactly setting the world on fire with his leadership skills. Not that Anara was my girlfriend or anything like that, but I confined myself to sleeping with her, and her only. I'm not committing to her or of that bullshit, but I'm happy with our arrangement. I would be even happier if Reign or Dante never find out.

"What about me?" Her eyebrow cocks in annoyance.

"It's a big job, Anara, I need someone experienced. Besides, you have *temperament* issues," I say, sniggering slightly.

"It was a one-time thing," she says, gritting her teeth as we reminisce back to the Raphael fiasco.

"I'm going with Ra and that's final. It's too dangerous for any amateur mistakes."

"I'm not a fucking amateur," she seethes.

"Drop it, Anara, because it's not happening."

She pushes me away and slams out of the room.

I exhale deeply, this situationship was getting out of control, but I can't find it in myself to end it. Well, I couldn't end it if I wanted to. She has become my drug of choice, dangerously addictive, and every time I have her I want another fix. My mind switches back to work and I reflect on the fact that payment seems to be a little short from our Bronx collections- the old Salvatore territory. It seems like one of our distributors has been skimming off money.

Not only that, but he's begun asking questions about our other warehouses and suppliers. In our world, you don't ask questions. Questions equal suspicions, and his questions had definitely riled mine. He's either an informant or working for someone else. Things had quieted on the threat front since the Salvatore peace treaty, but there is always someone else who wants to challenge the hierarchy.

My mind switches back to that night. So many things seemed to happen in one short period of time. Sapphire, Padrone, and Eleni. Anytime I mentioned her name in the past year to Dante, all I received was white hot laser death stares. In his distorted reality it didn't happen. She never existed, and if I persisted with talking about her then he would leave the room or change the subject rapidly. I know he hasn't forgotten about her, but he refuses to acknowledge it point blank. I pick up the phone to call the person Dante won't. I need my best on the street, and he was trained by me, so he's one of the fucking best.

"Ajax, I need you back in New York."

***

Nine Months Earlier

Ajax

"You're not going to sell Dante this hotel, are you?" I say, exasperated after the millionth meeting with Alessandro Da Costa.

He pauses for a second, looking sheepish. "I think there is something you should know."

"What?" I say, lighting a cigarette then changing my mind, remembering I am supposed to be quitting.

"She got to you then?" he says, smirking. "I would say my daughter is quite fixated with you, Ajax, considering the normal trash she likes. I have to say I like you considerably more."

"Well, thanks, I guess," I say, rolling my eyes.

I had started seeing Sophia shortly after my third month in Miami. After Eleni left, I was in no rush to go back to New York. I still feel an ache in my chest every time I think of her, wherever she was, I hoped she was happy. If she is with someone else, I pray they will give her everything I couldn't. Sophia pursued me for a while. I can wholeheartedly say I was not interested, but there was something about her I eventually found exhilarating. I learned behind the brattish Mafia princess persona, there is something much more alluring. I'm enjoying my stay in Miami, although I'm pretty sure Alessandro will never sell Dante this hotel.

"Before you even got on the plane to Miami, I told Dante point blank I wouldn't sell the hotel."

"What?"

"He told me to keep you here for a while and to keep you busy," he says sheepishly.

"Are you fucking kidding me?" I say angrily. "When were you fucking going to tell me?"

"I'm telling you now because I want you to stick around here. I think Sophia would like it if you stuck around too."

"What about New York?"

"Fuck New York. What is there anyway, apart from Dante? He doesn't seem to like you much."

Present Day

"I'm not going back to New York, Nic, no way," I say, speaking into the receiver. Sophia looks up at me, leaning on my chest, agreeing with what I'm saying.

"I need you, Ajax."

"Dante sent me here for nothing. Find someone else. I'm settled now."

"Ah, so you know about that. Well, that was then, and this is now. Dante gave you a job when you had nothing. Time to repay the loyalty."

"I've repaid it enough."

"I'll make you a captain; you know what that means. You'll be a made man in New York. Not many guys under thirty can say that."

"Fine," I say, exasperated, knowing I can't turn this down as I watch Sophia's face fall.

"Good man, I'll see you tonight at the compound. Dante and I look forward to your arrival."

I groan and hang up.

"What the fuck was that about?" she says, looking incensed.

"I can't say no to being a made man."

"What about me? Was I just something to keep you occupied? What about my father? He thinks you work for him."

"Your father will understand, after all I'm a Dischanel man. I could never be a captain of the Da Costa family it doesn't work like that."

"What about me?" she repeats again, and I can see the anger building up on her face.

"I'll be back for you, Soph, just be patient."

She gets up and walks into the bathroom, slamming the door.

I guess being understanding is not her strong

point.

***

Six Months Ago

Dante

"I don't like you watching me sleeping," he says, irritated.

"I'm not watching you, Dad," I say, rolling my eyes.

"You're checking if I'm still alive?"

"Seriously, Dad, shut up."

He coughs slightly and reaches for the water glass. His hands shake, spilling it everywhere, so I hold it steady for him.

"Just fucking shoot me now," he groans.

"Dad, you've had a heart attack and a stroke, you're lucky you're not dead."

He swears under his breath in Italian as he adjusts his IV drip.

The last six months have been a fucking whirlwind since that fateful night.

The way he dropped to the floor clutching his chest, I honestly thought I killed him. Everything seemed to freeze as time slowed down. Thankfully, he survived the heart attack, but not long after that he had suffered a stroke. He was slowly beginning to recuperate, but the doctors said it would be a long road to recovery, the problem being my father was not a patient man.

"Dante," he says slowly.

"Yeah, Dad."

"What happened to that girl…I'm sorry." He says it slowly. This is the first time we have properly acknowledged her since that day six months ago.

"It's fine, Dad," I reply mechanically.

"No, it isn't. I know you cared about her; I just didn't want you to get hurt—"

"Dad, just cut it out. It's fine."

"You punched me, Dante."

"I know, and I'm sorry, like I have said a thousand times."

"I deserved it."

"Probably." I smile at him and he smiles lopsidedly back.

"It's time for you to be Don now, properly."

"No, Dad, you will still make some of the decisions."

"We both know I can't. What kind of leader can I be if I can't even hold a fucking cup? No, Dante, it's your time to be the official head of the family with Nico as your Capo."

"Dad—"

"No arguments, this is your time."

"Okay," I say, swallowing hard. I am the Don, but everybody knows Dominic Dischanel is the head of the family. Now everything is changing.

"Make sure all the families know formally."

"Sure, Dad."

"And Dante?"

"Yeah."

"I'm truly sorry about the girl."

Before I have a chance to answer he has fallen

asleep.

Not as sorry as I am that I even met her.

That night had been a complete blur. I didn't get a chance to fully process her being gone until Dad had started to recover. At first the loss surged through me like poison. I wanted to find her, I wanted to bring her back home. But then it switched to anger. She left without saying a word. She should have *known*; she should have *known* me enough to believe that I would never want to be with Sapphire. She should have *known* I would never agree to my father offering her money to leave.

Finally, I had taken to blocking her out completely from my mind. Nico and Farook on occasions had attempted to speak about her, and in those situations I would either ignore them, walk out, or change the subject. That part of my life is *over*. She is a small blip on my landscape. Any feeling that I might have or thought I had for her is dead. It wasn't even a feeling; it was an infatuation, but most of all, it is *over*.

Present Day

Ring.

Groan.

Ring.

Fuck, my head is banging.

"Dante, you're fucking late. Where are you?" Nico's voice blasts through my ears.

"I'm in—traffic," I reply, lying.

"Sure, you are, get your fucking ass here now!"

Nico clicks off, knowing I'm not in traffic. My

eyes open, acclimatizing to the bright light. On either side of me there are two girls lying there naked, with two more sprawled out on the floor.

Last night was fucking wild, emphasis on the fucking.

In fact, every night is pretty much like this with interchangeable faces and names that were all forgotten once they walked out the door. I stand up. My head is pounding, and I can taste every sip of liquor I had last night. "I want you all gone by the time I come out of the shower," I say hoarsely, slapping one of the girls' asses.

I open the door, and my maid Rosa shakes her head when she sees me, which she has been doing a lot lately. I step in the shower, the heat deafening my thumping head. Ever since I knew my father would be okay; I had started to step into old habits. The old Dante had come out from the shadows and he had no intention of retiring. This way of living is much better for me, no feelings, just fucking, the way it was always meant to be. Spending my time partying kept my mind occupied so I didn't have to think about…things that I wanted to stay hidden in the enclave of my mind, buried deep in my subconscious. The things that only came out late at night in my darkest moments and made me ache all over again.

***

Eleni

France,   Spain,   Belgium,   Greece,   Turkey,

Dark Temptation

Cyprus, Switzerland.

Now I'm on the yellow sands of Mykonos sitting next to my mother, who keeps shooting furtive glances at me. I hadn't told her the whole story. Let's be honest, would she even believe me? When I looked back, everything seems to blur into a haze. Did any of it really even happen? Then I think of the familiar pang in my chest that I haven't been able to evade in God knows how long, and every feeling, touch, memory, and taste comes hurtling back to me.

I thought coming home would cure me, but it didn't. I've milled around Europe for months, trying to be normal, but it didn't seem to work for me. I feel like something is missing.

Late at night is the worst time for me, the times I remember Dante's body wrapped around mine, falling asleep in his arms, waking up beside him. All of that seemed to be a distant memory as I remember that he had his new life now, with his new child. My heart sinks in my chest when I realize the baby would have been born by now. I wonder whether it is his? Does it look like him? I don't want to think about him, but the more I try to suppress it, the more I can't get him out of my head.

"Eleni?" A voice jerks me out of my thoughts.

"Hm?" I reply back, still half distracted.

"Whatever it is you're running from, your head won't let you get away from it. *Go back to America.*"

Chapter Forty

Reality Check

Nico

Where is Dante? He needs to be here for this. For fuck's sake, he has to be acting really badly if I am the responsible one.

"Sebastian is ripping us off. He's diluting the product. If we start selling that shit on the street, we'll be in trouble. There won't be a fucking business. I know cocaine and that shit is not it."

"Let me talk to Dante and get back to you."

"Sweet," he says, walking off.

The door slams and Dante appears, yawning and showing us his multitude of hickeys without any hint of coyness. I feel Ajax's body tense next to me, realizing this is the first time they have seen each other since Dante sent him to Miami on a sham mission.

"Don," Ajax says in a curt voice.

426

"Ajax, looking good. Miami must have agreed with you," Dante says with a smirk.

"I look better than you, that's for sure, but I guess that isn't anything new. Nico let me know what we're doing next, so I can update Farook and Zeek." He walks out without acknowledging Dante and I see the familiar rise of anger in Dante for a second.

I guess some rivalries never die.

Dante

"It wouldn't hurt you not to be a jackass." Nico rolls his eyes and I ignore him. Dante Dischanel never forgets and Ajax and...*her* is not something I will let go of easily.

"Where would the fun be in that?" I reply, smirking at Nico's annoyance. "What did I miss?"

"Sebastian is definitely ripping us off, the question is why?"

"I think a little trip to our West Coast friends is in order. Maybe we need to lay down the law a little and remind them who the Dischanel family is."

"Do you even know what your name is after last night, Dante?"

"What is that supposed to mean?"

"Another all-nighter, Dante. Jesus, I thought I was bad, but you're going to be a candidate for a new liver soon if you don't take it easy, Hef."

"You're giving me morality advice? You. Wow, I've really heard it all now," I say, lighting a cigarette up. I catch my own eye in the mirror and am alarmed slightly at the tinge of grey to my skin.

"Exactly," Nico says knowingly, and I hate him for reading me so well.

"Shut up, let's head out to Los Angeles. You, me, Ajax, and Anara."

"Not Anara," Nico says mechanically.

Although I'm still half-drunk I know Nico has been hitting it for a long time and has conveniently forgotten to tell me. There are noticeable changes in his behavior, not enough for everyone to notice, only somebody who knows him well. He seems happier, although I do miss him as my wing man, and nights without him weren't quite as wild.

"Why not?" I say, staring at him blankly, waiting for him to conjure an excuse.

"Temperament issues," he says, rolling his eyes.

"Fine. Peyton."

"Peyton? The blonde? Yeah, we need someone hot in case we need a seduction mission, that's why I suggested Anara. She's got a great body, don't you think?"

"What do you mean by that?" he says sharply, and I hold in my laughter, seeing him get visibly annoyed.

"She's hot, what's the problem?"

"No problem at all, just…don't let Reign hear you say that."

"Right, yeah, he would definitely snap my legs in two."

"Yeah." I hear Nico swallow and his face pales.

Sucker, I think as I stare at him, contemplating what is worse, whether I thought Anara was hot or whether Reign snapping him in two would be more painful. Definitely the latter, having physical pain was much worse than anything else…something I knew *too well.*

***

Eleni

"Another day and you'll be ready to go home," I say to the young child in front of me as I insert her IV drip." She smiles at me shyly as I watch her eyes flicker before she falls asleep.

"You're a natural." I turn around and Noah is leaning on the doorframe, smiling at me as the bright Californian sunshine streams through the window.

I'm not ready to return back to New York, too many ghosts are still there. I can't face returning back to Dante's happy family life with Sapphire, California is close enough for me. *The past should remain in the past.* I need that Dante-shaped hole in my chest to heal, to finally move on.

"How's your day going so far?" Noah walks closer and flicks a strand of hair out of my eyes.

"Four cracked ribs and a drunk," I say, smiling at him.

"Interesting day."

"Interesting decade." I snort at him.

"Eleni, about what I asked you."

Uh-oh, I knew what was coming next. Noah had asked me out countless times, but I always reject him. I'm not ready for that, to give myself away so freely again. I like Noah and I enjoy spending time with him, but hesitation still edges between us.

"I'll wait however long you want me to, you're worth it."

"You're sweet, Noah, but I don't want you to waste your time on me. I'm a lost cause." I say it lightly, hoping he'll understand I don't think I'll be ready anytime soon. If ever.

"How does a wedding sound?"

"Wedding?" I stare at him blankly.

"One of my friends is getting married this weekend, seeing as I haven't found anyone suitable for that plus one, how about it?"

"Noah, that sounds awfully date-like."

"Hey, friends only. Just promise you won't try to take advantage of me at the free bar."

"As friends," I say slowly so he gets the message.

"Friends." He smirks and I know the message has gone in one ear and out of the other.

Friends with a handsome, smart doctor who is desperate to go out with you.

What the hell is wrong with you, Eleni? Why won't you let him get close to you?

But I already know the answer, those five little letters that still have a hold on me.

***

Ajax

"Oh, it's you," I say, looking at Dante coldly as he walks in.

"Yes, me, your boss. The one who could kill you

in the blink of an eye." He smiles back at me and I can see the dark shadows around his eyes. Clearly being a jackass and a man whore is his way of coping with Eleni's departure.

"We all know that Alessandro Da Costa controls the flow of weapons from Cuba all the way to Miami and LA."

"Yeah, so what?" Dante looks unimpressed. I want to break his jaw because he's not understanding what I'm saying. Saturday is Selene Da Costa's wedding."

"Alessandro's daughter is getting married? I can't remember if it was her I screwed or her sister?' Dante replies, snorting and sending my rage into overdrive.

"Definitely not her sister," I reply, gritting my teeth. Just because he took one woman from me, I definitely wouldn't let it be a habit.

"Yeah, so what's the big deal?"

"A Sicilian cannot refuse a request on the day of his daughter's wedding, so if you were to ask him for enough manpower to take on Sebastian..."

"He will have to honor it; in fact, it might be a good idea to get a permanent stake in the West Coast. Alessandro won't mind as long as he can wet his beak with some of the profits. Good plan, Batman, aren't you happy I sent you to Miami now?" He smirks and I smile back icily.

"All you need now is a date to the wedding, preferably someone you don't have to pay per hour."

"Unlike you, I don't have any problems in getting a date."

"So witty, Dante, they should have you doing movies."

"I already do *plenty* of movies," he says, smirking.

"Whatever," I reply, rolling my eyes and walking off.

***

Dante

I roll my eyes in irritation as Carmelo tries to put a line on the pretty blonde in front of him without any luck. Jesus, he is the ultimate jackass. I'm in a rush, but I will let this play out before I interject.

"Carmelo, you've used that line on four of us already this week. Seriously!"

"Because you're all so beautiful, *Gattina*."

"I'm bored, Carmelo, you may leave," she says pointedly, dismissing him.

"But—"

"Like she said, Carmelo, piss off." I cough, announcing my arrival, and Peyton's amber eyes fixate on me hungrily as Carmelo's narrow in anger.

"Dante, I'm a little busy here—"

"Carmelo, fuck off unless you want to see what life without kneecaps is like."

He shoots me a look of disdain and walks off. I focus my gaze back on Peyton.

"What can I do for you, Don?" She's done it smoothly enough, enunciating the words huskily while flicking her eyes up at me seductively.

"Did Nico mention anything to you?"

432

"Yeah, a job in Los Angeles."

"Things have changed, you'll be accompanying me to a wedding."

"Wedding?" It was like I fucking proposed. Her eyes light up and she smiles up at me with a wild look in her eyes.

"No," I say firmly, wanting to quash any ideas that were forming in her head.

"No what?" she says, ignoring me.

"No, don't get any ideas about anything else going on. This is business only."

"Then why not take Anara or Ra?" she replies smugly.

"Because I want a classy date, not one who will start a brawl."

"Fine, I will accompany you."

"It isn't a fucking choice," I snap at her; she is wearing down my patience quickly.

"Just make sure you do something about your appearance, you look like you haven't slept in a week."

"Whatever, make sure you look the part. Think classy, Peyton, not dollar store whore, and remember, this is not a date."

"Sure," she replies breathlessly.

"Not a date!" I shout at her as she walks off with a spring in her step.

This isn't going to end well.

***

Nico

"Why didn't you call me, Ra?" I walk in and Dre and Ra spring apart guiltily, clearly I'm not the only one in the team mixing business and pleasure.

"Call you?" she replies, looking at me, confused.

"I told Anara I was looking for you about a little team I'm putting together for a trip to L.A."

"I haven't even seen Anara, that's why I came here. She's supposed to collect from Slash, but she never turned up."

"She didn't?" I say slowly. Anara never missed payments, and I always send them out in pairs, especially when it's someone like Slash, whose name coincidentally rhymed with what he was, trash.

"She wouldn't go on her own, right?" Ra interjects my thoughts, looking alarmed.

"No way."

Unless she was trying to prove a point, that she was just as good or even better than Ra.

"Why so angry, little cousin?" Carmelo walks in and smiles at me.

"Have you seen Anara?" I say, trying to ignore the temptation to punch him.

"Yeah, she was here earlier."

"I thought you were taking her to the Bronx." I'm speaking through gritted teeth and I can feel my temperature rising dangerously.

"Oh that, I was in the middle of something with Peyton. I told her to be patient, but she stormed off. A little time out would be good for her spoiled ass anyway. She was acting like a real bitch."

Storm clouds seem to erupt on my horizon, and I see Dre and Ra look nervously at each other.

"Was that a bad call?" Carmelo says, taking in my stormy appearance.

"Very fucking bad."

Thump.

I punch him hard, knocking him clear out. Padrone would ride me about it later, but I don't care. I start dialing her number, willing her to answer, but it just keeps ringing…

***

Two days later

Anara

"Anara, I know you're awake." I squint and see Ra's shadowy figure in front of me.

I ignore her and concentrate on the pain working through every nerve in my body. What felt like a good idea in the heat of the moment turned out to be the worst fucking thing I had ever done. Not only had Slash completely beaten the hell out of me, but I had also not gotten paid and everybody knew what had happened. My reputation is shattered, and not even Reign can pull me out of the mess I caused. What scared me the most was the look in Slash's eyes. I can still see the piercing darkness and feel the hot heat of his breath on my neck. Who knows what he would have done if Nico and Dre hadn't busted in? Even though I was half out of consciousness, the rage in Nico's eyes still burns through me as if he were in this room. I'm about to lose him; I know it, and I feel my chest pang as a tear falls unashamedly down my cheek.

"Does it hurt, Anara? Should I call the doctor?" I feel her hand tap me tentatively.

"I just want to leave," I say, finally opening my eyes. I see the pity in hers and it makes everything a hundred times worse.

"He didn't—" she trails off.

"No, he just beat the crap out of me. No big deal."

"Everyone was really worried. Carmelo got a black eye for letting you go on your own."

"Who did that?"

"Nico."

"Really?"

"*Really*," she says, catching my eye meaningfully. "Maybe that isn't such a good idea, Anara, Nico is…Nico."

"I could say the same for you and Dre."

"I don't know what you're talking about," she replies. Her eyes narrow at me as if daring me to challenge her.

I won't, I've got enough shit to deal with and this is only the beginning.

Later on, I'm lying on the couch, flicking through channels, trying to get something to take my mind off the ache in my chest. The doorbell sounds and I ignore it. I'm not in the mood for company. It's probably Ra again with her sympathetic eyes. I don't need that. The doorbell dings again but this time the person doesn't take their finger of the buzzer.

"All right already." I hobble over to the door; my body aching more than ever.

I open the door and Nico almost flies through and pins me up against the wall.

"What the fuck were you playing at, Anara?" he hisses as his hands tighten around my neck, eyes ablaze in anger. He suddenly drops me, and I sink down the wall, trying to get my breath back.

"I wanted to prove to you that I'm not weak…that I am as good as Ra." I say in a small voice realizing how stupid I sound.

"You didn't want to look weak, so you almost got yourself killed? Do you know what men like Slash are like? Do you? Because it could have been a lot worse than a few broken ribs."

"I know I messed up. I'm sorry." I whisper the words, not wanting to catch his eyes.

"We're over, I'm done with your games. You deliberately put yourself in danger to spite me."

"I didn't mean to."

"Do you know what you put us through today? All of us? Do you even care? I thought you were dead, just like Zosha ended up dead."

"Nico, I'm sorry."

"I don't want you near me. If you see me at the warehouse or anywhere else, don't talk to me, don't look at me. We're through."

"Get out, then! Do what you do best and run away when it gets a little tough!" My own fury explodes, and I just want him as far away from me as possible.

He leaves, slamming the door, nearly taking it off the wall from the force he uses. I slink back to the couch, refusing to acknowledge what has even happened, burying it deep in the recesses of my mind.

***

Dante

"My father will end you."

"Not before I end you first, Daischel."

"There is no going back from this, you're a dead man."

"I'll take my chances." The gun cocks and Daischel stares him straight in the eye, unblinking.

"Start digging your grave, because after this my father will end you."

"I think the only grave that will need to be dug is yours."

Three shots rang out of Amaury Vasquez's gun straight into the chest of Daischel Dischanel. He was already dead before he hit the ground.

"Your father will be joining you soon, kid."

Gunshots approach and Amaury walks off, stepping over Dash and the pool of blood that now encompasses his body. Disappearing into the night, victorious.

"Dash?" I'm momentarily frozen by the sight in front of me.

I run over to him, pulling his head on my lap, willing him to wake up, but his eyes remain shut.

"Dash?" The words come out as a whisper as my heart begins to thump noisily in my chest.

"Dash, wake up." Panic now wells up inside of

me. This can't be happening.
"Dash!"

"Dante, wake up!"
"Dash?"
"Dante, you're having a nightmare."

My eyes open and my father is staring over me with his eyebrows creased in concern.

"What time is it?" I say groggily, my mouth feeling dry like the Sahara.

"Time for you to get a good night's sleep and stop partying so much," he replies, rolling his eyes and sitting next to me.

"I don't know what you're talking about."

"I'm worried about you, Dante. Why were you calling out Dash's name?"

"It's just a nightmare…I was reliving that night again. I haven't had it for a while."

"All the more reason for you to get your rest. It's time to be more Don material and less of a playboy."

"Can't I be both?" I smirk, looking for a reaction.

"No, you can't. All eyes are on you now I am officially retired unless you want me to come out of retirement?"

"No, Dad, I'm just kidding. I'll be in Los Angeles this weekend behaving myself."

"Since when have you ever behaved yourself?"

"Good point."

Four days later—Los Angeles

"As soon as Alessandro has finished Daddy duties, we move in," I say, pulling at the collar of my tux in irritation. The heat is stifling, and I am already getting irritated.

"You two should dance to blend in, I'll keep a lookout." Ajax smiles broadly at me and Peyton lights up beside him.

"I don't think that will be necessary," I say drily, watching two pink hues appear on Peyton's cheek.

"I'll be in the ladies if anybody notices I'm not here," she says before stalking off.

"Ouch. I think you upset her."

"Like I give a damn."

"What's the issue? She's hot and you sleep with anything these days."

"I prefer brunettes, Ajax, you of all people should know that."

"Well, you seem to prefer anything, by what I see you with at the club."

"What has it to do with you? When was the last time I saw you with a woman? Don't hate the player, hate the game."

"Do you ever wonder where Eleni is?"

"Do you ever wonder what it would be like to live life without the use of your legs, Ajax? Because if you ask me that again we'll test that theory." I can feel rage started to seep through me as Ajax's eyes narrow in irritation.

I wasn't going to talk about her to anyone, especially him.

"I'm going to get another drink."

"You do that," I say tonelessly.

Peyton walks back a couple of minutes later shooting me glacial looks, which pisses me off even more.

"Are you even going to compliment my outfit? Are you even going to acknowledge I'm here?"

"Peyton."

"Yes."

"Shut the fuck up and look pretty, that's all I need you to do. Like I told you, this isn't a date, so don't expect any of that crap."

"So, we're not even going to smash?" she asks, looking at me incredulously.

"No, Peyton, this is just business."

"Why have business without the pleasure?" she purrs, tracing her finger down my face.

"I don't touch any of the girls in the crew, Peyton," I reply irritably, pulling her hand off me.

That isn't what I heard is what she's thinking, but one look at my stony face tells her to drop it.

***

Eleni

"This is some wedding." I take in the lavish surroundings, even the flowers were embellished with Swarovski crystals.

"I'm looking at the best thing in this whole place," Noah says, looking straight into my eyes.

"Now you're just exaggerating." I laugh, trying to melt the tension away, but it was a little difficult as we were on the dancefloor, our bodies inches away from each other. Noah is giving me *that* look, and I know it will be hard to dissuade him from making a move on me. In fact, why am I so worried? A very sexy, smart doctor wants to date me, and this is what I'm worried about? I clearly have issues; he's perfect for me in so many ways, but there is something inside of me holding back.

"Who do you know, the bride or groom?" I ask as he spins me around, then pulls me closer.

"The groom."

"How do you know him?"

"Just through mutual friends."

I want to ask more, but he ends the conversation with such finality that I know the subject is closed. *Why is he being so evasive?* I have spent enough time with Dante to know when a man is lying to me; spent enough time amongst gangsters and mobsters to pick out the subtleties of understanding the context of body language and tone.

Am I being paranoid?

Noah has never given me any reason to doubt him before, maybe I am sabotaging this before it even began. I'm trying to hold onto Dante by keeping Noah at arm's length, but I won't do it anymore, and this time when he leans in to kiss me, I don't pull back.

Chapter Forty-One

Secrets

Ajax

"How many fucking people need to dance with the bride?" Dante says, lighting a cigarette with his usual scowl plastered on.

"Relax, Dante, Alessandro has already agreed to see us."

"Dante Dischanel, charming as ever."

My head whips around to that familiar voice and it's *her*. Sophia Da Costa, the girl I left behind, the girl who hadn't returned a single one of my calls since I had left Miami.

"Sophia."

"Ajax," she says coldly, barely meeting my eyes. "I guess some things never change, Dante."

"It ain't easy being sleazy."

"Alessandro is free, Dante," I cough politely, so he will get the hint and leave.

Dante looks at me, then at Sophia, and smiles.

"Oh, I see, a little *something something* went down in Miami. You want me to leave you alone so you can have some quality time together?"

I roll my eyes at him in annoyance, he has become even more insufferable than he was the last time.

"Fuck outta here with that bullshit, Ajax."

"Gladly, as long as it's away from you!" Sophia stalks off into the crowd and I feel myself deflate.

"Miss you too, sweetheart!" he shouts after her and smirks at me.

Relax, Ajax, don't break his jaw…at least not at Sophia's sister's wedding.

Later that night

"I guess it was worth suffering through that wedding, now we know Alessandro will back us."

We're at a bar in downtown Los Angeles for a meeting with Sebastian, somewhere busy so we don't draw too much attention to ourselves. Although we have Alessandro's backing, L.A isn't our turf, and we don't need any more trouble than what we already have going.

"Yeah, I guess spending all that time in Miami really worked out for you."

"Clearly it did. If you were banging Da Costa's daughter, you got something out of it. Are you still mad that I cock blocked you? Again." He snickers, looking at me for a reaction. Underneath all of this bullshit there is still tension between us, we will always share a history of Eleni. Although I'm not in love with her anymore, I still have a lot of affection toward Eleni, but that's where it stopped. Underneath all of Dante's bravado and promiscuity, he still loves her, I can see it in his eyes when I mention her. He's hurting, and no amount of strippers or alcohol can ever numb that longing. Her departure has impacted him, even though he will never admit it.

"Are you even listening to me, Ajax, or are you daydreaming about rainbows and fucking unicorns?"

"I know what I'm doing, Dante, shut your hole and get on with it," I snap and he stares at me for a second, deciding whether to start something or not, but Sebastian walks in and diverts his attention.

"Gentlemen, and a very beautiful lady," he says, eyeing Peyton with interest.

"Cut the crap, Sebastian, why the fuck are you ripping me off and why do you think you can get away with it?" Dante's voice is calm, but the tell-tale warning signs are there.

"I don't know what you're talking about," Sebastian replies tonelessly, but I can tell he's lying when his eyes swivel toward the exit.

"Stop lying, Sebastian, we can do this the easy way…" I interject. I want answers and I want this weekend to be over even more.

"Or we can do it the Dischanel way," Peyton cuts in, lifting her jacket a little to show the gun neatly tucked in her pocket.

"I have no hesitation in getting creative, trust me." Dante's voice drops, and the temperature plummets several degrees.

"We have the backing of Alessandro Da Costa,

that might loosen your tongue." I smile at him, watching the surprise pass through his face.

"You don't understand…he made me," he whispers, his face going grey.

"Who made you?" Dante replies.

"He'll kill me if I tell you."

"We'll kill you first. Start talking, Sebastian." Dante moves forward threateningly, revealing the silver gun in his waistband.

"He made me hike up the price…he wanted to lure you here."

"Who?' I'm genuinely confused now and I'm starting to have a bad feeling about this.

"Sebastian, you better start talking—"

"He's here!"

We all look around as gunshots explode into the bar. Sebastian takes four in the chest and drops to the floor.

It was a trap.

Eleni

One more hour to go.

I stifle a yawn, looking up at the clock. Night shifts on weekends are not a favorite of mine.

"How do you manage to look so good after a double night shift?" a familiar voice echoes from the doorway.

"I'm living off caffeine and adrenaline." I smile at him. Things have definitely shifted after the wedding, but when he asked to come up to my apartment that night, I said no. I wasn't ready for that. *Baby steps*.

"I have one more patient to see in the emergency room, then I'm done for the night," he replies, yawning. I can see the circles under his eyes.

"I'll see them. Leave, Noah, you look like you could do with the rest."

"Really?"

"Yeah, go to bed."

"Maybe you'll join me after you finish here?" he says hopefully.

"Maybe you could take a cold shower instead," I say, rolling my eyes.

"Touché. She's in room five. I'll call you later. You're a star, Eleni." He kisses me on the forehead and walks out.

***

Dante

"Do you think we should be out in the open like this?" Ajax looks around to make sure we haven't been followed.

"We need to get to Peyton before the cops arrive. They'll want a statement from her, and when they see her record it will arouse suspicion. We can't take the chance of anything leading back to us or Sebastian. Alessandro has sent a cleaning crew to the bar to eradicate any witnesses, but we still need to be careful."

"I wish we got a look at the shooter, at least we would have something to go on."

"It doesn't matter, it was all a trap. Whoever it

was lured us there for a reason. As soon as we pick up Peyton, we're on the Red Eye out of here."

"Why am I picking her up? She's your date."

"It will look suspicious if we both go."

"Then you go."

"You're such a bitch, Ajax."

"Enjoy your romantic reunion." He snorts and waits in the car while I enter the emergency department.

"Peyton Robinson," I say to one of the nurses. She blushes when she looks up from her screen and I smile back at her. I need to get out of here quick and turning on the charm would ensure that.

"She is currently with Dr. Valentine—oh, actually she's with Dr. Konstantinou. Are you a close relative?"

"I'm her brother, can I see her? I'm desperately worried about my little sister."

"She came in with a laceration gunshot wound to her shoulder, but she's stable now. She's in room one, sir, if you would like to see her."

"Thank you, Nurse."

"You're welcome." She winks at me and discreetly slips her number to me.

***

Eleni

"It's an artificial wound, it won't leave any damage," I say, stitching up the pretty blonde in front of me.

"Thank God for that, I'm way too pretty to be

scarred."

"If you don't mind me asking, how did you get shot? You know I have a duty to inform the authorities about this."

"Oh, it's nothing. Bar brawl. Two guys fighting over me, and it got a little rough."

"If someone is hurting you, I can help. There are shelters that can protect you from whoever you're trying to cover for."

"Shelter?" she replies, clearly startled.

"Yes, for domestic violence victims. I can put you in touch with them if you would like."

"Victim? I'm wearing Chanel, do I look like a freaking DV victim to you?"

"The offer's always there if you need it."

"That won't be necessary. My boyfriend will be here to pick me up."

There's a tap at the door, and she raises her eyebrow at me, as if to indicate that it's him.

I open the door and I feel a lightning bolt rip through me. Dante is leaning on the doorframe. My medical clipboard clatters to the floor as I see the shock in his eyes reflects mine. We stand there in stunned silence for a while before Peyton interjects.

"Finally, can we leave now?"

"This is your boyfriend?" I ask, shocked.

Dante is with this bimbo?

"Boyfriend? No fucking way."

"Who the hell is she?" Peyton asks, confused, looking between our expressions.

"Peyton, this is Eleni."

"*The* Eleni?" Peyton's jaw drops in apparent recognition.

I turn my head back toward Dante, and I can feel his emerald eyes burning into mine, taking every inch of me in. He's trying to mask his reaction, but it's too late. His eyes have already betrayed him. I clear my throat nervously, and the coldness of his reaction returns back.

"I'll wait for you outside, Peyton." He gives me one last chilling stare before walking out.

"So, you're the famous Eleni?" she says, appraising me.

"I wouldn't be so sure about the famous part."

"You're Dante's type. *Interesting*."

"I don't think Sapphire would like you saying that."

"Sapphire? Who cares about her? She's *dead*," she says, rolling her eyes.

"What?"

"She's dead." She repeats it to me as if I am slow.

"I don't understand. When I left she was pregnant—"

"Oh honey, you have been gone for a long time. Sapphire wasn't pregnant with Dante's baby, it was Lorenzo's. Sapphire was the snitch; she was the one feeding information to the Salvatores all along."

"It can't be," I whisper. My heart is thudding so hard I think I will pass out.

"It sure is. The Salvatores and Dischanels have reached a truce, and Padrone went into retirement after his stroke. Dante is officially the Don. Are you okay? You've gone really pale."

"I'm fine. Ask the nurse at the desk for a prescription and you're good to go."

She nods and walks out, leaving me reeling from the blow. I have to see Dante. I run down the hall, almost skidding. He's not there, and I'm about to walk back in when I see his familiar profile, and before I know it, I'm running toward him.

"Dante!"

His head swivels back but he turns back around and continues walking away.

"Dante—wait, please."

"What?" He turns back around and glares at me.

"Peyton just told me about Sapphire.. If I had known…I—"

"If you had bothered to ask instead of running away…if you actually trusted me. If you believed me when I told you I didn't want Sapphire. Are those the if's, buts, and maybes you're referring to? It's all irrelevant, we are *irrelevant*."

"I heard your father had a stroke, how is he?"

"He's fine," he replies gruffly. I can tell he is mollified that I even asked about Padrone.

"I know what he did, he shouldn't have offered you the money."

"I never would have taken it."

"I know."

"Do you still think about me?" I blurt it out before I could even think of the consequences.

"No, I don't. That part of my life is over." He says it so quickly that the response stings.

"Do you really mean that?"

"Yes, I'm glad you left. It allowed me to be the man I was always meant to be."

"Man? Or man whore? " I snort at him, watching him trying to front this out.

"What the fuck are you talking about?"

"That's your girlfriend in there? I always knew you had trash taste, but I thought you could do better." Jealousy pierces me and I don't know why.

"She's not my—"

"No, Dante," I reply, exasperated. I was getting caught up all over again. "I'm sorry, I shouldn't even be commenting on her, it's not my business. I should go."

"Eleni?" We both swivel around, and Noah is there waiting, with his eyebrow creased. "Aren't you going to introduce me to your *friend*?" I can sense the tone in that final word.

"Who is he?" Dante says in a clipped tone. I can see him taking in Noah's boy next door appearance and he isn't impressed.

"Noah, Dante, Dante, Noah. Dante Dischanel is an old friend from New York. We go way back...and Noah is my—"

"Boyfriend," Noah says smoothly, offering his hand to Dante. "Any friend of Eleni's is a friend of mine." Noah's blue eyes lock with Dante's as they shake hands, Noah winces slightly as his hands turn chalk white and Dante's nostrils flare in amusement.

"I have a flight to catch. Goodbye, Eleni," he says flatly before walking away.

It takes all my self-control not to stop him. This time it's him walking away from me, a sure sign that we are not meant to be. Two ships colliding in a storm.

"Eleni?"

"Hm?"

452

"Are you okay?"

"Yeah, just a little tired." I want to be alone and not explain any of this to him.

"How about we go for breakfast?"

"I'm actually a little tired, rain check?"

"Are you sure you're okay? Who was that guy?"

"Just somebody I used to know."

***

Sabrina

"Get up!" The corkscrew-haired woman takes out her gun and points at the chest of the now rousing police detective.

"Who are you?" he replies, looking both startled and disheveled.

"How rude of me not to introduce myself. Sabrina Salvatore."

"Salvatore?" he says slowly, his brain finally registering recognition. "As in Lorenzo Salvatore?"

"His wife actually, or widow. However you want to look at it."

"Get the fuck out of my house," he growls, reaching for his gun, but she cocks her pistol at him and he freezes.

"Not yet."

"What do you want crazy bitch?"

"Tsk tsk, manners don't cost a penny."

"What do you want?"

"I want you to drop all charges against Dante Dischanel." He snorts at her and she smiles back calmly, a little too calmly.

"Why would I do that? Are you out of your fucking mind?"

It was probably her marriage to Lorenzo that had pushed her over the edge. Losing him had definitely done something to her. They endured a passionately toxic love-hate relationship for so long that suddenly Sabrina didn't know how to cope with the Lorenzo-shaped hole in her life. It wasn't that she missed him or held deep affection for him—not anymore, anyway. It was more habit, and despite how fucked up they both were, he completed her. Cheating had been one thing but having a baby—something she had wanted so badly—with another woman had done something to her deep inside. It hurt her so deeply it was like a wound that could never heal.

"Dante Dischanel can't go to prison; I have bigger plans for him."

"Oh sure, let me just change the law to please some Mob wife."

"Like I said, I have plans for him. When he thinks he is the happiest he has been, when he thinks he is untouchable, that is when I will unleash fury on him." She smiles, a maniacal smile that sends a shiver down the detective's spine, and he wonders how sane this woman actually is.

"Let's go somewhere else to discuss this," he says slowly, if he can bring her out into the open. Then there would be more chance for him arrest her.

"I don't think so." She pulls the trigger at Aiden Fonseca. He is dead as soon as the bullet hit him square in the chest, his face still carrying the look of surprise.

"I bet you didn't see that coming." Sabrina smiles to herself, the first stage of her plan is coming into action. It is all coming together.

***

Bogotá, Colombia
Three Months Ago

"Jefe?"

"Que pasa?"

"The packs are ready to be sent to America."

"Good, and we're going with them."

"Jefe…I don't think it's such a good idea. You know what will happen if you go back."

"Rumor has it that Dominic Dischanel has retired. His son isn't as tenacious as him. I think it will work."

"Jefe, if you go back to New York, they will know."

"We won't go east; we'll go west and plan. We need to revive some of our old contacts. Call my son and tell him I'm coming home."

"Jefe…"

"*Muevete!* What are you waiting for?" the older man replies, looking visibly irritated.

"Jefe…Nacio is not your biggest fan. I think that conversation should wait for a while. He didn't take your fall from grace well, he lost everything when you did."

"He'll get over it."

"He said you are dead to him, leave him with his

books. The college boy was never cut out for this life."

"I'll wait until I'm settled, but I want my son by my side when I take back what is mine. I killed your brother, Dante, now I'm coming for you."

Chapter Forty-Two

Fire In The Water

Dante

Adrenaline fires through my body as I walk out of the hospital into the parking lot.

Did that actually just happen?

Eleni is here? All this time she has been a plane ride away. I'm surprised, but even more surprised that her boyfriend is a weedy little jackass whose hand I nearly crushed.

"How's Peyton doing?" Ajax's voice distracts me from my thoughts.

"She'll be out in a minute; I want to get out of this city as soon as possible," I say, lighting a cigarette. I'm starting to feel claustrophobic. I want to be back in New York, away from every thought that is beginning to seep into my consciousness.

"What's wrong, Dante?" Ajax replies slowly, his eyebrow is creased.

"Eleni works at this hospital." I don't even know

457

why I told him, I just needed to say it to someone. *Anyone.*

"No fucking way. Are you serious?"

"As a heart attack."

"Did she say anything to you?"

"Nothing that I'm interested in."

"Is she coming back to New York?"

"For what?" I snort. "There is nothing there for her anymore."

"Maybe you should go back and talk to her properly. I'm sure there are a lot of things you want to say to her, Dante."

"Drop the subject, it's over. I just want to get out of this city."

"I'm making a detour before I go home."

"Why?" I ask sharply.

"I need to make a stop in Miami before I go back to New York."

"She must really have you pussy whipped if you're flying five hours to hit it."

"Shut up, it's not like that."

"Sure, you're just flying there for air miles." I smirk and watch his cheeks flush.

"I'll be back in New York by tomorrow."

"You better be. I don't care how much you want to get laid."

Ajax hails a cab and I watch him disappear as I smoke my third cigarette in less than ten minutes, waiting for my legs to carry me away from this hospital, but they don't seem to want to move.

***

Dark Temptation

Anara

"Are you actually going to move or what?"

"Is not an option?"

"Anara, you're going to work today."

"I'm still sick."

"Sick or *lovesick*?"

"I don't know what you're talking about."

"Stop feeling sorry for yourself because you got dumped. Everyone knows you two were a thing, they put two and two together after Nico nearly broke Carmelo's jaw."

"Is nothing private anymore?"

"Not when you're sleeping with the underboss, no, it isn't. You're not the first and you won't be the last to have their heart broken by Nico Dischanel."

"Thanks, Ra, I feel so much better now," I snort, trying to push back down the tears that are threatening to form.

"You'll be over it in no time." She smiles at me and I ignore her.

If you only knew.

"You're going to the warehouse today."

"I'm fucking not, no way."

"Nico isn't there, he's at La Guardia picking up Dante and Ajax. I wonder how the wedding went?"

"Probably went out with a bang, knowing Peyton."

"Do you really think she slept with Dante?"

"Really, Ra? Of course, she did, Dante is straight hoeing these days."

We both laugh and for a second I forget that painful twinge in my chest.

"Talking of…you're looking very smiley these days, Ra.' Now it's her turn to be put on the spot and a look of awkwardness passes her face before she brushes it off.

"I don't know what you're talking about."

"Sure, you don't." I pretend as if I don't know she and Dre have been seeing each other for months.

"Be at the warehouse in an hour. If you're not, I'll drag you there." She slams out and leaves me sitting there alone.

I stand up and stare at myself in the mirror. I hadn't changed. Not really. The bruising has gone down, and I feel less sore. I concentrated on my midriff, looking for a tell-tale sign, but nothing. It was all so new; it's been three days since I discovered I am pregnant. I took a dozen pregnancy tests, praying it was a false positive, but it wasn't. I went for my first scan yesterday and after hearing the heartbeat, I knew I want to have this baby, more than anything. I never thought I wanted a baby but holding that scan in my hand made me re-evaluate everything. This is my priority now; nobody knows and that is how I'm going to keep it until I figure out a plan.

"Pick up those boxes, will you?"

"You've got arms, you fucking do it."

"How about I give you a black eye to match the last one I gave you, Diezel?"

"You've got a fucking screw loose, Anara."

"I know it, and I love it, now move the fucking boxes."

"No wonder Nico binned you, you're a fucking

headcase."

I picked up the box cutter and threw it at him. It narrowly missed his ear and he stormed off, slamming the door.

He really hit a nerve; I will get in big trouble for reacting like that, but I don't care. I just want to get out of here. Every moment I'm in the warehouse is a reminder of Nico. I didn't realize how much of a process losing him would be. I physically feel like I am aching for him. Sometimes I wake up in the middle of the night and the pain is almost too much to bear. It is like grieving for someone, but he's still alive. I look around at the boxes of ammunition that need to be sorted and I think fuck it, I want to be out of here. I turn around to pick up my jacket and see smoke billowing under the door frame.

"Help! Diezel! Anyone!" The fire alarm goes off and I try to go through the door, but it's too late. The doors have an auto lock program when the fire alarm is activated. The smoke has become dark clouds of black as I push myself against the wall, trying to breathe, but it's too late, and I feel myself sidling down the wall. An explosion rips through the building, but *I'm already unconscious.*

***

Eleni

"Are you okay, Eleni?" Noah cuts through my thoughts.

"Yeah, I'm fine." I try to smile at him, but I can't seem to make it convincing.

461

Dante sits invisibly between us. He rolls his eyes when Noah makes a joke. He scowls when Noah places his hand on mine, and he winks at me when I pull away from Noah's touch.

Even though Dante is long gone, his presence still remains.

"Who was that guy from the hospital?"

"Just somebody from the past, seeing him again just threw me off. I'm fine, really."

"Are you sure that he's from the past?" His voice is light, but I can feel the subtext in his tone.

"He's nobody, Noah, just an old friend from the past. He's left the city now, so I'm not even thinking about him now."

We drive back to the apartment, my mouth goes on autopilot, trying to pretend that I'm okay inside, when the only thing I want is to be on my own, to deconstruct everything. We pull up outside and Noah turns my face toward him and kisses me hard, passionately. The kind of kiss that should make me quiver inside, but it doesn't. I try to close my eyes, but it's no use. I'm just going through the motions.

"Thanks for breakfast, Noah, I'm sorry if I'm a bit off today," I say, breaking the kiss.

"Are you sure I don't have anything to worry about with Dante?" He holds my gaze, and I don't look away.

"No, he's history."

"In that case…" he says, curling a tendril of my hair around his finger, "why don't I come upstairs?"

"Not yet, Noah, rain check?"

"Sure." I see a flicker of annoyance pass his face but when I look again his expression is impassive.'

I leave the car after another passionless kiss with Noah and head upstairs; my head is pounding from the twelve hour shift I have put in, and the ghost of Dante that stays on my mind. I put the key in the lock and feel relieved that I am finally on my own in my own space. Stripping everything off, I step into the shower, the heat melting away the building tension. I was doing fine since I saw him, I was moving on, and everything seemed to be moving along nicely. Now, I'm back to where I was when I left New York. The toxic cloud of Dante is now filling every part of my psyche. I need to try to make this work with Noah; he's a good man. The type of guy that most girls would want to be with, so what the hell is wrong with me? I hear the doorbell ring, was that Noah? I'm not expecting anyone else. I trudge out of the shower, wrapping a towel around me, and yank open the door to the familiar face in front of me.

"Hello, Eleni."

***

Dante

"What do you mean I can't come back to New York?" I'm about to pull up to the airport when Nico's call comes through.

"There has been an explosion at one of the warehouses. I want you to stay out of the city in case something else is planned."

"You're right, it could be a trap."

"I'm sending a private plane to pick you up

tomorrow; I'm not taking any chances on a commercial flight. Where are you going to stay tonight?"

"I'll figure it out, it looks like we're going to the mattresses. I want everyone prepared because it looks like a war is coming."

"Done, where are Ajax and Peyton?"

"I put Peyton on the earlier flight, I couldn't bear to spend any more fucking time with her. Ajax went to Miami, long story. Any major casualties?"

"Anara was in the warehouse at the time, I'm waiting for Chang to update me." He says it in a clipped tone, but I can tell he's distracted.

"Keep me posted about everything, I'll see you tomorrow."

"Call me tomorrow from a payphone, and I'll give you the details of where I'm sending the plane."

He clicks off, and I wonder where the fuck I'm going to stay tonight. I don't want to check into a hotel. Too many people would have access to me, and I'm alone in a city where I don't have the muscle to protect myself. I made a quick call to Zeek to find the location of one of the few people I could depend on, hoping she wouldn't slam the door in my face when she saw me again.

***

Nico

"I told Dante not to come back tonight."

"Good, we can't risk it. Someone is playing a

dangerous game."

"But who?"

"Good fucking point, surely not the Salvatores? The worrying thing is if it isn't them, then there is someone else who wants us dead."

I light up a cigarette, my mind ticking like a clock, trying to think of every angle that this mystery assassin is coming at us with.

"Nico, you can't smoke in here, it's a fucking hospital."

"Sue me," I reply irritably. "Maybe I should leave you here to speak to Chang."

"Like you have anything better to do, the strip club isn't open yet."

"I do other things."

"Like what? One night without sex isn't going to kill you."

"Are you a doctor?"

Chang walks in, interrupting our little tête-à-tête. I look at his face, searching for a tell on Anara's condition. I think back to getting the call from Diezel, and my chest sinking when I found out she had been caught in the explosion. I hadn't seen her for weeks, I purposely made sure I was never around when she was. I had moved on and didn't need any reminders of her. I was almost back to myself. A different girl in my bed every night with the last one's name being firmly forgotten by the time I kicked them out.

"How is she, Chang?"

"A lot of bruising from the impact of this explosion, and she is pretty beaten up from the last one too. The smoke inhalation hasn't damaged her lungs too much, the good news is the baby is fine."

There is radio silence when Farook and I look at each other stunned, wondering what baby he is referring to. "What baby?" I say slowly. I can feel an uncomfortable feeling beginning to build up.

"Anara is three months' pregnant; you didn't know?" Chang asks, creasing his eyebrows.

"No," I say hoarsely as Farook shakes his head.

"Any idea who the father is? Anara could really do with someone to look after her once she's discharged."

"No, we'll take care of it," I say quickly.

"Right." Chang shoots me a curious look and walks off.

"Nic?"

"What?" I turn around to face Farook, and he's looking at me quizzically.

"It's yours, isn't it?"

"No."

"Nico." Farook sighs in exasperation and I avoid his glance. "Dante and I have known for a while about you two. Is it yours?"

"Maybe, I don't know. There could have been someone else."

"You think you weren't enough man for her that she had another guy to supplement her needs?" he says, his eyebrow cocked in amusement.

"I don't know, Farook, is this a fucking inquisition?"

"Do you really think she was sleeping with someone else?"

"Fuck no, but how did this happen?" I run my hands through my hair, trying to work this through my head.

"Do you want a fucking diagram?"

"I was careful."

"Always?"

"Well…most of the time. Fuck, I'm screwed."

"It's kind of poetic, you screwed her, now she's going to screw you for life."

"Fuck you, Farook."

"Reign is going to kill you when he finds out."

"You're really not improving the situation."

"You need to speak to her, figure out what you're going to do."

"Or you could speak to her for me."

"Time to man up, Nico, you're going to be a *father* now."

And with those words, I crumble a little inside, as for the first time in my life I don't know what I'm going to do next.

***

Eleni

"Don't look pleased to see me or anything." He smirks as his eyes take in my partially covered form.

"What are you doing here? How do you even know where I live?"

"How about you let me in, and I'll fill you in."

I reluctantly let him in past me, the familiar smell of nicotine and Bleu de Chanel engulfs my senses.

"What do you want, Dante?" I say stiffly. So

much for getting him out of my head when he's less than two feet away from me.

"A little unfriendly of you, Eleni."

"How did you find me?"

"I think you're forgetting who I am, it wasn't that hard."

"I know exactly who you are, Dante, don't let the door hit you on the way out."

"Wait, let me explain." The smirk drops off his face and I can see his face tense.

"What's wrong?"

"What do you mean?"

"You're worried about something, what is it?"

"How do you know I'm worried about something?"

"I think you're forgetting who I am," I mimic him, and he snorts.

"There was an explosion in New York. I was due to come back tonight but I can't risk walking into a trap, nor can I risk checking into a hotel, so…"

"And you couldn't tell me this over the phone?"

"Would you pick up?"

"Probably not."

"Is anyone hurt?" I say worriedly.

"Not majorly. Can I stay with you tonight?" A nervous shiver erupts down my spine when those words come out.

"I guess so. Do I have any choice? You're pretty much inside already."

"I'm forever indebted to you." He smiles at me and I feel a million butterflies take flight.

"I'm going to get dressed, then I'll bring you a comforter and pillows. You'll be on the couch.' I say this pointedly in case there were any doubts on where he would be sleeping.

"You don't have anything I haven't seen before, Eleni."

"That was then, this is now," I say, walking away and closing the door behind me.

My heart is thumping hard in my chest as I stand behind the door. On reflection of myself in the mirror I can see that I look a flushing mess. My cheeks have two spots of color and my eyes look wild. I need to compose myself. I walk into my wardrobe to find the most unflattering nightwear that covers every inch of me.

"I didn't know you were a Dodgers fan."

I turn around and Dante is eyeing the huge Jersey I am about to put on. "Dante, get out!"

"No." He walks toward me, his face strangely expressionless as he moves inches away from me.

"What do you want?" My voice comes out barely as a whisper as I back myself up, the mirror behind me.

"Why did you leave New York?"

"What? Dante, that was a long time ago—"

"Tell me why? I need to know. I have to know!"

"The past is in the past, Dante, let it go."

"I can't let it go when it is standing in front of me."

"I left because of Sapphire; I didn't want to be second best to her. Can we drop it now?"

"That's bullshit, and you know it." His eyes lock with mine, he can see through me so easily.

"Why didn't homeboy stay the night?"

"Huh? You were spying on me?" I look at him,

incredulous, but he doesn't even look ashamed.

"No, I was waiting for you to come home. Don't flatter yourself. You never answered the question. Why didn't he stay the night?"

"Not everything is about sex, Dante," I reply irritably.

"Wait." Comprehension finally dawns on him and his face lights up. "You mean you and he haven't—"

"Dante, I'm warning you shut up!" I feel visibly flustered.

"Why haven't you slept with him? I'm curious now." I look away, but his gaze is electric, pulling me in.

"Because I haven't. Just because you can't keep it in your pants doesn't mean everyone else can't."

"I don't seem to remember you complaining, Eleni."

"Just shut up and go to sleep, Dante." I pick up the comforter and pillows and push them into his arms as I walk past him, but he pulls on my arm and brings me toward him.

"You don't want him because you still want me."

"No!"

"Then look me in the eyes and say that." He drops the comforter out of his hand and pulls my arms up above my head, so I have no choice but to look at him.

"Tell me you want me, Eleni, I don't want to be alone tonight." His mouth is inches away from mine and I can see the moisture on his lips.

"Dante." I moan out his name slowly as his

mouth finds the curve of my neck.

"Tell me you want me...because I want you too." A spark of electricity runs through my body when he says those words and I feel myself light up.

"I want you, Dante." I say it loud and clear, my heart rate accelerating like crazy as his mouth finds mine and I feel like a desert that has finally found an oasis.

"Let's say goodbye properly this time." He leans his head against mine and everything I ever tried to suppress comes flowing back to me as I nod at him slowly in agreement.

He unfurls the knot in my towel. As it drops to the ground and I'm naked under his touch, his mouth moves down to my breast, hungrily sucking. I start to unbutton his shirt, wanting to feel his skin on mine. Wanting to taste him in every way. He pulls me up by my legs, so I'm tightly woven around him as his mouth moves back up to meet mine, my hands running through his dark, thick locks again as he walks me to my bed and lays me down flat with him on top of me. We don't say anything for a second. I know he's thinking of the first time we were together because so am I, how much has changed since then. How much we have changed since then. Our lives have taken us in different directions, and I know after tonight I won't see him again, this is a clean break. Something purely physical that we both need to conclude our epic story. His green eyes stay fixated on me as his body moves against mine in lithe expertise. He knows me too well; he knows every part of me. His kisses and touch sweep across my body like a tide and I brace myself for the storm of Dante Dischanel for the last time.

***

Dante

I watch her as she sleeps peacefully, her black hair splayed over the pillow like a halo. The sun will be rising soon, and I want to be gone before she wakes up, but I can't find it in myself to leave just yet. I did everything I could to forget you, to get rid of your mark, your touch, but I can't. You're still a part of me like an invisible tattoo. I'm trying to convince myself that it's just another one-nighter, but it could never be that with you. This is meant to be closure, but how can it be closure when I can't seem to let go? This is meant to be goodbye, but it is proving a lot harder than I expected.

***

Rage builds up inside of me as Dante walks out of the apartment the following morning. I feel ice flood my insides. His clothes are crumpled, and his shirt buttons clumsily fastened, which gives me no illusion to what he was doing last night. Betrayal seems to flow through me like venom.

This isn't over by a long shot.

***

Nico

I had been standing here for twenty minutes, trying to figure out what to do next, what to even say next. Farook had left me here to 'man up,' and all that entailed so far was sitting next to Anara's bedside thinking of what to say next. I'm not like Dominic or Farook, I can't be someone's father, I don't know how to be responsible. Hell, I can't even be faithful. Anara definitely pushed all of my buttons and I winced slightly, thinking how I acted the last time I saw her, and how forcefully I had thrown her against the wall. What kind of man am I? Anara deserves a lot better than the little I can offer her. Her eyes flicker but then quickly close.

"Anara, I know you're awake, Chang told me you're conscious…why didn't you tell me?"

"Go away, I don't need you. I can take care of myself," she mutters, her eyes remaining shut.

"You don't need to; we can work out our options together."

"Options?" Her eyes snap open. "Do you think I'm going to get rid of my child to please you? Get lost, Nico, I mean it!" She tries to lift her body up but lays back down.

"I never said that, Anara, I just mean we can work out—"

"There is no we, it's just me and my baby. Get out, Nico, I don't need you, and I never did."

"Anara, that is not what I meant—"

"Get out!" She screams so loudly that her voice begins to shake. Chang comes running and indicates for me to leave.

I look at her again, trying to find the right words to salvage the situation, but they never come, two lines of tears roll down her cheeks, and hot shame begins to fill me.

***

"You putas better hurry up filling those packets." Esteban wipes his forehead, this city heat is killing him. He hates the brightness of LA., he longs to be in the nitty gritty streets of New York.

"What's the hold up?" Virgil walks in, eyeing the women in lingerie filling up the packets of cocaine.

"Five minutes."

"Good, I have a date later. I love this city—all the women here with their fake asses and tits. *Bellissima!*"

"You're not Italian, asshole, and I hate this fucking place with a passion. When are we going back to New York? I would rather be back in the Colombian wilderness than here."

"It doesn't look like we'll be going back any time soon, that idiot Sebastian shot the wrong person. Dischanel will be in hiding for now."

"Guess we'll have to keep blowing up his warehouses until we bring him out into the open."

There is a knock on the door and both Esteban and Virgil reach for their guns. Nobody knows about this place apart from them and Jefe. Had Dischanel found out their location?

"Show yourself." Esteban points the gun at the door, ready to blow off whoever's head that is waiting on the other side.

"I hope you know what you're doing with that gun," a clipped voice replies, and Esteban lowers his gun in shock, knowing whose voice that belonged to.

"What are you doing here, Ese?" Virgil snorts as a hooded figure walks through the door.

"I thought the college boy was too good for this life." Virgil puts his weapon back, smiling at the youth in front of him.

"That isn't for you to decide," he replies pointedly, his blue eyes narrowing coldly.

"You don't belong in this world, go back to the library, kid."

"I want to see my father."

Esteban shrugs and takes him upstairs; it is up to Jefe to decide what to do with his wayward son.

Nacio pushes the door open, his father has his back to him, staring through the window. It is coming up to mid-morning. The bright sun is beaming through, illuminating the dark, decrepit room.

"I thought I could hear your voice, what do you want?"

"I want to talk to you."

"I have nothing to say to you, you are no son of mine." He doesn't turn around to say it, the iciness of his voice enough to end the conversation.

"What if I have something to change your mind? What if I tell you I know where Dante Dischanel is right now?"

"I already know where he is. New York."

"No, he's in Los Angeles. He isn't back in New

York—not yet anyway—and if you act quickly, he might not ever make it back."

"How do you know that?" Amaury turns around to face his younger son, his eyes carrying a maniacal excitement.

"I have a mutual friend who knows him."

"Who?"

"Never you mind. Look at this as a peace offering. I'm ready to be your son again."

"Kill him first and then we'll discuss whether you can be my son again."

"Not yet, I want to make him *suffer* first."

***

Eleni

I wake up alone, sunshine streaming through the blinds. I knew Dante wouldn't be here when I woke up, I guess that was the whole point of last night. Parting on good terms, *very good* terms. I ashamedly roll onto the other side of the bed and inhale his scent. Last night doesn't feel like it's supposed to, in fact it made it even harder for me to let go. Even though so much time has passed, he has a pull on me. Nobody else can ever captivate me the way Dante Dischanel does. I pull myself out of bed, putting my hair up with an elastic band and grab a sweater. I feel a little pang in my chest as I think of Noah. How can I explain this to him? *Sorry, I slept with my old flame despite me telling you there was nothing for you to worry about, but hey, it's nothing to stress about, as I probably won't see him again as he is an international Mafia boss.* Perfect, I'm sure he'd be happy with that explanation. I realize that after this there is no way I can be with Noah, not when I'm still in love with somebody else. I know it will never work out with Dante, but it's unfair to string Noah along. I pause as I hear a rustling sound. I am alone, right?

"Hello?" I call out. Surely I'm being paranoid, but the noise keeps getting louder.

I walk toward the apartment door, as the noise is coming from the other side, and yanked it open—but there is nothing outside. Did I really just imagine that? I turn to walk back in but the next thing I see is darkness as a chloroform-soaked napkin was pushed over my mouth, I struggled for what felt like hours before I fell to the floor, unconscious.

***

Dante

"I have a car rented under David De Luca," I tell the blonde behind the counter, handing over the fake driving license.

"That seems all in order, Mr. De Luca." She hands over the keys and smiles flirtatiously at me.

I am heavily distracted as I drive to LAX, part of me is thinking about the million and one things I have to do when I get to New York, and the other half of me doesn't want to leave last night behind. My phone trills, probably Nico wondering what time I'm coming back,

"Yeah."

"It's been a long time, Dischanel."

"Who is this?" My blood runs cold, that voice is so *familiar*.

"I thought you would recognize my voice, Dante; it was the last voice your brother heard before I killed him." He laughs softly, waiting for my response.

"Vasquez."

"In the flesh."

"You are behind all of this, Sebastian and the explosion?"

"Look at it as me trying to get your attention."

"You have it now, and when I find you, you're going to regret not staying hidden in whatever shit hole corner of the earth you were."

"I'm cowering in my boots, Dante; however, I'll be calling the shots."

"What gave you that fucking idea?" I'm gripping the steering wheel so tightly I think I might rip it off as rage and adrenaline course through me.

"Because that pretty thing you were knocking boots with last night…I've got her with me."

"You're lying," I say through gritted teeth, even though I'm sure he isn't. Amaury Vasquez is not one for bluffing.

"You know I'm not, Dante, I don't have to."

"If you touch her…"

"You'll what? Put the phone down on me? Her life for your life. I'll be in touch with the directions once you've had some time to think about it."

The phone clicks off and I call Nico hurriedly, but there is no response. I have to call the one other person I know I could grudgingly depend on.

"Ajax?"

"Yeah?"

"Where are you?"

"Waiting for a flight back to New York. I had to change at San Diego, some bullshit baggage handler strike or something."

"Vasquez has Eleni."

"What? As in *the* Vasquez."

"Get to Los Angeles now and get a trace on the number that called me. That is where I will be."

"Dante, wait—"

But I hang up and do a U-turn, causing honks and horns from a multitude of other drivers until I am off the freeway and back into the City of Angels, where I would meet my fate.

Chapter Forty-Three

Unfinished Business

Eleni

"Rise and shine." A voice comes out of the darkness, it's so distorted that I can barely make it out. I try to move, but my hands and feet are tied up. I can't see anything and there is a gag in my mouth, making it hard to breathe.

"Help me," I say in a muffled voice, but the voice just laughs. He pulls the gag out of my mouth and the blindfold from my eyes, and I gasp.

"Noah!"

"Surprise." He's smiling at me but not his usual smile, his eyes sparkle with malice.

"Noah...I don't understand."

"You will soon...so many questions."

"Who are you?" I say as chills begin to work their way down my spine. I realize I am only wearing a sweater over my bare body, something that hadn't skipped Noah's attention. His eyes drink every pore of me in.

"What am I doing here? I don't remember anything." My mind feels blank and I'm struggling to put a coherent thought together.

"Let's just say you are my guest, waiting for another famous name to make their appearance."

"What are you talking about? How did I get here?" I'm struggling against the ropes, but I know it's hopeless. I'm trapped.

"My men brought you here."

"Your men?" I say slowly, the ramifications of that sentence beginning to settle.

"My men," he says, smiling at me.

"Who are you?"

"My name is Ignacio Vasquez, son of Amaury Vasquez. Heir to the Vasquez cartel."

"Cartel? As in *drug cartel*?" I ask, horrified.

"*Ding, ding, ding,* Eleni. Somebody is a clever girl."

"You've been pretending to be someone else this whole time." I say, horrified. The last couple of months were all a huge lie. I had run away from one dangerous situation into another with somebody much worse.

"I didn't pretend, Eleni; I was trying to be someone I'm not. You can relate to that, right? Like when you said Dante was somebody from your past, but it didn't look like that when he walked out of your apartment this morning."

"You were spying on me?" I ask, half affronted, half horrified.

"Don't flatter yourself, you were part of a much bigger picture."

"Like what?" I snort at him, trying to act like he was some kind of visionary.

"My father was Consigliere of the Dischanel family a long time ago. When he wanted to break away and start his own family, Dominic refused. The hard-headed bastard thought he could stop him, even though my father was more superior than him in every way. A war started between my father's faction and the Dischanel family. It ended when my father shot his rival's heir."

"His heir?" My mind immediately went to Dante, but he was still alive…

"Are the pieces coming together, Eleni?"

"He killed Dante's brother."

"A move he would end up paying dearly for. The rest of the New York families sided with Dominic and he was run out of New York with a huge bounty on his head. My family were disgraced and forced to flee back to Colombia. I stayed. I was furious with my father. My life had been ruined by something I didn't even want to be a part of. Nacio Vasquez became Noah Valentine. I worked hard, went to college and medical school to save lives. I tried to be the nice guy and I ended up falling in love, and we know how that ended up, Eleni."

"We were barely dating, Noah, don't put this on me."

"We could have been happy if you didn't act like such a slut. Dischanel was in your bed when you were telling me you weren't ready. Such bullshit, Eleni, but I guess I have to thank you. If it weren't for your actions it wouldn't have put me back on track. Back to the man I was meant to be."

"No.."

"Yes, as soon as I saw him at the hospital I recognized him. I knew what I had to do; it was burning inside of me like a blazing inferno. My father killed one Dischanel, now I'm about to kill the other. The Dischanel line ends tonight."

"You can't touch him, he's in New York far away from you," I spit at him, rage burning inside of me.

"He's on his way here now, Eleni, when Dante heard we had you he was beside himself with rage. I guess it's true love after all, so sad that neither of you will get to have a happily ever after."

"He won't come without backup."

"Au contraire, Eleni, that is part of the terms. He comes alone."

"What terms?"

"His life for yours."

"No! He can't do that."

"You're not really in a position to dispute that, Eleni, and if you even try, I will shoot you dead."

***

Nico

"Ajax, what is your location?"

"I've just come out of the airport, send me the address."

"Done. Do you think you and Dante can handle this alone?"

"Well, I haven't got much fucking choice. Why didn't Dante speak to us first before he did this?"

"Because it's Vasquez, and sometimes you can't control your emotions when it comes to deep shit like that."

"Alessandro is sending men there as we speak; I hope it's not too late."

"Me too." I clicked off, feeling a weight on my chest.

"Anything?" Dominic asks, his face drawn.

"Nothing, radio silence from Dante."

"Dante doesn't want Amaury to know that we are aware of this, that is the only conclusion I will allow myself to make."

"We have a location on Amaury."

"Yeah, Farook has sent it through to Ajax."

"At least Ajax is in shooting distance, that is our only saving grace."

"So, the girl is back?"

"Yeah, Dante was a little vague in the voicemail, but it seems like Eleni was working at the hospital when they took Peyton to after the attack."

"Are you pissed that Dante has risked it all again for her?"

"Sometimes it's better to fight for something than to have nothing."

"Didn't you try to pay her to leave? I'm a little confused by your one-eighty, Padrone."

"I thought if she left Dante would become a leader, but I was wrong, he has become a complete train wreck. I know Dante, inside he's unhappy, it's his way of acting out. Maybe I was selfish thinking he couldn't lead this family with her as a distraction, what is meant to be will find its way."

"Well, that isn't confusing, Padrone."

"What about you, Nico? Will you be settling down or is that a stupid question?"

"You son of a bitch! You knocked up my sister!" Reign comes thundering through the penthouse doors with Farook and Zeek behind him, who clearly failed at holding him back.

"I'm going to fucking snap you in half, Nico!" He lunges toward me, but Padrone steps in front of me, despite Padrone being twice Reign's age he manages to hold him back.

"I will deal with this Reign, go."

"My fucking sister!" Reign screams at me as Padrone pushes him back.

"Reign, cool down, that is a direct order."

"This isn't over!" Reign turns around and walks out with Zeek and Farook running after him.

"It's not what it sounds like."

"What does it sound like then, Nico? You better start talking, boy."

"Okay, it might be what it sounds like. Anara and I were having—relations, but now we're not. I broke it off before Dante left for L.A. I didn't realize she was pregnant until the explosion."

"Would that have changed anything if you knew?"

"Honestly, I don't know." I light a cigarette to calm my nerves down.

"Do you love her, Nico?"

"Love? Are you kidding me, Padrone? I'm more of a—"

"Yes, Nico, we're all aware of your reputation, but nothing lasts forever. If your father were here, he would tell you to make this right."

"I'm not cut out for this, Padrone; you know I can barely take care of myself."

"When someone else comes into the picture, you adjust."

"What if I can't do it, Padrone? What if I screw up?"

"What if you don't? I have faith in you as if you were my own son, which you are in many ways, Nico."

"She doesn't want me near her, Padrone."

"Actions speak louder than words, Nico, show her who you really are. Life is short and there is no greater joy than your own child." For the first time in my whole life, Padrone has a look upon his face that I had never seen—regret.

My legs feel heavy as they walk down the hospital halls. Ajax isn't answering, and neither is Dante—this was in God's hands now. I wasn't a believer, but I pray that they will come through this. The thought of losing Dante is too hard to contemplate, like losing a piece of myself forever. Anara is sitting up and talking with Ra, and when she sees me, her face freezes.

"Oh, hi, Nico." Ra clears her throat and looks sheepish.

"Can I have a minute with Anara?"

"Sure." She tries to leave but Anara grabs her hand.

"No, get out."

"Speak to him." Ra untangles her hand from Anara's, walks out, and gives me a wink.

"What do you want?" She folds her arms at me like a petulant child.

"Just—" I fiddle for my lighter and cigarette, I need a crutch.

"You can't smoke in here, Nico," she says irately.

"Chang won't mind."

"It's bad for the baby!" She's looking at me like she wants to punch me, and I can't blame her.

"Shit, I forgot." It sounds stupid and reaffirms my belief that I'm not cut out for this.

"I'm glad that the baby is high on your list of priorities."

"It is, which is why I'm here. Where do we go from here, Anara?"

"I'm keeping the baby, so don't even think about paying me off like some whore."

"Why do you automatically expect the worst from me?"

"Because I know you."

Touché.

"I never thought I would get to have any of this, it wasn't in my plan. I don't think I even had a plan."

"What are you saying, Nico?" Her voice switches to apprehension.

"I'm saying that I want to have this baby with you. I want us to try and be a family. I don't want to half ass it and be a weekend dad or any of that bullshit. I want to do this with you because there is nobody else who has even come close to you…even Zosha. I shouldn't have reacted like I did after the Slash incident; I was scared I would lose you. Breaking up with you was easier as it was on my own terms rather than something happening to you."

"Do you really mean what you're saying, Nico, or is this just another game?"

"I've lost too much to lose you as well, Anara, I think I—you know."

"What?"

"That word. The word that I'm not going to say."

"*Love?*" She snorts at me.

"What?"

"You don't."

"Somebody has trust issues. I'm ready to try, Anara. I can't guarantee I'll be perfect, but I'll do my best for you, for us, for our baby. How does that sound?"

"That sounds…like a deal."

"I feel like I need to do something to cement the moment.'

"Like what? Please don't tell me you're proposing, Nico."

"Are you fucking crazy? I mean something a bit more like…" I sit on the bed and move closer until my mouth finds hers, and I feel my body react to my touch as her arms wrap round my neck. Our foreheads are against one another as she picks up one of my hands and puts it against her tiny bump.

Just the three of us.

***

Dante

"Dischanel, you came."

"Unlike you, I never run from a fight." We are in

what I can only assume is an abandoned warehouse.

"You came alone as requested."

"Yes."

"Good." He smiles at me and rage bubbles inside of me. Looking into the eyes of the man who murdered my brother turns my blood cold. I have to clench my fists to stop myself from ripping him apart. First, I need to find Eleni, then I will deal with Vasquez.

Without warning, his two minions hold me down as Vasquez punches me hard across the face. Blood drips down my mouth, but I refuse to cower in pain. He continues his assault and I feel every punch hitting bone until he finishes, smiling.

"That was for your father."

"Where is she?" I spit at him, tired of his games.

"With my son."

"Your son?" I repeat blankly, I thought he was some spotty teenager. Even Eleni could probably take him.

"My son, the doctor. You've already met, I heard. Trust him to go after your sloppy seconds."

"Take me to her before I rearrange your face," I growl as the puzzle pieces slot into place. Noah must have alerted Daddy Dearest as soon as he saw me in the hospital. He must have had eyes on me as soon as I went to Eleni's last night.

"Why do you need to see her? It will make it so much worse for her, Dante, when she knows you're giving up your life for hers."

"I want to see her, one last time."

"That better be all, Dischanel."

I follow him down narrow steps to some kind of

basement, where I can see Eleni being held tightly by that piece of shit, Noah. Vasquez makes a signal and nods to his son before disappearing., When he releases Eleni, she comes running toward me.

"Dante! What have they done to you?" Her face is staring at me in alarm, and I know I must look terrible.

"Eleni, I need you to get out of here." I put her little face in my hands and watch as tears start to drip out of her eyes.

"This is my fault, Dante, I led them to you. Noah—"

"I know, and it isn't your fault. This would have happened sooner or later. This is unfinished business."

"I'm not leaving you, Dante, not again." She hiccups as tears cling heavily to her ebony lashes.

"Spare me the *Notebook* scene, I'm going to barf," Noah interjects, and I can see the rage in his eyes. "Eleni isn't going anywhere, she is property of the Vasquez cartel, and if she plays her cards right, my fiancée."

"No." She looks at him, dumbstruck.

"We had a deal."

"I changed my mind. I want to take you on *mano a mano* for your woman and your empire."

I turn around so my back is toward Eleni, and signal at the gleaming gun on the inside of my jacket before I take it off. Vasquez's goons hadn't even thought to search me properly when I came in.

"You know what to do," I whisper to her.

"Dante, I can't do this."

"If you want us to live, you will when I make the

signal do it."

"Let's go, *puta*," Dante goads him before one more meaningful glance.

Noah shrugs his own jacket off, but his physique is probably one quarter of mine. I smirk at him and he shrugs.

"I'll let you throw the first punch, *Princesa*."

"My fucking pleasure." I serve him an upper cut so hard it nearly takes his head off, but he snickers at me before producing two heavy blows that hit me straight in the chest.

"Brass knuckles, always a necessity."

"Fucking cheat," I spit at him.

"If you can't beat them fairly, beat them any way you know how."

The blows reign mercilessly down on me and I look at Eleni to signal her, but her mouth is agape in horror as I drop to the floor, and Noah begins kicking me hard. Blood starts dripping hard from my mouth.

"Guess the best man won, Eleni," Noah says, smiling, giving me one last kick. "Say goodnight to Dante, babe, it's lights out."

"Say goodnight yourself." The gun is in her hand as she points it at Noah.

***

Eleni

"Put the gun down, Eleni," he says firmly, walking toward me. Anger is painted on his face.

"Fuck you, Noah Valentine." My hands are

shaking, but I pull the trigger twice and drop the gun like it is made from fire. Noah stands there transfixed for a second before falling down.

"My son!" Amaury runs in and takes a look between Dante, Noah on the floor, and me with the gun. "You bitch! You will pay for this!" He points his own gun at me, and I wait for the bullets to hit me, but they don't. Ajax and three other burly men walk through the warehouse as a plethora of gunshots explodes around us.

I drag my broken body toward Dante and stroke his cheek. His face is a bloody mess and felt icy cold. "Dante, wake up, Dante?"

I am so focused on Dante that only the pool of blood emanating from where I am sitting made me realize I have been struck by a stray bullet. I put my hand to my side. Blood pours out as I feel my eyes start to blur and my vision of Dante begin to distort. I turn around to see if I can find Ajax, but Amaury is standing in front of me and his gun is inches away from me. Everything feels like it is going in slow motion. Then there is only darkness.

Chapter Forty-Four

Aftermath

Nico

"I wish he was still here, Padrone." We're all stand by the graveside looking somber, the sky is gray, fitting with the mood of the occasion. If only things could have been different."

"They say everything happens for a reason, but sometimes I have to question that rationale," Padrone replies, his voice slightly shaky but calm. "We gave him retribution; he is at peace now."

"It doesn't feel real, none of this does. How have nine years passed since Dash died?" Ajax says quietly as he polishes Dash's gravestone.

"I can stand here proud that we fought for his vengeance." Padrone kneels down as if he is talking to Daischel himself. "You didn't die in vain, son."

"Good job, Ajax." I nod at him; he is the last-minute hero in this.

"You avenged his death, Ajax, and I am forever

493

indebted to you." Dominic acknowledges Ajax, who is looking a little sheepish.

"I would say Eleni is the real hero, she took out Nacio. Considering I doubt she's ever held a gun before; the girl did good."

"I plan to thank her personally when she wakes up. Chang said she is making good progress after surgery."

"Dante is on the mend too, punctured lung and a few broken ribs, but they still couldn't take him down." I chuckle and take a sigh of relief. *It was finally over*, at least for now.

"What happens to Vasquez's Colombia operation?" Ajax asks, rearranging the sling on his shoulder. He had taken a bullet to the shoulder, but it was nothing serious.

"We absorb it, Carmelo is already on it."

"Carmelo." I groan.

"Carmelo is here to stay; life is too short for grudges, Nico."

"Yeah, yeah," I reply irritably.

"This one is for you, Dash." We all take a bottle of Dash's finest whiskey and proceed to pour in respect for our fallen brother, fallen comrade, fallen son who we will never forget.

"I finally feel like I can breathe easily now."

"Me too, Padrone." My phone beeps and I'm reminded I have an appointment.

"Someone has you on a short leash, I take it," Ajax snorts.

"Says the guy who flew to another state because of some p—"

"Nico! We're in a cemetery, have some respect."

"Sorry, Padrone, you know what I mean. I take it you will be spending more time in Miami."

"Sophia might stay here for a while now things have calmed down."

"Whipped."

"Didn't Anara put you on curfew?"

"No comment." Ajax and Dominic chuckle, and for the first time ever, I know I have something better than all of this waiting at home for me.

***

Eleni

The sound of the hospital monitor is the first thing I hear when I wake up. Where am I? I inhale but there is a mask over my mouth. I scrabble to pull it off but somebody else does it for me.

"Glad to see you are awake, Eleni." Emerald eyes twinkle at me but not the ones I am used to.

"Dominic?" I say, confused.

"Yes."

"Where am I?"

"New York, I had you air-lifted here for surgery."

"I'm back." I look around at the familiar room which doesn't feel so familiar anymore.

"Yes, you are, and luckily you are more or less unharmed."

"What happened to me? Dante?" I say, putting my hands to my mouth as memories come rushing back.

"Is fine, everybody is fine. Ajax got there in the

nick of time before things went south."

"How long have I been here?"

"A month."

"A month? Shit! My job, my apartment, I'm screwed!"

"It's all been taken care of," Dominic says, as if reading my mind. "I believe I owe you an apology, Eleni. I shouldn't have interfered in Dante's life. I was worried that with you there it would distract him, and he would have a similar fate to Dash. I saw you as a threat."

"I, uh—"

"Do you accept my apology?" He looks at me with unwavering sincerity.

"Yes. Whose things are these?" It looks like a second person has been staying here.

"Mine. I split my time between you and Dante. I didn't want you to be alone."

"Thank you, Dominic." I'm a little stunned and don't know what to say.

"Don't let this old man keep you, I'm sure there is somebody else who wants to see you."

"I, um, I don't know if that's such a good idea. I was the one who led Noah—Nacio to Dante, this is kind of my fault," I say in a small voice.

"This fight was always going to happen, Eleni; it was written long before you were even in the picture."

"Does he want to see me?"

"Why don't you find out?"

He leaves the room and I stand there a little stunned.

"Eleni?" A familiar voice accompanies the head

496

peering through the door.

"Chang!"

"Good to see you up and running. Before you leave, there are some blood results I want to go through with you."

"Sure, I just need to—"

"See, Dante?" He smirks at me. "True love never dies, plus he's been driving me crazy every day to see you, so go ahead."

"Thanks," I say shyly, walking out.

My legs feel like lead as a I walk down these familiar halls. I'm just about to walk into Dante's room when I see *him*. Everything stops for a second.

"Ajax?" My voice cracks.

"Eleni?" His face breaks into a smile and my heart lifts.

"I'm sorry," we both say in unison, then laugh.

"I shouldn't have left that way; I was afraid I would disappoint you. After everything you went through, I didn't want to let you down again. I ran away to Miami instead of saying what I really felt."

"I should have tried to understand where you were coming from instead of shutting you out, I shouldn't have avoided your calls."

"Can you forgive me?"

"Only if you forgive me first. Thanks for taking care of Vasquez Junior, by the way."

"Don't remind me," I groan. "I'm supposed to save lives, not take them."

"I think if you're about to be killed, you get a pass."

"Thank you, Ajax, for saving me. You were

always good to me. Do you think we could move on from how we left it?"

"Sure, you know I'll always have a soft spot for you, Eleni."

"I'll always love you, Ajax…but I'm not in love with you like that."

"I'm not in love with you either, not like how I used to be. I've met someone else and she is the one."

"Really?" My heart floats and I'm genuinely happy for him. By the way his eyes light up when he talks about her, I know it's real.

"Do you believe in soul mates, Eleni?"

"Sure."

"The definition of a soul mate is somebody you are infinitely connected to. Ever since we met, Eleni, I have felt something between us. Before we even got together, I knew you would always be in my life. Even though we have both moved on, a piece of me will always love you.' He chuckles. "Wow, that was really heavy."

"No, I like it. I feel the same way."

"Can we be friends without it being crazy weird?"

"We'll always be friends, Ajax, always."

"What are you doing milling around? Shouldn't you be resting?"

"I'm looking for—"

"Dante?"

"Yeah," I say sheepishly.

"First door on the left."

"I take it you two are back on?"

"Honestly, I don't know, it's—"

"Complicated?" he interjects and we both laugh.
"Exactly."

"Dante isn't exactly my favorite person, but he's been a wreck the last year, Eleni. He missed you even though he will never admit it to himself. You balance him out, you make him a better person. After everything that has happened, it would be silly to let it go."

"I just don't want to get hurt again."

"The only thing worse than getting hurt is regret, Eleni." He walks forward and kisses me on the cheek, then disappears, leaving me to marinate over my thoughts before I walk through a door that will change everything.

***

Dante

"How is the patient doing?" Nico and Farook walk in the door, smiling at me.

"Bored out of my fucking skull," I say, picking on a thread on one of the sheets. "How was today?"

"Good, it felt right to be there. Dash would have been proud. It took us ten years, but we did it."

"We thought the worst had happened when you didn't pick up the phone, jackass," Nico says, playfully punching my arm.

"I told Vasquez I was coming alone; I didn't want any fuck ups in case he hurt Eleni. One wrong move could have jeopardized everything, especially after the other night."

"What happened the other night?" I can feel

Farook's brown eyes boring into me.

"A little reunion between the sheets, hey?" Nico winks at him and they both smirk.

"Mind your fucking business, I just realized a couple of things. Let's leave it at that."

Nico pulls out a cigarette and lighter, but then puts it away. I frown at him.

"I'm trying to give it up. Anara is on my fucking case about it, which is a fucking crock because she used to smoke as much as I do—*did*. Fucking women."

"I believe that's what you got you in your current situation.' Farook snorts and makes a whipped sound. "Are you together? What is the current situation?"

"We're trying and seeing it where it takes us."

"But she's at your place every night?"

"It's complicated, considering Reign wants to kill me. We're just keeping it low-key for now."

"How can you be keeping it low-key when she's knocked up?" Farook rolls his eyes in exasperation.

"Well, look at it this way, she can't get knocked up again."

"There is something very wrong with you," I snort at him and Farook doesn't even bother to answer.

"I just don't want to screw this up, it's not about me and her anymore, there is someone else to think about. Did I tell you she's going to let me name the baby if it's a boy?"

"What if it's a girl?"

"No, it's a boy. I feel it. Besides, I've seen what having daughters has done to Farook, so it's a definite pass."

"Touché, Nico. So Dante, Nico is about to be a daddy and you are ready to be a one-woman man?"

"I never said that."

"Denial is not just a river in Egypt."

"Where is Padrone?" I say, changing the subject.

"With Eleni. You know he said he was wrong about her," Nico says, giving me a meaningful look.

"Take the hint, Dante, it's a fucking sign."

"If you let her walk away, you will regret it." With those words Eleni walks in and every doubt I ever had seems to vanish on the spot.

"We'll leave you to it."

"Good to see back on your feet, Eleni."

They walk out and there is an awkward silence between us.

"How are you feeling?" I say quietly, not knowing what else to say.

"I've been through worse, you?" she says nervously.

"Like I've done ten rounds with Tyson." I stand up so we're standing opposite each other. "Do you know what happened?"

"Ajax gave me the highlight reel just now."

"Ajax." I wondered when he would come into this. "I suppose you had a little reunion."

"You're so transparent, Dante, there is no need to be jealous."

"I'm not jealous." But I can hear from my tone I sound like a petulant child.

"You don't need to be, Ajax has moved on, and I'm happy for him. I don't have any romantic feelings toward him anymore."

"Oh."

"Can you make sure you thank your father for all of this? I didn't expect him to go to all this trouble for me. I didn't even think he liked me after...everything."

"My father respects loyalty, and if you show that to him, then he'll always be in your corner. Why can't you thank him yourself?"

"I have already, but if I don't see him before I leave, then I want him to know that I am thankful."

"Leave?"

"Yes, back to Los Angeles. Where I live."

"You're leaving?"

"Yeah, unless there is a reason why I should stay?" She looks at me and our eyes lock.

"I don't want you to leave, Eleni. I'm really bad at this kind of shit. I just found you and I don't want to lose you again...I love you." I finally say it and mean it. "The day you walked into my life, you turned everything upside down. You didn't give a shit about who I was, you saw right through me. You caused ripples in the life I thought I knew so well, only you could make me question myself when I was wrong. You made me feel things I didn't think I was capable of. Finding you was chance, losing you was the worst thing that ever happened to me, and I don't want to go through that again. Eleni? Say something?"

"I don't know what to say, Dante...I never expected you to say any of these things."

"I didn't treat you right the first time. I broke your heart because I didn't have one myself. I hurt you because I switched off my emotions a long time ago. I never wanted to fall for you, I never wanted to be invested because it broke every rule I had, but I was always fighting a losing battle. When I was in jail I made a vow to fight for you, but once again fate ripped us apart. I spent a year in a haze trying to demolish you from my thoughts. Only in my darkest hours of consciousness you would appear in my mind. You are ingrained so deeply within me I can't forget you; I don't want to lose you again, Eleni, *ever*."

***

Eleni

"Do you believe in fate, Eleni?" He takes a step toward me, taking my face in his hand and pushing a loose tendril of hair behind my ear.

"Yes," I say softly, enjoying the touch of his skin against mine.

"Fate has put you in my path again for a reason. It is not a coincidence that you are back in my life. If we are not meant to be together, then why are you standing in front of me? I can't let you walk out of my life again. I will fight for you until my last breath. The other night was meant to be goodbye, but I realized I don't want a life without you in it. I made a mistake letting you go once; I don't want to repeat it."

"You asked me why I left, and I told you it was because of Sapphire. It wasn't, and I think you know that just like you know me so well." I move closer and shut my eyes as his thumb strokes my cheek. "I left because I was scared of you, what I felt for you. How deeply I loved you, and I was scared that you could never love me back. We have gone through a million different lifetimes together. Seeing you again...nearly losing you...it made me realize that I don't want to be without you. Is this what you really want, Dante? Are we really going to do this?" I say nervously, my heart pounding through my chest.

"I only want you, Eleni, nobody else." He puts his hands on either side of my face and leans forward to kiss me slowly. I feel heat spread through all of my bones. "Besides, how many other girls have got shot twice for me?" He smirks, and I playfully push him away.

"Don't remind me."

"It's a good thing we're together, your taste in men is trash." He laughs and I fold my arms at him.

"Too soon?"

"Way too soon! When you say together, Dante...do you mean—"

"One hundred percent official, like I said, Eleni, I don't want anybody else. *Ever*. Put it in the *New York Times* if you want, Dante Dischanel is officially off the market."

He pulls me in for another kiss. This time it's longer and more tender. A thousand butterflies explode within me as every touch sets me alight.

"I love you, Eleni, *sempre e per sempre*."

Three Months Later

"What's up, Dante? You're acting really

strange." He's being so evasive lately, it was really making me feel on edge.

"What are you talking about? I'm fine." He smiles at me but not convincingly.

"You're distracted, I feel it," I say sharply, taking in the scenery around us. We are spending a weekend in the Hamptons at one of Dante's properties, a beachfront house with a sprawling view of the sea, but everything felt on the verge of being ruined.

"You're overthinking things, Eleni."

"I'm not, are you breaking up with me?" I say the thing that is bouncing on top of my head.

"Eleni, just stop." He rolls his eyes at me in exasperation.

"We're on vacation, and you hate leaving the city, and you're not in a suit, Dante. I'm seeing red flags. Are you having second thoughts? Do you want to slow things down?"

"Just turn around, Eleni, please."

I swivel my head around and my jaw drops. On the beach behind me he has arranged seashells to spell out, "Will you marry me?"

"Dante, are you serious?" I turn back around and he's on one knee in front of me with a huge diamond ring in a Tiffany box.

"Remind me not to try and surprise you again. I've been working on getting everything perfect for days, and yes, I'm serious. I know we haven't been together long, but I've been thinking about this since you came back into my life. The way I feel about you voids any time or distance. You're the only person I see with me forever, so let's make it infinite. Marry me?"

"Yes!" I choke back the tears as he slips on the ring and stands up.

"I love you, Eleni."

"I love you too, Dante, *always and forever*."

Three days later

Dante

"Quit looking at me like that." I smirk as I see Eleni's eyes on me in the car mirror.

"I never knew you were into such romantic gestures, Dante. I never even thought you would want to get married."

"Neither did I. Who knew one hundred grand could change so many things?"

"Was I the gamechanger?"

"I think you re-invented the whole fucking game, Eleni."

"Who knew you were such a big softie deep down?"

"Nobody, and let's keep it that way."

"How do you feel about Colombia for our honeymoon? Great weather."

"Do you want to take me there for the great weather or the fact you have business to look into?"

"You really do know me too well; this could be dangerous."

"I think we're past that." She snorts at me. "Almost home."

After that day in the hospital, Eleni moved back to New York. She is working with Chang again, but now as his practice partner instead of his assistant. We are living together, but not in the penthouse. Too many things had happened there for us to start fresh. What she didn't know was I had just purchased a house on Staten Island, but that is the second part of the surprise. The phone trills and I put it on loudspeaker.

"Dante, it's me. Anara had the baby."

"We're on our way." I click off, things were changing for all of us.

***

Anara

"Are you disappointed it isn't a boy? Nico?" I turn my head around to face him, but he's transfixed by the pink bundle in his arms. She has her tiny hand wrapped around Nico's finger and I can't seem to read his reaction.

"I could never be disappointed, she's perfect." His voice cracks a little and I beam with pride.

"Anara, I—" he starts but doesn't finish as Eleni and Dante walk in with balloons.

"Congratulations." Eleni walks over and hugs me and kisses Nico on the cheek.

"I thought you knew it was going to be a boy." Dante smirks at Nico and kisses the baby's forehead gingerly.

"Either way, I'm happy."

"I guess congratulations are in order for you too." I smile at Eleni and pick up her left finger. "Wow, that is some ice."

"You knew?"

"Of course, Nico can't keep a secret to save his life."

"You two are next."

"That's a long long long way in the distance, like from here to space."

"Who said I wanted to marry you, Nico?" I look at him square in the eye and he looks affronted.

"Who else are you going to marry?"

"Carmelo." I smirk and everyone starts laughing, apart from Nico.

"Have you decided on a name yet?" Eleni asks while stroking her face.

"Yeah, I have."

"We have?" Nico looks surprised and hands her back to me.

"Nicole Alara Dischanel."

"Nicole as in—"

"Don't get all soppy, Nico." We lock eyes, then look away awkwardly.

"Nicole, I like it."

"Welcome to the world, Princess Nicole."

***

Eleni

One month later

"Thanks for letting me know, Chang." I click off and bite my nail, wondering how I am going to explain this.

"What's up?" Dante walks through the door,

perfect timing or not.

"Nothing, just packing for the new house."

"How many shoes do you have, Eleni? Damn, it's like a Louboutin factory in here."

"Says the man who has rows and rows of black suits."

"Are you sure you're okay with selling the penthouse?"

"Very sure. I would rather not treasure some of those memories."

"What's up, Eleni? Something is bugging you."

"I just want to make sure you're ready for all of this. That you don't have any second thoughts before next week. I love you and we can wait, there's no rush. We don't need to do this right now."

"I don't need to do this, I want to. I have waited too long for you; I'm not waiting anymore. I want everyone to know that I love you and you're mine. Unless you're having second thoughts?"

"No, Dante. I just love you so much I get a little scared."

"You don't need to be scared." He walks forward and kisses me hard on the lips, lifting me up so my legs wrap around his torso. "I think we may need some practice before the honeymoon."

***

Dante

"You may now kiss the bride." The minister nods at us for the one moment I had been waiting for in the ceremony.

I walk toward her slowly, wanting to ingrain this image in my mind forever. She looks perfect like an angel in white with her dark hair cascading around her like a halo.

"I love you, Eleni Dischanel."

"Back at you, Mr. Dischanel."

Everybody applauds as I kiss my new wife and I imagine Dash standing next to my father too. This is not the life that I thought I would have that day when I held my dying brother in my arms. This is better, nothing can top this moment.

***

Nico

"Anara?"

"Yeah." She twiddles with my bowtie as we move against one another on the dancefloor.

"About what I said in the hospital."

"What did you say?"

"About not wanting to marry you."

"Yeah, so charming of you."

"I didn't mean it; I was just being an ass. If I wanted to put a ring on it, what would you say?"

"I would say you need to stop taking advice from Padrone. I know you're not ready to get married and neither am I."

"Why do you know me so well?"

"It's a gift and a curse, besides my brother wants to kill you. Hardly a great time to have a wedding."

"He'll get over it…eventually."

"He will if he wants to see his niece."

"Anara, I know we've had two chaotic years, but I just want you to know that—"

"I know Nic, me too."

He kisses me on the forehead, and I put my head under his chin, two hearts syncopated against each other. Both had been broken beyond recognition but had now started to heal.

***

Eleni

"I think this may be the best day of my life." Dante dips me back and kisses me slowly.

"I second that."

"What do you think of the new house?"

"I love it, so many rooms."

"I know we've just been married for a couple of hours but seeing Nico with his own baby has kind of made me think about us having one. You're so good with Nicole, Eleni."

"You might get that sooner than you think,' I say, looking at him coyly. I was going to wait to drop the news until later, but this is perfect timing."

"What do you mean?" His eyebrows crinkle but I see a smile starting to build.

"Los Angeles…that night we spent together. Chang thought it was a false negative, but he re-checked my blood work and it's confirmed. We're having a baby. Well, actually, we're having twins."

"Like the luckiest man in the world, our new story awaits us."

Epilogue

"Hush, little baby, don't say a word, Mama's going to buy you a mockingbird, and if that mockingbird don't sing, Mama's going to buy you a diamond ring." Sabrina smiles at the blue bundle in her arms, everything she ever wanted was looking up at her with big blue eyes, *Lorenzo's* blue eyes. For years she had watched her body fail her as she tried to hold a pregnancy, in vain she thought both of them were to blame. That clearly wasn't the case anymore. The truce with Dante was not something she cared particularly for, to make peace with the man who killed her husband and brother. Her blood just boiled thinking about it, but then her brain clicked into gear and she arrived there and played her part like the victim Dante thought she was. She even fired the gun to make it look like she killed Sapphire for authenticity purposes. Sapphire wasn't dead at that point, she needed to be alive so the baby would survive the delivery. As soon as he was born, she was disposed of appropriately.

She looked at him closely, he was almost Lorenzo's

doppelganger, and had little or no remnants of Sapphire's likeness on him. He was *hers*, from the day he was pulled out of Sapphire, he *belonged* to her. Sapphire could barely function as a human, let alone a mother to somebody as precious as what she was carrying in her arms. Despite her having to marry Lorenzo's older brother to cover it up, it would be worth it. She had a clear end in sight, a goal. In Sicilian tradition, a childless widow can marry a sibling, so it all made sense, it all fit together. So many lies cobbled together to eliminate any future questions. As Leo got older, people would start to notice the resemblance of him to Lorenzo, which would alert the wrong people too soon, so this little move would quell any rumors. To the world, Leo is Ludovico's son until the time is right to reveal otherwise. Sabrina had a plan, and she didn't care how long it would take to unfurl. The slow knife dripping poison is more painful than the fast hand who acts on impulse.

"Leo Rey Salvatore, you will rise up against those who wronged us, you will rule over those who oppressed us. Our enemies will kneel before you in defeat, and most importantly, you will *destroy* Dante Dischanel."

Acknowledgements

Thank you to everyone who helped me on this journey.. Especially my publishing team.

About The Author

In between being a dreamer and procrastinator Sarah Amelle lives and breathes reading and writing, if she isn't thinking about her next dramatic cliff hanger she is probably reading her favourite dark romance stories.

Sarah Amelle specialises in Mafia bad boys, especially the complicated ones with dangerous minds and even darker hearts. Her weakness is a hot alpha male and an even feistier female protagonist. After amassing almost twenty million reads across online interactive apps Sarah decided to take it to the next level with her latest book Dark Temptation part of the Dark Hearts series.

Social Media Links

Goodreads:
https://www.goodreads.com/book/show/57389107-dark-temptation

@sarahamellestories

Join our Reader Group on Facebook and don't miss out on meeting our authors and entering epic giveaways!

Limitless Reading

Where reading a book
is your first step to becoming
limitless...

LIMITLESS PUBLISHING *Reader Group*

Join today! *"Where reading a book is your first step to becoming limitless..."*

https://www.facebook.com/groups/LimitlessReading/